John Boyne is the author of thirteen novels for adults, six for younger readers and a collection of short stories. His 2006 novel *The Boy in the Striped Pyjamas* has sold more than 11 million copies worldwide and has been adapted for cinema, theatre, ballet and opera. His many international bestsellers include *The Heart's Invisible Furies* and *A Ladder to the Sky*. He has won three Irish Book Awards, along with a host of other international literary prizes. His novels are published in over fifty languages.

Also by John Boyne

NOVELS

The Thief of Time
The Congress of Rough Riders
Crippen
Next of Kin
Mutiny on the Bounty
The House of Special Purpose
The Absolutist
This House Is Haunted
A History of Loneliness
The Heart's Invisible Furies
A Ladder to the Sky
A Traveller at the Gates of Wisdom

NOVELS FOR YOUNGER READERS

The Boy in the Striped Pyjamas
Noah Barleywater Runs Away
The Terrible Thing That Happened to Barnaby Brocket
Stay Where You Are and then Leave
The Boy at the Top of the Mountain
My Brother's Name Is Jessica

NOVELLAS

The Second Child
The Dare

SHORT STORIES

Beneath the Earth

THE
ECHO
CHAMBER

JOHN BOYNE

PENGUIN BOOKS

TRANSWORLD PUBLISHERS
Penguin Random House, One Embassy Gardens,
8 Viaduct Gardens, London SW11 7BW
www.penguin.co.uk

Transworld is part of the Penguin Random House group of companies
whose addresses can be found at global.penguinrandomhouse.com

Penguin
Random House
UK

First published in Great Britain in 2021 by Doubleday
an imprint of Transworld Publishers
Penguin paperback edition published 2022

'Rhythm Is A Dancer', p.111, performed by Snap!, lyrics by Benito Benites,
Michael Münzing, Luca Anzilotti and Thea Austin.
'Hey Jude', p.186, performed by The Beatles, lyrics by John Lennon and Paul McCartney.

Every effort has been made to obtain the necessary permissions with
reference to copyright material, both illustrative and quoted. We apologize
for any omissions in this respect and will be pleased to make the
appropriate acknowledgements in any future edition.

A CIP catalogue record for this book
is available from the British Library.

ISBN
9781529176742

Typeset in 11.5/15 pt Dante MT Std by Jouve (UK), Milton Keynes
Printed and bound in Great Britain by Clays Ltd, Elcograf S.p.A.

The authorized representative in the EEA is Penguin Random House Ireland,
Morrison Chambers, 32 Nassau Street, Dublin D02 YH68.

Penguin Random House is committed to a sustainable
future for our business, our readers and our planet. This book
is made from Forest Stewardship Council® certified paper.

For Chris Meyler

'Social media gives legions of idiots the right to speak when they once only spoke at a bar after a glass of wine, without harming the community. Then they were quickly silenced, but now they have the same right to speak as a Nobel Prize winner.
It's the invasion of the idiots.'

UMBERTO ECO

'The snowflake never needs to feel responsible for the avalanche.'

JON RONSON,
So You've Been Publicly Shamed

PART I

4 February 2004

In a waiting room at St Mary's Hospital, Paddington, George Cleverley sits quietly, looking at his five-year-old son Nelson and four-year-old daughter Elizabeth, at their sleepy expressions and unkempt hair. They were never supposed to be here at this time, so early on a Wednesday morning. They're frightened and confused.

'I thought we weren't going to have another baby for six more weeks,' says Nelson, who's been keeping a time chart on his wall, counting down the days to what he hopes will be the arrival of a younger brother. He's wearing a cowboy costume, although he forgot his hat and toy gun.

'That was how it was supposed to be,' says George, putting his arm around the boy and pulling him close. 'But sometimes, babies arrive a little earlier than expected.'

'Is Mummy going to die?' asks Elizabeth, who heard the anguished screams of her mother as the ambulance arrived and watched as the blood soaked into Beverley's nightdress.

'Of course not,' replies her father, although he's not certain. The first two children's births took place without any fuss, but this pregnancy has proved very difficult. He's done everything he can to help Beverley, and the problems she's encountered have brought them as close as they've been in years; the idea of losing her is almost too much for him to bear. And yet, it is to this dark place that his mind strays. The notion of being left to look after Nelson and Elizabeth on *his own is overwhelming. He would need to be strong, he knows that, but what kind of life could he possibly hope to give them without the support of the woman he loves? He's never been a religious man, but he finds himself praying.*

A young nurse wanders past, glancing in his direction. He knows what she's doing. She's passing by simply to get a look at him, to tell people that she saw that George Cleverley off the telly and he's shorter in real life, or taller, or fatter, or thinner. Generally, he takes pleasure in his celebrity, but at moments like this, it's too much. Even the ambulance drivers seemed impressed, and he was certain that one came close to asking for an autograph.

'Whatever happens,' he tells his children now, keeping his voice calm and strong in order to reassure them, 'we are a family. We love each other, we will always love each other, and nothing, absolutely nothing, can ever come between us. Do you understand?'

'Yes, Daddy,' they both say, and he pulls them in closer.

A door opens and a doctor steps out, pulling a mask from around her face. George stares at her, knowing that her expression will immediately tell him everything he needs to know.

The doctor is smiling.

'She's fine. She's lost a lot of blood but she's having a transfusion now and I don't envisage any difficulties.'

'And the baby?'

'A little boy. Premature but healthy. We'll have to keep him here for a few weeks, but I think he's going to be okay.'

George starts to cry, and Nelson and Elizabeth stare at him in bewilderment. He holds them tightly. He loves his family. He's in love with them all.

And at that precise moment, in a dorm room at Harvard University, a nineteen-year-old boy presses the return button on his computer keyboard and watches as the first post on something he's called 'The Facebook' appears:

Mark Zuckerberg changed his profile picture
just now

Monday

THE MILLINER AND THE NOSE

George Cleverley had always prided himself on being a thoroughly modern man, a free thinker who held no truck with the historical bigotries of the previous generation, the societal prejudices of his own or the belligerent intolerances of the next.

After the birth of each of his children, at a time when childcare was still considered the primary domain of the mother, he had done his fair share of nappy-changing, often sitting up with his wife while she administered sleepy midnight feeds and reading aloud to her as she nursed their latest progeny at her breast. He went on marches, protesting against anything that seemed even vaguely objectionable, and wrote newspaper columns criticizing American presidents, African dictators and Russian despots alike. He named his eldest son Nelson, after Nelson Mandela, adding Fidel as the boy's middle name. On his weekly chat show, one of the most popular programmes on British television, he made a point of ensuring that an even gender ratio was maintained among his guests and, when actresses featured in the line-up, never referred to their bodies or sex lives during the conversation, preferring to focus on their craft and philanthropic pursuits. He considered himself fiscally conservative but socially liberal, was a prominent opponent of blood sports, and had twice been a weekend guest of Charles and

Camilla's at Highgrove. Politically, he was held in high esteem by both the Left and the Right, who considered him a fair and balanced journalist. Although he never publicly discussed his political leanings, he always voted for the person, not the party, and so, over the years, had cast ballots for Tory, Labour and Liberal Democrat candidates alike. In the 2019 general election, exhausted by Brexit, he had even voted for a Green. He sponsored eighteen goats in Somalia and had attended seven Pride marches in the capital, waving the rainbow flag vigorously.

And yet, despite all his hard-earned Woke credentials, his first thought when Angela Gosebourne informed him that he was going to be a father again was: *You planned this, didn't you? To trap me.*

At the time, George and Angela had not been conducting their affair for long, no more than five months, and he hadn't really considered it a proper affair at all, more of a dalliance. He'd never been unfaithful to Beverley before and hated seeing himself turn into that sort of man, but his marriage had become strained in recent years, much of their communication taking place over WhatsApp rather than face to face, and Angela's attraction to him had taken hold of his ego and given it a good shake.

Although he was fond of her, he had never imagined their relationship would have any long-term consequences. She had a tendency to pepper her speech with foreign phrases co-opted into the language, a too desperate sign of her erudition, and had a laugh that grated, forcing him to keep witty remarks to a minimum. Ultimately, he'd decided to end the liaison but, a few days after the break-up, she'd phoned, asking for one final roll in the hay and, being weak, he'd succumbed to her erotic invitation, which, in time, had led to today's meeting in a Kensington wine bar, where she'd delivered the news by placing her hand over her glass when the waitress tried to pour, saying, 'I can't. *Je suis enceinte.*'

'I don't want anything from you,' Angela insisted now, taking a compact from her handbag and dabbing at her face with a powder puff, another habit that aggravated him. 'You can be a part of this baby's life or not, exactly as you wish. If you'd prefer to have nothing to do with him, then naturally, I'll understand. But there's no changing things. It's a *fait accompli.*'

'Him?' asked George, a small twinge of paternal pride asserting itself over the dismay. 'It's a boy, then? You're sure?'

'Well, not sure, no,' she admitted. 'But a mother can sense these things.'

'Nonsense,' he replied.

'You've never been a mother, George, so you can't know.'

'Perhaps not, but I don't hold with old wives' tales.'

'I'm not an old wife,' countered Angela. 'You're confusing me with Beverley.'

'I mean, it's all very well to say that I can be as involved as I like,' he continued, ignoring the barb, 'but it's not quite as simple as that, is it? If I throw myself into fatherhood again, which I'm loath to do at my age, then I'll almost certainly lose Beverley, and the children will take her side, as they always do, so I'll lose them too. But if I don't, if I just walk away, then I'm a scoundrel and, twenty years from now, when I'm in my dotage, he, she or they will show up at my front door complaining of abandonment and blaming me for everything that's gone wrong in their life. I'll be eighty years old by then and, frankly, I won't need the grief.'

'They?' asked Angela, frowning. 'Is there a history of twins in your family?'

'No. Why do you ask?'

'You said *they*?'

'I understand that some people prefer the third person plural for a pronoun,' he replied, having recently interviewed a pop singer on his show who'd insisted upon this, leading one of the cameramen to be fired for calling them Sibyl, after the Sally Field movie about the woman with multiple personalities.

'Well, as he's still the size of a peanut,' said Angela, 'he hasn't yet made any such preferences known. So, let's not overcomplicate matters.'

'But you take my point,' said George, summoning a waiter over and ordering an Old Fashioned on the rocks with two twists of citrus rind rather than the traditional one. 'Now that you've told me, I'm obliged to react in some way, even if that reaction is to do nothing at all. If I choose not to be involved, then I'm still involved by the nature of not being involved. Do you follow?'

'I suppose so.'

'And then there's the financial aspect.'

'Now that's beneath you,' she said. 'If you think I'm after your money—'

'I don't think that at all,' he replied. 'But you'd be entitled to some. And so would the child. Obviously, I wouldn't shirk from paying my fair share. I wouldn't want him to suffer any deprivations as a consequence of his bastardy.'

'You know, for such a dyed-in-the-wool liberal, you use some very archaic terms. It's rather *de trop*, if you don't mind my saying.'

'These are legal terms, nothing more.'

'I'm not sure that's true,' said Angela.

'And I couldn't keep something like that from Beverley. She goes through our bank statements every month, with all the urgency of a sniffer dog at international arrivals, just after the planes from Thailand have got in.'

'George!' she said, laughing a little. That grating laugh.

'Well, it's true. A few weeks ago, we got into a ferocious argument about why I'd spent thirty pounds in Simpson's of Piccadilly when we have an account at Hatchards.'

'Well, I'm not surprised,' replied Angela, taking a sip of her water. 'Since Simpson's closed its door in the mid-nineties.'

'You know what I mean,' he said with a sigh. 'Waterstone's, then. With an apostrophe, I might add. It offends me that a book chain, of all places, cannot punctuate correctly.'

'Speaking of which,' said Angela, nodding at the canvas bag resting on the table between them, a large W emblazoned across the front. 'You've been back, I see. What did you buy?'

'A new biography that interested me,' he said, passing the book across. 'Eight hundred pages long. When was the last time you read an eight-hundred-page book? I never seem to read any more,' he added. 'I'm always on my laptop or my phone. Anyway, my point is that if I suddenly start transferring huge wodges of cash from my bank account to yours every month, Beverley's going to ask why. And if she finds out that I've fathered a love child, she will almost certainly divorce me.'

'And would that be the worst thing in the world?' asked Angela.

'It would, yes. I love my wife.'

'Then why did you cheat on her?'

'I don't like that word,' he said, grimacing a little. 'Cheating is for cardsharps, carnival barkers and presidential candidates, and I am none of those things.'

The Old Fashioned arrived but with only one citrus rind, the waiter explaining that the bartender had declined to make it with two.

'What do you mean, he declined?' asked George, looking up at him irritably. 'What gives him the right?'

'François posts images of all his cocktails on Instagram,' replied the young man. 'So he can't take the risk. Last month, he substituted Aperol for Campari in a Negroni and he received death threats from purists.'

'Oh, for God's sake,' said George, waving him away, too weary to argue.

'Of course, if she threw you out,' continued Angela, 'it's not as if you'd be homeless.' She looked down at the table-cloth and tapped her fingers against it. 'I mean, you could always come and live with me, if you wanted. Live with us, that is. The baby and me.'

He narrowed his eyes, hoping that she was joking.

'But you live in Croydon,' he said.

'What on earth has that got to do with anything?'

'If you don't know, then there's very little point in me trying to explain.'

'I'll have you know that Croydon is becoming quite gentri-fied these days.'

'I just prefer a postcode that begins with a SW, that's all,' said George. 'My father instilled certain values in me from the start that have stood me in good stead over the years. Carrying a monogrammed handkerchief, for example. Having a good tailor. Matching one's belt with one's shoes. The stuff of civil-ized living.'

'You can't make life decisions based on letters of the alphabet.'

'I don't see why not.' He took a sip from his drink, then a larger draught, then finished it entirely. 'I suppose you want this baby, do you?' he asked, keeping his tone casual and his implication vague.

'I'm thirty-eight years old,' she replied. 'So yes, I do. I might not get another chance.'

'You do know the world is overpopulated as it is?'

'Then one more won't make much of a difference, will it?'

'Of course, the Chinese had the right idea with the one-child policy.'

Before they could debate this, the Shadow Home Secretary, who had been seated on the other side of the room, stopped by to say hello and George stood up, kissing her on both cheeks and congratulating her on her recent promotion.

'I must say, you look marvellous,' he added. 'Power agrees with you. Or shadow power, anyway. And, correct me if I'm wrong, but you're wearing Caron Poivre, aren't you?'

'How did you know?' she replied, beaming.

'I have a good nose,' he said, smiling as he tapped the proboscis in question. 'Arturetto Landi once gave me a tour of his studio and said that I could have had a career in it.'

'Being a nose?'

'Being a nose.'

'It's good to have options. Hello,' she said, turning to Angela.

'Hello,' replied Angela, standing up and shaking her hand.

'This is a friend of mine,' said George, looking a little rattled. He would have preferred if Angela had pretended to be a deaf-mute and kept to her seat. 'Angela Gosebourne. Angela is a milliner.'

'A milliner?'

'Yes, a milliner.'

The Shadow Home Secretary considered this for a moment, as if she was not entirely sure that she understood the word. 'Do you mean hats?' she asked.

'Yes,' replied George. 'Hats. And, you know, fascinators. And what have you . . .' he added, trailing off.

'How interesting. I don't wear hats very often. I don't think I have a head for them.'

'Everyone does,' said Angela. 'You just have to find the right hat for you, that's all.'

'No, you're quite wrong,' replied the Shadow Home Secretary, who had been concerned about the size of her head since childhood, when the children in her school suggested that she had been immortalized on Easter Island. 'But I wish you well in your endeavours all the same.'

'Thank you,' replied Angela, sitting down again.

Some more conversation was exchanged between the principals before George resumed his seat too.

'That was very odd,' said Angela. 'Why did you tell her that?'

'Tell her what?'

'That I'm a milliner.'

'I momentarily forgot that you're a therapist, that's all.'

'What nonsense.'

'All right, I didn't want to say anything incriminating. She knows Beverley. It wouldn't do if news of this lunch got back to her.'

'And why is being a milliner any less incriminating than being a psychotherapist?'

'I don't know,' he said, throwing his hands in the air. 'I panicked, that's all. Sometimes, I find myself at a loss to explain my actions.'

'The milliner and the nose,' said Angela, considering the careers they might have had in the alternate universe he had created. 'It sounds rather like a children's fairy tale, don't you think?'

'Children's fairy tales are notoriously dark,' he replied, ordering another drink and wondering whether it would betray his emotions too much if he ordered a double. 'Full of gruesome murders and anthropomorphism.'

'And cannibalism,' she added. 'Think of Hansel and Gretel locked away in a cage above the witch's fire. Being fattened up for the slaughter.'

'I'll avoid that one when I'm reading our son to sleep.'

'So that's something that you can see happening?' she asked, looking up hopefully.

'Well, possibly. We'll see.'

'But you'll give me an answer at some point, though? About whether you want to be involved?'

'Of course,' he replied. 'I'm not saying yes, but I'm not saying no either. I'm sorry I can't be clearer, but I need some time to think. Is that all right?'

Angela sighed and stood up, putting on her coat. 'I suppose it will have to be,' she said. 'Sometimes I wonder what it is that I ever saw in you, George, I really do.'

She leaned over to kiss him on the top of his head. His thick white hair was one of his most attractive traits, reminding her of a bichon frise puppy. 'Enjoy your book,' she said. 'All eight hundred pages of it. I'll wait with bated breath for your call.'

DEVIL WOMAN

While George was coming to terms with the concept of being a father again at sixty, his wife of almost twenty-five years was sitting in a Heathrow Airport coffee shop, saying goodbye to Pylyp, her lover of five months, who was leaving London for Odessa, his home city in Ukraine, to attend the funeral of his father. And he'd just upset her greatly by admitting that he would be staying till the end of the week.

'Oh no!' she cried, raising her voice in dismay. 'Wouldn't

two nights be more appropriate? Or even just one? It's not as if he's going to come back to life the longer you stay.'

'But is my mother,' replied Pylyp, looking at her through the dark brown eyes that had mesmerized her on their first encounter and had continued to make her feel like a teenage girl ever since. It wasn't just his eyes, of course. It was his face, his hair, his body, his muscular chest and arms, his tight ass, his accent, his entire sexy self. 'Is in need of big son now that she alone with eldest son rotting to dust in grave and husband corpse now too.'

'Of course,' replied Beverley, who had heard the story of Pylyp's brother's untimely passing on several occasions during their time together and was, quite frankly, tired of it. Pylyp liked to maintain that he had been killed fighting the Russians, martyring him as he grew into legend, but the fact was that Borysko Tataryn had actually died en route to a military training camp when he'd been stung by a bee, suffering an allergic attack that left both him and his anthophilous assailant dead within minutes. 'But sometimes,' she continued, 'a person needs to be left alone to grieve. That way, they can come to terms with their loss more quickly. After all, it's not as if you're going to return to Ukraine permanently, is it?'

'I do not plan on this, is true. My life is here. In London. My tortoise is here. In London. And you are here. In London.'

Beverley tried not to betray how maddening it was to find herself relegated to the bronze medal on his list of affections. She knew how much he loved Ustym Karmaliuk – named in honour of the great Ukrainian folk hero – but it bothered her to think that, faced with a choice between the two of them, she would probably lose out to a vertebrate reptile currently enjoying his one hundred and fifteenth summer.

'I wish I could come with you,' she said.

'This would only confuse my mother,' he replied, shaking

his head. 'You have six more years than her and, in my country, you would be seen as devil woman.'

'Right,' said Beverley. 'Good to know.'

'Of course, I know that you are not devil woman.'

'Thank you.'

'But she would think so. She would call you slut, say you are person with deranged mind. Even whore.'

'Yes, all right.'

'Tramp and Jezebel. Harlot, lady of the night—'

'Yes, I've got it, Pylyp,' said Beverley, raising her voice in irritation. 'You don't need to go on.'

'She would ask friends to stone you in street. Behaviour of women in England very different to behaviour of women in Ukraine. At home, women have . . . what is word?'

'Less progressive attitudes towards relationships between older women and younger men?'

'No, I think word is *self-respect*. Maybe is not. I need learn of these words.'

Beverley looked away, trying not to feel too wounded, but felt comforted when he reached across to take her hand in his own. She glanced down, observing the contrast between his impossibly smooth, tanned skin and her own, which was pale and paper thin, and shuddered a little. She was still a beautiful woman, there was no question about that, and she prided herself on the fact that she had never once injected any foreign bodies into her face. But in her youth, she'd been an absolute knock-out. Back then, she couldn't walk into a room without feeling the eyes of every man present turning to look at her. Now, she sometimes felt as if she was invisible. The last time she'd found everyone turning in her direction was a couple of months earlier, when she'd strolled into the bar at Claridge's after an afternoon's makeover and everyone, men and women alike, had stopped talking and stared in her direction. For a moment, she felt as if she was reclaiming the power she'd wielded in her twenties, but the sensation did not last for long, for she quickly realized that they were actually looking at Judi Dench, who'd wandered in behind her and was searching the room for Maggie Smith, who was seated at a corner table with a bottle of champagne and a bowl of dry roasted peanuts, being acerbic to anyone who dared approach her.

'You will miss me, yes?' he asked, smiling at her now. 'You will miss my big Ukrainian dick?'

'Well, quite,' she replied, laughing a little. A woman at the next table, also in her late fifties but with a lot more upholstery and a lot less refurbishment, glanced across with a disgusted expression on her face. Beverley noticed that the woman was reading her most recent novel, *The Surgeon's Broken Heart*. 'You do have a very nice dick,' she agreed, slightly louder now, for she enjoyed scandalizing women of her own age. 'I wouldn't be human if I didn't feel withdrawal symptoms.'

'My body will be in Odessa,' replied Pylyp, 'but my dick will remain here in London. With you.'

'What an odd thing to say,' said Beverley, considering these words for a moment before deciding that they hadn't come out quite as romantically as he had intended them. Still, she told herself, it was the thought that counted.

Beverley and Pylyp had originally met the previous year when she took part in the television series *Strictly Come Dancing*, where he was one of the professional dancers and, to her delight, was assigned as her partner. His lean body, impressive pectoral muscles and shoulder-length brown hair had overwhelmed her and, although she had never betrayed George before, it seemed to her that her husband barely noticed her these days and so the attentions of a handsome twenty-four-year-old had ultimately become too much to ignore. She hated thinking of herself as a cheat, however. It diminished a marriage that had, for so long, been rather wonderful and proved the bedrock of her existence.

Dancing was a skill that came quite naturally to Beverley and, while she could never have been a professional, she was certainly a gifted amateur, and survived quite far in a show that, over the years, had gone from being a bit of light entertainment froth to something that captivated the British public in ways not seen since the heyday of *Opportunity Knocks*. Desperate C-list celebrities made it known that they wanted to take part, evicted twenty-somethings from freakishly sexual reality shows told interviewers that they longed to perform the Viennese waltz in front of millions of viewers, while the dimwit and frankly unemployable children of superstar footballers made it known that they'd be open to an offer from Auntie. It would, after all, increase their social media following by hundreds of thousands. Before the cameras, the contestants gave off an air of devil-may-care frivolity, but behind the scenes there were more knives on display than at a convention of Michelin chefs.

Pylyp glanced at his watch now, saying it was time he made his way through security, and she glanced mournfully towards the large cardboard box he had brought with him to the airport and that she had, in a moment of weakness, reluctantly agreed to take care of during his absence. He lifted the lid and reached down to kiss Ustym Karmaliuk on the head. When she saw the tears in his eyes, she had the good grace to feel a little embarrassed that she was so attached to this boy.

'Remember,' he said, growing serious now. 'Only must be the plant-based foods. Leafy greens, vegetables, the things for the skinny people who hate the red meat. And crickets. Ustym Karmaliuk is the crazy tortoise for the crickets. A half-dozen every day at least.'

'I'll speak to my cricket man,' replied Beverley. 'And I'll let Harrods know that there's a new guest at the table. Anything else that his palate might appreciate? Smoked salmon, perhaps? Lobster thermidor? Beluga caviar?'

'No, the freeze-dried fish food is only fish food that he likes.'

'Well, naturally. He's a tortoise of taste. He's been well raised.'

'And the worms. You must wake up early, when the grass is still wet.'

'If you say so.'

'You must go outside when you are still the sleepy-eyes.'

'I will. I promise.'

'Because the worms is everything to Ustym Karmaliuk. They are like the breast milk to the newborn baby.'

'It's a good job you're so handsome,' said Beverley, offering a deep sigh. 'That's all I'll say.'

They stood up now and made their way to the security gate, where Beverley showed her Fast Track card and the security officer declined to let her lover through the VIP lane, since the name on the card was Beverley Cleverley and the name on the boarding pass was Pylyp Tataryn.

'Oh, don't be such a jobsworth,' she said, employing the stare she had perfected over many years of dealing with the lower orders. 'What difference does it make to you?'

'Rules is rules,' replied the officer, who reminded her a little of Engelbert Humperdinck in appearance. Jowly. Sideburny. Sexy, if he had been forty years younger.

'And that's who you are, is it?' asked Beverley. 'A rules man? No independent thought? Just doing what the bosses say?'

'They're the ones who pay my wages,' said the man. 'I'm afraid your son will have to use the regular line like everyone else.'

Beverley took a step back, rather impressed by the man's subtle insult.

'Touché,' she said, before turning back to Pylyp and throwing herself upon him, like Elizabeth Taylor launching herself on Montgomery Clift when he agrees not to give her a frontal lobotomy in *Suddenly, Last Summer*. She would have liked to kiss him on the lips, but photographers were usually lurking around Heathrow in search of minor celebrities, not to mention members of the public with their smartphones, and she couldn't take the risk. 'Well, stay in touch,' she said. 'Call me every day. And enjoy the funeral. No, that's not quite right, is it? One doesn't enjoy a funeral. What should I say? Experience the funeral? Try not to let it upset you too much?'

Pylyp smiled and ran his fingers along her cheek, causing her to purr like a cat. 'One week,' he said. 'Then I will be back. And I will bring my big Ukrainian dick with me.'

'I thought you were leaving that behind in London?' she asked, regretting the remark immediately, for he looked utterly confused. 'Never mind,' she said. 'Bad joke. I've got the tortoise. I suppose he'll have to do for now.'

PRO-SEMITIC

There were delays on the Tube and a dreadful whisper was spreading among the commuters that a man had thrown himself under a train at Sloane Square. Like the rumour, Nelson Cleverley found himself making his way slowly along the platform at Victoria Station, which was crowded with passengers, most of whom were betraying their impatience by pushing

23

against each other as they fought for every square inch of available space.

He was wearing his pale blue scrubs, which at least meant that he didn't feel that he was going to pass out with the heat. Everywhere he looked, beautiful young people were talking to each other or scrolling through their phones, and they seemed so comfortable in their own skin that it bewildered him. The girls all wore summer dresses and he stared at their legs, which were lean, tanned and sexy, trying to feel some flicker of desire. The boys, too, seemed so confident in their shorts and T-shirts, silver rings on middle fingers, string brace-lets strapped across wrists. He looked at their legs, too, and wondered why they seemed so much trimmer and hirsute than his own, which verged on flabby and hairless. He counted the items of clothing on his body and it came to a total of five: polyester scrub top and trousers, boxer shorts, socks and a pair of old trainers. Standard hospital wear. And even though he knew that he was probably the least fashionable person in London and the South-East, he appreciated the fact that his outfit made him stand out in the crowd. As he made his way along the platform to the exact spot where he knew the train doors would open, should it ever arrive, people stepped aside to let him through, as if he was en route to an emergency. He took some pleasure from this rare sense of authority.

In the pocket of his trousers, his phone buzzed, and he took it out to read a message from his mother:

Beverley Cleverley
Do u know nething bout tortoises?

He frowned. There were several aspects of this that he deplored. The first was his mother's casual use of text speak.

Was it so difficult for her to spell out the words correctly? She was a writer, after all. Also, the lack of any introduction or sign-off. He hated such informality. He tapped a quick response,

Nelson Cleverley
Dear Mum,
Nothing, I'm afraid.
Best wishes,
Nelson Cleverley

before returning the phone to his pocket. When he looked up again, he noticed a young woman standing a few feet away looking directly at him, so he forced himself to smile, just as Dr Oristo had taught him. She smiled too and, to his horror, began walking towards him. He could feel his back breaking out in a sweat and his heart rate increasing. The palms of his hands grew damp, moisture seeping from them like a squeezed sponge, and he rubbed them against his trousers, hoping they wouldn't leave a stain.

'I'm sorry for staring,' she said when she approached him. 'I just have this thing for guys in scrubs.'

'They're very practical,' replied Nelson. 'I don't normally wear them outside of the hospital, but I had an appointment, you see. With my orthodontist. I have aggressive molars, but they're being treated and should become placid soon. I could have changed clothes but I didn't have time. Fortunately, I don't have any blood on these ones, they're quite fresh. A lot of the time, scrubs are covered in blood or bodily fluids or fae-cal matter so they really shouldn't be worn outdoors but, as I say, these ones are clean. Brand new, in fact. On a hot day like this, I suppose I'd be better off wearing shorts and a T-shirt, but this was all I had in my locker.'

'Okay,' said the girl, frowning, and he guessed that he had said too much. *Always stop when you have plenty more to say.* Another thing that Dr Oristo had drilled into him. *Don't keep talking, like some deranged sociopath.*

The girl stared down the track, as if this might hurry the train along, but there was nothing. He took her in in a glance. About five foot seven, with shoulder-length red hair, pale skin and blue eyes. Lots of freckles around her nose. She was absolutely perfect and he wondered whether it would sound ridiculous to ask her to marry him.

'They say a man threw herself under a train,' said Nelson. 'That's why there's such a delay.'

'Who says so?' asked the girl, turning back to him.

'It's what I've heard.'

'But from whom?'

He nodded towards the other end of the platform. 'The people up there,' he said. 'They're more clued in, I think.'

The girl considered this.

'I feel like we're going to grow old down here,' she said, checking her watch.

'There are worse places to grow old,' he replied.

'Are there?' she asked. 'Such as?'

He racked his brain and felt his heart thumping even harder in his chest, and tried to recall the coping strategies that Dr Oristo had taught him. *I am a pleasant and attractive young man,* he told himself. *There is nothing to be frightened of.*

'A concentration camp,' he said eventually. 'It would be worse to grow old in a concentration camp. Although, I suppose, when you think of it, very few people did grow old in concentration camps because they died there. It was very sad, really. Nazis were horrible people, don't you think?'

'Well, yeah,' she replied. 'I mean, obviously.'

'Sorry,' said Nelson. 'I don't know why I'm talking about Nazis. They don't make a good conversation topic. Maybe it's because I watched *Schindler's List* last week so they've been on my mind. *The list is life*, that's what Ben Kingsley says in it. Apparently, he insists on being called Sir Ben Kingsley in real life. I don't know, I've never met him. Have you?'

'I have, actually,' said the girl. 'I sat next to him on a plane once.'

'Did he make you call him Sir Ben Kingsley?'

'Not that I recall. I don't think we chatted much.'

'*The list is life*,' repeated Nelson. 'I'm sorry, you're not Jewish, are you?'

She looked distinctly unsettled now and peered down the platform again.

'Don't get me wrong, I'm not anti-Semitic,' he continued. 'Quite the opposite, in fact. If anything, I'm pro-Semitic. Is that a phrase? Pro-Semitic? I'd love to be Jewish. I'm actually Presbyterian, sort of. I used to enjoy going to church when I was a child. I found it a very peaceful environment, although I never felt particularly spiritual.'

But she was already gone. He sighed, shaking his head, and thought that, if nothing else, this encounter would make a good story to tell Dr Oristo when he saw her.

From further along the platform, a commotion broke out and he turned in the direction of the noise. To his dismay, the crowd seemed to be dividing in the centre, like the Red Sea parting under Moses' command, and a narrow corridor opened up before him. At the far end, an old man was sitting on the ground while his wife held his hand and called out for a doctor. And there was Nelson. In his scrubs.

The entire platform turned in his direction.

He began the slow walk towards the stricken man, enjoying

27

the reverential silence of the onlookers but dreading arriving at his destination. It reminded him of prize-giving ceremonies at school, where he'd been forced to walk through the Great Hall to collect his trophy while his bully, Martin Rice, laughed at him and lobbed chewed-up bits of paper at his head.

'Is everything all right?' he asked, kneeling down before the sick man, who was pale and shaking. He was at least ninety years old and didn't seem to have his teeth in. His unshaven chin was covered in some sort of ectoplasm and there was a smell of urine about his person. When Nelson looked down, he noticed a stream of piss seeping towards him.

'Jesus fucking Christ!' he shouted, jumping up and leaping out of the way. The crowd let out a collective cry of disgust and he felt a desperate desire to run away, but the woman pulled him back down to her level.

'He's had a funny turn,' she said, a blast of cheese-and-onion crisps on her breath. 'His name's Eric. I told him we shouldn't go out in this heat, but would he listen? Never listens to me, the daft bugger.'

'Perhaps we should leave him be,' suggested Nelson. 'See whether he gets better on his own.'

The woman's forehead wrinkled into so many lines that Nelson felt it might be quite calming to count them.

'Well, aren't you going to take a look at him, then?' she asked. 'See what's what?'

'Would you like me to?' he asked.

'You're a doctor, aren't you?'

'A nurse,' he replied.

'Same thing, when it comes down to it. Both overworked and underpaid. Go on, do your job.'

Nelson nodded and did exactly as instructed. He took a look at him.

'There he is,' he said, nodding his head. 'Old Eric.' He took the man's wrist in his hand and pressed his index and middle finger against it. 'Feeling a bit unwell, are we?'

'And you can fuck off too,' said the man, pulling his hand back. 'There's nothing wrong with me. That fella over there, that black fella, he tried to push me under the train. So is it any wonder I had a turn?'

Everyone turned now to look at the man in question and several people took out their mobile phones to film the exchange. A tall, slim, handsome black man wearing a suit and holding a briefcase was standing near by and he, too, looked around, assuming that Eric was describing someone else, before realizing that he was the person of interest.

'Me?' he asked, pointing a finger at himself. 'I did no such thing.'

'Here,' said Eric, grabbing Nelson by the collar and pulling him forward. 'He's after my money. Figured he'd push me on to the tracks, then jump down and save me before the train came along and get a nice little reward for himself. But the joke's on him. I haven't a pot to piss in.'

'It was probably just an accident,' said Nelson. 'You might have lost your footing.'

'He tried to push me!' insisted Eric. 'That's what they're like.'

'What who are like?' asked a young woman of Caribbean descent, pushing her way to the front and raising her voice. 'You gonna come out with some racist shit now, old man? 'Cos if you are, I'll push you under the train myself!'

'Such manners!' said Eric's wife, looking up at the latest player in the farce. 'I don't know what they teach you in your part of the world, but here in England—'

'You shut your mouth, old woman! Bloody old people

saying the black man pushed him. It always the black man, ain't it? Never the white man!'

'And I didn't touch him anyway!' said the accused, looking mortified by the accusation. 'Why would I?'

'Of course you didn't,' said another woman, who was standing near by and carrying an enormous Mamas & Papas bag before her like a shield. 'He's just gone a bit doolally, that's all. We all have, with the heat.'

'Dozy bitch,' said Eric, pulling himself to his feet.

'Who you callin' a dozy bitch?' she asked.

'Me, most likely,' said Eric's wife. 'It's one of his many terms of endearment. Now look, you,' she added, turning back to Nelson. 'What do you think? Does he need to go to hospital?'

'I'd have to do a full examination, to be sure,' he said. 'And I don't think that would be possible down here.'

'So you're just going to let him carry on as if nothing's happened? What if he drops dead in thirty minutes, who should I blame then?'

'I'm happy to help,' protested Nelson. 'It's just that this is such an enclosed space, which makes things difficult.'

From down the tunnel, the sound of a train approaching could be heard and the crowd adjusted itself instantly, the medical emergency taking second place in importance to continuing their journey. The noise grew louder and Nelson watched as the lights began to illuminate the back wall and then, to his delight, he saw a pair of paramedics making their way down the steps towards him. Of course, everything was captured on CCTV these days. The moment the man had fallen over, someone in a room upstairs had probably despatched them. He breathed an enormous sigh of relief, knowing he wouldn't have to touch Eric again.

'I'm sorry, I have to go,' he said, turning to the couple. 'But these two men are here to help you now.'

Eric's wife looked aggrieved but, when she saw the para-medics approaching, she transferred her attention to them while Nelson scuttled back down the platform, returning to his original spot just as the train arrived and the doors opened.

Once on board, he managed to find an empty seat just as his phone buzzed again. He took it out of his pocket and read the message:

Beverley Cleverley
Do u think they like After Eights?

ROUND EARTHERS

The conversation in the wine bar haunted George throughout the rest of the afternoon, which he spent in his office at the BBC with his producer, Ben Bimbaum, whose full name George always struggled to pronounce. In his left hand, he held the solitary balloon that remained from a sixtieth-birthday celebration the production team had thrown for him a few days earlier and, as he stared at it, the silver numbers glared back from the lurid pink foil, distorting his image and turning him into a bug-eyed monster.

'Sixty,' he muttered beneath his breath.

'What was that?' asked Ben, looking up from his iPad.

'I'm sixty,' he repeated.

'Yes, I know. I was at the party.'

'Sometimes I feel like I'm seventy.'

'You don't look it,' said Ben.

'I don't look seventy?'

'No, you look sixty.'

George frowned, uncertain how to take this remark, and released the balloon from his grip. It rose tentatively towards the ceiling and pressed itself against the plaster. Like the human occupants of Broadcasting House, it longed for an escape but feared that it was trapped there for ever, like a prisoner serving a life sentence for an unspecified crime.

'I'm going to name seven people,' said George, sitting down now, depressed to notice how he'd started grunting whenever he either rose from or sank into a chair. 'And I want you to tell me what they have in common.'

'All right,' said Ben, brightening up considerably. 'I love quizzes!'

'Teddy Roosevelt,' said George. 'Gary Cooper. General Patton. Bob Fosse. Sergio Leone. Calvin Coolidge. Leon Trotsky.'

Ben pressed a finger against his lips and frowned. 'Is it that I don't know who any of them are?' he asked.

'Really?' said George, appalled. 'Not even Trotsky? I thought you'd be all over him.'

'Is he a footballer? I'm afraid I don't know very much about football.'

'Smart boy,' replied George, looking away. 'Yes, he's a full-back for Liverpool.'

'Well, I know *they're* very popular.'

'They are, yes.'

'My father used to support Nottingham Forest. He took me to the City Ground once when I was a child and I was interfered with in the toilets.'

George stared at him and, for once, found himself at a loss for words.

'It's fine,' said Ben, waving a hand in the air. 'It was, like, a hundred years ago and I've dealt with it. So are they people who you'd like us to invite on to the show? I'm not sure how well they'd go down with our viewers, since none of them is actually famous. Say their names again. Trotsky. Teddy Roosevelt. Who else was there? Oh, this is like the end of *The Generation Game*! Barry Cooper. Bob Coolidge. A cuddly toy.'

'Trotsky doesn't play for Liverpool,' said George, interrupting him. 'I was mocking you.'

'Oh,' said Ben. 'Who does he play for, then?'

'He doesn't play for anyone. He's not a footballer. He was a Soviet revolutionary, instrumental in the Bolshevik Revolution of 1917. He helped to bring down the Tsars. You've heard of the Tsars, I assume?'

'I think so,' replied Ben, crinkling up his face in a way that always reminded George of a pug, only less photogenic. 'They were, like, kings?'

'Effectively, yes,' said George. 'And stop saying "like", unless you're using it as a preposition or to express enjoyment of something. It irritates me.'

'Sorry,' said Ben.

'Anyway, my point is that he died aged sixty. Just like all the other people I mentioned. That's what they have in common.'

'Okay, I get it,' said Ben. 'You're having intimations of mortality brought on by reaching a landmark birthday. It's something we could do a show on, I suppose. We don't do enough themed shows. Let's see who else is turning sixty this year.' He picked up his iPad and returned to his digital symphony. 'George Clooney,' he said, brightening up. 'Boy George. Oh, both Georges like you! Maybe we could do something on

33

that? Barack Obama. He'd be good. Ghislaine Maxwell. Well, perhaps not her.'

George stared gloomily up at the balloon, which continued to press its case against the ceiling.

'How many children do you have?' he asked after a moment.

'I'm sorry?'

'Children,' he repeated. 'You're a father, aren't you?'

'Yes,' said Ben.

'How many do you have?'

'Two,' he replied, pushing his spectacles along his nose. 'Harry and Bess.'

'Houdini or Truman?'

'I'm sorry?'

'Did you name them for Houdini or Truman? I assume you know that both Harry Houdini and Harry Truman were married to women named Bess and that your choice of names is not a mere coincidence. Oh wait, let me guess. You don't know who they are either.'

'Sorry,' said Ben with a shrug.

'Cambridge, wasn't it?' he asked.

'What?'

'Where you took your degree.'

'My undergraduate degree, yes. But I went to Harvard for my masters.'

George felt like laughing hysterically.

'How old are you?' he asked.

'Twenty-six.'

'And Mark? How old is he?'

'Who's Mark?'

'Your husband.'

'My husband's name is Matthew.'

'Well, how old is Matthew, then?'

'Thirty-one.'

'When you get home tonight, ask him whether or not he's ever heard of Harry Houdini or Harry Truman. If the answer is no, then I congratulate you. You're in for a long and happy life together.'

He stood up and made his way to the window, looking down over Portland Place, an uninspiring view that somehow continued to entrance him, despite the decades he'd spent there. Following widespread public outrage over the culling of a popular voice actress from *The Archers* – her character had been kicked to death by a concupiscent bull – a security cordon had been erected that morning, requiring everyone who approached the building to display their staff badges to one of the guards on duty, and it was causing delays. He made a point of never wearing his own lanyard, assuming that everyone would or should recognize him. A black limousine pulled up now and he watched as a liveried chauffeur jumped out to open the back door. A Russian oligarch who had recently been cleared of murdering his fiancée stepped out and looked up towards the heavens with an expression on his face that suggested he was considering getting one of his henchmen to do something about the weather.

'How did you do it, if it's not too personal a question?' he asked, turning around again and looking at Ben.

'How did I do what?'

'You and Mark. How did you get your children? Did you adopt them or employ a surrogate?'

'Matthew. And yes, we used a surrogate.'

'You're awfully young to have children, don't you think?'

'Not really. I think it's better to have children when you're young enough to enjoy them.'

'And when you share a similar mental age.'

'Exactly. And then, by the time they're out of the house, we'll be middle-aged and, hopefully, solvent and we can see the world.'

'No one who has allowed themselves to become a parent is ever solvent,' said George. 'You'll be spending money on them for the rest of your lives. Children are an endless drain on the finances. My three still live at home and don't show any sign of wanting to move out.'

'We're teaching Harry and Bess to be independent,' said Ben. 'Neither of us has travelled much and we're determined to make it part of our future.'

'People always say that,' said George. 'But in reality, does anyone actually enjoy travelling? The packing, the airports, the food, the hotel rooms. Having to talk to your significant other all day long. When it comes to it, wouldn't we all prefer to stay at home?'

'But I've always wanted to visit Australia,' protested Ben. 'And Canada. And Japan. I never did a gap year, you see. Mother wouldn't let me.'

'You should have stood up to her.'

'Oh no,' said Ben, frowning. 'No, that wouldn't have been possible. Mother was a woman of very determined views.'

'So go on holiday, then. You don't have to have children, rear them and exile them just to feel that you've earned a trip abroad. I was almost thirty-eight by the time I had my first child, did you know that? Then Elizabeth arrived exactly a year later, and Achilles four years after that. The funny thing is, each one was born in February. I must have been at my randiest, and Beverley at her most fertile, in April.'

'Fascinating,' said Ben, who didn't sound in the least fascinated.

'The second, the ninth and the fourth. That's their birthdays.'

'May,' said Ben.

'May?'

'February minus nine months is May. You must have been, you know, at your most amorous in May.'

'No, that's a common misconception,' said George, shaking his head. 'The average length of human gestation is two hundred and eighty days, or forty weeks. Which is ten months, not nine. Why we always talk about nine months has been a mystery to me my entire life.'

Ben looked down at his iPad.

'Hey, Siri,' he said. 'How long is the gestation period for humans?'

'The duration of a pregnancy for humans is forty weeks,' replied Siri, which had been programmed to replicate the voice of a sexy young Australian surfer with blond shaggy hair and washboard abs.

'Told you,' said George, irritated that the younger man could not take his word for this without consulting the Internet. Ben was the eleventh producer he'd worked with over thirty-one years of *Cleverley* and they'd almost all been in their mid-twenties. The host kept growing older, but the producers remained the same age, a little like Leonardo DiCaprio and his girlfriends.

'Who are you, Ben?' he asked now, leaning forward and looking his colleague in the eye.

'I'm sorry?'

'I said, who are you? Tell me who you are.'

'I'm Ben Bimbaum,' said Ben, looking uncomfortable. 'Don't you remember? You're not having a stroke, are you?'

'I don't mean your name. Pretend that I'm a complete stranger and I've asked you to tell me who you are. What do you say?'

'Well, I'm a producer at the BBC,' replied Ben, whose face was flushing scarlet now. 'I work in light entertainment on the *Cleverley* show.'

'And that's it?' asked George, looking disappointed. 'That's all you are? That's what defines you?'

'I'm also a father,' added Ben. 'And a husband. I enjoy fly-fishing but can never get the time to pursue this passion. I'm an Anglican and my faith is strong.'

'That's more like it,' said George, smiling as he slapped the table. 'Now don't stop. Tell me more. I want to hear your deepest, darkest secrets.'

'I'm a fervent royalist but believe that Princess Diana was not quite as saintly as some people like to think. And if Prince Philip did something to the brakes of her car, which is often rumoured, then maybe she had no one to blame but herself. Although we must remember that it was the Queen herself who was a mechanic during the war so, if anyone knows how to disconnect a brake line, it would be her.'

'I met Diana many times,' replied George, developing a glassy-eyed look at the memory. 'Charming lady. Gorgeous skin. But you're not wrong. She was as mad as a box of frogs.'

'Did you ever have her on the show?'

'Of course not. Royalty don't go on chat shows. I mean, Fergie's always reaching out, of course, but she doesn't count. Carry on. Tell me more.'

'I'm a member of a book club, but it's been seven months since I managed to get through one of the novels,' continued Ben, warming to his theme now. 'I usually just glance at a couple of online reviews before going to the meetings and pass off their opinions as my own. The last one I tried, well, it didn't even seem to be written in English.'

'That's pretty common these days, I understand. But I

bought an eight-hundred-page biography earlier today and I'm determined to read it from cover to cover. Anything else? Any other defining points?'

'Not really, no. I think that just about covers it.'

'All right. Now tell me something about yourself that you've never told anyone before.'

'Such as?'

'Well, how should I know? Tell me one of your secrets. Something you've never even told Mark.'

'Matthew,' said Ben.

'It's the biblical names,' replied George, waving this away. 'That's why I keep getting mixed up.'

Ben thought about it and looked as if he might start crying. 'I don't want to,' he said, sounding as anxious as a fourteen-year-old boy with a bad case of acne being dragged into a game of Spin the Bottle.

'I don't care. Tell me something ridiculous or disgusting you've done that you'd rather people didn't know about.'

'I had sex with a woman once,' said Ben.

'Not good enough, we've all done that. Tell me something else.'

'I'm not wearing any underwear.'

'That's just unhygienic. Try again.'

Ben thought about it, opened his mouth, then closed it.

'Come on,' insisted George. 'You were about to say something.'

'I can't. You'll mock me.'

'I won't, I promise.'

'You promise?'

'I just said that I promise.'

'All right, then.' He took a deep breath. 'I'm a member of the Flat Earth Society,' he said.

George sat back down in his seat and frowned. 'The what?' he asked.

'The Flat Earth Society.'

George stared at him, uncertain whether or not the younger man was playing him for a fool. 'I'm sorry,' he said, shaking his head. 'You're telling me that you don't believe the world is round?'

'Let's just say that I'm sceptical,' said Ben. 'And anyway, Round Earthers have had it their own way for centuries and no one ever questions them. No one dares. They have it all sewn up, you see. But perhaps it's time to challenge the consensus.'

'Of course it is. Why accept basic reality when you can live in a world of fantasy instead? Pretend the Earth is flat and get children to believe you, that'll help with their education. And while you're at it, stand up against trained scientists when they want to administer medically proven vaccines because you heard some right-wing conspiracy theorist say on her live stream that they're not safe, despite her not having had a single day's worth of medical training in her life.'

'Well, I wouldn't go that far,' said Ben.

'I bet you protested against wearing masks last year.'

'I did not,' insisted Ben. 'I wore one with Shawn Mendes' lips on it.'

'It's because of that thing,' continued George, pointing at Ben's phone, which was lying on the table between them. 'If you were an American, you'd be one of those people insisting that Donald Trump had won the election.'

'There were irregularities in—' began Ben, but George cut him off.

'That's enough,' he said, standing up and walking towards the window, wondering whether he should simply open it up and push this idiot out. The Earth might not be round, but it was certainly hard, and a six-storey drop would put a fine dent in Ben Bimbaum's head.

THE SURGEON'S BROKEN HEART

Although Beverley was sitting in the drawing room of the Cleverleys' five-floor Belgravia home, trying to maintain a polite interest in the conversation she was holding with a ghost, her mind was far away, soaring 35,000 feet above Europe, on an aeroplane headed for the north-western shore of the Black Sea.

'You're awfully young,' said Beverley, who had been examining the ghost's resumé in search of anything objectionable and had found it quickly enough, in the line that detailed her date of birth. She studied her up and down, wondering which particular branch of Oxfam she shopped in, for unlike her own daughter, who kept up scrupulously with the latest fashions, this girl was dressed like one of the maids from *Downton Abbey* when she pops into the village for a dozen eggs, a slice of best tongue and a flirt with the shy but sexy blacksmith.

'I'm twenty-five,' admitted the ghost. 'But I feel much older.'

'How old do you feel?'

'Ancient, sometimes. Like, thirty.'

Beverley resisted an urge to slap the girl across the face and politely returned her attention to the pages that her publisher had sent her earlier in the week. This was the third potential ghost that she had interviewed recently and the selection process was proving tiresome. The first had been dismissed immediately on the grounds that she was an American and, as Beverley pointed out, an American simply couldn't understand what her readers expected from her. They didn't have the nuance, darling. The second was rejected because she displayed stalker-like tendencies that Beverley found unsettling. It was one thing, after all, to be a fan of her novels, but another thing entirely to have such an encyclopaedic knowledge of them. But number three, sitting before her now, seemed to have potential, particularly as she claimed to be more interested in journalism than novel-writing.

'So I won't be any competition for you in the future,' she added helpfully.

'Oh, I don't worry about competition,' replied Beverley, who disliked many of the authors she encountered on the festival circuit, particularly those who made no secret of how much they looked down on her books. 'Life's too short for pettiness. What I always say is, there's room for us all.'

'Of course you're right,' said the ghost. 'But it's refreshing to hear a writer of your stature feels that way.'

'I think you'll find I'm very much a live-and-let-live type of person,' continued Beverley, warming to the fictional character she was creating, loosely based on her own life. 'Every year, as the Booker Prize longlist is being announced, I tune in and never feel any sense of resentment that my name isn't included. Indeed, I say "Bravo!" to those young writers whose books are the sensations of the season but who will never be heard from again once the paperback is published. I shout "Hooray!" at those ageing white men who've been writing the same novel over and over for decades and still don't seem to have got it right.'

'It's good to know you're not bitter,' said the ghost.

'The thing is,' said Beverley, smiling through gritted teeth, 'I may not have a shelf-ful of prizes but I have what many of those people do not have.'

'Money?' asked the ghost.

'No, dear, not money. Although I do have a lot of that, it's true. No, I was referring to readers. I met one only this morning, for example, in Heathrow Airport, where I was seeing a dear friend on to a plane, and she came over to congratulate me on the success of *The Surgeon's Broken Heart*. In fact, she said it reminded her of *Wolf Hall*. Just without all the boring historical bits.'

'I couldn't write a book like yours if I tried for the rest of my life,' said the ghost. 'I mean, I think I could write *as* you, but not *like* you. Does that many any sense?'

'None whatsoever. But then, I'm looking for a ghost, not a member of Mensa. Would you like some tea? Or something stronger, perhaps? I might have a G and T myself.'

'No, thank you,' replied the ghost.

'You don't drink?'

'I do, yes. But generally not while I'm on a job interview. It tends to give the wrong impression.'

'You haven't been a ghost before, though?' Beverley asked, glancing down at the résumé again.

'No.'

'But the idea appeals to you?'

The younger woman nodded enthusiastically. 'It does,' she said. 'I'll be quite honest with you, Mrs Cleverley, it's very difficult to live in London. It's so expensive here, as I'm sure you know. Taking on a job like this would help me get a place of my own, which would mean I'd be more on the spot, so to speak, if a journalistic opportunity arose.'

'And where do you currently reside?'

'In Oxford, with my parents.'

'Well, if you're looking for a place to live,' said Beverley, 'I did notice a two-bedroom apartment for rent just around the corner on Eaton Terrace the other day. Very close to the gardens too.'

'I suspect that would be rather out of my league,' replied the ghost. 'I'd probably need to look at something a little cheaper. A room in a shared house, most likely.'

'Oh no,' said Beverley, grimacing. 'Who knows what kind of diseases you could catch in such places. Eaton Terrace. That's the ticket.'

The ghost smiled, seemed on the verge of saying something, then decided against. She took off her glasses, extracted a small pouch from her handbag and removed a piece of microfibre cloth which she used to wipe her lenses, holding them up to the light for a moment before, satisfied with the result, repeating the sequence in reverse.

'You know, you're a lot prettier without glasses,' said Beverley, intrigued by the ritual. It reminded her of a summer at Wimbledon, when she'd noticed how Rafael Nadal always touched the court with the tip of his right foot before serving, then adjusted his shorts, tucked his hair behind his left ear, then his right, wiped his forehead and bounced the ball. This unchanging routine had had an equally hypnotic effect on her and resulted in her flirting with him at the party on the final night. 'Why don't you get laser surgery?'

'Again, it's quite expensive,' explained the ghost. 'And I don't mind wearing glasses. Appearances don't interest me.'

'Yes, I can tell.'

'I think that what I look like is the least interesting thing about me.'

'Oh no,' said Beverley. 'I'm sure there are many less interesting things about you than that. The surgery is a lot less painful than you might imagine. You hear the sound of the laser cutting through the cornea, of course, and there's a smell of burning, but other than that it's fine.'

'Even still,' said the ghost. 'I don't like anything coming near my eyes.'

'Do you have a boyfriend?'

'No.'

'A girlfriend?'

'No.'

'You're not a virgin, are you?'

The ghost frowned. 'I'm not really sure what any of this has to do with the job,' she said.

'Nothing at all, really,' said Beverley with a shrug. 'I'm just making conversation, that's all. I'm interested in people, you see. Well, you have to be when you're a writer. I suppose you heard what happened to my last ghost?'

'I heard something, yes, but to be honest it sounded a little fantastical.'

'What did you hear?'

'That she was eaten by a lion.'

Beverley nodded. 'It's partly true,' she said. 'She was on safari in Kenya and made the mistake of stepping out of her jeep in the middle of an unsafe area. She wandered a little too far from safety to capture photographs for her social media accounts and was in fact mauled to death by a lion, not eaten. Although I daresay it took a few, you know . . . chunks. By the time they got her to a hospital, however, her injuries were too great for her to be saved.'

'How awful!'

'It is awful, yes, and she hadn't quite delivered the final draft of *The Surgeon's Broken Heart*, so that took some fixing. But I thought I might use her dismemberment as a scene in my next novel, as a sort of homage. I assume that Philippa has explained to you how this all works?'

'A little, but she said that you'd go into more detail.'

'The thing is,' said Beverley, leaning forward, 'I'm an incredibly creative person. I always have been. Inspiration runs through my veins. And I absolutely adore literature. I read six or seven books a year, if you can believe it, which is probably why I'm one of the most popular writers in the country. But, you see, with my family responsibilities and philanthropic duties, I simply don't have the time to actually write them myself. Which is where you come in.'

'Of course,' said the ghost.

'Naturally, I insist upon remaining very hands on during the creative process. The stories are mine, so the hard work is already done for you. Really, all the ghost has to do is take my ideas and type them up. I suppose you could compare it to how Leonardo da Vinci took on assistants and pupils, told them what he wanted and then they just got on with it. I feel a great affinity to da Vinci, actually. He's been a tremendous influence on my work.'

'I'm afraid I don't know much about him,' admitted the ghost. 'Although I've read *The Da Vinci Code*.'

'I saw the film,' said Beverley. 'Now don't get me wrong, I'm not comparing what I do with what Leonardo da Vinci did. His work is probably a lot better than mine. But, as fellow creatives, I imagine we would share a certain sympathy.'

A noise came from the corner of the room and both women turned to look towards its source.

'There's a box over there,' said the ghost. 'And it appears to be moving.'

'It's not my box,' replied Beverley.

'It's in your drawing room.'

'I know. And I wish it wasn't. It contains a tortoise named Ustym Karmaliuk. I'm taking care of him for a friend.'

'Ustym Karmaliuk, the great Ukrainian folk hero?' asked the ghost, opening her mouth in surprise. 'The Robin Hood of post-Napoleonic Europe?'

'I'm surprised you've heard of him,' said Beverley.

'Hasn't everyone?'

'I wouldn't have thought so, no.'

'Well, the truth is, I have a great interest in the region,' explained the ghost. 'My grandparents emigrated from Kiev in the fifties and, when I was growing up, they told me many stories of their history.'

'Really,' replied Beverley. 'How interesting. And have you been there yourself?'

'Not yet,' said the ghost. 'The flights are quite—'

'Expensive, yes. You've mentioned your financial difficulties. You see, there *is* something less interesting about you than your looks, after all.'

The ghost smiled and blinked a few times. A curious silence ensued and Beverley began to feel that they were two unprepared actors on a stage, each one convinced it was the other's line.

'May I take a look at your tortoise?' asked the ghost eventually.

'As I explained, he's not my tortoise, but feel free. Just don't expect too much back from him. He's not like a puppy or a child, always demanding attention and, you know, love.'

The ghost stood up and walked across the room, lifted the lid from the box and looked inside. Beverley could hear her whispering something, and then she appeared to be singing slightly out of tune. Finally, she replaced the lid and left Ustym Karmaliuk to reflect upon their conversation as she returned to her seat.

'Beautiful,' she said. 'Simply beautiful. Did you know that tortoises can live for up to two hundred years?'

'I didn't,' replied Beverley. 'They're not really my area of expertise. Although I'm reliably informed that this one is a hundred and fifteen. Now, tell me, since you're currently unemployed, you'd be able to devote all your time to my new book?'

'Oh yes. Of course. Philippa said that a timetable is usually put in place?'

'Ten weeks,' said Beverley. 'That's usually enough time. If you spend any more time on a book, it just feels overworked. We need a finished manuscript by the end of the summer if it's to be ready for publication in March, as I always publish my novels in the week leading up to Mother's Day.'

'And do you have an idea for the new one?' asked the ghost.

'I do,' said Beverley, smiling widely. 'It's about a young man from Eastern Europe who becomes a ski instructor in Verbier and falls head over heels in love with an English woman.'

The ghost nodded and waited for more information, but none seemed to be forthcoming.

'And what happens then?' she asked finally.

'Oh, there are any number of misunderstandings and chance encounters. Some witty dialogue and obstacles to their love. You can figure out all those minor details, I imagine. But they get past them and, in the end, marry.'

'I see,' said the ghost. 'But I expect you provide a more detailed synopsis at the commissioning stage?'

'Not really, no,' replied Beverley cheerfully. 'I think there's more than enough there for you to be getting on with, don't you? What do you think, does it fire up your imagination?'

'Well, it gives me a lot to play with, certainly.'

'Good. And remember, my readers don't like an awful lot of description. No need to spend pages and pages describing clouds and wallpaper and fields filled with flowers. Sometimes the sky is just blue, all right?'

'And what is your philosophy of writing, if you don't mind my asking?'

'My what?' asked Beverley, frowning.

'Your philosophy of writing. As in, what do you think a novel should be?'

'Ah,' replied Beverley, considering this. 'Well, a novel must have interesting sentences that gather together to make fascinating paragraphs. I believe very strongly in the idea of the chapter – that's crucial. And good spelling. I mean, if a writer can't spell, then what use is she? And the characters are very important to me. It might sound simplistic to say that they should be clearly divided into what one might call "the good guys" and "the bad guys", but art must imitate life and, in life, I find these are the categories into which most people fall. You're not taking notes, I see?'

From the hallway, there came the sound of the front door being opened and, a moment later, George stepped into the room.

'Hello,' he said, surprised to see a stranger sitting there. 'Who are you?'

'I'm a ghost,' said the ghost.

'Splendid. Hello, darling,' he added, leaning over and kissing Beverley on the cheek. 'Pleasant day?'

'No. Terrible.'

'Trust me, it couldn't have been as bad as mine.'

'Anyway, we're just finishing up here. I'll see you out, dear,' she added, standing up and leading the ghost towards the hallway to retrieve her jacket, which looked as if it had been sourced from a skip behind a homeless shelter. 'It's been a pleasure meeting you,' she said.

'So should I wait to hear from you?'

'Philippa will send a contract through, but I'm happy to go ahead if you are. I get a good sense from you. I think we can work well together. Just stay away from London Zoo, all right? If something ridiculous was to happen to you, too, it would simply be more than I could cope with. I'll text you later tonight, as I'll need to meet you at Selfridges tomorrow morning.'

'Selfridges?' asked the ghost, uncertain why they would be going shopping, but before she could ask any further questions, the door was closed in her face.

Returning to the drawing room, Beverley was confronted by a frowning George.

'There's a tortoise in a box,' he said, nodding towards the corner of the room. 'Just over there. A tortoise. Where no tortoise should be.'

'I know,' she replied. 'He's come to stay for a little while. You don't mind, do you?'

LOVE WHISTLE

Dr Twyla Oristo, tall, slim, the recipient of three separate PhDs, sat down opposite Nelson in her office, a pad and paper resting by her side, wearing the inscrutable smile she'd been perfecting since her earliest days as a therapist. Originally from Jamaica, she had come to England in 1979, on the same morning that Mrs Thatcher was first elected to high office. Although Nelson had been her patient for only eighteen months, she considered him the most likely to be upset by what she had to tell him today. For this reason, she had decided to hold off breaking her news until the end of their session.

'So tell me about your week,' she began.

'It was terrible,' he said. 'I joined a gym.'

'But that's wonderful,' she replied, brightening up. 'I'm sure you're familiar with the phrase *mens sana in corpore sano*?'

'Healthy men make healthy soldiers?'

'Well, not quite. But are you enjoying it?'

'No.'

'Why not?'

'I'm afraid I've already been banned.'

'Oh.' She paused and tapped the end of her pen against her knee. 'Are you going to tell me why?'

'Why I joined or why I was banned?'

'Either. Both.'

Nelson shrugged his shoulders and looked around the room, as if he might find the answer in one of the paintings on the wall. 'The thing is, I've seen men and women go to gyms in movies,' he said. 'They always have flirtatious and amusing conversations that lead to dinner dates and sex, so I thought I might give it a try.'

'Remember how we talked about not confusing real life and movies?' said Dr Oristo.

'Yes, but I thought this might be one of the occasions where films were based on true events. Like *Titanic* or *Gandhi* or *Avengers: Endgame*. So, I decided to give it a go. I even went out and spent a lot of money on the . . . what do you call it? The workout clothes.'

'What did you buy?'

'Green Lycra shorts and a matching tank-top.'

'Lycra isn't always the best idea for a man. And a tank-top

often looks better on someone with more definition in their upper arms.'

'I thought I looked rather good in it,' replied Nelson, slightly offended. 'Although there was a clear outline of my . . . you know. In my shorts.'

'Nelson,' said Dr Oristo, smiling benevolently at him. 'You know we don't use by-names in therapy. We call things what they are. We're both adults, after all.'

'Still, I'd rather not,' he said.

'Then I'm afraid I won't be able to understand what you're talking about.'

'I'm sorry I brought this up now.'

'We don't have to talk about the gym if you'd prefer not to.'

'But I do want to. All right, then. There was a clear outline of my gentleman's part in my shorts.'

'Your what? Your gentleman's part?'

'My phallus.'

'Better,' said Dr Oristo. 'But not quite there yet. Try again.'

Nelson sighed. Names from the pornography he occasionally watched ran through his mind but none seemed appropriate to use in front of a woman.

'My family jewels,' he said.

'You were carrying rings and bracelets about your person?'

'My disco stick.'

'Excuse me?'

'My meat and two veg.'

'Nelson—'

'My love whistle,' he said.

'Oh, for pity's sake!' she shouted, throwing her hands in the air in frustration. 'Just say *penis*, can't you?'

'My penis,' he muttered, looking down at the floor. 'I'm sorry, I think I got carried away there.'

'Yes. But we've established in the past that anxiety makes you do that.'

'You're the one who made me say it.'

'I know, and I am filled with regret. Now, tell me what happened when you went to the gym.'

He sighed and threw his mind back to an afternoon a few days earlier that he would rather forget.

'Well, as I said, it was my first time there so I didn't know quite what to do. I wasn't intending to exercise, after all, but to find love. So I walked up and down a couple of times and, after a few minutes, I saw a nice-looking woman standing on one of the mats doing stretches. She was pulling a leg behind her in a way that seemed erotic.'

'Did you find it erotic?' asked Dr Oristo.

'Not really, no. I thought it looked quite painful.'

'All right. And what did you do?'

'I did what you always tell me to do. I told myself that I was a pleasant and attractive young man, that there was nothing to be frightened of, and I went over to speak to her.'

'While she was stretching?'

'Yes.'

'And what did you say?'

'I told her that I had been admiring her calf muscles from afar and wondered whether I might be allowed to touch them.'

'And what happened then?'

'She told me to f-word off.'

'And did you?'

'Of course. I f-worded off to a different part of the gym, where I saw another woman on a rowing machine, and she was sweating terribly so I offered her the use of my towel. She declined and, since we were then engaged in what I thought was an agreeable conversation, I asked her whether she might like to have dinner with me at the restaurant of her choice.'

'Just the offer of the towel and then the offer of dinner?'

'Yes.'

'Nothing else?'

'No.'

'All right,' said Dr Oristo, placing her hands together with the tips of the fingers touching like a steeple. 'I see we need to revisit some of our sessions. But first, Nelson, I'm afraid I have to return to the issue of clothes. I see you're wearing scrubs today.'

Nelson looked down at his body as if this was news to him. 'I am, yes,' he said.

'We've spoken about uniforms before, haven't we?'

'Have we?'

'You know we have. On at least a dozen occasions. And what have we said?'

He hung his head low. 'That I shouldn't wear them in public,' he replied. 'That I need to be myself and not pretend to be something I'm not.'

'Exactly. And you're not a doctor or a nurse, Nelson, are you? In fact, to the best of my knowledge, you have no medical training whatsoever. What if an emergency was to take place and people mistook you for a professional? The consequences could be devastating.'

'I just feel more confident when I wear a uniform,' he protested. 'People take me more seriously. And it's not as if I'm hurting anyone, is it?'

'I'm not sure that's true. There's one person you're hurting.'

'Let me guess. Nelson Fidel Cleverley.'

'Exactly,' said Dr Oristo. 'And it's not as if people look at you disparagingly when you're not wearing one, is it?'

'Martin does.'

'Ah yes. Martin Rice,' replied Dr Oristo. 'And how have things been with him this week?'

'The same as ever. He made a joke about me in assembly in front of all the boys. He called me Nelson Stupidly. I think some of the students have adopted it as a nickname for me. It's what he used to call me years ago when we were children. You'd think he'd have outgrown it by now.'

'It's unfortunate that you and he ended up teaching in the same school,' said Dr Oristo. 'But I thought you were going to speak to the headmaster about the way he treats you? Bullying in the workplace is not as uncommon as you might think. As it happens, I've made my own receptionist's life very difficult over the years.'

Nelson shook his head. 'There's no point,' he said. 'Martin and Mr Pepford go drinking together after school, they even play five-a-side football and take showers afterwards. Men who shower together after sports, well, there's a bond there, isn't there? It borders on the homoerotic but, of course, no one ever points that out. No, if I even tried to say something to the headmaster, he'd just laugh me out of his office. Or he'd tell Martin about it and things would get worse.' He put the heels of his hands to the corners of his eyes and held them there for a moment before looking up at the ceiling. 'God, what's wrong with me?' he asked, blinking back tears. 'Why am I such a coward?'

'You're not a coward, Nelson,' said Dr Oristo. 'You're a kind, intelligent young man who has difficulties with social situations and with confrontation. There are always going to be people out there who take advantage of other people's good nature and, while I don't know this man, it seems to me that Martin Rice is one of those people. But all of this will continue until you stand up to him.'

'I know,' said Nelson. 'And when I'm talking to you, it all seems so simple. But then the days pass and I start struggling again. On my way here, I tried to talk to a woman at the Tube station. I followed your advice and somehow ended up saying something stupid about concentration camps being bad places.'

'But concentration camps *are* bad places,' said Dr Oristo, looking a little confused.

'I know, but you don't bring them up within sixty seconds of meeting someone, do you? Nazis should be kept until the third date, I feel.'

Dr Oristo burst out laughing and Nelson stared at her in surprise. This was something that had never happened before.

'I'm sorry,' she said. 'That was unprofessional of me.'

Nelson smiled. He never made anyone laugh, let alone women.

'And did you strike up this conversation or did she?' asked Dr Oristo.

'She did. She was looking over and made a remark about my clothes. She said she'd always had a thing for men in scrubs.'

'Which you shouldn't have been wearing.'

'I know but . . . well, I was. And we got talking. I didn't run away; I actually stood there and spoke to her. She seemed very nice. I liked her freckles.'

'She was attracted to you.'

'I doubt it.'

'Nelson, she was. Women don't approach strange men on Tube platforms and start talking to them unless they think that man looks friendly and interesting. And, believe me, you're a very strange man. She must have been attracted to you.'

'Well, if she was, it only took a few minutes for her to see sense.'

'But at least you engaged with her, and you should be proud of that. That's what these sessions are all about, remember? Building your confidence. Trying to help you talk to people without feeling such anxiety.' She paused for a few moments, waiting for Nelson to agree, but when he said nothing, she spoke again. 'How are things with your parents these days?' she asked. 'I presume you're still living at home?'

'Of course. Where else would I be living?'

'Many twenty-two-year-olds have their own places these days.'

'Not in London, they don't. And if they do, it's a cardboard box by the banks of the Thames. Anyway, I like it at home. I feel safe there. Although, earlier today, Mum arrived home with a tortoise. So that's a worry.'

'A tortoise?'

'It belongs to a friend of hers, apparently. She's minding it. I didn't like the way it looked at me. I thought a reptile would be the last thing Mum would want in the house, but she seems to be fond of it because, when I left, it was sitting on her lap and she was stroking its shell.'

'And what about your father? How is he?'

'Fine, I suppose.'

'I saw him on television this weekend,' said Dr Oristo. 'Interviewing Mick Jagger. I thought he looked rather tired.'

'Which one?'

'Well, both of them, I suppose. Perhaps the burdens of father-hood just happen to be weighing on his mind right now. He sees you struggle, and from what you've told me, living with Eliza-beth and Achilles isn't always easy. Perhaps he's looking for a way to connect with you all? You should allow that to happen if that's what he's after. I'm sure he loves you very much.'

'I know he does,' said Nelson. 'I know they both do. I have

no terrible dark secrets from my childhood so I don't understand why I'm so messed up. A twenty-two-year-old virgin who can't talk to women and is being bullied at school by the same man who bullied me when we were pupils. Achilles is five years younger than me and he's so much better evolved.'

Dr Oristo glanced at the clock. Their session was coming to an end and she had yet to tell Nelson her news. It was bad timing, but there was nothing she could do about that now. She put her notepad away and leaned forward.

'Nelson,' she said. 'I have something to tell you and, at first, you might find it upsetting, but I want to assure you that you have nothing to worry about. I need you to trust me and to remain calm. Can you do that for me, Nelson? Can you trust me and remain calm?'

He stared at her and thought about this for a long time. 'It seems unlikely,' he said eventually.

SANGERS FOR SKANGERS

A few months earlier, Elizabeth Cleverley had read a novel about a girl born with a halo above her head. Having spent the morning preparing sandwiches for the homeless, she felt she could relate to the girl's predicament and longed for her shift to be over so she could go somewhere with Wi-Fi to post pictures of her philanthropy online. She, too, deserved a halo, she believed. A digital one, anyway.

Sangers for Skangers – the 'g' was hard in both cases – was

an initiative dreamed up by her boyfriend, Wilkes Maguire, who spent his evenings trawling through supermarket dumpsters in search of stale, discarded bread before toasting every slice, adding past-its-sell-by-date ham, turkey or cheese, and wandering the streets, handing out his efforts to the homeless, before kissing their hands, taking a selfie and assuring them that he saw them.

Wilkes's grandmother was Irish and 'sangers', he explained to Elizabeth, was Dublinese for sandwiches, while 'skangers' was a term used for those unfortunate nomads who spent their days sitting on O'Connell Bridge begging for money. It had always been meant in an offensive way but, by reclaiming the term, Wilkes said he was removing its injurious effects. Intuitively, he understood the struggle of the dispossessed, he insisted, and it was important that others realized just how deeply he felt it, which was why he documented his every charitable move on Facebook, Twitter, Instagram, Tumblr, Snapchat, Pinterest, Reddit, YouTube, Flickr and TikTok, and kept a spreadsheet documenting how many likes each of his posts received and the monthly increase in his follower count.

It was Wilkes's total obsession with social media that had first drawn Elizabeth to him, along with his perfectly spherical head, scrappy beard and strange, baby-like features that made him look as if he'd spent much of his life as an infant before transitioning to adulthood, skipping all the usual stages in between, both physically and mentally. Others might have found this particular quality repellent, but it sparked a curious desire in her and she'd followed his endless, self-serving tweets – sometimes more than fifty a day – for months before wandering into one of the soup kitchens where he volunteered. As she locked eyes with this modern-day Mother Teresa over an enormous tureen of leek, bacon and potato soup, he told her that hers were the colour of consommé, which she took as a compliment, despite the fact that consommé makes for a rather bland and unexciting meal, although, like Elizabeth herself, it was essentially fat free.

From the start, Wilkes (he / him) had told her that he saw it as his mission to make the world a better place and longed to document his trips to Africa, Asia or South America on social media, where he would help to build houses for those who currently lived in ditches and ate live rats and cockroaches.

'Do a lot of them live in ditches and eat live rats and cockroaches?' she asked, sceptical that things hadn't moved on in those places in quite a big way since Live Aid.

'Oh God, I hope so,' he replied. 'I feel it's my destiny to help them. I've written to Bill Gates, asking him to stop throwing his money at these problems until I've had a chance to do my bit.'

'I'm not really interested in charity work,' she said on their first date. 'I mean, don't get me wrong, I approve of it in principle, but it's not really my area. I'm more interested in becoming an influencer. Couldn't your parents just fund your trip if you wanted to go?'

'That would be such a *bourgeois* thing to do,' he said, smiling a little at her *naïveté*. 'And if you don't mind me saying so, it's a little *jejune* of you to suggest it.'

Elizabeth didn't mind in the slightest, since she didn't understand a word of it, and that same evening, Wilkes took her to a needle exchange, where he got some great pictures with a recovering heroin addict who had once stabbed his grandmother in the foot when she wouldn't hand over her pension. A few days later, on their second date, he took her to a medical clinic, where he posted a photo of himself giving the thumbs-up sign while witnessing puberty blockers being administered to a child. On their third, they went to *Les Misérables*. And on their fourth, and most disappointingly, to bed, although he insisted on her logging into a special sex app on his phone first to confirm that she was giving consent. Otherwise, he said, he would feel like he was committing rape. Throughout the eight months of their relationship since then, however, not only had she been forced to give official online consent every time they slept together, but he had refused to stay overnight in Elizabeth's bed, claiming that he could not possibly justify sleeping in a house that could comfortably fit thirty people but in which only five currently resided, returning to his own apartment as soon as their passion had been spent, which was generally quite quickly.

'There's a tortoise now,' Elizabeth told him. 'So now we are six, as A. A. Milne would say.'

'Amazing to think that a tortoise is living better than most humans,' he replied, shaking his head and immediately posting the comment to Twitter.

'It's hardly his fault,' she protested. 'He was just shoved into a box and handed over to my mum. I'm sure if he knew about the plight of the homeless, he'd be very sympathetic.'

'It would behoovened you not to make such comments,' said Wilkes, turning away from her. 'It would really behoovened you.' And she shrugged, making a mental note to look that word up later, since she was certain that it wasn't actually real. 'Still, I appreciate you.'

'I appreciate you too,' she replied, knowing how important it was to Wilkes that he say this as often as possible, rather than 'I love you.' The phrase 'I love you', he claimed, was too focussed on his feelings, which only sustained the patriarchy, while 'I appreciate you' recognized her special qualities.

Wilkes had chosen to devote himself to social media in the hope that someone, somewhere, would listen to him. He'd always longed to have a voice in the world, to feel special, but his previous attempts at creating a public persona had ended in abject failure. He'd tried being a singer/songwriter, hoping this would give him the attention he craved, but it turned out he hadn't a note in his head, so he had a go at stand-up comedy instead, to the eternal embarrassment of his friends, who knew that his sense of humour was on a par with Hitler's. Having been laughed off a stage at an open-mic night, and not for the right reasons, he accepted that he simply wasn't funny and spent four days writing a novel in his local library. The book remained on his hard drive, a testament to his genius, but publishing houses across London, Europe, America and the Far East had all declined the opportunity to add his name to their list. Finally, feeling depressed and misunderstood, he set up a Twitter account, and the rest, for him, was history. At last, he had discovered a place where people would listen to the magical thoughts that ran through his mind. Almost 1,800 people, in fact. Two or three of whom occasionally liked something he posted.

Despite her general indifference to a life of philanthropy, Elizabeth had spent a lot of time doing Good Works recently, and at least it filled her days, stopping her parents from asking when she would get a real job, for since graduating with what she called 'a strong third' in sociology, she'd been living under George and Beverley's roof and was showing no interest whatsoever in pursuing a career of her own.

'When I was your age,' Beverley pointed out later that evening as they sat around the kitchen island eating dinner, 'I was working for the Department of Education.'

'And I was a rookie journalist,' added George.

'Yes, we know the story of your terrible, early struggles,' said Elizabeth, pushing her bouillabaisse around her bowl with a spoon. 'You don't have to repeat it for the zillionth time.' Wilkes had recently been discussing the idea of both of them going vegan, and she wondered whether she should stockpile meat in the freezer in case that day ever arrived. Although there was a McDonald's near by that she could always slip out to in case of emergencies.

'I'm just saying that we were both gainfully employed,' said Beverley. 'No one handed us anything on a platter.'

'Your father left you an inheritance of about five million pounds,' said Elizabeth, looking at her mother. 'And you, Dad, went to Eton and Oxford and immediately got a job at the BBC. So let's not pretend that you're a couple of working-class kids made good.'

'Be that as it may,' said George, 'your mother is right. With or without her inheritance or my father's insistence that I be educated at an actual university rather than, I don't know, a polytechnic with notions, we still would have made a success of our lives. And I, for one, did not bring up my children never to do a day's work, live off family money and generally be parasites on society. I'm not Prince Andrew.'

'It's not that I don't *want* to work,' said Elizabeth, 'I just don't think that it's the right thing for me. I can't be stifled, you know? I'm not the kind of person who can just take the Tube into some office every morning. Like, I'm really creative and individual and spiritual. I need time just to do me.'

'To do you?' asked George, frowning. 'I don't understand what that means.'

'To do me,' she repeated. 'You know, you do you, and I'll do me.'

'Does any of this make sense to you?' asked George, turning to his wife.

'No, but what I want to say is this.' Beverley folded her arms and gave her daughter the outraged stare she'd perfected over many years of feeling disparaged. 'I find it a little offensive that you have the audacity to call yourself a creative. You don't create anything. As a novelist, I'm the creative one in the family.'

'You're not a novelist. You have a ghost.'

'I come up with the stories!' snapped Beverley, who was highly sensitive to any accusation that her work wasn't entirely her own.

'Actually, now that you mention it, I've thought about doing some writing,' said Elizabeth. 'But I'm just not sure that anyone would really understand my work. I have this, you know, like, this *depth*?' She paused and looked at both her parents in turn, waiting for them to agree.

'Was that a question or a statement?' asked George. 'Your voice rose at the end of it and yet it didn't seem as if you were asking us anything. Hence my confusion.'

'I think I might make a brilliant poet,' she said. 'I live like a poet, don't you think?'

'Only in the sense that you contribute nothing to society,' replied George.

'Speaking as a mother,' said Beverley, a phrase she liked to employ whenever possible, even if it had no direct connection to what she was saying, 'there's no money in poetry. I mean, when was the last time a poem was made into a film?'

'It's just . . . poetry really speaks to me,' said Elizabeth.

'I have never seen you read a book of poems in your life,' said George. 'I'd be less surprised if I came home to find you saying you wanted to be a kangaroo.'

'That's so unfair, Dad,' said Elizabeth, banging both fists on the table, something she'd been doing since her earliest years and which had, for a long time, brought some terrific results.

'I don't identify as a kangaroo. But I *do* live for poetry. I really do. It has soul. And I'm a very soulful person. I'm really in touch with my inner child. Wilkes told me that.'

'Yes, but Wilkes is a moron.'

'He's not a moron! He's a humanitarian!'

'Of course he is, dear,' said Beverley. 'But you might tell the humanitarian that there are plenty of Fairtrade deodorants on the market if he'd like to give one a try.'

'You say that you live for poetry,' said George. 'Fine. Then tell me this. Who's your favourite poet?'

Elizabeth thought about it for quite some time. The kitchen clock's second hand could be heard moving around the dial, sounding almost embarrassed to be the focus of so much attention. 'Emily Dickinson,' she said eventually. 'Oh my God, I *love* Emily Dickinson.'

'Every sixth-former throwing up her lunch and cutting her arms with a compass says she loves Emily Dickinson,' said Beverley with a sigh. 'So unoriginal.'

'Quote for me one of her poems, any of her poems,' said George. 'Do that and I will write you out a cheque for a thousand pounds right now.'

'Oh, it's all about memory, is it?' she asked. 'It's all about forcing beautiful words into my head and then reciting them back to you like a parrot?'

'Ten thousand pounds,' said George, upping the ante. 'A hundred thousand. But my offer expires in three minutes, so it's up to you.'

'Fine,' she said. 'I'll do it.' She paused for a moment, then stood up, closed her eyes, and adopted a tragic voice while extending both her palms out to her parents in the manner of a statue of the Virgin Mary, or perhaps the Little Matchgirl, while saying the following:

> *'When Death arrived – I was not home –*
> *I'd gone to town – to buy some socks –*
> *He rang the bell – He called my name –*
> *But that's just Death – He never knocks –'*

'That's not Emily Dickinson,' said George, rolling his eyes. 'That's just something you made up on the spur of the moment. You're not getting a penny out of me for that.'

'Yes, but at least it proves that I'm a poet,' she said. 'And you can keep your money, I don't want it. God, I hate capitalists!'

'Says the girl who lives in a multimillion-pound house in Belgravia,' remarked Beverley. 'Speaking as a mother, I wonder that you can bear to stay here at all with such high principles. If you really wanted to show us, I suppose you could always move out and find a place of your own, like most other girls your age do.'

'If you want me to move out, you only have to say so.'

'We want you to move out,' said George.

'So you're making me homeless?'

'Well, it's not as if you don't have friends among that community, is it?' asked Beverley.

'We're not making you homeless,' said George, standing up and putting an arm around his daughter's shoulders. 'You can stay here as long as you like, you know that. But both your mother and I think it would be good for your personal development if you got a job. Call it a favour to us.'

'Oh my God,' she said. 'So I have to do favours for you now, do I? I'm your daughter, you know, not your best friend.'

'Still, it would be much appreciated.'

'Fine!' shouted Elizabeth, standing up and marching towards the door. 'I'll think about it. And in the meantime, if anyone is looking for me, I'll be upstairs. Writing poetry.'

RUM AND COKE

At a corner table of the Churchill Arms in Kensington, Jeremy Arlo, six weeks short of his fifty-first birthday, was seated at a table, pretending to read the *Evening Standard*. He was of average height, with thinning grey hair, and had chosen to wear a pair of chinos that were too tight around the waist. An ill-advised check shirt, also a size too small, made his stomach swell, parting the fabric at his navel to reveal an unappetizing glimpse of furry skin. He glanced at his watch and wondered whether he had time to run down to the high street to buy something more appropriate to his girth, but it was already three minutes past seven, and the shops were probably closed by now.

Before he could decide for sure, however, the door swung open and Achilles Cleverley stepped inside with a bemused expression on his face. Achilles had never seen a bar so bedecked with Union Jacks before. He caught his own reflection in a mirror – jeans, Sex Pistols T-shirt, biceps freshly pumped – and felt out of place, an anachronistic figure brought back from the future to tell the drinkers gathered there that the world they cherished would one day come to an end, their empire would crumble, and this would be its last remaining outpost.

He glanced around and spotted Jeremy instantly. A new victim was always easy to identify. He'd be the one person who looked absolutely terrified to be there.

'Mr Arlo?' he asked tentatively, approaching the table and

feigning shyness as he brushed his blond hair away from his forehead in imitation of a young Leonardo DiCaprio, an actor that Achilles was frequently compared to in terms of looks and physique. Jeremy stood up immediately, almost upsetting the half-empty glass on his table.

'Nick,' he said, extending his hand. 'It's good to meet you. You found the place all right?'

'Yes, no problem.'

'Oh good.'

They stood there smiling at each other, saying nothing, and when things got awkward, Achilles asked whether they might sit down.

'Of course, of course,' said Jeremy, indicating the seat opposite him.

'To be honest, I wasn't sure whether you'd show up,' said Achilles. 'You probably have a lot better things to do with your evenings than meet random strangers.'

'Not at all,' replied Jeremy with an anxious smile. 'Well, I mean, yes, naturally, I have a busy life. I do have, you know, friends and so on. But I was so looking forward to talking with you in person. There's only so much that one can say over text messages.'

'That's true, but I got a really positive sense of you from them.'

'As did I with you. Is that right? It sounds ungrammatical. Sorry, I'm a little nervous. I wasn't entirely sure if this was a good idea.'

'Why not?'

'Well, it is a little unorthodox.'

'I suppose.'

'But as the day wore on, my bad angel began shouting down my good angel, and before I knew it, I was standing at the bar ordering a drink.'

Achilles nodded, slightly concerned by the man's use of the word *angel*. Was he some sort of religious nut, intent on saving his soul in time for the Rapture? If so, this might not work out as planned.

'Did you come far?' asked Jeremy after an awkward silence.

'You sound like the Queen. Isn't that what she asks everyone?'

'Yes, I think so,' he replied, laughing.

'You wouldn't like it down my way. This is much better than I'm used to.' Achilles looked around innocently, as if he'd never been in a building with a roof before, let alone in a room with tables and chairs.

'It's private, too, which I thought was important. We don't need everyone knowing our business, do we?'

Achilles glanced at the man's pint before looking back up pointedly.

'Oh yes, can I get you a drink?' asked Jeremy.

'I'll have a rum and Coke,' said Achilles. 'And you might need this,' he added, handing across his fake ID, which added ten extra months to his age and carried his fake name. 'Just in case they look over and think I'm not eighteen.'

'You are eighteen, though, aren't you?' asked Jeremy.

'It says so on the card,' replied Achilles. 'So I must be, mustn't I?'

Jeremy smiled and stared at it for a few moments. Achilles remained silent, watching as a cloud of hesitation passed across the man's face. Once or twice in the past, one of his marks had chosen this moment to make an early escape and he'd never heard from them again. But more often than not, desire took a lead pipe to the man's conscience, beating it senseless and leaving it on life support.

'Well, yes,' said Jeremy finally. 'Rum and Coke it is, then,' he muttered, walking away, and as he made his way to the bar, Achilles glanced around at the old men dotted around the room, staring wordlessly into their pints. The place was creepy as fuck, he decided, but at least there was absolutely no chance of running into anyone from school. No one he knew would be seen dead in a place like this. Behind the bar, a woman standing with an elbow on one of the pumps studied the boy's ID before looking in his direction, and he gave her his most charming smile, the one that rarely failed him, and he watched as she handed the card back to Jeremy and turned around to reach for a bottle of Captain Morgan. A younger girl wearing a low-cut top and too much make-up passed by, carrying a tray of empties, and glanced at him.

'Parents let you out on a school night, did they?' she asked.

'Fuck off,' he said, flashing her the pearly whites too. She wasn't much older than him, and she laughed, already smitten.

'One rum and Coke,' said Jeremy, returning to the table and putting the drink down before him, along with another pint for himself.

'Thanks a lot, Mr Arlo.'

'Please, call me Jeremy. Calling me Mr Arlo makes me sound like your teacher.'

'Oh yeah?' asked Achilles, taking a sip from his drink; to his annoyance, the barmaid had gone light on the rum and heavy on the Coke. 'Is that what you'd like, then? To be my teacher?'

'No, no,' said Jeremy, shaking his head quickly and blushing. 'No, I didn't mean anything along those lines. You've got me all wrong.'

'I was just joking,' said Achilles, regretting what he'd said. It was far too soon to indulge in any flirtatious teasing. He needed to put the mark at ease. 'Sorry.'

'I just wouldn't want you to think that . . . Well, this is very unusual, of course. It's certainly not something that I've ever done before.'

'Me neither,' said Achilles, the lie slipping out without any particular effort on his part. 'Actually, to tell you the truth, I'm a bit nervous too.'

'Well, please let me say from the outset,' said Jeremy, 'that if you feel uncomfortable at any time, then you must leave. I don't want you to think that I'm keeping you here against your will.'

'Of course. You're a Guinness man, I see,' he said, nodding at Jeremy's pint.

'I'm not much of a drinker at the best of times, to be honest. But tonight, well, I thought it might take the edge off.'

'I like my rum and Cokes,' said Achilles. 'Sometimes a few tequilas go down well. A beer on a warm day. I'll drink whatever's given to me, I'm not fussy. My mum used to put vodka in my bottle when I was a baby to shut me up, or so the story goes.'

'I remember when I was your age, my father took me to a pub like this for my first drink. He said, "Jeremy, you'll never forget this moment." And he was right. I never did.'

Achilles stared at him, waiting for the punchline, but none came.

'So, have you been using that site for long?' he asked when the silence between them started to become uncomfortable.

'Not long, no,' said Jeremy. 'Actually, you're the first person I've met from it. I wasn't sure what to expect when I signed up.'

'Me neither,' replied Achilles. 'I got loads of messages from creeps. Yours was the only decent one.'

'Oh, I'm glad,' said Jeremy, looking relieved. 'Not that you got loads of messages from creeps, I mean. But that I came across differently.'

'Completely differently.'

'Obviously, it's not the ideal way to meet someone.'

'Well, I don't know,' said Achilles with a shrug. 'It's 2021. People are so busy with their lives that where else can you meet people other than online? I'm sure if I just randomly walked up to you in a bar and started talking, you'd think I was some crazy kid, punching above my weight.'

'And I'm sure you'd never just randomly walk up to me in a bar. I'm old enough to be . . . well, your much older brother anyway.'

'How old are you, if you don't mind my asking?' asked Achilles. 'Thirty-five? Thirty-six?' He looked at Jeremy, hoping he wasn't being too ingratiating. It never did to push things too far too soon.

'A little older than that,' said Jeremy, looking down at the table. 'I'm fifty. I might as well be upfront about that right now. No point in starting off with a lie.'

'You don't look it,' replied Achilles. 'You're in great shape for fifty. It's good to see that you take such good care of yourself.'

'Thank you, yes,' said Jeremy, who was aware that he was in anything but great shape. 'And you? Have you met many people?'

'Oh no,' said Achilles, shaking his head. 'I only went on the site for a laugh, and then you messaged me, and I thought, this guy seems quite cool. I can't talk to people my own age. They're all so dumb. And I don't have a father, you see.'

'You didn't know him or he's dead?'

'Dead. A couple of years ago now. I miss him. Someone to give me advice and help me out, you know? Someone to keep me on the right track.'

'Well, it looks like your mum's done a fine job with you anyway,' said Jeremy. 'You seem like a wonderful young man.'

'Thank you, yeah, I try to be. God, it's so easy to talk to you. I'm so glad I came.'

'I am too. It's funny, but when you're actually in conversation with someone in real life, the age difference just slips away, doesn't it? Honestly, Nick, I feel as if you're just one of my regular friends. Even though you're not much older than my son and—'

He stopped suddenly and Achilles watched as Jeremy bit his lip. That was a slip-up on his part. The marks never wanted to talk about their own families, especially not their kids. He stepped in for a quick save.

'In my head, I'm a lot older than my years,' he said. 'I've been through so much already. I guess I really look up to people your age who've achieved something, you know? I've achieved nothing so far.'

'Well, you're young,' said Jeremy. 'It's all in front of you.'

'Yeah, but it takes money, doesn't it? I shouldn't complain. I do okay. Even though my mum's a single mum and works every hour she can to put food on the table, she's always put me first. One day, when I'm rich and famous, I'm going to buy our flat from the council and give it to her as a present.' He breathed in and did that trick with his tongue at the back of his throat that always made tears come to his eyes, before taking a tissue from his pocket and wiping them away. 'Shit, what's wrong with me?' he asked, laughing a little. 'Proper little cry-baby, aren't I? All this fuss over my mum.'

'It's wonderful to see,' said Jeremy, leaning forward and touching Achilles' hand for a moment. 'So many young people these days don't think about their parents at all.'

'Just a son you have, is it?' asked Achilles, and he watched as the man struggled for an answer.

'Yes,' said Jeremy. 'I'm . . . well, I'm a widower.'

'Oh,' said Achilles, feeling an unexpected stab of guilt. 'I'm sorry.'

'Thank you. It was a few years ago now. So I've been alone with my son ever since. And, not so long ago, my sister and her husband broke up, which has left my niece in a very troubled place, so I've been doing my best to look after her too. But that's the modern world, isn't it? Nothing lasts for ever, it seems. But look, let's not talk about them. You don't want to be bored senseless by my problems.'

'I don't mind.'

'Well, I do. Will you have another drink?'

'If you're having one, yes. I don't want to keep you, though, if you have plans.'

'I don't have any plans,' said Jeremy with a smile. 'I'm all yours.'

Achilles broke into a wide grin, a flash of white teeth dazzling the older man. 'Then I'm all yours too, Jeremy. Same again, please. And this time, tell Peggy Mitchell there's two ingredients in a rum and Coke, yeah? Not just one. Cheers, ears.'

@TRUTHISASWORD

In her bedroom, Elizabeth made her way along the bookshelves, convinced that she would find innumerable works of poetry there that she could take downstairs to prove to her father just how wrong he had been. Running her finger along the spines, though, all she discovered was the first three volumes of the Harry Potter series, the first two of *His Dark Materials*, a complete collection of Mallory Towers and a hardback series of classic nineteenth-century novels, not one of which had ever been opened. Next to them were eight works of fiction and non-fiction by Katie Price, each one well thumbed and much loved.

I could be a poet, she told herself, refusing to be bowed by her apparent lack of interest in the form. She sat down at her desk and removed a piece of A4 paper from her printer before taking a pen from a drawer. Within two minutes she'd composed the following:

> *Whenever I can,*
> *I think of a man,*
> *Who said I had eyes*
> *The colour of consommé soup.*
> *We were in a group*
> *Together*
> *In Kazakhstan.*

She read it back and nodded her head. 'I mean, that's kind of brilliant,' she muttered to herself, making a note to take out all the capital letters when she started her second draft and right-justify it so it would look extra poetic. Putting it to one side, she wondered whether she might be able to come up with an entire collection by bedtime. In the meantime, she turned on her computer, feeling a buzz of adrenalin course through her veins at the fun she was about to have.

Some people had drugs.

Some people had Nintendos and played *The Legend of Zelda: Breath of the Wild* all day.

Elizabeth had this.

She logged on to Twitter's desktop site but, rather than using her own personal profile, she typed in the fake one she'd created a few months earlier, @TruthIsASword. Removing a notebook from the top drawer of her desk, she glanced down at the list of phrases she'd written there and which she kept regularly updated. The first was #SingleMother and, when she typed this into the search engine, she looked at the first tweet that came up, posted by a woman in her early twenties who said that she hated spending so much money on nappies, especially since they were so bad for the environment, but that washing reusable cloth ones was proving to be a huge hassle. Elizabeth considered this for a few moments before typing a reply:

@TruthIsASword mebbe if u didnt sleep around you wouldn't be on your own u grubby slut u even dirtier than ur skanky nappies lol #filthybitch

She watched the screen for a few moments, waiting for the likes to come in. As the numbers flipped up towards five, and then fifteen, and then thirty, she emitted a low groan of pleasure.

Turning back to her notebook, she read the next phrase: #PrideMarch. Apparently, planning was underway. There were thousands of mentions, but she focussed on a profile of a boy in his late teens who said that he was excited to go on his first #PrideMarch and wondered who else was going.

@TruthIsASword satan will be going tell him I said hi #BumBoy #BeKind

She sniggered and walked over to the mini fridge that she kept in the corner of her room, extracted a bottle of sparkling water and once again watched as the replies, retweets and likes flooded in. She answered a few, increasing the venom each time, before growing bored of the subject and moving on.

This continued for another half-hour or so, during which time she picked on former *Big Brother* contestants, Holocaust deniers, @SalmanRushdie ✅, Tories, the Welsh, fans of Ariana Grande, cyclists, eco warriors, and, for no particular reason other than she felt like it, the British Bird Lovers Society, before she returned to where she'd started and began reading some of the replies to the messages she'd posted earlier, most of which were just as abusive as hers and gave her an opportunity to feign outrage. A familiar surge of excitement built inside her body, as it always did after spending time on Twitter, starting at her crotch, and she pressed her left hand between her legs, touching herself as she searched for @GretaThunberg ✅ and told her that the world was going to end before she was thirty:

@TruthIsASword and you'll be sorry u didnt have more fun then lol lol lol get laid crazy bitch xxxx

As waves of desire began to take her over, she returned to her list, posting the most outrageous things she could think of. Finally, getting close to orgasm, she arrived at her three favourite targets and began to read their most recent tweets.

From @GeorgeCleverley ✅ she selected the following:

What an honour to catch up with Sir Mick Jagger and to learn of his deep love for his eight children. Still rocking at 75!

And replied thus:

@TruthIsASword sick old pedo knocking up girls young
enuf to be his great-granddaughter bet u do the same u
dirty old nasty bbc perv #jimmysavile

From @BeverleyCleverley ✔ she chose:

Many thanks to my wonderful readers for giving The
Surgeon's Broken Heart a 30th week on the Top 10
Bestsellers Chart. I write for all of you, not for the critics!
xxBC

And responded:

@TruthIsASword u dont even write ur own books u dozy
old cow doubt u even read dem

And finally, she opened up the Twitter profile for her boyfriend, @Wilkes4Love. His most recent tweet mentioned the
plight of a homeless man who'd been pissed on by a group of
teenagers after a drunken night out and related how he had
wept upon hearing what they'd done, vowing not to urinate
for twenty hours in solidarity. As her body began to shiver into
orgasm, Elizabeth typed the following:

@TruthIsASword u never get tired telling the world how
virtuous u are do u i hear u like ur women 2 shag u up de
arse with a rolling pin and call u betty lolz

She stared at her post for a few moments, watching and

hoping, and when a reply appeared, she jumped on it like a starving man at a buffet:

@Wilkes4Love What a vile thing to suggest. Seek help. Peace and love. #BeKind

At which point, she came.

HELPMEHELPYOU.COM

The website was called HelpMeHelpYou.com and Achilles had discovered it one bored afternoon almost a year earlier. It was aimed, it said, at sugar daddies and sugar babies, the former being men who, through pressures of work and an on-the-go lifestyle, struggled to form romantic connections but longed for the company of a younger woman, or man, for a night, a weekend or a holiday. Pictures on the homepage portrayed men who, in real life, would have had absolutely no trouble whatsoever in finding a romantic partner, for they looked like Brad Pitt's better-looking younger brother, while the girls who clung on to them pressed an index finger seductively against their lower lips, as if they were trying to remember exactly what took place at the Diet of Worms or how many different chancellors had served under Harold Wilson when he was prime minister.

Achilles felt the whole thing might be a bit of a lark, so he set up an account and posted a few photos of himself, one with his shirt open to the waist and the top button of his jeans undone, revealing a whisper of pubic hair, and waited to see whether anyone might get in touch. An hour later, when he logged back in, there were twenty-three messages, most of which came from men over the age of forty who were not shy in suggesting the things they would like to do to him. These he deleted right away, focussing his attentions instead on those who disguised their lust as indifference, pretending to be interested in him as a person while making subtle suggestions about their disposable income.

The first man he met was a married father of two from Battersea, the indent on the fourth finger of his left hand making it clear that he'd removed his wedding ring on the journey to the pub. Achilles went for a drink with him several times before asking whether he could help him out with a 'loan' of £1,000 because, he claimed, his landlord was threatening to throw him out on to the streets, and when the man proved hesitant to hand over any money, Achilles asked whether he might move in with him if he was made homeless, at which point they made their way to the nearest ATM. It was the easiest £1,000 that Achilles had ever made, but he deleted the man's number afterwards as he wasn't interested in any long-term blackmail plots. Anyway, it was clear from the website that there were hundreds, even thousands, of men who would willingly pay for his company and then be equally generous in their desire for him to leave them alone. By the time he worked his way through them all, he realized, he could be old enough to be a sugar daddy himself.

Achilles had promised himself that he wouldn't engage in carnal acts with any of his victims. It wasn't that he had any moral objections to prostitution as such, more that he didn't particularly want to go to bed with a middle-aged stranger, regardless of any financial incentive to do so. He wasn't a rent-boy, he told himself, he was a con artist. A grifter. And like any other ordinary decent criminal, it was important to uphold certain standards.

His second and third marks had behaved much like his first, so he quickly upped his ask to £2,000, then £5,000. Less than a year in, he'd managed to earn £35,000 in cash. If he continued like this, he figured he could earn enough in ten years to live comfortably for the rest of his life without ever having to work. And all it took was a night or two out every week in a nice bar or restaurant, making small talk with a lonely older man. There were worse ways to make a living, after all.

THE CLOSET DOORS

Afterwards, Elizabeth lay on her bed for a little while, staring at the ceiling, without a single interesting thought passing through her mind, rousing herself only when a knock came on her door. Sitting up, she watched as it slowly opened, and her older brother looked inside.

'Nelson,' she said. 'What's up?'

'Actually, I was looking for Dad.'

'Well, he's not in here.'

'Or Mum.'

'Also absent without leave. They were downstairs an hour ago, if that's any help.'

'Well, they're not there now. And then I knocked on Achilles' door, but it looks like he's gone out.'

'So basically, you're stuck with me.'

'Yes. Well, I tried the tortoise, but he gives nothing back.'

She beckoned him forward and made room for him on the bed. 'I don't like that tortoise,' she said, crossing her arms defensively. 'Do you remember when we were children and we begged Mum and Dad for a dog, and they point blank refused?'

'I suppose we could get one now that we're adults.'

'I've lost interest,' said Elizabeth. 'I can't even remember what breed I wanted.'

'It was a guide dog,' said Nelson. 'Achilles offered to poke your eyes out, if it would help.'

'Oh, that's right. I liked the little yellow coats they wear. And they're so well behaved when they're standing by traffic lights. Imagine, Mum and Dad said no to a guide dog and yet now there's a reptile living downstairs. It's ridiculous. Anyway.' She sighed and glanced across the room at her laptop, wondering whether she'd left her Twitter page open, but the screen had gone into sleep mode. 'What did you want to talk about?'

'Dr Oristo,' he said quietly. 'She's retiring.'

'Is that all?' asked Elizabeth. 'I thought it was something serious.'

'This *is* serious.'

'You liked her, then?'

'I trusted her.'

'Was she helping you?'

'I think so.'

'Did she manage to figure out what's wrong with you?'

Nelson shrugged. 'It's a range of things,' he explained. 'Social anxiety. Crippling shyness. Unresolved issues from childhood bullying. Fear of women.'

'I'm a woman.'

'You're my sister. You don't count. You're basically invisible to me.'

'Fair enough. What else?'

'My inability to interact with others in a normal way. The uniforms.'

'I didn't like to say,' said Elizabeth. 'But now that you mention it, I see you've come dressed as an extra from *Holby City*. Is this a new career direction or just one of your fancies?'

'They're actually very comfortable, you know. I don't know why more people don't wear scrubs in daily life. They don't wrinkle when you wash them.'

'What are they made of?' asked Elizabeth, reaching across to feel the material.

'Polyester.'

'Good God! I don't think we've ever had any polyester in the house.'

She took a bottle of hand sanitizer from her bedside drawer and applied it liberally to the affected areas. 'Have you saved anyone's life while you've been wearing them?'

'No, but a man collapsed at the Tube station and I did my best to help him.'

'So what are you going to do?' asked Elizabeth. 'Find another therapist? We live in London. There must be thousands of them out there. Everyone has been suffering from some form of breakdown since last year.'

'It took me eighteen months to get used to Dr Oristo,' replied Nelson, looking miserable. 'I don't know if I can go through all that getting-to-know-you stuff again. Building trust and what have you. She gave me the name of one of her colleagues, someone she recommends, but she's a relatively young woman, and I don't think I can talk about things like sex with someone her age.'

'But you don't have sex, Nelson,' said Elizabeth. 'So why

would you talk about it? Surely your sessions are just fifty minutes of uncomfortable silences?'

'It's because I don't have sex that I need to talk about it. Dr Oristo says I have a blockage.'

'So call a plumber.'

'Aren't most plumbers men?'

'Sexist. Anyway, maybe you want to have sex with a man. Have you ever considered that?'

'I don't know,' he said. 'I don't think I do, but then again, I don't think I want to have sex with a woman either. I just feel as if I'm supposed to.'

'There must be someone you fancy.'

'I will admit that,' said Nelson, 'on occasion, I am drawn to someone.'

'Who?'

'Princess Anne.'

Elizabeth blinked. 'All right,' she said. 'Anyone else?'

'I liked one of the contestants from this year's *Bake Off*.'

'Which one?'

'I can't remember her name.'

'But it was definitely a her?'

'Oh yes.'

'Is it always a her?'

Nelson blushed a little. 'Well, not always,' he admitted.

'Go on, then. Confess.'

'You won't tell anyone?'

'I can't promise that. I mean, if it's funny, then Achilles will have to know.'

'Do you remember that guy Mum was paired with on *Strictly*?'

'Oh God, yes,' said Elizabeth enthusiastically. 'Pylyp. He was gorgeous. As it happens, I had a little go on him myself.'

84

'You did?'

'Yes. I didn't go back for seconds. He was a bit self-involved.'

'Gosh,' said Nelson, uncertain how to take this, for, while he was still technically a virgin, he did have one sexual escapade to his name, when Pylyp had invited him to fellate him backstage at a *Strictly* rehearsal and he'd decided to give it a go.

'So that's it – Princess Anne, some random girl from *Bake Off* and Pylyp.'

'Once or twice I've thought about Helen Mirren.'

'Well, you're only human.'

'And Will Young.'

'The singer?'

'Yes.'

'Interesting choice.'

'And Mark from Westlife.'

'We're moving into much more male territory now.'

'And Emma Stone.'

'And the closet doors are re-opening to usher you back inside. Look,' she said. 'If you trust Dr Oristo, and Dr Oristo trusts this other doctor, then perhaps you should just give her a chance. What's her name anyway?'

Nelson reached into his pocket and extracted a card. 'Dr Angela Gosebourne,' he said, standing up and wandering around the room, picking up some of his sister's knick-knacks and examining them before putting them down again. The closer he got to her laptop, however, the more anxious Elizabeth became, particularly when he sat down in front of it, staring at the black screen.

'Do you mind if I look her up online?' he asked. 'Dr Gosebourne, I mean. Just to see what she looks like?'

'Can't you do it in your own room?'

But he was already fiddling with the trackpad and the screen had come to life. To Elizabeth's relief, Safari had been closed, but she hadn't cleared her search history and dreaded to think what might pop up once he started tapping letters into Google.

'I'll just be a minute,' he said, typing away, but she jumped off the bed and, using her hip, knocked him out of the chair, sending him sprawling to the floor.

'Hey!' he shouted. 'What was that for?'

'Sorry,' she said, sitting down. 'But it really only responds to my loving touch. What did you say her name was again? Gosebourne? Spell it for me.'

'G-O-S-E-B-O-U-R-N-E.'

Elizabeth typed in the name and a website called Psychology Today popped up.

'There are two Angela Gosebournes, if you can believe it,' said Elizabeth as Nelson returned to the bed. 'One is in Melbourne and one is in London.'

'I think we can safely assume that she's the London option.'

Elizabeth clicked on the icon and an image of an attractive blonde woman appeared on the screen.

'Holy moly,' said Nelson as she turned the laptop to face him.

'Indeed,' said Elizabeth. 'She's quite the looker. For such an old woman.'

'Read what it says about her.'

Elizabeth scrolled down. '*I work in a person-centred way, drawing from various modalities, depending on your needs. Being human is difficult for all of us. Life is tough and we are often faced with challenges that seem difficult to surmount. My goal is to help you to explore your difficulties and develop a new outlook on life. I offer a safe and non-judgemental environment, a dialogue between you and me.* And then there's a lot more, but it all looks like a bunch of hippy-dippy shit. Oh, and it says she's currently expecting her first child, so maybe she's not a good choice.'

'Why not?' asked Nelson.

'Maternity leave. You don't want a therapist who's going to bugger off for six months while you're swinging from a lamp-post, do you?'

'She really is very beautiful,' he muttered, staring at the screen.

'And presumably taken, if she's having a baby.'

'I don't want to have sex with her,' replied Nelson. 'But if I can talk to her, then maybe that will help me talk to other women. Dr Oristo is nearly seventy, after all. Maybe the reason I wasn't getting any better was because I wasn't intimidated by her. Dr Gosebourne looks much more daunting.'

'So give her a try,' said Elizabeth, stepping away from the laptop but clearing her history this time. 'What's the worst that could happen?'

A BUSINESSMAN

A television was on in the pub, its sound muted, showing a repeat of the previous weekend's episode of *Cleverley*. Achilles glanced up at it and saw his father in conversation with Mick Jagger, both of them laughing like a couple of puffed-up old peacocks who knew they were richer, more famous and had far brighter plumage than any of the mere mortals watching them.

When he was a child, his father's celebrity had confused Achilles. By the time he was twelve, people had stopped wanting autographs and were brandishing smartphones instead. He'd always hoped that George would tell them to leave him alone, that this was his private time with his son, but he never did, maintaining a broad façade of bonhomie in the face of these unsolicited intrusions.

'It's important to keep the punters happy,' he said whenever Achilles complained. 'To you, I'm just Dad. But to them, I'm George Cleverley off the telly. Without them, there'd be no fancy houses, no expensive schools and no luxury holidays.'

Achilles liked the first, tolerated the second but could have done without the third. When he was thirteen, the entire family had been photographed by a paparazzo on a beach in Spain and one of the tabloids had run pictures of a nearly naked Achilles, who, already feeling awkward with the onset of puberty, had felt utterly humiliated when he saw his scrawny body, clad in a pair of ill-advised yellow Speedos, spread across several pages of the paper. He'd been bullied mercilessly for it at school, but the embarrassment had provoked him into joining a gym, where, with very little effort, he'd put on some muscle and developed a six-pack. Within a few months, he'd grown into his looks and the teasing ended as a succession of girlfriends began showing up at his front door.

'I happen to know that man,' said Jeremy, following Achilles' gaze towards the television set.

'Mick Jagger?'

'No, George Cleverley.'

Achilles glanced across the table, intrigued.

'Oh yes?' he asked. 'He's famous, right? Well, I suppose he must be if he's on TV.'

'He's very famous. Has been for decades. Started out as a

journalist but quickly made it on to the Beeb. Has an opinion on everything, of course. Loves the sound of his own voice. You know, the amount of times he's—'

He paused for a moment before making the zip sign across his mouth.

'Oh, come on,' said Achilles, giving him his most flirtatious smile. 'You can't tease me like that.'

'No, Nick, I shouldn't. It's a private matter.'

'Who am I going to tell? It's not like I move in those circles.'

'I can't, I'm sorry,' said Jeremy. 'It's a confidentiality issue. I'd get into a lot of trouble at work if anything was to get out.'

Achilles sat back and considered his options. He'd been playing this game long enough to know that it was pointless trying to push anyone to reveal anything that they'd prefer to keep private.

'Speaking of which,' he said, 'you didn't tell me what it is you do. For a living, I mean.'

'Oh, well,' said Jeremy. 'I'm, you know, in business.'

'What sort of business?'

'I suppose you could call me a businessman.'

'That's very broad.'

'What about you? What do you want to be when—'

'When I grow up?'

'When you're older,' he said, his face flushing a little.

'I don't know yet,' replied Achilles. 'With my background, it's not easy to have ambitions. I might end up working in food.'

'A chef?'

'No, McDonald's.'

'I'm sure you can aim higher than that.'

'Nothing wrong with Maccy D's. We can't all be rich,' he added, lowering his head and allowing his hair to fall over his eyes as he gave his best impression of a Dickensian urchin before reaching across to take the man's hand in his own. Jeremy leapt up, as if he'd been touched by an electric cattle prod.

'I'm just going to run to the loo,' he said. 'And then I'll get another drink in, if you like? Rum and Coke again, or something different?'

'Surprise me,' said Achilles.

Jeremy stepped away from the table, descending the stairs in the direction of the toilets. The moment he was of sight, Achilles reached forward and put his hand in the inside pockets of the man's coat, taking out his wallet, but it wasn't money he was after. He flicked through it quickly and found what he wanted. A business card.

Jeremy Arlo

it said.

Arlo, Quill, Fitzgerald & Connolly
Solicitors-at-Law
1 Temple Chambers
London WC2

Interesting, he thought as he glanced back up at the television screen, where his father was shaking hands with Mick Jagger and wrapping up his show. *What have you been doing that you shouldn't, Daddy?*

PART 2

21 March 2006

It's the Cleverley family's last morning in Dublin – George has been recording a special St Patrick's Day edition of Cleverley in the RTÉ studios in Donnybrook – and they're wandering around the Princess Grace suite of the Shelbourne Hotel, finishing their packing. Beverley has been quiet recently, filled with anxiety at the notion of being pregnant again. She loves her children with all her heart, but the idea of adding a fourth to their brood is too much for her, particularly since she'd almost died giving birth to Achilles.

She hasn't said a word to George about being late, but she knows that he's guessed something isn't right as he's been particularly solicitous of her since their arrival in the city. Beverley watches him now, checking his passport is in his hand luggage, and smiles. He's a kind man and theirs is a good marriage.

Sensing that he's being watched, he turns around.

'What?' he asks.

She shakes her head. 'It's nothing,' she says.

He puts his bag down and comes towards her.

'It's not nothing,' he tells her. 'You've been acting very strangely since we got here. What's going on?'

Beverley bites her lip. She can hear the children arguing in the next room and knows that this isn't the time to broach the subject but, without warning, tears come to her eyes and start streaming down her cheeks.

'Good Lord, Beverley,' says George, stepping back a little. 'What's wrong? What's happening?'

There's no way around it other than just saying the words.

'I think I might be pregnant,' she tells him. 'Again.'

He remains silent, a deep sense of worry building at the pit of his stomach. He can still feel the horrible distress he'd experienced two years earlier, on the night Achilles was born, when he thought that he might lose her.

'No,' he says.

She nods and the tears fall even more. Both of them know what this might mean. The consequences. The decisions that will have to be made. He wraps his arms around her.

'I can't . . .' she begins, the words growing muffled as she buries her face in his chest.

'I know,' he says, feeling his own eyes begin to grow damp. 'But if you are, then you are. And we will deal with it.' He hesitates. He knows what he wants to say, what he needs to say, but isn't sure whether it's too soon to express such an idea. 'I can't lose you, Beverley. I won't even run the risk.'

She smiles at him, overwhelmed with love. He is such a good husband. Kind and understanding. She places a hand to her stomach, protective and fearful at the same time.

And at that precise moment, in San Francisco, a twenty-nine-year-old man named Jack Dorsey, having finished creating the operating system and website, tweets this:

@jack: "just setting up my twttr"

Tuesday

AIDAN DOESN'T EXIST

George Cleverley had had so many dealings with the firm of Arlo, Quill, Fitzgerald & Connolly over the years that he'd come to loathe the place. Even stepping out of the lift on to the third floor, where his solicitor's office was located, gave him a nauseous feeling in the pit of his stomach, comparable only to the smell of chlorine, which took him back to the humiliating swimming lessons of his childhood.

And then there were all the accoutrements that came with such an expensive firm, each one designed to project the idea that you were relaxing in the lobby of a luxury hotel and not seeking help for a legal problem that was, most likely, going to bring extraordinary levels of stress crashing down upon your head. The sound of pan-pipe music, for example, delivering a bilious version of Abba's 'Money, Money, Money'. The ironic eighties sweets gathered in a bowl on the receptionist's desk. The incongruous framed picture of Warren Beatty and Faye Dunaway being riddled with gunfire in the closing scenes of *Bonnie & Clyde*.

He glanced over at the young woman seated behind the reception desk, tapping away at her computer. He hadn't met her before and was impressed by how she was resisting the urge to ask for a selfie. Office protocol, he expected. Drumming his fingers on the side of his chair, he sighed dramatically and waited for her to initiate a conversation. When she didn't, he felt that he would pass out with boredom if he didn't say something, so he cleared his throat as he turned in her direction.

'No Aidan today?' he asked.

'I'm sorry?' replied the woman, looking up.

'I said, no Aidan today? The male receptionist. Is there a specific word for a male receptionist?'

'Yes,' said the woman.

'Are you going to tell me what it is?'

'It's *receptionist*,' she replied.

'I see. Got it.' He remained silent for a few moments, aware that he had been chastised, then slapped his left hand with his right, hoping to make her smile. Not even an acknowledgement. There was a time when the ladies loved this type of playful behaviour, but not any more. Only last week, he'd held a door open for a young female intern and she'd practically taken his head off for it, telling him that she was perfectly capable of gaining ingress into and egress from the office without the assistance of a man.

'It's strange, isn't it,' he mused aloud, 'how the words for some occupations define the gender of the employee, while others don't? Waiter and waitress, for example. Actor and actress. Tailor and dressmaker. Each one tells us whether it's a man or a woman performing the job. But then there are others, like engineer or doctor or teacher, which tell us nothing at all. I wonder why that is.'

'A woman can be a tailor and a man a dressmaker,' replied the receptionist. 'In those cases, it refers to the clothes that are being made, not who's making them.'

'Yes, that's true, I suppose.' He paused and thought about it. 'Steward and stewardess, there's another. On a plane, you know? Although a pilot can be either sex. I've actually flown on planes where the pilot was a woman.'

'And you remained on board?' asked the receptionist in a dry tone.

'Nothing I could do,' replied George with a shrug. 'By the time they start announcing themselves over the tannoy you're already taxiing towards the runway. Now, I have to say that I've never approved of the word *poetess*. I think it's pretentious and, let's face it, poets don't need any encouragement on that front. And then there's fireman. We don't say firewoman, do we? Although there probably aren't any. That's more of a job for men, I think.'

'Actually, these days, we say firefighter,' replied the young woman. 'It's a gender-neutral term. And yes, there are plenty of women employed in that field. My cousin, in fact, is a firefighter.'

'And is she a woman?'

'Well, no,' she admitted. 'But there are women there. In the fire station.'

'Cleaners, perhaps.'

'Not cleaners, no,' she snapped.

'Office personnel, then. Organizing the rotas and what have you. I wouldn't be keen on my daughter being a firefighter, I have to say.'

'And what does your daughter do?'

'Absolutely nothing,' he said. 'Well, I say nothing, but she claims to help out at soup kitchens and places like that. I'm not sure that she really puts in a lot of effort, though. The home-less. That's gender neutral too, isn't it? That phrase gets bandied around a lot these days, doesn't it? They're talking about having gender-neutral toilets at the BBC. It doesn't bother me in the slightest; it's the women I feel sorry for. I don't believe they really want to go to the loo when there's a nasty, smelly man in the next stall, do they? I said that to one of my colleagues and she accused me of being sexist, but I was genuinely trying to help. Then she told me that I was helping in the wrong way, which made no sense to me at all. I try to keep up, I really do, but every day something else has changed and it's impossible to stay abreast of it all, don't you agree?'

'I haven't given it much thought,' she said, leafing through some papers.

'And who makes these random determinations, I wonder? About what we should and shouldn't say.'

'Society.'

'Well, you know what Mrs Thatcher said about society, don't you? That there's no such thing, just individual men and women and families.'

The receptionist ignored this remark and George glanced at his watch. Really, this was too much. The last time he'd been kept waiting this long was on one of his visits to Highgrove, and one expected it there. Welcomed it, even.

'Well, if you're talking to him, tell him I said hello,' he said eventually.

'Talking to who?'

'To Aidan.'

'Aidan doesn't exist,' replied the young woman, taking a folder from her drawer and putting some papers in it before staring across at him defiantly.

'I'm sorry?'

'I said, Aidan doesn't exist,' she repeated. 'He never did, really.'

George laughed. 'What a peculiar thing to say,' he said. 'Are you telling me that he was a figment of my imagination?'

'Not yours, mine,' she replied, standing up and disappearing into a sort of kitchen area located to the rear of the room.

George stared at where she might have been had she not had the rudeness to walk out on him and blinked a few times. There had been an Aidan, hadn't there? That hadn't been somewhere else, like his agent's office, or the Salford studio or his doctor's surgery? But no, he was sure of it. He could picture the chap sitting right there behind that same desk. They'd spoken a hundred times.

The receptionist returned now with a cup of coffee, having not offered to bring him one, and took her seat again, and George felt a burst of resentment building inside him. Who the hell did she think she was to condescend to him like this? He was George Cleverley, after all. The fourth-highest-paid presenter on the BBC. One of the few television personalities over the age of fifty without a criminal record.

'I don't mean to be rude,' he said, leaning forward and glaring at her. 'Nor do I wish to labour the point, but I can categorically tell you that a chap named Aidan had your job before you.'

'Aidan never existed,' repeated the receptionist, and this time his irritation blew up into a full-blown rage.

'No, of course you're right,' he said, throwing his hands in the air. 'I'm making it all up. There never was an Aidan. I've completely invented him. And the Berlin Wall is still standing too. As is the USSR. And Al Gore won the presidency.'

The receptionist frowned. 'What's the Berlin Wall?' she asked. 'And who's Al Gore?'

He sighed and sat back in his seat. This was ridiculous. He wasn't going to continue engaging with her if she was going to be so obtuse. It was a waste of everyone's time. Fortunately, at that same moment, Jeremy appeared from behind a glass door and George rose from his seat with some difficulty and rather a lot of indecorous grunting.

'Finally,' said George, feeling petulant now as he shook the solicitor's hand.

'Are you all right?' asked Jeremy. 'If you don't mind me saying so, you look a little peaky.'

'I'm fine,' he replied. 'Let's go to your office. We'll talk there. And you,' he added, turning to the young woman. 'Well, I don't know what to say to you. But I assure you that I am right, and you are wrong, and that's the end of the matter. Also, the water out of that machine is tepid. If it has a blue tap and a red tap, then the blue should be cold. Otherwise, it's false advertising, and this is a firm of solicitors, after all. You wouldn't want to get sued.'

ARCHIBALD ORMSBY-GORE

'I should probably say from the outset that I know who you are,' said Angela Gosebourne, taking a seat opposite Nelson in the same consulting room that Dr Oristo had used. Although the setting was a familiar one to him, he didn't feel quite as comfortable as he once had, perhaps because the walls had, overnight, been stripped of their artwork, while the bookcases, which until recently had overflowed with volumes on psychotherapy, nutrition and Caribbean cooking, now lay empty. There was no soft music playing either, no flowers on the cabinet by the window, no box of tissues resting on the table between them. Even the scent in the air was different, for where Dr Oristo had favoured a soothing fragrance of orange and lemon, Dr Gosebourne seemed more partial to Dettol, which made Nelson want to put on a pair of rubber gloves and find a sink to clean. Looking around, he felt as if he'd wandered into a crime scene where most of the evidence had already been taken away by forensics. 'So, if you'd prefer to work with someone else,' she continued, 'then I'm happy to make a referral.'

'When you say you know who I am,' replied Nelson, 'I assume you mean that you know who my father is. But, as he's one of the most famous people in the country, it's hard to imagine that you'd be able to refer me to someone who hasn't heard of him. Unless they've been living in a cave for the last thirty years, that is.'

'The thing is,' said Angela, 'I don't just know him from television. As it happens, we have a passing acquaintance.'

'Really? Well, it's not as if you'll discuss anything I say with him, is it?'

'Of course not,' she replied. 'I'd be struck off if I did, and rightly so.'

'Then I'm happy to go ahead.'

'All right,' she replied. In fact, she had been a little anxious about accepting this patient, knowing that she was carrying his half-sibling in her womb, but her curiosity had got the better of her and any opportunity to gain more insight into George and Beverley's home life was irresistible.

'I was actually quite glad that Dr Oristo recommended another female therapist,' said Nelson. 'I don't think I could discuss my problems with a man. Somehow, it would make me feel emasculated.'

'You've been experiencing difficulties with women, I understand,' said Angela. 'Anxiety about social interaction?'

'That's pretty much it, yes.'

'And yet, if I may say so, you appear quite confident with me.'

'I don't see you as human,' he told her. 'Just an authority figure. Somehow, that's less intimidating to me.'

'I see. Does that explain your interest in uniforms? Dr Oristo notes that it has become something of an obsession.'

Nelson looked down at the floor and frowned. 'I prefer to think of it as a coping mechanism,' he said. 'Akin to carrying around a treasured childhood toy like What's-His-Name in that book.'

'What book?' asked Angela.

'You know. The one with the teddy bear. A posh fellow carries him around everywhere. And there's a war on.'

'*Brideshead Revisited.*'

'That's the one. Dr Oristo felt that I should learn to live without my uniforms, but I have to wear clothes, don't I? So why not a uniform? They're as good as anything. And, a lot of the time, they're actually quite comfortable.'

'Are they, though?' asked Angela, noting the fact that today he was dressed like a construction worker in a pair of many-pocketed trousers, a waterproof jacket, a hi-visibility vest, steel toe-capped work boots with leather uppers and had placed a hard hat on the floor next to his chair. Around his waist, he wore a multi-purpose belt carrying pencils, a tape measure, a small torch, two penknives and a roll of gaffer tape. 'You're presenting a false front to the world. Have you ever engaged in any construction work, for example?'

'I put together a flat-pack IKEA bookcase for my bedroom a few months ago,' he said. 'Does that count?'

'Not really, no,' she said. 'I'm thinking of those men who work on building sites, not some bloke who can twiddle an Allen key on a Billy bookcase.'

'I think that's a little harsh,' he said. 'They're actually more complicated than they look. Especially if you're not naturally gifted with your hands.'

'What intrigues me,' she continued, 'is that you call this a uniform, but it's not a uniform at all, is it?'

'Isn't it?'

'No, it's a disguise. Which is a very different thing. And you wear it even though you know it won't convince me that you are, in fact, a construction worker. So neither of us believes it and yet here we are, complicit in some strange fantasy. You could have just worn, I don't know, a pair of jeans and a T-shirt, for example. It's a nice day out, after all.'

'But I had to get here,' said Nelson. 'And I feel more comfortable on the Tube wearing something like this.'

She scribbled a few sentences in her jotter and glanced out of the window for a moment, Nelson following her gaze, both of them remaining silent. He wondered whether she was waiting for him to say more about his journey.

'Let's talk about women,' said Angela, turning back to him with such a dramatic twist of her head that he jumped a little. It reminded him of Rita Hayworth, tossing her hair back in *Gilda* and declaring that sure, she was decent. 'Do you have a wide circle of friends?'

'*Wide* is a rather subjective adjective,' said Nelson.

'Well, who is your best friend?'

He thought about it. 'Probably my sister, Elizabeth.'

'All right,' she replied, nodding. 'And after her?'

'My younger brother, Achilles. Although I don't mean to suggest that I love him any less than I love my sister. I've just known her longer, that's all.'

'But apart from your family,' said Angela. 'You must have some friends who don't share your DNA, for example?'

'Not really,' he said.

'You don't have a close female friend?'

'Of course I do,' said Nelson.

'Who?'

'My mother.'

'Apart from your mother.'

He breathed heavily through his nose as he thought about it, then seemed to brighten up considerably.

'Actually, I met a new woman recently,' he said. 'And we seem to be getting along quite well. Although it's early days.'

'Okay. That's good to hear. When did you meet her?'

'Today.'

Angela stared at him. 'Are you referring to me, Nelson?' she asked after a pause.

'I am, yes.'

'But we're not friends, as such. I'm a doctor and you're my patient.'

Nelson shrugged his shoulders and looked embarrassed.

'That doesn't mean we can't be friendly.'

'We can certainly be friendly. In fact, it's a good thing if we are. But you must never mistake that for friendship.'

'Charming,' he said, drumming his fingers on the side of the seat. Angela looked down at her notes again and turned a few pages.

'And you're currently working as a teacher, is that right?'

'Yes,' he said. 'But I don't think I'm really cut out for the pedagogical life.'

'Why not?'

'Well, to be honest, I can't stand children.'

'No?'

'No. In fact, I loathe them.'

'That's not good.'

'Well, it's exhausting, isn't it? Getting up every morning to go to the same building. Making small talk with the other teachers in the staffroom. Preparing classes. Trying to keep the kids quiet as you explain what happened at the Battle of Agincourt or why Catherine Howard got her head lopped off. Phoning parents. Issuing detentions. Dealing with bullies. Attending staff parties. Socializing. Dragging yourself home again in the evenings. Doing it all over again the next day. I don't know why we all do it.'

'Most people do it in order to put a roof over their heads,' said Angela. 'And to put food in their stomachs.'

'But I'm fine on that front,' said Nelson. 'My parents don't charge me rent and they give me quite a generous allowance. To be honest, I'd like to quit work entirely and live off my wits, but my parents have said that they won't support me if I do.'

'When you say live off your wits—'

'I mean that I could be an entrepreneur. Or I could invent something. Maybe go on *The Apprentice*.'

'Would you like to go on *The Apprentice*, Nelson?'

'Oh no,' he said, shuddering at the idea. 'I don't know why I mentioned that. It's my idea of hell. I couldn't do all that "people call me the Velociraptor of the spreadsheet" nonsense and I wouldn't be comfortable sharing a bedroom with a stranger. Also, I don't like Lord Sugar's beard. It always looks to me as if it doesn't know whether it's coming or going. He's Jewish, you know, Lord Sugar.'

Angela frowned. 'Is that relevant in some way?' she asked.

'Not really. I mention it purely for biographical reasons. I might just as well have said that he was born in 1947, has a wife named Ann or was once the chairman of Tottenham Hotspur Football Club. Although, having said that, I have to admit that

'I've long been drawn to the Jewish faith. I'm not a religious man, but if I had to sign up to something in that line, then I think it would be Judaism. But I could never do that thing they do with their hair. You know, the long ringlets. My own hair is already starting to thin, you see, so it's completely out.'

'You're thinking of Hassidic Judaism,' said Angela. 'A lot of Russian and Ukrainian Jews are Hassidic.'

'Really?' asked Nelson. 'When my mother took part in *Strictly Come Dancing*, her partner was Ukrainian.'

'Pylyp,' said Angela.

'You watch that show?'

'Of course,' she said. 'Everyone does. Pylyp is one of the few men on the planet who can pull off Latin trousers and a mesh shirt. In fact, I probably shouldn't tell you this, but I had a bit of a fling with him once. We met in a bar and were just drawn to each other. It didn't last very long, but it was wonderful.'

'Really?' said Nelson, astonished. 'You'll never believe this but—'

'We're getting side-tracked. We were talking about your living arrangements. Perhaps the fact that you still live at home means that you don't have as many opportunities to meet women as you might like.'

'I'm not sure I want any opportunities,' he said. 'That's the thing.'

'Do you like women, Nelson?'

He thought about it. 'Well, you know. They're fine.'

'Name me a woman who you like. One who isn't related to you.'

He thought about it.

'Kylie Minogue,' he said.

'Okay. Good. Name me another.'

'Dannii Minogue.'

'Someone whose surname isn't Minogue.'

'Madonna. She doesn't even have a surname. Nor does Cher, for that matter.'

'And do you like them in a sexual way?'

'I don't think so, no. Although I'm twenty-two years old, so I suppose I'd be in with a shot if I did.'

'Do you have posters of any women on your bedroom wall?'

'Just one,' he said.

'Who?'

'Princess Anne.'

Angela sighed.

'Don't you think that, really, you're old enough to look after yourself?' she continued. 'And that your father should keep his money for his other responsibilities rather than spending it on his grown children?'

'What other responsibilities? We are his responsibilities.'

'Yes, but you never know what might come along in the future. A change in his circumstances, for example. What if he lost his job?'

'That wouldn't happen,' said Nelson, shaking his head. 'He's far too popular. People say he's a national treasure. Well, *he* says he's a national treasure, but I assume others have said it to him and he's just relaying the information back.'

'Some people might say that you're taking advantage of his good nature.'

Nelson frowned. 'That's a bit judgemental, don't you think?' he asked.

'I'm not saying that *I* think it,' she said. 'I'm saying that some people might say it.'

'Who are these people?' asked Nelson. 'Are any of them in

this room? They don't know me. They don't know about my struggle.'

'Your struggle?' asked Angela, trying not to laugh. 'And what struggle would that be? As far as I can see, you've had a very easy life of it.'

'Dr Oristo was much kinder than you.'

'I'm not Dr Oristo,' replied Angela. 'And I'm not here to pander. I'm here to challenge you. This is good work we're doing and I need you to trust me. Tell me about your job.'

'Well, I teach in the same school that I attended as a boy. I don't know why I applied there because I was ruthlessly bullied when I was a pupil and I don't think I've ever quite got over it. Perhaps I went back to see if I could ever be happy there.'

'Why were you bullied?'

'Because my father was on television. And because of my name.'

'Cleverley?'

'Yes. For some reason, people have always found it funny. There was one bully in particular, Martin Rice, and he made my life a misery. Only he went on to become a teacher too and came to the same school, so the whole cycle has started all over again. He calls me Nelson Stupidly and does everything he can to make the boys laugh at me.'

'Have you stood up to him at all? This *bête noire* of yours?'

'Oh no, I couldn't do that,' said Nelson, shaking his head. 'He's bigger than I am.'

'But Nelson, you're a grown man. What do you think he's going to do to you? Flush your head down the toilet?'

'I just wish he'd found a different school, that's all. Or, you know, been murdered or something.'

Angela, who had been trained to watch out for warning signs like this, looked up from her notepad.

'You're not considering any form of violence, are you?' she asked.

'No, of course not. It was just a figure of speech, that's all. Like saying, *I want to have him whacked.*'

'Is that a figure of speech?'

'It is in Martin Scorsese movies.'

'The thing is, Nelson, I should point out that while it's true that everything said within these walls is confidential, if I thought that you were planning on committing an illegal act, I would be professionally bound to report it to the police.'

'I promise I'm not,' he said. 'I have no plans to murder Martin Rice. I only meant that if someone else had any such plans, and saw them through, then I would not mourn his passing.'

Angela pressed the clicker at the top of her ballpoint pen repeatedly in a way that Nelson found irritating. He felt a strong urge to grab it from her hands and fling it out of the window. He hoped this wasn't a tic that she was going to continue through more of their sessions. 'And how about the female teachers?' she asked.

'There's only a few under the age of thirty.'

'And how do you get along with them?'

'I pretend they don't exist.'

'But there must be some occasions when you're forced to interact. Staff meetings, for example? Or if you're discussing a problem pupil?'

Nelson shook his head. 'If we spent the time we needed discussing problem pupils, we'd have to cancel classes for the entire month. No, if there's something important I need to ask one of them about, then I leave a note in her locker and wait for her to write back. I believe that's how the Queen communicates with other members of the royal family, only rather than using their lockers, she sends a footman with a note on a velvet cushion and whoever it is, Prince William, say, or the Duchess of Cornwall, they write a reply and send it back the same way.'

'I see,' said Angela. 'Do you think that you and the Queen have a lot in common?'

Nelson thought about it. 'We both like dogs,' he said.

'Do you have a dog?'

'No.'

'All right. And you don't go on dates?'

'Lord, no,' said Nelson, shivering a little at the idea of it. 'And neither does she, I expect.'

'So you're not sexually active?'

He shook his head, blushing furiously now. 'Not with another person anyway,' he said. 'Although I nearly had a threesome the other night.'

Angela looked up, surprised by this unexpected revelation. 'Really?' she asked.

'Yes. All I needed was two other people.'

She smiled and cocked her head to one side. 'I'm surprised you can joke with me like that,' she said. 'That was rather *risqué*, if you don't mind me saying so.'

'I told you, it's because you're in a position of authority. It makes things so much easier.'

'Can I ask, have you ever had a girlfriend?'

'Only once,' he said. 'And she wasn't really a girlfriend. She was just someone I liked. And I think she liked me too. We went out for a drink. Or rather, we found ourselves in the same pub having a drink at the same time and decided to have our drinks at the same table.'

'Strictly speaking, that doesn't make her your girlfriend. But you talked to her?'

'I did.'

'What did you talk about?'

'The usual things people talk about on first dates. Films we liked. The metric system. The Elgin Marbles.'

'And did you arrange to meet again?'

He nodded. 'She was going away on holiday a few days later,' he said, 'and we arranged to have a drink in the same pub when she returned. But, sadly, she never came back.'

'Why not?'

'She died.'

'Oh no!'

'Oh yes! She was eaten by a lion.'

Angela's eyes opened wide. 'She was what?' she asked.

'Well, mauled to death by a lion, to be more precise. She was on safari and got out of her jeep when she shouldn't have. And a lion got hold of her. By the time they got her to hospital it was too late.'

'Good Lord,' said Angela. 'How awful. The poor woman.'

'Yes.'

'She was a ghost, you know.'

'You think she's a ghost? You've seen her since she died?'

'No, of course not,' he said, frowning. 'I'm not insane.'

'Sorry, I must have misunderstood you. But this must have been very upsetting for you.'

'Well, yes and no,' said Nelson. 'Obviously, I felt sad for her. No one wants to be eaten by a lion. But it's not as if I knew her very well, is it? We'd only spent one evening in each other's company, although I had high hopes for what might take place upon her return. I'm very sorry about what happened to her, but the truth is, I find it hard to picture her face now.'

'Still,' said Angela. 'You finally get talking to a woman,

arrange to meet for another date, and then she's killed in what can only be called a catastrophic event. You don't think this might have affected your psyche in some way?'

Nelson looked down at the floor. He picked up his hard hat and put it on his head.

'Do you mind if I wear this for the rest of the session?' he asked.

'I do,' replied Angela. 'No disguises, remember? But our time is up anyway, so don't worry, you can leave it on for now, if you like. I want you to think about what we've discussed, all right? And when I see you tomorrow, you are to be dressed in a normal fashion. No uniforms. Okay?'

'I'll try,' said Nelson. 'But I can't promise anything.'

EVERYTHING I'VE TOLD YOU IS TRUE

When Achilles first encountered Rebecca Jones, he was in Schuh, trying on a new pair of trainers, while she was browsing on the opposite side of the store. He became aware of her glancing in his direction and experienced that familiar tingle beneath his navel that quickly twisted into a shiver of anticipatory excitement.

For as long as he could remember, girls had liked him. Boys, too. It was as if there was a natural magnet located somewhere beneath his skin that simply drew people towards him. His earliest memories were of women in the street running their palms along his cheeks when he was out with his mother or nanny and telling him what a heartbreaker he was going to be one day. 'I could just eat you up,' they would say and, even then, he felt a willingness to let them. At pre-school, boys had tussled with each other to be his best friend. In primary school, girls had giggled when he looked in their direction. As a teenager, he learned how to take advantage of his charms, losing his virginity at fourteen to a friend of his older sister's who, despite the age gap, stalked him for several months afterwards. People just wanted to be near him, to talk to him, to touch him, to kiss him, to discover what exquisite delicacies lay beneath his clothes. He knew that it wasn't just his good looks that made this so, although they were certainly a part of it, but that there was something more mysterious and indefinable to his allure that no amount of study could ever explain.

And so, while he wasn't particularly surprised that a stranger was crossing the floor to stand in front of him, he was intrigued by the words she chose to introduce herself.

'That's disgusting,' she said.

'I'm sorry?' he replied, looking up at her and brushing the hair away from his eyes.

'I said, that's disgusting. You're disgusting.'

'What a bizarre way to initiate a conversation,' he replied, cocking his head to the side. 'Are you always this rude?'

'You couldn't have worn socks?' she asked, looking down at his bare feet. 'What if you don't buy those trainers? You think the next person who tries them on wants to catch all your foot funguses?'

'Firstly, it's fungi,' said Achilles, stretching his legs out and wiggling his toes. 'And secondly, I don't have any such disorders, thank you very much. I'm extremely hygienic and I pay particular attention to my feet, which is why they're in such excellent shape.'

'I hate feet,' she said, turning away.

'And yet you were mysteriously drawn to mine. You can touch them, if you like. I love a good foot massage.'

'Vile,' she said, rolling her eyes and walking back in the direction of the wedges.

This was not the sort of dialogue that Achilles was accustomed to. Typically, if a girl struck up a chat with him, the exchange would lead to a coffee, a kiss and either a quick shag in the disabled toilets or a taxi back to his for something more substantial. Instead, this girl had seemed repulsed by him, which he found both fascinating and insupportable.

Thirty minutes later, carrying the bag that contained his new purchase, he spotted her sitting in the window of a coffee shop and went in to join her.

'Just to set your mind at rest,' he said, holding the bag high, 'I bought the trainers. So no one else will have to catch my horrible diseases. And I picked up some new socks too. You were right. I should have worn some in the first place. I apologize for my crimes against humanity. If you still feel you need to despatch me to The Hague to stand trial, I will completely understand.'

'My father is a chiropodist,' she replied, looking him up and down as she sipped her latte. 'So I know what can happen when someone unwittingly wears shoes that someone else has worn before them. There are any number of afflictions. Warts, verrucas, athlete's foot—'

'I'm not much of an athlete.'

'Corns, calluses, blisters, bunions, heel spurs, gout—'

'Jesus, I'm not Henry VIII.'

'I'm just saying.'

'I knew a chiropodist once,' said Achilles. 'He bought me a pair of Bang & Olufsen headphones. The sound quality is tremendous. There must be good money in feet.'

Rebecca narrowed her eyes a little, sizing him up, before turning to look out of the window.

'Well, if you're not going to leave,' she said, turning back to him, 'then you may as well get something to drink. And I'll have one of those marshmallow cakes at the front of the display case.'

He grinned, put his shopping down by the side of the table and went to the counter to purchase an Americano, another latte and two cakes. When he returned, she was messaging someone on her phone, although she put it away as soon as he sat down. In her bag, not on the table. He was pleased, if not surprised, to have her full attention.

'So, what's your name?' he asked.

'Rebecca,' she replied. 'Like the first Mrs de Winter.'

'I'm sorry?'

'You don't get the reference?'

'I'm afraid not.'

'That's disappointing. I hoped you would. Somehow, I thought you'd be a reader.'

'I'm not really,' he replied. 'But my cousin Rachel is.'

Rebecca smiled. 'Nice,' she said, and he laughed, trying to keep his smugness under control. 'And yours?'

'Achilles Cleverley.'

'That sounds more like a character in a spy movie than a real name.'

'Maybe we are in a spy movie,' he said. 'And, any minute now, a man is going to come in and hand me a flash drive with all the codes on it.'

'The codes to what?' she asked.

'I don't know,' he said. 'I hadn't thought that far ahead. I mean, I could keep the scenario going a little longer if you like, but I feel it's run its course.'

'I agree,' she said.

'Nothing worse than a joke that's past its sell-by-date.'

'Tell that to Boris Johnson. So, I suppose, with a name like Cleverley, you must be related.'

'To who?'

'To the man with the chat show.'

'I'm his son. The youngest child of three but by far his favourite.'

'Then the others must be absolute monsters.'

He stared at her, uncertain whether she was being flirtatious or just downright rude.

'So, do you have a boyfriend?' he asked.

'Why do you assume that I'm straight?'

'Because ninety per cent of people are,' he said. 'So it's not an unreasonable assumption. You're not going to get all Woke on me, are you? Because I'm allergic to self-righteousness. Anyway, you didn't answer my question.'

'About whether I have a boyfriend? It just seems like a peculiar question to ask a complete stranger.'

'Small talk isn't really my thing. Have you ever been to Africa?'

'No, why?'

'Are you interested in astronomy?'

'Not in the slightest, why?'

'Do you give money to charity?'

'Sometimes, why?'

'Do you have a boyfriend? It's as valid a question as any of those.'

'Hmm.' She thought about it. 'No, I don't, if you really want to know. How about you?'

'Do I have a boyfriend?'

'Yes. For some reason, I feel like you might.'

He shrugged.

'I had one once,' he said. 'Well, not really a boyfriend as such, more a guy I had a fling with. A dancer. A friend of my mother's. He was very handsome and I was interested in trying it out, just to know what it would be like. But it didn't take. I tried vegetarianism once, too, but couldn't get into that either. So I think I'm destined for a life among women. My older brother, on the other hand, is a total flamer.'

'Do people still use that word?'

'I do.'

'And does he have a boyfriend?'

'Oh God, no,' said Achilles, laughing. 'He's so far back in the closet he's got one foot in Narnia. But it's only a matter of time. I fully expect to wake up one morning and find a skinny-assed boy with a bad haircut and a spotty back coming out of his bedroom with a look of utter disappointment on his face. Anyway, the point is, I'm currently single and available for selection.'

She smiled and took a bite of her cake. One of the tiny marshmallows stuck to her upper lip and he reached across to wipe it away, but she reared back in her chair as if he'd been about to hit her.

'Sorry,' he said, genuinely surprised by her reaction. 'I was only—'

'My fault,' she said, shaking her head. 'I don't like people touching me unexpectedly.'

'I'll submit future requests in writing, then.'

'That would be preferable. So, if you're not a spy, I can only assume that you're something much more mundane. Like a schoolboy.'

He opened his arms wide in acknowledgement. 'I am, as you suggest, a lowly schoolboy.'

'How old are you?' she asked.

'Seventeen,' he replied. 'And you?'

'Eighteen.'

'I love older women,' he said.

'That's probably for the best. If it was the other way around, you'd be a paedophile.'

'Please. My father's worked for the BBC all my life. I practically grew up around paedophiles. Jimmy Savile used to drop round on Christmas Eve with presents for me.'

'Do you still have them?'

Achilles thought about it. 'I think I have a *Jim'll Fix It* badge somewhere, but I don't really know what it means. Dad explained it to me once, but it's so long before my time that it doesn't hold any resonance for me. Although I believe they were quite prized items back in the day. I could probably get a lot of money for it from some nonce on eBay. I did really well with my collection of Nazi memorabilia.'

'Does it get exhausting?' asked Rebecca.

'What?'

'Keeping the patter up.'

He smiled. 'It does, as it happens. But hey, it's all I've got. I'll need a nap when I get home.'

She looked him directly in the eye and he felt, for a moment, discombobulated. 'I think you have a lot more than that,' she said. 'I mean, it's obvious that you have . . .' She waved a hand up and down in the air before him. 'All of this.'

'My genetic make-up.'

'Yes, that.'

'Do you like it?'

'I've seen worse,' she said. 'I suppose I'm wondering what's behind the good looks. Tell me something about you that nobody knows.'

He thought about it and looked away, searching for a funny answer but deciding against it. He would risk the truth.

'I've never taken drugs,' he said. 'Nothing. Never smoked a cigarette, never had a joint.'

'Really? That's unusual.'

'But true. Just doesn't appeal. Your turn. Something about you that—'

'I'm learning Russian. I take classes every Tuesday evening.'

'Interesting,' he said. 'Why Russian?'

'Don't know. Just felt like it.'

'I guess you've left school by now so ... are you in college?'

'Yes, I'm training.'

'To be what?'

'A musician. A harpist, to be precise.'

He sat back in his chair, smiling a little. 'Okay,' he said. 'Now I don't know whether you're messing with me or not. A harpist? Seriously?'

'I'm completely serious. Why would I make that up?'

'I made up that bullshit about me being a spy.'

'Yes, but that was to impress me. And it wasn't credible anyway. I'm not sure being a harpist is all that remarkable.'

He considered this, then shook his head. 'Actually, I think it is,' he said. 'It's not as if I have a whole bunch of harpist friends who get together every Saturday night for a jam session. All right, then, let's test you. How many strings does a harp have?'

'Forty-seven.'

'Why are some strings different colours?'

'So the harpist can find his or her place. The C-strings are all red. The F-strings are all black.'

'Impressive,' said Achilles. 'But you may have tried this trick on other innocent schoolboys in the past, so you've learned them off.'

'I doubt you're particularly innocent.'

'What are the strings made of?'

'Usually metal, nylon or catgut.'

'And what is catgut when it's at home?'

'The intestine of a sheep.'

'So can a vegetarian be a harpist?'

She looked up at the ceiling for a moment as if she was hoping to find the answer there. 'I don't know,' she said. 'And actually, that's a very good question. I'll ask Dr Lefèvre when I next see him.'

'Let me guess,' said Achilles. 'Dr Lefèvre is your harp teacher.'

'He is, yes.'

'I can't quite get a hold on you, Rebecca,' said Achilles, finishing his Americano. 'I don't know if you're making all this up or not.'

'Everything I've told you is true,' she said. 'Whether you believe me or not is up to you.'

She stood up, gathering her bags, and he frowned.

'What's happening?' he asked. 'You're not leaving?'

'I have a lesson.'

'Then where's your harp?'

She laughed. 'It's not a violin, Achilles. I don't carry it around with me. It's at the music school.'

'That does make sense. So, are you going to give me your number?'

'One dick pic and you're blocked.'

'Scout's honour.'

'Were you ever a Scout?'

'I was a Cub,' he said.

'You're still a cub,' she replied, scribbling her number on a napkin and handing it across. 'Don't wait too long to call, though,' she said. 'I might meet someone else before the day is out. I'm a very popular girl.'

And with that she was gone, and Achilles was left in a dizzy state of rapture. Usually, he didn't feel any great romantic longings for anyone and was happy enough with sex for its own sake, but there was something about this girl that intrigued him. He wanted to see her again. He wanted to keep talking to her. He put the napkin in his pocket and left the coffee shop, thinking about her all the way to the Tube and all the way home. It was only when he put the key in his front door that he remembered he'd left his new trainers behind.

HASHTAG MESSIAH

Elizabeth had spent the morning under the direction of Wilkes at Sangers for Skangers and had now been dragged to a soup kitchen to decant a tureen of something turgid and greenish that he inexplicably referred to as 'vegetable soup' into bowls for several dozen of London's homeless. Although she longed to return north of the river for a hot shower, Elizabeth was feeling virtuous and hoped that her Good Works might mean they could go to MNKY HSE or Sushisamba later for some real food. If she caught her boyfriend in the right mood, she might even be able to persuade him to join her for an afternoon at the spa of one of the five-star hotels on Park Lane, where they could scrub the greasy film of poverty from their skin with a meso-infusion body hydration treatment and a cryotherapy energy facial. She couldn't be expected to be virtuous and honourable every minute of the day, she told herself – she wasn't Jameela Jamil, after all – and she'd already gained almost forty new followers by posting a picture of herself on Instagram with her arm around, but not quite touching, the shoulders of a destitute young man who looked into the camera lens with disgust.

@ElizCleverley Feels so good to give back! We take luxuries like food for granted in the western world & need to remember there are people out there who don't share our good fortune. #homeless #SoupKitchen #VegetableSoup #Recipes #Kindness #Goodness #Decency #FirstWorld #KimKardashian #Smell #Rancid #Humanity #BobGeldof #Gross #PleaseHelp #Indigent #Indigenous #Indignant #AGoodWash #Soap #MoltonBrown

'Can we have a talk?' asked Wilkes, sidling up behind her and wrapping his bony arms around her waist. He'd spent the last hour going through the Twitter account of a famous writer to make sure that she wasn't following anyone objectionable, then offering her up for the world's condemnation when he saw that she was. A constructive use of his time, he told himself.

'Jesus fuck,' she said, putting a hand to her chest. 'Don't creep up on me like that.'

'Sorry,' he said, backing away and holding his hands in the air. 'That was wrong of me. I should never have touched you without your permission.'

'I don't mind you touching me, Wilkes, I just don't want to have a heart attack when you do it.'

He shook his head and looked as if he was about to cry. 'No, I'm entirely to blame,' he said. 'That was a non-consensual incursion on your personal space, and I should have asked first. I'll totally understand if you feel that you need to take the matter further.'

She stared at him, remembering previous boyfriends who had treated her body like it was theirs to molest whenever they felt like it and how distressing that had been. But at the same time, this level of chivalry was a bit much. Couldn't there be some happy medium? And who would she take the matter to, even if she wanted to? She was hardly going to report him to the Metropolitan Police.

'I forgive you,' she said. 'But learn from this moment, Wilkes, all right? Be better. *Do* better.'

'I will,' he said. 'I promise. I appreciate you.'

'And I appreciate you too. But if I'm going to die young and beautiful, then I want it to be on a beach in Dubai with a frozen Margarita in one hand and a Cecelia Ahern in the other, not ladling out gunge to a bunch of strangers at the back end of Brixton.'

He smiled, his sanctimonious, ghostly white face glowing like a five-watt bulb. Elizabeth hated being one of those women who only felt valued if she was with a man, but the truth was that she'd had a boyfriend every day of her life since she was fourteen years old and couldn't imagine being single, and Wilkes was, to date, the one she liked the most. It wasn't just that he paid more attention to her pleasure in bed than his own – he preferred not to orgasm in her presence, believing it was a symbol of male dominance over women – or that he had the kind of empty mind and childlike expression that she found so devastating in a man. Nor was it his understanding of all the world's injustices and his determination to address them. She was all in favour of that, naturally, although she didn't think he needed to talk about them quite so often or to be constantly writing in a notebook that had the words *Global Inequalities, by Wilkes Maguire (he/him)* scrawled across the front. No, the thing she liked most about her paramour was that he was neither impressed by her wealth and privilege nor repulsed by it. In the past, some of her exes had come to her home and spent more time with her father than with her, luxuriating in the pulsating glow of his celebrity, while others had scoffed at the five floors and the expensive artworks, while partaking of the pleasures of all. Wilkes, however, never seemed to notice his surroundings. He was like a puppy, full of energy, desperate for attention and with a surprisingly weak bladder.

'So, what's up?' asked Elizabeth as they sat down at an empty table, facing each other. She leaned forward, placing her elbows on the woodwork, before immediately regretting it. The tables hadn't been washed down after lunch yet and the sleeve of her blouse attached itself to the surface. She peeled it off, making a mental note to throw it away later.

'An opportunity has presented itself,' he said.

'Does it involve ESPA Life at the Corinthia?'

'No.'

He reached into his back pocket and removed a piece of paper, passing it across with so much reverence that it might have been a scan of their first child, which, he had already informed her, would be brought up gender neutral. In fact, it wouldn't even be allowed to look at its own genitals until it was eighteen.

'Have a read of this,' he said. 'And try not to get too excited.'

'I'll do my best,' she said, unfolding the page and scanning it quickly, trying to avoid looking at the picture that accompanied the article. It didn't take her more than a few moments to know that she would rather bore a hole to the centre of the Earth with her tongue than have anything to do with it.

'A leper colony,' she said quietly, more as a statement than a question. She couldn't remember ever having used these words before and they didn't sound quite right as they emerged from her mouth. It was as if she was talking about something that she was ninety-nine per cent sure didn't actually exist but that just might have in the distant past. Dragons, for example. Zombies. Honest Republicans.

'That's right,' replied Wilkes with a wide grin. How did he have such white teeth, she wondered? He claimed never to use whitening strips, saying they were bad for the environment, but those gnashers sparkled like a clutch of blood diamonds hanging around Naomi Campbell's neck.

'You want me to go to a leper colony?'

'Well, not on your own, no. I want us to go together.'

'We couldn't just go to Paris?'

'I don't think there are any leper colonies there. If there were, I'd certainly consider it.'

'But I don't understand,' she said. 'I thought leprosy had been eradicated.'

'It has been, for the most part,' he replied. 'But, luckily, there's still a few small pockets of the world where the disease is rife. I found this small island just off Indonesia where they're crying out for help. I know it sounds a little frightening, but just think about it. How many people in the twenty-first century get to spend time around lepers?'

'Kevin Spacey's lawyers?' she suggested. 'Prince Andrew's boot boy?'

'This isn't funny, Elizabeth,' said Wilkes, frowning. 'Leprosy is a horrible disease that affects tens of people every year and we as a society do nothing to help them. There hasn't been a march, a charity record, there's not even an awareness ribbon for supporters of the disease.'

'Well, you'd hardly support it, would you? You'd be opposed to it.'

'Support the obliteration of it, I mean. AIDS has a red ribbon, breast cancer has pink, bladder cancer has yellow. The cancers have it all sewn up, to be honest, and they haven't left much room for anything else. Perhaps I should create one.'

'You could go for something with nasty red splodges on it.'

'Or spots!' said Wilkes, feeling he'd had a Eureka moment. 'You know, as in—'

'I'm pretty sure that's leopard,' said Elizabeth.

'Oh, right.'

'But isn't it all a bit . . .'

'A bit what?'

'A bit gross? Aren't lepers covered with scars and open, pus-filled wounds? Don't their arms and legs fall off without any warning?'

'I don't think that happens,' he replied. 'Although, naturally, we'd have to take precautions so we didn't contract it ourselves. I still have a bunch of hemp masks left over from last year, so they should help. But you have to admit, if we arrived back in London and stood in the middle of Trafalgar Square ringing bells and shouting "Unclean! Unclean!", it would really make people sit up and think. I bet your father's never had a leper on his chat show.'

'He had Gary Glitter on a few times back in the day.'

'If he booked us, it would create a media storm.'

'Yes, but then we'd have leprosy. Is it worth it?'

'It would be if it stopped people spending all their time on social media and made them actually live their lives instead.'

'But Wilkes,' said Elizabeth, reaching across the table to

place her hand on his, 'you're on social media. You're very active on it. You practically have carpal tunnel syndrome in your right wrist.'

'I have to be,' he replied. 'I'm educating strangers on how they can live better lives. And making sure that those with the wrong opinions are held to account.'

Elizabeth smiled and realized once again what an incredible person her boyfriend was. His giving nature. His empathy. His indestructible conviction in his own moral superiority. 'I don't know why they always give out honours to politicians and movie stars,' she said. 'It's people like you who are the real heroes. You should be Sir Wilkes Maguire.'

'Naturally, I could never accept any honour that invoked the spirit of the British empire,' he replied, shaking his head. 'But at the same time, if such a thing came my way, it would be an amazing boost for the homeless. And the lepers.'

'I'm sure Daddy knows people at Number Ten,' she said. 'I'll have a word.'

'Well, if you must,' he said, as if it was neither here nor there. 'But let's get back to what we were discussing.'

'Oh, I thought we had finished talking about that.'

'We've barely even begun!'

'It's just . . . well, how many people can we really help there?' she asked, not wanting to sound too negative. Along with his weak bladder, Wilkes was prone to tears, particularly now, during hay-fever season. He perspired a lot too. Basically, he was a leaker. 'Don't you think we're better off doing good at home? We're in a soup kitchen in the middle of the day, after all, discussing leper colonies in Indonesia.'

'No, we need to wake people up. To make them see how much suffering there is in the world and how deeply it affects me. Not everyone's like you and me, you know. Take your family, for example. Do you know, last week, I saw Nelson eating a tomato?'

'What's wrong with tomatoes?' asked Elizabeth, baffled.

'It was an *Italian* tomato, Elizabeth, and Italy exploits migrant workers in order to fill supermarket shelves around Europe. They barely pay them and then kick them out at the end of the season. It's practically slave labour.'

'You ate a pizza last week,' said Elizabeth. 'We were in Pizza Express. And pizzas have tomato bases.'

'Yes, but I posted a picture of it online and pointed out the troubling politics and twenty-four people thanked me for drawing attention to the problem. And then there's Achilles. Every time I see him he's carrying a disposable cup from Starbucks in his hand. Can't he buy a reusable one?'

'Oh, that's just Achilles,' she said. 'He's an idiot.'

'But it's not just your family. It's your friends too. And your family's friends. And your friends' families.'

'Yes, I get the point. Don't go on.'

'You're always saying that you really want to make a difference in the world – well, this is how to do it.'

'What I mean is that I want to be an influencer.'

'But this is *how* you influence people. By gaining as many followers as possible and making them believe in you, even if you have no knowledge or training in your particular subject. That's how Jesus did it, after all. And look at Christianity. It's huge.'

'Jesus wasn't on social media,' countered Elizabeth.

'Only because it wasn't around then. But can you imagine if he'd tweeted from the cross?'

'Dying,' said Elizabeth, looking into the distance as she considered this. 'Nails in my hands and feet. Back in three days. In the meantime, #BeKind.'

'Exactly. Or if he'd made a TikTok and posted it as he rose

from the dead? What about an Instagram video of him turn-ing water into wine? Content like that would have broken the Internet. Hashtag Messiah!'

She thought about it, wondering how she could transfer his compassion to something less disgusting. Sick puppies, for example. Everyone loved a sick puppy.

'How many lepers are on this island anyway?' she asked eventually.

'Around twenty,' he said.

'You don't think it's a bit white saviour?'

'No!' he cried, appalled. 'We'd just be transporting know-ledge, support and medical supplies to a people who have suffered for too long in silence.'

'But neither of us has any professional training,' she pro-tested. 'And you don't like blood. You nearly passed out last week when you got a splinter in your foot. I thought I was going to have to sedate you when I was taking it out.'

'That's not fair,' he said. 'The heel is a notoriously sensitive part of the human anatomy. And I wasn't crying from pain. I was crying because I realized that you appreciated me enough to help prevent my leg from turning gangrenous. Just think, if you say yes, we could be pulling splinters from the limbs of lepers this time next month. Can you imagine anything more exciting?'

'I can,' she said. 'But we don't have all day so there's no point in me starting a list. Do they even have Wi-Fi on this island of yours?'

'Look, I don't need you to decide right now,' he said with a sigh. 'I know I've thrown this at you out of the blue. All I ask is that you think about it, okay? Keep an open mind. Read up about it. Consider how much good we can do in a part of the world that is desperate for people like you and me, and how this is a completely unexploited hashtag on social media. #WilkesHelpsLepers.'

'I'm happy to think about it,' said Elizabeth, standing up and resolving to think about anything but this for the rest of the day. 'But in order to do so, I need to go home and have a long, hot bath. I always think best in the bath.'

He nodded. 'Do you want some company?' he asked hopefully.

She thought about it. He did look adorable, sitting there in his oversized cardigan with a bunch of old elastic bands inexplicably wrapped around his tiny little wrist. But all this talk of leprosy had eradicated any sexual desire she might have felt. She needed some time alone.

'No thanks,' she said. 'But I'll post a photo once I'm submerged.'

AFTER EIGHT

Beverley waited until the house was empty to contact Pylyp. He'd been gone less than twenty-four hours but she was already missing him, so much so that, the previous night, she'd had an erotic dream about shirtless Ukrainian peasants charging Russian soldiers with pitchforks as they attacked each other across the Carpathian Mountains. Waking in a state of disarray, she'd given serious consideration to nudging George, who was lying asleep next to her, and inviting him to take advantage of her arousal, something that neither of them had proposed in quite some time.

A few hours earlier, she'd texted her lover to say that she would Skype him at this time, when she was sure to be alone, and he answered now on the second ring, appearing on the screen before her in a tank-top, his face damp with perspiration, as if he'd just completed a workout.

'Hello, you,' she said, already turned on by the casual manner in which he lifted his right hand to brush the hair out of his eyes, revealing the taut muscles and hirsute underarms that gave her an erotic charge that she'd experienced only twice before in her life: when she'd first fallen in love with the handsome young George and when she'd danced with Anthony Hopkins after the premiere of *The Silence of the Lambs* and he'd pressed his teeth against her neck. 'I haven't heard a peep out of you since I left you at the security gate. I thought maybe you'd died too.'

'As well as my father?' he asked, frowning. 'This is not funny joke.'

'It wasn't meant as a joke. You said you'd text me when you landed, and you didn't. I was genuinely worried. I don't know what goes on in that part of the world, but one hears things on the radio and—'

'I am sorry,' he said, interrupting her. 'Yes, you are right. I mean to contact you every hour of the minute but am so busy making plans for funeral—'

'I thought he was being buried this morning?'

'No. He is still on display.'

'To whom?'

'Population.'

'Charming.'

'And I am making food for neighbours who call in night and day. Door is broken from so many knockings.'

'Can't you just turn them away?'

'I from Ukraine,' said Pylyp, sounding outraged. 'Not

Moldova. This is thing Moldovan man will do. But I from Ukraine,' he repeated defiantly.

Beverley nodded, realizing that she hadn't understood how deeply this remark would cut the sensibilities of an Eastern European.

'In London, neighbours often stop by after a bereavement,' she told him, 'but they know not to intrude if no one answers the door. Maybe they'll leave a lasagne on the doorstep. Or, you know, a quiche or something.'

'On doorstep? For dogs of street to eat?'

'Well, I mean they leave it in a sealed container. A Le Creuset casserole dish, or whatever they have to hand. I feel like I'm rambling. Oh yes, you were saying about your neighbours stopping by constantly. Are you eating? It's important that you keep your strength up. Don't let your muscles atrophy.'

'This morning, I eat dead chicken. And last night, dead rabbit. Tonight, I will eat dead pig.'

'Well, you're choosing the right period of their life cycle anyway. And how are your spirits?'

Pylyp frowned. 'My spirits?' he asked.

'You know, are you crying a lot? Are you depressed?'

'A man dies, is normal,' he replied with a shrug.

'Still, your father.'

'Who beats me when I am a child and calls me the pansy for dancing.'

'You mustn't dwell on bad memories,' suggested Beverley. 'Try to remember the good. What was the nicest thing he ever did for you?'

Pylyp thought about it. 'When I am thirteen years old,' he said, 'he is taking me to whorehouse.'

'You're not serious.'

'I am very serious. I am serious as the cancer. You know this song? I am serious as the cancer when I say the rhythm is the dancer?'

'I think I've heard it. It always struck me as a little distasteful, if I'm honest.'

'The rhythm is the dancer,' said Pylyp, starting to sing in a tuneless voice. 'It is the soul companion. You must be feeling it everywhere.'

'At least you know what to do if you do start to feel upset.'

'And what is that?'

'Dance,' said Beverley. 'It's what you love, after all. Have you danced since you returned home?'

'I cannot dance the month my father is dead,' replied Pylyp, shaking his head. 'I from Ukraine. Not—'

'Not Moldova, yes. Is that something they do over there?'

He turned his head and spat on the floor in disgust. 'They are having none of the respect,' he said. 'This is why I despise them. But their sunflower seeds are better than anyone else's. You have eaten the Moldovan sunflower seeds?'

'I mean, I suppose it's possible,' said Beverley. 'I've eaten bread with sunflower seeds on it, but I've never enquired about their provenance.'

'I bring some back to London with me. They make you crazy.'

'But you won't be going to Moldova.'

'Oh yes. Is good point.'

'You'll be coming straight back to London.'

'Is plan, yes.'

'And it's important to stick with plans. Otherwise, things fall apart.'

'Like the house of Lego.'

'A house of cards, I think you mean.'

'The Lego cards.'

Beverley sighed and glanced across the room, where a photograph stood of her and George on their wedding day, next to the enormous eight-hundred-page biography that her husband had brought home the previous day. They both looked deliriously happy and in love. George's mind, his intellect, his wit had wrapped around her like a warm blanket back then. What had gone wrong in the meantime, she wondered? How had they lost each other?

She turned back to the screen, where Pylyp appeared to be counting his fingers to make sure they were all still present and correct.

'And your mother?' she asked. 'How is she holding up?'

'She rips out the hair and cries through the day and the night. I must not leave her alone for long or she hangs herself from the lightbulbs. But I do not want to talk about Odessa any more. There is someone I miss so badly in London.'

'Oh yes?' asked Beverley, brightening up.

'Yes, I think about him constantly.'

'Him? Don't you mean her? I know pronouns are a subject of much mind-numbing debate these days, but I can assure you that I am, and will always remain, a she.'

'I mean Ustym Karmaliuk, who is boy.'

Beverley tried not to give away her irritation that Pylyp's first thought was for his tortoise rather than her. 'He's quite well. Look, he's here with me now.' She adjusted the laptop's camera and angled it towards her lap, where the tortoise was sitting comfortably, munching on an After Eight. It paused for a moment, looking up slowly as if it was aware that it was the subject of attention.

'Hello, Ustym Karmaliuk,' said Pylyp, adopting the peculiar voice he always used when addressing the reptile. 'Are you behaving like the good tortoise for Grandmother Beverley?'

'Christ, don't call me that.'

'What is this he eats?'

'It's an After Eight.'

'A what?'

'An After Eight. You know, a mint chocolate.' She noticed the look of horror on Pylyp's face and immediately changed tack. 'It's mine. It must have fallen into my lap. Sorry.' She whipped it away from Ustym Karmaliuk's mouth and tossed it halfway across the room, where, to her delight, it landed directly in the wastepaper basket.

'You must not feed him these things,' insisted Pylyp.

'I didn't, I promise. It just fell!'

'I tell you this in airport. Only the leafy greens. And the crickets. He is the crazy tortoise for the crickets, I tell you this!'

'But you don't know how hard it is to get crickets in this part of London,' protested Beverley. 'Perhaps if I lived in the north, it would be easier, but here—'

'None of these After Nines.'

'After Eights. I can't believe you've never had them, actually. They're divine.'

'You must obey me on this!'

'Oh, Pylyp,' she said, laughing a little. 'You've gone all masterful. It's quite a turn-on. Anyway, don't worry, I'm taking good care of your little pet.'

'He is not pet. He is best friend of me. We are like the poets, Byron and Shelley. Locked in the eternal embrace.'

'As it happens, I'm growing rather fond of him,' said Beverley. 'Honestly, when you gave him to me, I didn't know how I was going to cope. But I've started to understand why you're so fond of him. He's very loyal, isn't he? He follows me everywhere I go, although, of course, if I leave the room it takes him so long to get out that I'm already back before he can make it to the door. And he causes no fuss. George nearly sat on him last night, though.'

'What?' cried Pylyp.

'Nearly,' said Beverley, waving her hands in the air. 'I said nearly. I shouted at him before he landed on the sofa. Anyway, when will you be home? I need you.'

'I am not sure. My mother—'

On cue, the sound of wailing rose from the room behind him and he turned around for a moment, shouting something out in Ukrainian.

'What on earth was that?' asked Beverley.

'Is my mother.'

'It sounded like a goat being castrated.'

'No, we do not do that in house. It was definitely her. Is eleven fourteen in morning. And she always starts crying at eleven fourteen.'

'Any particular reason?'

'This is when my father collapses and finds out that he is dead. Is strange bizarrity, but she spends entire life complaining about him, telling everyone what shit man he is, but now that he rots into the corpse, she says she cannot think of the life without him. Maybe she misses having someone to kick around.'

'Get her a dog.'

'My mother would never kick dog. She not Moldovan.'

'Is there anything that might distract her? Does she have a job?'

'She is brain surgeon.'

Beverley blinked. 'I'm sorry?' she said. 'I thought you said that she was a brain surgeon.'

'I did say this.'

'All right, well, that's unexpected. You never mentioned that before.'

'She is brain surgeon for many years. She cuts open the heads with the scalpels and plays with all the brains inside.'

'I see. Well, it's good that she's a career woman anyway. It will give her something to focus on. Widowhood can play strange games on the bereaved. I wrote a novel once about a woman who went so out of her mind with grief when her husband died that she tried to persuade her son to come home and live with her, but he refused. He'd built a wonderful life with an older but still very attractive woman in England and knew that was where he should be. Eventually, he—'

She stopped mid-sentence, noticing a figure moving behind Pylyp. A young woman had wandered into the room wearing a pair of barely-there shorts and a T-shirt that Beverley recognized as one that she had given her lover a few months earlier. The girl walked over to the fridge, removed a soft drink, glanced in Pylyp's direction, saw the open computer screen and then scurried out of sight again.

'Who was that?' asked Beverley.

'Who was what?'

'That girl. The one who just came into your kitchen.'

Pylyp turned around and looked, even though she was already gone. 'There is no one,' he said. 'Is my mother perhaps?'

'Is your mother around twenty years old, with big tits and legs that go all the way down to the floor?'

Pylyp considered this. 'She is quite chesty,' he admitted. 'And where else would legs go? They must not stop in mid-air or she falls over and lands with the bang.'

'It's a saying. I didn't mean it literally. Anyway, you must know who I'm talking about. She was standing right behind you.'

'Was ghost, maybe.'

'Pylyp, it wasn't a ghost. It was a person.'

'A ghost of person.'

'Pylyp!'

'Was maybe my cousin, Ulyana. She stays here for now to help look after my mother.'

'I see,' said Beverley, unconvinced. 'So why didn't you just say that when I asked?'

'I forget,' he replied. 'My mind is in the upstairs and downstairs place and I not thinking clearly. I miss my tortoise. And I miss my father, who beats me and calls me the pansy.'

'And me? Do you miss me?'

'Of course. Then you.'

'It's nice to know how deeply you care.'

Beverley drummed her fingers on the desk and glanced towards the corner of the screen when an alert pinged. An email from her ghost had arrived with the subject line *Pages*. She clicked the red *x* in the corner to make it disappear.

'And how is my beautiful Beverley?' asked Pylyp.

'I thought you'd never ask.'

'I ask now.'

'I'm fine. I'm lonely. But I'm keeping busy. The new novel is taking all of my attention. I hired a new ghost yesterday and she seems very dedicated. She was messaging me all last night with questions about the characters and the plot and the this and the that and the blah blah blah. Honestly, I'm absolutely exhausted. At this rate, I might as well be writing the bloody thing myself.'

'This is not something you like to do?'

'Well, I basically do anyway,' she said with a sigh. 'I mean, the stories are mine and I come up with the titles, so all the ghost really has to do is think up the actual words and put them on the page.'

The young woman appeared again in the background,

saying something to Pylyp in Ukrainian, and he turned around to answer her. She kept her hand on his shoulder throughout the exchange, then leaned forward and stared into the screen, her face filling Beverley's laptop so completely that she looked as if she was about to burst through it, like the little girl in *The Ring*.

'*Stara zhinka*,' she said, spitting out the words, and Beverley scribbled the phrase down on a notebook phonetically, thinking that she might look it up later. She glared at the woman and the woman glared back.

'Pylyp,' she said. 'Pylyp, could you tell your cousin to step away from the camera?'

He said something and the girl disappeared.

'I don't see any family resemblance,' she said. 'Are you sure she's your cousin?'

'She is being adopted when she will be little girl,' said Pylyp. 'My uncle and aunt could not have the babies of their own. They find her by side of road under huge pile of cardboard boxes and take her in.'

'I see,' replied Beverley. The doorbell rang and she looked around, rather relieved to be able to bring this conversation to an end. 'I'd better go,' she said. 'There's someone at the door. Shall we talk again tomorrow?'

'Of course,' said Pylyp. 'Goodbye, then. Kiss Ustym Karmaliuk for me.' And with that, he hung up the call before Beverley could even say another word, leaving her a little stunned.

'Charming,' she muttered, but nevertheless, she reached down and did exactly what he had asked, resting her lips on Ustym Karmaliuk's shell for a few moments and ignoring the insistent chiming of the bell, which rang through the house, echoing off the empty spaces and making her feel more alone than ever.

ABSENCE IS PRESENCE

Unlike the reception area, Jeremy's office was a testament to good taste, with a bespoke wooden KARE desk, a pair of floral armchairs from Anthropologie and a sequence of framed album covers on the wall, displayed to suggest that he might be a boring old solicitor but he still liked to kick it big time with the kids. The two men took a seat opposite each other, manspreading with such ferocity that a sturdy bridge could have been constructed between their crotches.

'Before we get started,' said George, holding up his right hand like an Indian chief in a fifties Western, 'tell me that I'm not going insane.'

'You're not going insane,' replied Jeremy.

'Your receptionist out there. You used to have a chap called Aidan, didn't you? Your new girl told me that he never existed. But I'm certain that I remember him. Or have I completely lost it?'

'Ah,' said Jeremy, nodding his head. 'Technically, you're correct. Or, technically, she's correct. One of you is technically correct but, honestly, I'm not sure which one.'

'I'm not following you.'

'That, in fact, *was* Aidan at the reception desk,' explained Jeremy.

'But that was a girl.'

'Indeed. The thing is, Aidan now identifies as female and

has asked that we call her Nadia. She's, you know, transitioning. Or rather he's transitioning. I think that's right, isn't it? He's transitioning into a she? Or have I got it wrong? Was she always a she? To be honest, the whole thing's a minefield. All I know is that I keep using the wrong pronoun and, every time I do, you'd think that I was expressing support for a campaign of ethnic cleansing.'

'That was Aidan?' asked George, leaning forward, his mouth dropping open in surprise. 'That girl out there?'

'Yes.'

'Well, now,' he said, shaking his head as he considered this. 'I have to say, he's done a bloody good job of it. I never would have guessed. He looks just like a girl. Quite an attractive girl too.'

'You can't say that.'

'What, I can't say that she's attractive? But she is!'

'No, you can't say that he looks just like a girl. There is no he. There's just a she. And she doesn't look like a girl, she is a girl. Although, yes, you probably shouldn't comment on her physical appearance either. You need to think before you speak these days, George, or they'll come after you.'

'They being?'

'The Wokesters.'

'The what?'

'People that are, you know, constantly alert to every injustice in society, every perceived slight, and who are just desperate to let you know when they've found one. They seek them out with all the urgency of truffling pigs.'

'My daughter's dating a chap like that,' said George, adopting a forlorn expression. 'He has terrible body odour. I don't know how she can stand it. He told me recently that he'd forced UCL to withdraw an invitation to a visiting American professor simply because he'd once served in the Bush administration.'

'Oh, he sounds terribly Woke.'

'The poor man wasn't even a Republican and had written a book defining some of George W.'s worst crimes. But the fact that he'd served at all was enough to make him *persona non grata*. In my day, we would invite people we didn't like to our campuses and then debate them. Put the bastards in their place. Not just ban them from the outset. It's cowardly. And shows a shameful lack of oratorical skills.'

'I think it's called de-platforming.'

'I'm sorry, but that's not a real word so I won't entertain it.'

'Then you're not Woke.'

'I'll have you know, I was Woke when everyone else was still napping.'

'You do have a good track record on this, it's true,' admitted Jeremy. 'Didn't you name one of your sons after Lech Wałęsa?'

'No, Nelson Mandela.'

'Oh yes. Very Woke.'

'And I named the other one after a Greek homosexual.'

'Even Woker.'

'Of course, I left Beverley to choose our daughter's name.'

'Ah,' said Jeremy. 'Well, that's not Woke.'

'Why not?'

'The man choosing the sons' names but leaving the girl to the mother? That's not Woke at all.'

'Well, all I remember is that I was awake every night with that girl when she was a baby,' he said. 'The boys weren't much trouble, but Elizabeth screamed the house down for about a year. In that regard, she hasn't changed much. She named her after Elizabeth Taylor, you know.'

'Wonderful actress.'

'No, the writer.'

'Well, who's to say?'

'Beverley is. She insists upon it. But anyway, getting back to Aidan—'

'Nadia.'

'Yes, Nadia. When did this all happen?'

'It's been in the pipeline for quite some time now, as far as I can tell. But Nadia herself only started coming into work a few weeks ago. Aidan left on a Friday at five o'clock as usual and Nadia turned up the following Monday shortly before nine with a look on her face that said, *One word and I'll have HR down on you like a ton of bricks.* Still, she seems happy with her decision, so good for her. No, not her decision, her choice. No, hang on, I don't think I can say that either, can I? It wasn't a choice. Her authentic self, that's what I mean. She seems happy with her authentic self.'

'Can one even say happy? Or self? Or with?'

'Probably not.'

'Can one use recognizable words at all or even speak in syntactically correct sentences?'

'It's risky.'

'Well, good luck to her, I say,' said George with a shrug. 'Whatever gets you through the day is fine by me. But I don't see why she couldn't have just told me that when I was out there rather than making me think that Aidan never existed. For a man my age, it suggests early onset Alzheimer's. How was I to know?'

'You weren't.'

'As it happens, I'm on her side. Or, to be more honest about it, I couldn't care less what she does or how she presents herself. I have enough problems in my own life without dealing with hers too. But why not just say, *Actually, Mr Cleverley, you knew me as Aidan over the last few years, but I've realized that's not the identity for me, and I'd appreciate it if you would call me Nadia from now on.*

Would that be so difficult? It just feels to me like she wants to be able to tell people that I didn't acknowledge her existence.'

'I wouldn't worry about it if I were you.'

'I'm not worried about it in the slightest,' said George. 'It just annoys me, that's all. Would it kill her to have some manners?'

'Shall we move on?'

'I suppose.'

'So, how can I help you?'

'Well, it's a matter of some delicacy,' said George, looking a little uncomfortable. 'One that will require some discretion.'

'Of course. Discretion is our watchword, you know that. You've nothing to worry about there.'

'The thing is, I seem to have got myself into a little bit of trouble.'

Jeremy reached for a notepad and his pen hovered over the blank page. 'Marital, business or financial?'

'Probably a little of all three, if I'm honest.'

'All right. You may as well just give me the details.'

'I met a woman. An actual woman.'

'Seriously, George, no jokes. If someone overheard you—'

'Sorry, I'm just feeling pissed off now. Anyway, this woman and I, we may have had . . . relations.'

'You may have had? You mean you're not sure?'

'Well . . .'

'You did or you didn't?'

'We did.'

'Frequently?'

'Many, many times. Over the course of five months.'

'And what? She's threatening to go to the papers? How much do you think she's looking for?'

'No,' said George, looking glum. 'It's worse than that. She

146

doesn't want publicity or money. If she did, that would make things a lot easier. No, it turns out she's pregnant.'

'Ah,' said Jeremy.

'There's life in the old dog yet, it seems.'

'Apparently so.'

'Me being the old dog,' clarified George. 'Not her. She's a very attractive woman, in fact. Although she has a laugh that grates on my nerves. Which was one of the reasons I broke up with her.'

'Can you tell me her name?'

'Angela Gosebourne. Dr Angela Gosebourne, in fact.'

'Does she work at the BBC?'

'Oh no. She's a therapist, as it happens. Helping, you know, nut jobs. People who've gone a bit doolally.' He rotated his index finger at the side of his right temple.

'I don't think you can use those words any more either, George,' said Jeremy. 'What you mean to say is *people with mental health issues*.'

'*Nut jobs* gets the sense across perfectly well.'

'It can be seen as offensive.'

'There's only you and me in the room. Are you offended?'

Jeremy considered it. 'Well, no,' he admitted.

'All right, then. She helps nut jobs. The point is, I'm reasonably sure that she's genuine about not wanting to hang me out to dry. It's not in her nature. Or, at least, I don't think it is. When you think about what she does for a living, it shows that she's a good person. She cares about people. About strangers, I mean. I've never given the slightest shit about strangers, have you? My fans, yes. I'm always polite to my fans. They're the ones who keep me on the box. But when I read about some tragedy in the newspaper, a plane falling out of the sky, say, well, it never really has any emotional effect on me whatsoever, although I act as if it does and I make all the appropriate sympathetic sounds on the chat show, then throw a few quid at whatever turgid song has been recorded to help the victims. But the truth is, I always think, well, that's just the way the world works, isn't it? Some people die, some people live. And the planet keeps turning. There's so many of us that God or Buddha or Elvis or whoever's up there needs to wake a dormant volcano every so often, just to keep the numbers down. It's been happening since the dawn of time. Dinosaurs and what have you. We can't care about everything. Even if we pretend to.'

'I'd like to think I'm a charitable sort,' said Jeremy.

'Well, we all would, wouldn't we? Listen, I have to do twenty minutes every time Comic Relief's on, so don't talk to me about charity. Last year I was forced into a One Direction skit with Jeremy Paxman, John Humphrys and David Attenborough and they made me play Liam. Liam! I mean, I ask you! I suggested they park me in the corner, smoking a fag and pretending that I was too good for any of this and we could say I was Zayn, but they weren't having any of it. Anyway, I was saying that Angela is a decent person. She cares about others.'

'So, she's not looking for money?'

'I don't think so, no.'

'And she wants this baby?'

'She says that she does.'

'And I presume that you don't?'

George shrugged his shoulders. 'I could do without it, if I'm honest,' he said. 'I'm sixty years old. I love my wife, even if there's been some distance between us over the last year or two. My kids hold the usual resentments, but they don't seem to hate me in any extreme way. They're all still living in my house, after all, despite the many hints I drop about them finding their own places. And the truth is, I don't want to lose them or hurt them. Nor do I want to lose Beverley or hurt her. I have my life exactly as I want it, do you see? So, I had a little bit of fun on the side. I shouldn't have to suffer any adverse consequences for that, should I?'

'I understand,' said Jeremy. 'It's perfectly natural that you wouldn't want anything to upset such a fine balance. I suppose the real question here is—'

Before he could complete that sentence, his phone buzzed and he glanced towards it. Normally, Jeremy would have switched it to silent until the meeting was over, but when he saw the name that appeared on the screen, he read the message carefully.

'Who's that?' George asked.

'My niece.'

'Well, can you tell your niece to fuck off until I've left, please? You're charging me by the hour here, remember?'

'Sorry,' replied Jeremy, sending a quick reply and setting the phone aside again. 'Her parents broke up recently and—'

'Jeremy.'

'Sorry, yes. You were saying?'

'I was saying that I've had my fun, but now I don't want it to affect my life in any negative way.'

'Do you want to play a part in the child's life?'

'Angela says that I can be as involved or uninvolved as I like. But as I pointed out to her, a lack of involvement *is* involvement. Just in a different form. Absence is presence.'

'You could just stay away?'

George shook his head. 'I couldn't do that,' he said. 'If a child of mine has the bad manners to be born, then I have an obligation to be there. I may be an asshole, Jeremy, but I'm not a complete prick. And I suppose I'd like to know the little bastard, to watch him grow up and to be a part of his life. I'm not the world's greatest father, I think my kids would attest to that, but I'm not the worst either. I do my best. I'm actually quite loving when given half a chance. But I can't see how to do all this without Beverley finding out.'

'You could just tell her the truth and throw yourself on her mercy?'

'It would be less painful to throw myself on a pitchfork. And the divorce would be horrendous. She'd take half of everything and the newspapers would have a field day with it. They're always looking to take me down a peg or two. And with the current temperature at the BBC, I'm not even sure that they'd back me. Although at least Angela is age appropriate.'

'How old is she?' asked Jeremy.

'Thirty-eight.'

'And you're sixty.'

'Well, that's age appropriate, isn't it? What do you expect, that I'll have sex with a woman in her fifties? If I wanted to do that, I'd just go to bed with my wife.'

'Can I offer you a piece of advice?' asked Jeremy.

'Of course you can. That's what I pay you for, isn't it?'

'These types of conversations. Never have them with any-one else. Just with your legal representatives. Or a priest. No one else. Never in public and never within spitting distance of a live microphone.'

'Oh, don't worry, I'm not a total idiot. I've been in this busi-ness long enough to know how it works. But I'm not a nasty old dinosaur either and I resent being treated as one, which is why your receptionist annoyed me so much. The real problem is, Angela doesn't want to break up with me. She'd prefer that I left Beverley and went to live with her instead.'

'That's unfortunate,' said Jeremy. 'It means that she might cause trouble.'

'Which is why I've come to see you. Because, if it's at all possible, I should like to avoid trouble.'

'I think the best thing would be if you left it with me for a while,' replied the solicitor. 'Let me have a think about how best to proceed. How does that sound?'

'Right,' said George, standing up. 'I suppose that will have to do for now. But remember, I want to do the right thing. Understood?'

'Understood,' agreed Jeremy as his phone buzzed again and he reached for it.

'You're popular,' said George, making his way towards the door. 'Having a little fun on the side too, are you?'

'No, no. Nothing like that,' he replied, laughing nervously. 'Just someone I met recently who . . . well, yes, I suppose it might resemble something like that. I mean, nothing's happened, as such.'

'Well, be careful, that's my advice to you. Don't find yourself in the same position as I have. Keep it zipped.'

GOAL

Nelson walked quickly along the edges of the playing field, filled with dread that the football might come his way. And then, naturally, it did, one of the boys kicking it with such an extraordinary lack of precision that it floated over the heads of the other players and flew across the pitch, landing only a few feet from him. He glanced towards the pitch, hoping to see one of the boys running towards him to retrieve it, but no, they were standing in a group, their hands on their hips, calling to him to send it back their way.

Nelson had never been any good at sports and lived in fear of moments like this, when he would inevitably be shown up in front of others as lacking in the basic skills that other men seemed to have instilled in them from birth. The only thing that lay ahead of him now, he knew, was humiliation. If he kicked the ball back to the players, it would inevitably fly over his head in some tragic boomerang movement, breaking one of the windows of the music rooms behind him. But if he refused to engage with it and hurried on his way, he would be left looking ridiculous. To make matters worse, Martin Rice appeared from the front doors of the school at the same moment, lighting a cigarette and grinning gleefully when he saw the scene that was playing out before him.

'Well, kick it back to them, Stupidly,' he shouted. 'Break's nearly over. They want to finish their game.'

Nelson glared at him before putting his backpack down on the ground and approaching the ball gingerly, staring at it as if it was some strange, unidentifiable animal that might leap up and bite him, were he to advance too quickly. In the distance, the boys were calling out his name, some being polite enough to add 'Sir', others using far less gracious terms. He looked in their direction, swallowing nervously. One of the taller boys had started to walk over, shaking his head in frustration, and Nelson realized that it was now or never. He pulled back his right foot and, keeping one eye focussed on the ball, aimed just below its centre, the toe of his shoe lifting it cleanly off the ground. He watched as it sailed through the air in a perfect arc, over the heads of the boys, all of whom turned to watch as it soared above the playing field, making its way along the length of the pitch before gradually starting to descend. The goalkeeper at the other end realized that it was coming directly for him and stretched his arms out in a desperate attempt to save it, but it was too late and the ball flew into the back of the net, top-right corner, as the entire playing field fell silent, every head turning towards Nelson, who was as stunned by what had just happened as everyone else.

He waited a few moments, nodded his head in satisfaction, retrieved his backpack and continued on his way into the school.

'Fucking hell, Nelson,' said Martin, staring at him. 'Shame no one was filming that. Might have gone viral.'

POPULAR FICTION

'Old woman.'

'I beg your pardon?'

'Old woman,' repeated the ghost. 'That's how *stara zhinka* translates.'

Beverley frowned and shook her head. 'Then I must have written it down wrong,' she said. 'It's more likely that it means something along the lines of *beautiful woman*.'

'That would be *prekrasna zhinka*.'

'Or *captivating woman*.'

'*Zakhoplyuyucha zhinka*.'

'I'm not sure your grasp of Ukrainian is quite as good as

you think it is,' said Beverley after a moment's pause, her smile as forced as one of Piers Morgan's co-presenters.

'Well,' replied the ghost, who took her language skills very seriously, 'I have been speaking it since I was four years old. It was very important to my grandparents that we all stayed close to our roots. But it's true that I don't get a chance to practise it as much as I'd like.'

'Then that explains it. You need to join a society of immigrants, my dear. There's probably some sort of organization somewhere in London. Regular conversation with native speakers will help to keep you proficient and you won't make such basic errors.'

They were walking through Selfridges department store on Oxford Street, looking at clothes, Beverley occasionally raising her hand to roar 'DON'T!' at any assistant who dared to approach her, atomizer in hand, preparing to douse her in unsolicited perfume. The shopping expedition was a ritual that Beverley had undertaken with all her previous ghosts when they were setting out on a novel, believing that if they could decide on the sartorial look of her central character, then the rest would fall into place. Her current amanuensis, however, did not seem entirely convinced, pointing out that every hour spent examining overpriced designer outfits that they had no intention of purchasing was an hour that she could pass more beneficially at home, writing.

'It's so good to be back, isn't it?' asked Beverley, breathing in the air and looking utterly enchanted by her surroundings. 'Did you find it as difficult as I did during the pandemic? When you couldn't come here to shop?'

'I've actually never been inside Selfridges before,' replied the ghost. 'I'm more of a Topshop girl.'

'Of course you are. What do you think of this?' she asked,

pulling a Vera Wang dress from one of the rails and holding it up to her body in the mirror. 'For the scene in the dentist's surgery when Carolyn meets Dr Westerley, before she learns that he spends his winters as a ski instructor in Switzerland?'

'You don't think it's a bit over the top?' asked the ghost. 'Women don't tend to wear gowns like this when they're getting the plaque scraped from their teeth. It's more the sort of thing one might wear to a New Year's Eve ball on a cruise ship.'

'But that's the problem with young women these days, isn't it?' replied Beverley with a sigh. 'They don't dress to impress. They never realize that today might be the day they finally encounter the man of their dreams. Instead, they just throw on whatever they find at the back of their wardrobe, something that doesn't smell too bad or isn't too wrinkled and might get them through the day without half the threads coming loose. DON'T! They wear polyester and rayon, jackets without a centre back seam, and – I SAID, DON'T! – match short skirts with plunging necklines. No, the women in my books need to look a million dollars from the second they wake up until the moment they slip into a blissful, silent sleep, where they dream of weekend breaks with Ryan Gosling on the Amalfi coast. So, make a note: red Vera Wang maxi-dress. Floral print, V-neck, silk wrap. To be used in Chapter Two.'

'Fine,' said the ghost, tapping this information into her phone and taking a photograph of the dress in question for future reference. 'I suppose she'll be wearing a bib anyway, so the dress won't get too stained.'

'A bib?'

'Yes, you know, those plastic bibs they give you when you're lying in a dentist's chair? To stop all the crud from your mouth falling on your clothes when they're polishing your teeth.'

'You really do live in some sort of sixties kitchen-sink drama, don't you?' said Beverley, looking appalled by these earthy descriptions. 'Every time you talk I half expect Alan Bates to come in and demand a plate of mashed potatoes and a pint of ale to wash it down. Let's be clear, there'll be none of that sort of thing in my book. No one needs that level of detail. What would you have Carolyn do next? Go to the toilet?'

'The characters in your books don't use the bathroom?'

'Of course not. Look, think about when you're sitting at home, enjoying one of your takeaway kebabs while watching a romantic comedy on television. There's Nicole Kidman drinking a glass of champagne as fireworks explode over Sydney Harbour Bridge. Behind her, Hugh Jackman gives her a shoulder massage while singing selections from *Les Misérables* into her ear. Now picture Nicole putting her glass down and saying, *Excuse me for a moment, Hugh, but I need to go and take a shit*. It rather spoils the mood, don't you think?'

'I suppose so,' admitted the ghost.

'It's fine for fiction to reflect reality,' continued Beverley, warming to her theme now. 'It just needs to be a lot more hygienic. You can attend every creative writing course in the country and I guarantee you that not one of the tutors will ever offer that piece of advice and, quite honestly, it's pure gold.'

A young woman with dark hair painfully scraped back from her forehead came over and stood next to Beverley, admiring the Vera Wang. She had immaculate skin and carried a scent of Chanel Chance Eau Fraîche about her person. 'It's beautiful, isn't it?' she said. 'And it's ten per cent off at the moment. Would you like me to see whether we have one in your size?'

'I beg your pardon,' said Beverley, turning around with a withering expression on her face. She wished that she'd been wearing a pair of sunglasses so she could have slowly taken them off and destroyed this insolent creature with a look. 'My *size*?'

'Yes, what are you, a fourteen? I think the one you're holding is a six. I can take a look in our stockroom, if you like. Vera Wang looks very elegant on the older woman.'

Beverley opened and closed her mouth several times, hoping that a series of lacerating words would emerge, leaving the sales assistant squirming in a pool of self-recrimination for the rest of the afternoon but, to her disappointment, nothing emerged. She turned to her ghost, wearing a *do-your-job* expression.

'We're not actually buying,' explained the ghost. 'We're just browsing. For Carolyn.'

'For who?'

'Carolyn Worthington. She's a secretary in a publishing house in Central London but dreams of marrying a wealthy man and living a luxurious lifestyle on the Côte d'Azur. Also, she needs to have her wisdom teeth removed as they've been giving her terrible gip. We're trying to find something for her to wear when she goes in for the operation.'

'Right,' said the sales assistant, nodding her head and appearing completely unfazed by any of this. 'Well, that is just so exciting!'

'DON'T!' roared Beverley as another atomizer came her way.

'I should probably point out that Carolyn is fictional,' continued the ghost. 'She's a character in a novel. We're just looking at what she might wear. If she was, you know, real. To give us a sense of her character.'

The sales assistant continued to smile, nodding like a bobblehead toy. She'd probably heard stranger things than this across the shop floor. 'Well, that's just super, and if I can help in any way, please do let me know,' she said. 'Would you like me to set you up with a dressing room?'

'No, we're fine, thanks.'

'My size,' muttered Beverley as the woman walked away. 'I could fit into this if I spent a week on a juice diet. I did one once, actually, but I ended up smelling of kale. Have you ever tried one?'

'A juice diet?' asked the ghost. 'No.'

'No, I didn't think so,' said Beverley, looking her up and down, eager to transfer a little of the body-shaming her way. 'Anyway, let's keep going. We need to think about shoes next.'

As they made their way further into the depths of the store, they passed the book section and Beverley glanced around the tables for a few moments before making her way towards the fiction shelves.

'I just want to see whether Jonathan Coe has anything new out,' she explained, running a finger along the spines before examining the books to the left of these, where copies of a novel by Chris Cleave were face out. 'How extraordinary,' she said, shaking her head.

'What's that?' asked the ghost.

'You don't see?'

The ghost looked at the shelf, uncertain at first what her employer was getting at, until, finally, the penny dropped.

'Cleave, then Coe,' she said. 'No Cleverley.'

'No Cleverley,' repeated Beverley, glancing around in search of a bookseller. 'Have a word with that young man, will you?' she asked, pointing in the direction of a tall, skinny man standing about ten feet from them, stacking a dozen copies of a new biography of Tsar Nicholas II on a display unit. 'It would be too embarrassing if I did it myself.'

'What do you want me to say?' asked the ghost.

'Just ask him why they're not stocking any copies of my books.'

The ghost looked mortified but caught the man's eye, offering him a little wave, and he wandered over with an obliging smile on his face. 'Can I help you with something?' he asked.

'Yes,' said the ghost. 'We were looking for books by Beverley Cleverley. Do you know her work at all?'

'Well, I haven't read any of it, I must admit,' said the man, whose name tag identified him as Declan. 'But I'm sure we have some in stock.' He leaned over and examined the shelves before standing up and frowning. 'Actually, she wouldn't be kept here,' he said. 'This section is all literary fiction. Beverley Cleverley would be on the other side of the room. In popular fiction.'

'Oh, I see,' said the ghost. 'Of course. Thank you.'

'Might I ask?' said Beverley, piping up now, her voice rising both in volume and tenor as she spoke. 'Might I just make the polite enquiry as to who makes these decisions and what criteria they employ in doing so?'

'I suppose it's the shop designers,' said Declan with a shrug. 'We carry much more popular fiction than we do literary fiction, so it makes sense to use the largest wall for them.'

'Not who decides what goes where,' replied Beverley, impatiently. 'But what is classified as popular and what is classified as literary? And is the latter, by its very nature, unpopular? Or is it more that popular fiction cannot be literary? I understand that Ian McEwan sells very well. As does Margaret Atwood, who's a personal friend. Doesn't that mean that they're popular?'

'I don't really know,' he said, scratching the place where his beard might have been, had puberty done its job more efficiently. 'Someone in head office, I imagine. There's a very nice woman called Leah who works in Central Buying. It might be her.'

'And you're perfectly happy to go along with these random choices, are you, Declan?' she asked, spitting out his name as if it was a piece of unripe fruit. 'You don't consider that these decisions create a sort of literary apartheid?'

'I'm not sure what that means,' he said.

'You've never heard of apartheid?'

'No,' he said.

'South Africa? In the eighties? When they segregated the blacks from the whites?'

'I wasn't born in the eighties,' said Declan. 'I'm only twenty-two. But if you're looking for books about South Africa, then I'm sure I can find some in the travel section. Also, the history section, probably. I can look it up on the computer for you, if you like?'

'I do not like, no. My point was that you have created an apartheid between the books that you or this Leah woman determine to be popular, which I assume you, or she, consider to be frothy and of little importance and, I daresay, are all written by women, while those you term literary novels, the ones of great weight and authority, are penned by men and given their own special piece of real estate in the store. Isn't that right?'

'Someone in head office . . .' repeated Declan, sensing that this was a battle he was ill equipped to fight.

'Yes, someone in head office,' repeated Beverley, waving him away. 'Always blame the mysterious someone in head office. It's so much easier than taking any personal responsibility for these things, isn't it? And I wonder, if I walked over to the popular fiction section, would I even find—'

'Mrs Cleverley?'

A voice made her spin around.

'I'm so sorry to interrupt,' said a woman, who was clutching a copy of one of her novels as if it was the last bag of frozen sprouts in Iceland on Christmas Eve. 'But you are Beverley Cleverley, aren't you?'

'I am, dear, yes,' replied Beverley with an ingratiating smile. 'How nice to meet you.'

'I should take this opportunity to get away if I were you,' whispered the ghost to Declan, who didn't have to be told twice and scurried off to hide in the children's section.

'I was just about to buy this,' continued the woman, brandishing a copy of *The Surgeon's Broken Heart*, 'when I happened to look across and saw you standing there. You don't mind me coming over, do you? I imagine it must get annoying to be approached by strangers in public, but I'm a great admirer of your work.'

'I don't mind at all,' said Beverley. 'It's always a pleasure to meet someone who appreciates my art. Would you like me to sign it for you?'

'If you would, yes. That would be very kind.'

Beverley rooted in her bag for a pen, and the ghost, having looked the woman up and down several times to make sure that she was not about to make a terrible error, spoke up.

'How far along are you?' she asked, nodding towards the woman's stomach.

'I'm sorry?'

'The baby. How many months?'

'Oh. Only a few months. I'm surprised you could tell. But I am starting to show a little, it's true.'

'Oh, many congratulations,' said Beverley, taking the book and removing the cap from her pen. 'I have three children of my own and they are the very lights of my life.'

'Three? How lovely! Do they still live with you?'

'I'm afraid they do. I can't get rid of them. Well, one's at school, so I suppose that's reasonable enough. But the other two . . . well, we've made it too comfortable for them, that's the problem. I imagine they'll move out eventually. Perhaps I need to change the locks.'

'And do you think your husband and you will stay together once they've all fled the nest?'

Beverley stared at her and burst out laughing. 'What an extraordinary question!' she said. 'But yes, I have no reason to think otherwise. Why do you ask?'

'Oh, it's just something I was thinking about. I worry about my own future, you see.'

'I don't think you need to concern yourself with such things for many years yet. You have the whole wonderful experience in front of you. Now, to whom shall I dedicate the book?'

'Angela Gosebourne,' replied the woman. 'Actually, if you could inscribe it for Angela and George. He's my fiancé. Or, rather, I hope he will be one day. He hasn't actually proposed yet but I'm hoping it's just a matter of time.'

'My husband's name is George too,' said Beverley as she turned the book to the title page and began scribbling away.

'Yes, I know. George Cleverley. I enjoy his television programme.'

'Do you? That's nice. I didn't know he appealed to a younger demographic.'

'He appeals to me,' said Angela, taking the book back, looking at the inscription and smiling. 'Very much so. I'll leave you alone now, but it's been a pleasure to meet you.'

She turned and offered a half-wave as she slipped back into the crowd, and Beverley stood there in the afterglow of the encounter. It was always thrilling to be recognized, but it was even better when someone else was there to witness it.

'Wasn't that nice?' she said, smiling at her ghost. 'Right, onwards to shoes. These characters won't dress themselves. DON'T!'

SOME DOTTY OLD MAN

After leaving Jeremy's office, George Cleverley made his way over to his solicitor's receptionist with a smile on his face.

'I'm leaving now,' he said.

'Thank you for keeping me informed,' she replied, looking up and adopting a suitably hostile expression.

'No problem at all,' he said, remaining exactly where he was as he narrowed his eyes and stared at her face.

'Is something the matter?'

'No, I'm just . . . well, you'd really never know, would you?'

'Never know what?' she asked with a sigh.

'That you're . . . that you were . . . that you are . . . Look, here's the thing.' He glanced around to make sure there was no one near by to overhear any of this. 'I'm a little confused. You said that Aidan never existed, but that's not quite true, is it? Aidan did exist once upon a time, but he doesn't exist any more. And that's perfectly fine. Admirable, even. I'm happy to acknowledge his permanent absence and your permanent presence. But why didn't you just explain that to me at the start? It doesn't matter to me in the slightest. If anything,

I applaud you for it. I think it's wonderful that we live in a world where, increasingly, people can be exactly who they want to be.'

'Who they *want* to be?' asked Nadia.

'Who they are, then. You see, all you're doing now is looking for something to get angry with me about. I'm trying to be supportive and you're scrutinizing my every word, desperate to find something to pick me up on.'

Nadia swallowed and stared at him. 'That's not what I'm doing at all,' she said after a moment.

'Oh, but it is,' he replied pleasantly. 'And if you think about it, if you're honest with yourself, you'll see that it is. So, again, I wonder why you didn't simply explain your new identity to me in the first place, since we've met many times in the past and always got along perfectly well. Why act as if Aidan never existed and I am some dotty old man?'

Nadia said nothing now, instead looking down at her desk.

'Could it be that you anticipate bigotry, that you actually long for it and can't bring yourself to imagine that a man like me hasn't an intolerant bone in his body? Because, if you took the time to examine my track record over three decades of public life, you'd see that's the case. But no, you're actually desperate for me to fulfil your own prejudicial expectations.'

'Mr Cleverley, I—'

'And if you can go home tonight and tell your friends that I'm exactly the kind of unevolved caveman that you need me to be in order to reinforce your victim status, then you can walk away feeling morally superior. Which is all you really want, isn't it? But the reality here is that you're the one being rude, not me. You're the one being disdainful and contemptuous, not me. And you're the one making baseless assumptions about a virtual stranger, simply because it fits the narrative that you want to construct around yourself, not me. Has it ever occurred to you that, of the two of us, you might be the intolerant one? That you might be the bigot?'

A ping from behind him sounded the lift doors opening and he raised a hand in farewell.

'Never mind, we'll chat another time,' he said. 'Have a pleasant day.'

Stepping into the lift he pressed the button for the ground floor and stared at his own reflection in the mirror, feeling rather pleased with himself.

A few moments later, back on the street, he took out his phone, opened his Twitter account and posted the following:

@GeorgeCleverley ✔ Much love to Aidan @AQFC as he continues his transition. Brave, authentic & inspiring. #TransRights #TransPride #BraveNewWorld #TotalSupport

And then, without bothering to read any of the replies that immediately began to flow in, he returned the phone to his pocket and continued about his lawful business.

SEX TAPES

Elizabeth was already in the bath when she realized that she'd left her iPhone on the charging stand in her bedroom. This was the furthest a phone had been from her hand in several years and she guessed that this was how a mother might feel when separated from her child for the first time. There was a noticeable fluttering in her chest, a dry sensation in her mouth and a condition she called 'itchy finger', whereby the index finger of her right hand continued to move in a spasmodic and uncontrollable fashion. She didn't feel like climbing out of the bath to retrieve it as the water was at the perfect temperature and the ratio of bubbles to body mass was ideal, but regretted missing the opportunity for a wonderful Instagram post. Short of calling out for one of her brothers to enter the bathroom and take a photo for her – which would have been weird – there was nothing, however, that she could do.

I'll only be half an hour, she told herself, channelling the valiant spirit of Joan of Arc as she rode into battle at the Siege of Orléans. *I can live without my phone until then.*

The room was filled with silence and, although she was alone, she felt strangely self-conscious.

So, what do I do now? she wondered, passing one hand gently through the water while she blew some of the bubbles from the fingertips of the other, like a girl in a commercial for bath foam.

I shall think, she decided.

I shall mull over my options.

I shall consider those less fortunate than myself.

It occurred to her that one of the advantages of travelling to an obscure Indonesian island to work with lepers was how amazing it would be for her brand. She had almost four thousand followers on Instagram, and if she could multiply that by, say, thirty, then she'd definitely be able to call herself an influencer. Most of her followers had initially clicked on her account because of their interest in her father's television show or her mother's novels, but their motivations didn't matter to her. After all, Kim Kardashian had built an empire by releasing a sex tape and her entire family had become billion-aires afterwards. Not that she was willing to go down that path again. She'd tried, once, with a former boyfriend, Tuscany Fields, but it had failed to cause the scandal she'd longed for and she still found the entire incident excruciating to recall.

She and Tuscany had only been dating for a few months when she came up with the idea of them making a sex tape of their own, releasing it online and then complaining about the invasion of their privacy. She'd met him one Saturday night when she was backstage at a recording of *Cleverley*. He'd been interning, tasked with keeping the production crew away from Scarlett Johansson, and she'd immediately been drawn to him. It turned out that he'd been brought up in a commune in Italy – hence the name – but had recently decided that he'd prefer not to spend his life eating lentils and saluting the sun. Instead, he wanted a Bose sound system, a seventy-eight-inch Sony television and a BMW. So, he came to London.

Once they started dating, Elizabeth made a point of taking him only to restaurants where there were sure to be paparazzi waiting outside and, although she did her best to cover her face and appear furious at the press intrusion whenever they walked in or out, the photographers had no idea who she was so didn't bother to take any pictures. Over time, she made her outfits more risqué, hoping this might encourage them to let off a few flashes in her direction, but still no luck.

In the meantime, her followers had plateaued and her social media creativity director, Trevé, had suggested that she do something dramatic if she wanted to increase her profile. No one knew who she was, Trevé pointed out, and no one cared. But everyone knew who her parents were. Embarrass them, and the country would follow her anywhere. Which was when she came up with the idea.

At first, Tuscany was wary about the camera she set up in her bedroom, wondering why they would want to watch themselves having sex after the event. It was like those people who went to concerts, he said, who paid no attention to the show but kept their arms extended, filming the whole thing on their phones. What are they going to do, he asked, go home and watch it again later and wish that they'd been there to enjoy it live?

'It'll be sexy,' insisted Elizabeth, ripping off his shirt and unzipping his trousers. 'When we're old and grey we'll be able to look back and remember when we were young and had fantastic bodies.'

'You think we'll still be together then?' he asked hopefully, thinking that his girlfriend had acquired a sudden romantic streak that had previously been missing.

'Well, no,' she admitted. 'Probably not.'

He remained unconvinced but gave in to her pleading and, he had to admit, when they watched it a little later, he did find it quite arousing. The following day, Elizabeth emailed the file to Trevé, who forwarded it to a specialist editing suite, who in turn chopped it down into a neat five-minute showreel of her and Tuscany's finest moments.

When the file was returned to her, she watched it over and over, wanting to ensure that it showed her at her most primal. Her instructions had been clear. She was happy to give viewers a glimpse of her breasts, but nothing was to be revealed between the waist and the knee, a courtesy that she did not extend to Tuscany, whose shortcomings were on display for the whole world to see.

A date was set for the leaking of the video, and several celebrity and pornographic websites were contacted in advance as official brand partners. Elizabeth would have been perfectly happy to give them the footage for free, but Trevé was clear that this was not the way these things worked. And so she accepted £2,000 from each of three sites, and on the agreed morning it was released online in sixty-minute time gaps, leading to her first tweet on the subject, which, despite its simplicity, she later discovered had taken more time to compose (23 days) than Anthony Burgess's *A Clockwork Orange* (21).

> **@ElizCleverley** Devastated that private moments of intimacy between @TuscanyFields and me have been leaked online by sick perverts. #tits #free #celebsexvideo #pleasedontlook #checkitout

This small taster allowed her followers to get a sample of what was to come and to conduct some private searches of their own now that the footage was freely available. Within an hour, she received hundreds of likes and retweets, along with supportive messages from people desperate for her to validate their existence. She waited a little longer before following up with:

> **@ElizCleverley** Can't get out of bed, can't eat, can't even pick up my phone, I feel violated. If this is the price of being a public figure, then I'd prefer to be anonymous. #freeporn #doggystyle #searchandyouwillfind

To her disappointment, this second tweet did not receive the attention of the first and, when she checked the celebrity blogs and the websites of the trashier newspapers, there was no mention of her public shaming. It was time to be a little more explicit:

> **@ElizCleverley** The sick people at daughtersofcelebs.com, privatesexvidz.com and bbcslutz.com should be ashamed

of themselves. They've destroyed my life by posting a private, intimate video of @TuscanyFields and me on their websites. Shameful. #watchforyourself #completelyfree

Again, there was a brief uptake in clicks, likes and retweets, but nothing substantial. She went to bed feeling miserable, and the next morning, only the *Daily Express* had bothered to run a piece on their online site, describing the 'shame of telly host's girl caught with her knickers down', an article that received even less attention than a piece about the funding of an art installation by a lesbian poet that featured her body-weight in Snickers bars.

'My followers have increased by only ten per cent,' she complained to Trevé when she dropped in to see him a few days later. 'You said that they would double. Even triple.'

'I may have overestimated the public recognition factor,' he said, admitting defeat in the face of general indifference. 'If it had been your father caught on a sex tape—'

'Don't be disgusting,' she snapped.

'But it's true.'

She'd stared at him contemptuously. 'Are you seriously telling me that a sex video of my past-his-prime father rolling around in bed with some twenty-five-year-old model would prove more popular with the public than one of @Tuscany-Fields and me?' She'd recently started to refer to her boyfriend by his full Twitter and Instagram handles, forgetting that, in real life, he preferred to be known simply as Tuscany.

'Of course,' he replied. 'The public know your father. Any opportunity to shame him is manna from heaven to them. You couldn't get your hands on one, I don't suppose? Perhaps if we were to release that and then you were to confront him outside Broadcasting House—'

He didn't get to make any more suggestions as Elizabeth had already left his office, firing him by email the following morning. The entire experience had proved utterly dispiriting.

Lying in the bath now, she could hear her phone ringing in the distance and groaned. She felt cut off from the world. What was she doing wallowing in a pool of her own filth anyway? She stood up, wiping the bubbles from her body, and jumped into the shower, scrubbing any remains of the homeless from her skin, before wrapping a towel around her and emerging from the bathroom on to the landing, where Ustym Karmaliuk stood waiting to greet her at the top of the staircase.

'How did you get up here?' she asked, lifting him up and turning him around. Another few hours and he'd surely make his way back down to the living room. Her phone rang again and she ran towards her bedroom, but it stopped before she could answer. She glanced at the screen. Two missed calls from Achilles. She threw it back on the bedspread. Whatever it was, it could wait.

CODE PURPLE

In the staff room, none of the teachers was aware of Nelson's extraordinary goal, and a moment that might have passed into legend quickly took on the shape of a dream. The boys, drifting back to classes in a fog of sweat and boredom, had already forgotten, while Martin, impressed and a little jealous, would certainly never refer to it again. But Nelson knew. He sat down in one of the ancient armchairs, the brown webbing beneath the seat slapping against the floor, and lifted a copy of that day's *Guardian* to scan the headlines but found himself unable to take anything in since all he really wanted to do was laugh.

'What are you smiling about?' asked Tina Holmes, the art teacher, who was seated across from him, drinking coffee from a pottery mug that she'd made herself, inscribing it with the words *World's Sexiest Teacher*. Miss Holmes had taught Nelson when he was a teenager and once, when he was fifteen, had sat next to him while he was alone in the art room, placing her hand on his lap, perilously close to his penis, which had withdrawn into itself, seeking sanctuary in his pelvic area, like Ustym Karmaliuk retreating into his shell when he sensed the presence of a potential predator.

'Was I smiling?' asked Nelson, adjusting his face so it reflected his usual melancholia.

'There's nothing more irritating than a boy having some private joke with himself,' she said. 'It's rude, it excludes others and I won't stand for it.'

'I'm sorry, Miss Holmes,' replied Nelson, who found it impossible to refer to any of his former teachers by their Christian names, not even Mr Salik, his erstwhile religious studies teacher, who was Muslim so didn't have one.

'So what is it, then?' she asked.

'Nothing,' he said. 'It doesn't matter.'

'Oh, for God's sake,' she said, taking a long slurp from her mug. 'I'm not telling you *not* to smile. I just wondered why you appeared so cheerful, that's all. You usually look as if you went to the theatre to see *Hamilton* but ended up at an understudies' performance of *Cats*.'

'Well, the thing is,' said Nelson, feeling that he needed to tell someone, if only to legitimize the experience, 'when I was on my way in, I was walking past the playing fields and—'

'Have you been working out?' asked Miss Holmes.

'I'm sorry?'

'Have you been working out? You look quite . . . fit.'

Nelson swallowed and stared at her, uncertain how to respond.

'Well, I did join a gym recently,' he admitted. 'But I got barred quite early on.'

'Whatever for?'

'It was a misunderstanding,' he said.

'Were you looking at other men in the changing rooms?' she asked, leaning forward and smiling lasciviously at him. 'Do men do that? Check each other out to separate the horses from the ponies?'

'No,' he said, looking appalled at the idea. 'It was women that I was harassing.'

'Oh yes? What did you do?'

'I tried to speak to them.'

Miss Holmes laughed. 'Well, that's where you made your first mistake,' she said. 'You're very nice to look at, Nelson, but you don't help your cause when you open your mouth.'

Nelson stared at her, the memory of his unexpected goal vanishing now. He wanted to ask her why she needed to be so unkind, but that would take words and he knew that he would not be able to find any. Instead, he simply looked down at his hands and examined the lines on his palms, as if he'd learned how to read the future and was eager to discover whether he'd live a long life and, if he did, would he find happiness.

At the front of the room, the headmaster clapped his hands together and asked for silence. As conversations came to a halt and all faces turned in his direction, Nelson felt a stab of anxiety at the pit of his stomach. Announcements always made him nervous. They rarely held anything but bad news.

'I'm afraid I have something rather unpleasant to report,' said Mr Pepford, looking around at the teachers, who, unlike Nelson, brightened up whenever an unexpected event occurred. A resignation, a sacking, a death. Anything to liven up an otherwise tedious Tuesday. 'We have a Code Purple in Year 10.'

There was a collective groan from around the room and Malachy Stout, the form tutor for that particular group, smacked his right fist down on the arm of his chair, causing one or two people near him to jump in surprise. 'Fuck's sake!' he roared. 'Fucking fuck's sake!'

'Yes, thank you, Malachy,' said the headmaster. 'We don't need to make a bad situation worse with vulgar language, do we?'

'Who is it?' asked Miss Holmes.

'Sarah Wilmot,' said the head.

'What, again? She's only just back from having her last sprog.'

'It seems that she has quite the maternal streak. She's turning into the Mia Farrow of St Thomas's.'

'And which poor bastard has got her up the duff this time?' asked Malachy.

'That seems to be the subject of some speculation at the moment,' the head replied. 'There are a number of suspects in the frame but, as of this morning, Sarah has declined to name her seducer.'

Martin Rice burst out laughing. 'Her seducer,' he said, shaking his head. 'We're not in a Jane Austen novel, you know.'

'So I think we should all be on the alert for a certain amount of tension in the Year 10 group over the days and weeks ahead,' continued Mr Pepford, ignoring this remark but smiling in Martin's direction to make it clear that they were still besties. 'The boys are all denying their part in these unhappy events while insisting that they could not be the father as they always use prophylactics. It seems they want to assert their sexual prowess while taking no responsibility for the results of any congress.'

'Why is it called a Code Purple?' asked one of the newer members of staff, a young woman, turning to Nelson, who blinked back at her many, many, many times. 'Are you all right?' she asked. 'You're not having a stroke, are you?'

'It's called a Code Purple because we don't know whether she's having a boy or a girl yet,' said Martin, leaning his head down between the two, the smell of nicotine causing Nelson to rear back in his seat. 'Mix blue and pink together and what do you get? Purple. It'll be Danny Thornton,' he added, standing up now and shouting over everyone. 'He's been putting it about ever since his cousin got to Boot Camp on *X Factor*.'

'Daniel is indeed one of the names in the frame,' admitted Mr Pepford. 'I've made a list of the usual suspects and Sarah's parents have asked me to interview them one by one. But until we know for sure who the guilty party is, there's nothing we can do.'

The meeting broke up with the teachers standing around and gossiping among themselves, and Nelson felt relieved when the phone rang in his pocket so he wouldn't have to join in the chatter. He took it out and looked at the screen before making his way outside to the corridor. It was Achilles calling. He frowned. Achilles almost never phoned.

This, he decided, pressing the 'Accept' button, couldn't be good.

Achilles hadn't heard a word from Jeremy Arlo since the previous evening at the Churchill Arms. That had been a near facsimile of many other first dates he'd set up, in that the older man had tried to behave as if there was nothing strange about their being together while remaining visibly anxious throughout their meeting. And while Jeremy had either been too polite or too frightened to suggest that anything more intimate take place, Achilles knew from experience that it was only a matter of time before the delicate subject of sex was raised, at which point he could pretend to be shocked and wounded by the misunderstanding while making a few financial demands to maintain his silence.

As he sat down to lunch at home now with his mother and her ghost, he began to feel a little insulted that Jeremy was not flooding him with text messages and decided that he needed to move things along himself. Something simple, he decided. Nothing that might scare the mark away.

Achilles Cleverley

Hey! Really enjoyed meeting you last night. Crazy busy here! xo

Beverley had prepared one of his favourite meals, an enormous bowl of chicken Caesar salad with home-made croutons, and he put his phone aside as she filled a plate for each of them. He was still trying to decide what he made of the new employee, who so far seemed impervious to his charms. The previous ghost, the one who'd been eaten by a lion, had also been unreceptive to him, and he'd once overheard her in conversation with Elizabeth describing him as 'cute, I guess, but kinda bratty', and while he recognized her description as an accurate one, it had nevertheless offended his sense of dignity.

'Your English is very good,' he said, and she gave him the side-eye as she crunched on a piece of romaine lettuce.

'Possibly because I was born and brought up in Oxford,' she replied. 'It's the first language there.'

'Oh. I thought Mum said something about you being Slovakian.'

'I said she had Ukrainian blood,' said Beverley, correcting him. 'Her parents came to England after the war.'

'My grandparents,' said the ghost, correcting her.

'And how do you see the job of a ghost?' asked Achilles, deciding that if she was not going to have the manners to slobber all over him, then he was honour bound to take her down a peg or two. 'It's a strange sort of role, don't you think? Mind you, there are some writers out there who I think would be better off if they hired one. I tried to read a novel recently that was so unintelligible that it seemed as if it had been translated from the original Serbian by someone who only spoke Croat.'

'A ghost is a sort of interpreter of dreams,' explained Beverley. 'Like Freud. Or that fellow in the Bible.'

'Daniel,' said the ghost. 'Although I'm not sure that Freud would approve of the analogy.'

'Was he not religious?'

'Men of science rarely are. The two are contradictory.'

'It's a little ironic, all the same, isn't it?' asked Achilles.

'What is?'

'Well, didn't Daniel end up in the lions' den? Or was that a different Daniel?'

The ghost thought about it. 'No, that was the same Daniel,' she agreed. 'And I see what you mean.'

'I'm not following,' said Beverley, looking up from her food with a baffled expression on her face.

'Daniel was accused of worshipping God over the king and was thrown into the lions' den for his troubles,' said Achilles. 'But he was saved by an angel. Your previous ghost ended up on a safari being mauled to death by a lion.'

'How do you know so much about the Bible?' she asked, putting down her fork. 'You're not being radicalized, are you?'

'Not that I know of.'

'It's impossible to know what goes on in schools these days,' she said, turning to the ghost. 'They let any type of person come in to give random talks to the children and the government approves them all. In my day, we were lucky if we had a member of the Women's Institute stop by to break up the tedium. I remember an elderly lady who gave us a talk once on "How to Satisfy Your Husband" and we all thought it was going to be some ghastly tale of lying back, closing one's eyes and thinking of England, but instead it had something to do with the correct way to roast a chicken and dispose of the giblets afterwards.'

'You do make a mean roast chicken,' said Achilles.

'Thank you, darling. But, speaking as a mother, I can't help but feel concerned about what goes on when my children are out of the house. One reads so much in the papers about ISIS and child brides and boys running off to fight whoever they're fighting in Syria, so you'll understand if I worry when one of my own starts quoting the Bible. We don't really do God in this house, you see. We never have. Sometimes, at Christmas,

George lets Him in for a few minutes before we eat but I always usher Him back out on to the street afterwards. God, I mean. Not George. Anyway,' she added, turning back to Achilles, 'all I'm saying is, please don't come home some day with a long beard and waving a copy of the Koran in my face. I wouldn't have the energy for it.'

'Can you even grow facial hair?' asked the ghost, peering at the boy's skin, which was so smooth that it looked as if he'd never had to buy a razor in his life. 'Some boys can't.'

'Of course I can,' he said, scowling. 'I have gone through puberty, you know. If I really put my heart and soul into it for about three months, I can squeeze a few hairs out of my chin. Anyway, don't change the subject. You still haven't told me how you interpret your job.'

His phone pinged at this same moment and he picked it up and glanced at it.

Jeremy Arlo
Busy here too. I enjoyed meeting you!

He frowned. Jeremy wasn't even hinting at getting together again. If anything, this felt like a brush-off. He wasn't accustomed to having to do so much of the running himself, but if he was going to earn the money he needed to keep his finances on track, then it seemed that he would have to work a little harder.

Achilles Cleverley
Fancy doing it again sometime?

'I imagine the entire arc of the novel and describe it,' explained Beverley. 'Then the ghost commits all my thoughts to the page.'

'I'd love a job like that,' said Achilles. 'Not the ghosting part, that sounds too much like hard work, but the imagining part. It would be great to say, *Oh, I'll just be an investment banker and imagine millions of dollars moving around the globe, but someone else can do the actual slog for me while I swan around on my yacht in the Mediterranean.*'

'You don't understand the process,' said Beverley. 'It's a lot more complicated than you might think.'

'And do you enjoy it?' he asked.

'It's not a question of enjoyment,' replied the ghost. 'Some of us have to work to pay the rent.'

'Ha,' he said, stuffing into his mouth a forkful of chicken coated in a shaved Parmesan that was so sharp it sent a shiver down his back. 'And do you plan on making a play for my brother while you're on the job, so to speak?' he asked, determined to annoy somebody, anybody.

'I'm sorry?'

'Well, you know that Nelson and your predecessor had something going on before she died, right?'

'What are you talking about, Achilles?' asked Beverley.

'Didn't you know? He was quite taken with her. Or so he told me. They went out for drinks one evening, apparently. He was thinking of asking her to move in with him.'

'Wouldn't that have been a little premature?'

'Well, you know Nelson. He got talking to her, so he figured, she'll do. Anything to put off focussing on the obvious.'

'And what obvious is that?' she asked.

'That he's a bender.'

Beverley rolled her eyes and turned back to the ghost. 'You'll have to forgive my son,' she said. 'He thinks he's being funny but, actually, he just likes to shock.'

'You talk to each other in a curious way,' said the ghost.

Beverley looked from her ghost to her son and back again, uncertain whether she was being insulted.

'There's nothing shocking about being a bender,' continued Achilles. 'Everyone is these days. I tried it myself once but, you know, there was just something missing. Or rather, there was something there that I wished was missing. You'll never believe who it was, Mother.'

'I don't want to know, thank you very much,' said Beverley, pouring herself a large glass of white wine but not offering any to either of her dining companions. 'Your sexual shenanigans are of no interest to me whatsoever. Or, I imagine,' she added, turning to the ghost, 'to you.'

'Not even slightly.'

'Clearly, you already find us terribly strange.'

'I do, a bit,' agreed the ghost, which made Beverley frown. She'd been hoping for some backtracking.

'My mother and I have always been close,' said Achilles, wondering whether he could make her blush. 'Tell her about Film Club.'

'Oh, I loved Film Club!' replied Beverley, looking nostalgic. 'Why don't we do that any more?'

'Mum likes to stay cultured, so when I was about fourteen, she set a night aside every week where she and I would curl up on the sofa and watch films together, then discuss them afterwards.'

'We started with that trilogy about colours,' said Beverley. '*Blue*, *White* and *Red*. By that Polish man.'

'It was about colours all right, but you've got the wrong ones. It was *Fifty Shades of Grey*.'

'Are you sure about that?'

'Perfectly. My psyche still bears the scars. Remember, I tied myself up a few nights later and then I couldn't undo the knots and Dad had to break down my bedroom door to set me free. Elizabeth took pictures and tried to upload them to Instagram, but they were deleted on the grounds of gratuitous nudity.'

'Oh yes,' she said, shuddering. 'I've tried to put that incident from my mind. And I shall ignore your inference about Nelson too. Until he tells me otherwise, I shall assume that he's perfectly normal.'

'That's not a very PC thing to say. You could be cancelled for less. And anyway, gay, straight or pansexual, he's anything but normal,' said Achilles. 'Maybe I'm wrong. Maybe he really did fancy the ghost. Anything's possible.'

Beverley shook her head, looking annoyed now. The last time she'd been this offended was the afternoon two summers previously when she'd been denied access to the royal box at Wimbledon due to the presence of what she referred to as '*parvenu* duchesses and their families, hogging all the best seats'.

'I didn't realize she was taking advantage of her position to infiltrate my family,' she continued now, shaking her head. 'An appropriate line needs to be drawn between an employer and the help. No offence, dear,' she added, turning to her ghost. 'I don't mind you eating with us. You have impeccable table manners.'

'None taken,' said the ghost. 'I don't consider myself the help anyway. I think of myself as a professional being paid to do a job.'

'Of course, it was easier in the olden days,' continued Beverley, ignoring this unexpected burst of Bolshevism. 'The staff were sequestered underground. Like the latrines. And the rest of us were gathered above stairs, engaged in improving conversation and whist.'

'What is whist?' asked Achilles.

'It's a card game. You've never played a rubber of whist?'

He stared at his mother. 'I genuinely feel as if you're speaking a foreign language to me right now,' he said.

'Never mind. My point is that a person instinctively knew where he or she belonged and they stayed there without ambition or complaint. I'm sure Nelson would have grown tired of her soon enough anyway. Was he terribly sad when the lion ate her?'

Achilles offered a half-smile. 'Well, yes,' he said. 'I mean, he wasn't thrilled.'

Jeremy Arlo
Love to. How's the rest of your week looking?

'I can't believe he never mentioned any of this to me,' said Beverley. 'Or, as far as I know, to your father. Are you sure you're not making all this up?'

'Why would I do that?' he asked.

'Well, I don't know, do I? But you have a history of making things up just to cause trouble.'

'Rubbish!'

'You're an incorrigible liar,' said Beverley. 'But I do love you so. And when it comes to Nelson, if this is in fact true, then I would hate to think that he's grieving and is unable to talk about it. I mean, these things happen, don't they? People get eaten by lions, one is sorry for them, but there we are.'

'Quite,' said Achilles, reaching for the black pepper. 'That's the wonderful thing about my mother,' he added, turning to the ghost. 'She has a very tender heart. Overflowing with sympathy and compassion for all.'

'Thank you, dear,' said Beverley, patting his hand. 'That's very kind of you to say. It's true that I do *feel* more than most people. Perhaps that's why I'm a writer. I have great empathy.'

'I saw a clip on YouTube the other day,' said the ghost,

'about a gorilla who saved a three-year-old boy when he fell into its enclosure at the zoo. The other gorillas tried to get to him, but she brushed them away, keeping him safe, then she carried him to the little door that the zookeepers use when they come in with food.'

'What has that got to do with anything?' asked Beverley. 'Why are you talking about gorillas?'

'We were discussing lions,' said the ghost. 'And I wanted to point out that sometimes animals can behave in unexpected ways. I know you're keen to have a lion scene in the new novel—'

'It should be handled very sensitively, though,' said Beverley. 'I wouldn't want your predecessor's ghost feeling that I was taking advantage of her misfortune.'

'The ghost's ghost?' asked Achilles, looking up. 'This gets better. What do you call a dead ghost anyway? Is it a double negative? Is a dead ghost just, like, a living person?'

'I mean her family,' said Beverley. 'Honestly, Achilles, must you always mock? You're like a teenage boy, never happy unless you're poking fun.'

'I *am* a teenage boy,' he replied.

'But that's no reason to act like one.'

'Regarding the lion scene,' said the ghost.

'Yes, let's just make sure that the lion never touches her face. Otherwise, the hero might not want to marry her. No one wants to dance with a girl who has great claw marks down her cheeks.'

'Wasn't that Dorothy Parker?' asked Achilles. 'Men don't drive cars, with girls who have scars.'

'I don't think so, dear.'

Achilles Cleverley
I'm free on Thursday. Bit short on cash right now though!

'I'll do my best,' said the ghost.

They finished their meal and Beverley stood up to clear away the plates while Achilles shamelessly looked the ghost up and down as if he was considering purchasing her but wasn't sure whether she'd go with his new jacket. She was quite sexy, he decided eventually. But in an understated way, which was always his preference. He waited for her to turn and look at him too, but she seemed more interested in investigating the condition of her nails. When she finally deigned to glance in his direction, she simply frowned.

'Is something wrong with you?' she asked.

'No,' said Achilles. 'Why do you ask?'

'You're staring at me in a weird way. Your eyes have gone all strange.'

'People always compliment me on my eyes,' he said.

'I wasn't complimenting you,' she said. 'I said that they'd gone all strange.'

'Good strange or bad strange?'

'Like the wind had changed and you'd been stuck like that.'

'Bad strange, then,' said Achilles, sulking. He drummed his fingers on the tabletop, deciding that he didn't care for this new ghost very much, but her indifference to him had left him with no choice but to consider seducing her.

Jeremy Arlo

Drinks are on me. And Thursday's good. I'll text you that morning with time/place. Still a bit nervous about this so maybe keep it to yourself?

'Have you heard of Peter O'Toole?' asked Achilles.

'Yes, of course,' said the ghost.

'Some people think I look like him. Back in his *Lawrence* days. Only younger, obviously.'

She sat back and examined him carefully for a long time before shaking her head. 'I don't see it,' she said. 'He was an incredibly good-looking man.'

Well, that settles it, thought Achilles. You, Missy, are in for a rude awakening.

Achilles Cleverley
Secrets make it even more exciting. Until Thursday xoxoxo

'Right, you,' said Beverley, clearing the rest of the lunch detritus away. 'Go away and do whatever it is you do when you're on your own, but please don't let it involve ropes. It took for ever to get that door fixed last time. And we have to get on with this bloody novel.' She paused for a moment, glancing at the clock. 'Hold on,' she said, turning to her son. 'It's Tuesday. Why aren't you in school?'

Achilles smiled. At moments like this, he truly loved his mother. 'It's taken you until one thirty to think of that?' he asked.

'Just answer the question.'

'Free morning,' he lied. 'Mr Rice told us all to go home and study.'

Beverley pulled a face. 'Awful man,' she said.

'The worst,' agreed Achilles, standing up now and kissing her three times on the cheeks, European-style, despite the fact that she was a staunch Brexiteer. 'And as for you,' he added to the ghost as he made his way out of the room, 'let's talk later, yes?'

'Why?' asked the ghost, frowning, as if he'd just invited her to take a hot-air balloon trip over Sri Lanka with him. 'What have we got to talk about?'

On the way to his room he checked his phone, but no more messages had arrived from the mark. He'd probably stay quiet until Thursday morning. He flicked into Twitter and was surprised to see his name, or his surname, trending, and scrolled down the page, his mouth opening wider with everything he read. Switching back to his phone, he opened his contacts list and pressed the number for his sister.

'What?' said Elizabeth when she answered.

'Something's happened,' he said. 'Dad's in trouble.'

After he had explained the situation, he hung up and called Nelson.

'Achilles?' asked his brother. 'Is everything okay?'

'Have you been online?'

'No. Why? What's happened?'

'Get on to Twitter right now. Dad's fucked up. Big time.'

PART 3

16 July 2010

It's Elizabeth who tells George and Beverley the truth about why Nelson doesn't want to go to school any more. Last week, he complained about a sore stomach and was kept off; this week, he claims to have an ear infection. Elizabeth has known the truth for months but waited until now to talk to her parents, not wanting to betray her brother's confidences.

They knock on his door and open it tentatively, looking inside. His eleventh- birthday cards are still standing on his desk and he's lying on his bed, wearing the Luke Skywalker costume he'd asked for, claiming that it made him feel brave. Looking at their son, curled up, holding on to a childhood cuddly toy that he immediately casts aside, he doesn't look brave. He looks frightened. And ashamed.

'Nelson,' says George, sitting down at the end of the bed and reaching out to lay a hand on his son's feet, although the boy pulls them away. He doesn't like to be touched, and they know this, although they both often long to throw their arms around him, to hold him close and keep him safe. 'We need to talk to you.'

'What's wrong?' he asks, sitting up and putting one of his pillows behind his back. 'My throat is still sore. I can't go to school tomorrow.'

'I thought it was your ears,' says Beverley.

'Oh yes, that's what I meant.'

'Is something . . . ?' George pauses, wanting to phrase this carefully, so he doesn't scare his son into silence. 'Is someone bothering you at school?' he asks. 'Is that the reason you don't want to go in?'

'No,' snaps Nelson, looking away, staring at his fingers, which are dancing anxious melodies upon the bedspread. 'Of course not.'

'Elizabeth says—' begins Beverley, but he cuts her off.

'Elizabeth doesn't know what she's talking about. She's just trying to cause trouble.'

'I don't think she is,' says George. 'Who is this Martin Rice anyway?'

Nelson says nothing for a moment, then, quietly: 'A boy in my class.'

'And he's being mean to you?'

Nelson nods.

'But why?' asks Beverley. 'Why would anyone bully you? You're such a loving boy.'

'He's not bullying me!' says Nelson, tears starting to form in his eyes now. He wipes them away. He doesn't want them to see him weak. Home is the one place he feels safe, and he won't have this taken away from him.

'Is he calling you names?' asks George.

There's a long silence, and they wait, saying nothing, until Nelson nods.

'And what else? Is he hurting you?'

The tears come now, and he breaks down and tells them the extent of the bullying he's been receiving. And not just from Martin Rice, but from the teachers too, who know what's going on but won't challenge the older boy, because he's good at football and, if they're honest with themselves, because they're frightened of him too.

A few days later, George and Beverley are seated in their Range Rover, parked in an unobtrusive spot near Ebury Mews. Beverley is holding a copy of When the Stars Align, her debut novel. It arrived in the post just as they were leaving the house and she'd opened the package while George was driving, letting out a cry of delight when she saw the finished book. Reaching across, George takes it from her and turns to the dedication page, smiling when he sees that she has dedicated it to him, with love.

'Well, this is marvellous,' he says. 'Simply marvellous. I'm so proud of you, my darling.'

Beverley feels a rush of love for her husband. He's been nothing but supportive of her since she declared an interest in writing and, when her book was finished, had agreed not to pull any strings with his industry contacts, so that if success came her way, it would come entirely on her own merit. And it has. A whole new life has opened up to her now.

'Is that him?' asks George, looking down the road as a stocky twelve-year-old boy walks slowly towards them, his schoolbag on his back. He seems weighed down by it, as if he already knows that his future is going to be more depressing than his present.

'That's him,' says Beverley, tossing the book on to the back seat without any ceremony. 'Are we sure about this?'

'I'm sure if you're sure.'

'I'm sure.'

George nods and waits a few extra moments until the child is practically level with them, then opens the door and climbs out.

And at that precise moment, near a taco stand in Mexico, a dog sits on the ground, panting and looking up hopefully, while a twenty-six-year-old man named Kevin Systrom takes a photograph of him, posting it to his brand-new Instagram account, and captioning it:

test

Wednesday

THE WOKESTERS AND THE POOTS

As he slowly drifted back towards consciousness, George emitted a lengthy groan, longing for a return to the erotic dream he'd been enjoying that featured him, Julie Christie and a water lilo. But it was pointless. The next twenty-four hours, he guessed, would be among the most irritating of his life. His mind was already flooding with memories of the evening before and the various humiliations that had been so quickly thrust upon him by a pitiless world.

He rolled over and lay on his back, staring up at the ceiling. It appeared to have been painted recently, for it looked startlingly white. On the bedside table next to him sat the eight-hundred-page biography that he had yet to open, along with his phone, which stood on its charger. His usual practice at this time was to sit up in bed, place both his and Beverley's pillows behind his back, and then reach for the phone and his glasses to discover whether anything interesting had taken place while he was asleep but, right now, it was the last thing he felt like doing.

In catching up with the news, he had a running order that he stuck to religiously.

First, AP and Reuters, to find out what had happened in the world overnight.

Then, the *Guardian*, to find out why this would cause all life on earth to end soon.

The *Telegraph*, to find out why the United Kingdom was alone among nations with the courage and resilience to survive this global catastrophe.

The Times, to find out how much it would cost.

Sky News, to find out what a group of middle-aged men down the pub in Bradford made of it all.

The New York Times, to find out why their journalists had been predicting this for years.

The *Mail Online*, to find out whether it might interfere with a Love Islander's holiday plans.

And, finally, *Fox News*, to find out why none of it was going to happen anyway because it was all a vast left-wing conspiracy dreamed up by a bunch of liberal elites and Hollywood perverts.

Today, however, he was afraid to look at any of these. Going to bed the night before, he knew that the last thing he needed was to have the bloody thing buzzing constantly as friends messaged to say how sorry they were that he was being put through such aggravation, even though he knew they were secretly delighted to see him being publicly shamed, and so he'd switched his phone off entirely.

A knock came on the door and Elizabeth poked her head around.

'You're awake, then?' she said.

'I am.'

'Do you want to know what's been going on since you went to bed?'

'I do not.'

'Well, you're on the front page of all the broadsheets. And the tabloids too. Actually, pretty much every newspaper is leading with you.'

'And if I'd said that I *did* want to know what had been going on, would you have left me alone and told me nothing?'

'It's better that you know,' said Elizabeth, glancing around a room that she had rarely entered since childhood. She could remember many happy Decembers searching for presents with her brothers in the wardrobes and under the bed. 'At least, this way, you're prepared.'

'You're very thoughtful,' he replied. 'The Cordelia to my Lear. Now get out.'

She shrugged her shoulders but, to his relief, left. Feeling so much anxiety that he worried he might be about to have a heart attack, he decided that he had no choice but to reach for the instrument of his potential downfall and face whatever monsters lay in store for him. It took about a minute for it to burst into life but, once it did, the texts began to pour in. He scrolled through the names, his thumb swiping up the screen as he scanned them quickly. Various journalists, a few politicians and a bunch of older celebrities all sending messages of support and saying that they didn't know what all the fuss was about. He'd delete them later. The only one he engaged with was from his producer, Ben Bimbaum, who told him that they needed to talk, and could he be at the BBC at eleven o'clock.

George Cleverley

I'm always at the BBC at eleven o'clock. You could set your watch by me.

He'd barely sent the message when the little dots appeared on the screen to show that Ben was replying. He must have been staring at his screen, contemplating the flatness of the Earth, waiting for George to turn his phone on.

Ben Bimbaum
Great! Looking 4ward to chatz!

'Oh, for fuck's sake,' he grunted.

The ridiculous thing, of course, was that he had been trying to be supportive. He'd always got along well with Aidan, the receptionist at Arlo, Quill, Fitzgerald & Connolly, and it was an incontrovertible fact that he rarely got along well with anyone. Particularly anyone under the age of thirty. And so, when he had learned that Aidan was now Nadia – oh! it was the same word backwards! he just got that! – he had tweeted a note of support, despite how rude he – *she* – had been to him earlier.

@GeorgeCleverley ✔ Much love to Aidan @AQFC as he continues his transition. Brave, authentic & inspiring. #TransRights #TransPride #BraveNewWorld #TotalSupport

The shit had hit the fan almost immediately without him even fully understanding what he'd done wrong. All right, he admitted to himself, he knew what he had *supposedly* done wrong. He'd called Nadia 'Aidan' in his tweet. And used the 'he' pronoun. But Christ alive, was that a hanging offence?

The whole commotion hadn't even been initiated by him, for his initial tweet had originally been liked by a couple of hundred people without any adverse comments at all. It was only when some idiot called @TruthIsASword had tweeted in response that things had started to kick off.

@TruthIsASword Sickened by this transphobic tweet. Man in ur position? Her name is NADIA. SHE is transitioning. Stop the hate, old man. #DeadNaming #MisGendering

There was scarcely a word of this that hadn't made him want to rip his eyeballs from their sockets, but @TruthIsASword seemed to have hit pay dirt because his/her/its reply had been liked or retweeted more than one hundred thousand times over the subsequent twenty-four hours and it seemed as if everyone wanted a piece of him now. Who was this @TruthIsASword anyway? A man? A woman? A gerbil? There was no photograph, just some stock image of the word *Peace* with no biographical profile, other than 'The truth is even sharper than a sharpened blade', which to his mind seemed both tautological and absurd.

As the day had worn on, the number of messages coming his way had made his phone threaten to burst into flames, like a Galaxy Note 7 on a long-haul flight. His agent, Denise, inundated with messages on her own social media accounts, had called to suggest that he offer an apology, but he'd refused, asking why he should have to apologize for something that was done with the best of intentions.

'Because these things are like snowballs,' said Denise. 'They have a habit of snowballing.'

'Your linguistic logic never fails to impress me,' he replied, wondering whether such pearls of wisdom really deserved ten per cent of his annual income.

'Just admit that you did wrong, it's a lot easier that way. People will accept it and move on.'

'But I didn't do wrong,' he protested. 'Does that count for nothing?'

'Not really, no.'

'So, if I was on trial for murder, but I'd happened to be away photographing penguins in the Arctic at the time the crime was committed, you'd say that I should plead guilty and go down for life because "it's a lot easier that way"?'

'I would in that instance, yes, because penguins live exclusively in the southern hemisphere, not the northern, so you'd be quickly caught out.'

'But you take my point. Why should I apologize for something that only someone looking to be insulted would find offensive? If anything, they should be apologizing to me for taking a message of support and turning it into something more sinister.'

'They being?'

'The Wokesters.'

'Who are they? Are they a family?'

'The Wokesters,' he repeated. 'You know, the POOTs.'

'The POOTs? I honestly don't know what—'

'The Permanently Outraged of Twitter. Look, I've been in this game a long time and I guarantee you that this will end up being nothing more than a storm in a teacup. It'll all be forgotten by tomorrow and someone else will be hauled over the coals for doing something just as offensive to public sensibilities.'

'George, if I may say—'

'You may not,' he replied, hanging up.

Only a few minutes later, however, the hacks had started calling, asking for quotes, and he made sure to litter them with so many expletives that they were essentially unusable. And by the time he made the mistake of opening the Twitter app on his phone in the late afternoon, thousands of messages had appeared on his notifications, all from the same compassionate, #BeKind idealists letting him know that he was old, fat, stupid, ignorant, a racist, a homophobe, an anti-Semite, a transphobe, a Remoaner, a misogynist, a hypocrite, a dinosaur, a child abuser, a fascist, a Frenchman, a twat, a prick, a dementia sufferer, a bad driver, a noisy eater, a rapist, a *Daily Mail* reader, a Tory, an Irish Republican, a Hamas supporter and a fan of Michael Bublé.

'Totally unfair,' he grunted, appalled by the insults. 'I've never bought a Michael Bublé record in my life.'

Later, when he got home, reporters were standing outside his front gate and, for some reason, Achilles was chatting away to them, wearing a tank-top to show off his biceps as he brought them cups of tea.

'What on earth are you wearing?' George asked, glaring at his son's arms.

'Sun's out, guns out, Pops,' replied Achilles with a grin. 'And don't worry about my style choices. The bigger question is, what have you got yourself into now?'

George had fought his way through the scrum, the smile so wide on his face that he felt as if his cheeks might crack. Still, he thought, it was good to have Achilles about the place. The boy was a complete idiot, of course, but at least he was amusing. Unintentionally.

'Shut up and get inside,' he said, pushing his son through the door and closing it behind him on the assembled vultures. As he walked into the living room, he found the rest of his family gathered, watching *Sky News*, where a group of reporters were live on television hassling some poor unfortunate man who was simply trying to get through his front door. The setting looked painfully familiar to him.

'And that was broadcaster George Cleverley returning home only a few moments ago,' said the presenter when the outside broadcast switched back to the studio. 'Apparently unwilling or unable to address charges of hate speech in a tweet he posted earlier today which has proved deeply upsetting to the transgender community.'

'Oh, for fuck's sake!' he roared, taking a whisky that some-how had been thrust into his hands by a strange woman who he only vaguely recognized as Beverley's new ghost.

A long conversation had ensued with his wife and children that had only made him angrier and, eventually, he'd retired to bed in a huff, turning off his phone before anyone else could contact him. Now, the following morning, to his disappoint-ment, if not his surprise, he saw that some public figures who he had counted as friends, or at the very least as engaging acquaintances, were taking the opportunity to use his discom-fort to boost their own Woke credentials. The Secretary of State for Culture, for example, a man who George had once observed snorting cocaine before appearing on the *Six O'Clock News*, had tweeted:

@SecStateCult ✅ We need a caring society, where those of all genders and identities can feel safe and welcome. The @BBC needs to remember this.

'And fuck off,' muttered George.
But the Secretary of State for Culture wasn't the only one.

@10DowningStreet ✅ Britain is a country that welcomes diversity and embraces kindness. Let's make 2021 a year for all our citizens, not just the London Elite.

There was something hilarious about being called a mem-ber of the London Elite by the current prime minister, he thought. What was next, the Queen criticizing his inherited wealth and privilege?

D-list pop stars chimed in, naturally, hoping for a little reflected attention. As did Z-list actors.

A model-slash-actress-slash-humanitarian-slash-philanthropist who he'd never heard of issued a press statement saying that she was boycotting his show until further notice because she felt 'unsafe'.

'Never invited, darling,' he said, climbing out of bed now and looking in the direction of the en suite with a sense of exhaustion that never boded well when it was still only eight thirty in the morning.

The phone buzzed again and, cursing, he picked it up to see a text message from Angela Gosebourne. He'd momentarily forgotten the other drama currently playing out in his life, that of impending fatherhood.

Angela Gosebourne
I need to talk to you.

'You and everyone else, sweetheart,' he said, flinging it at the wall.

REGULAR LONDONERS

Although she insisted on trading in her car for a new one every January, Beverley almost never drove in London, preferring to take black cabs wherever she went. They were quicker, more convenient and she liked the screen that protected her from having to make conversation with the driver. She had read somewhere that Stephen Fry had purchased his own black cab, even passing the Knowledge in order to be allowed to drive along the bus lanes, and she'd thought it rather a good idea, but didn't have the energy to remember so many thousands of street names herself, particularly when she had no intention of ever visiting any of them. She was familiar with the West End, of course, and Hampstead, Kensington and Belgravia, but avoided all the mysterious places that lurked menacingly, like malevolent suckers, at the end of each tentacle of the Tube map.

Today, however, she found herself driving along the eastern side of Hyde Park in the direction of Edgware Road or, rather, stuck in a convoy of dozens of other cars, buses and taxis.

'You'd think they could set up another lane,' she said, shaking her head as she stretched her neck, trying to see further along the road to what the hold-up might be. 'For people like me, I mean.'

'And what kind of person are you?' asked her ghost, who was seated in the passenger seat with a shoe box on her lap, into the lid of which a series of holes had been punched earlier by Beverley, using a fork and a stabbing motion reminiscent of Norman Bates when he surprises Marion Crane in the shower and has no intention of simply handing her a loofah. The action had utterly terrified the box's occupant, who had not experienced such extraordinary violence since the Polish–Ukrainian War of 1919, and he immediately took comfort in the presence of three After Eights.

'I pay an awful lot of taxes, dear,' replied Beverley. 'As does George. And this car isn't designed to stall. If there was an extra lane, say, just for those who could afford it, well, I'd be happy to pay whatever charge was imposed. Driving seems to me the only form of transportation where everyone, from the well-off to the hoi polloi, is thrown in together with no possibility of separation. Who are all these people anyway? What are they doing on the roads at this time of the morning?'

'Just regular Londoners, I expect,' said the ghost, who had been dragged away from her second day of writing in what Beverley had claimed was an emergency.

'Well, speaking as a mother, it's a huge inconvenience,' she sighed, pressing her hand on the horn for twenty seconds, hoping this might move things along. In the car in front, a small boy, aged no more than six or seven, turned around in the back seat and gave her the finger. 'Did you see that?' asked Beverley in outrage. 'Did you see what he just did?'

'Perhaps he thinks that blowing your horn won't make things move any faster,' suggested the ghost.

'Why isn't a boy of that age in school anyway?' asked Beverley, ignoring this remark.

The line of cars began to move at last and she pressed her foot on the accelerator, inching forward so the front of her Audi and the bumper of the Prius ahead were practically kissing. When the lights turned red once more, she uttered a profanity and pressed the horn again. This time, the little boy raised himself in the back seat, lowered his trousers and presented her with his bare bottom, wiggling it back and forth in great delight, and she looked away.

'If I had a child like that,' she said, 'I'd drown him. I would, I promise you. I would hold his head down in a bucket of water, and there isn't a jury in the land who would convict me.'

'I imagine they might find one,' said the ghost. 'If they tried hard.'

'You know what your problem is?' asked Beverley, sensing the sarcastic tone. She was already suspicious of the ghost, who had delivered some more pages earlier that morning, featuring a character having her first period while her family were skiing in Verbier, drops of blood spilling into the snow, which, in the ghost's words, 'it drank up quickly, the ice becoming increasingly vampiric with each womanly expulsion from Natalya's womb'. Beverley had read the passage in disgust and sent a terse email in reply, pointing out that, as discussed, the women in her novels did not menstruate, nor did they urinate or defecate. At a push, they could blow their noses, but only if they were seated in a doctor's surgery at the time and the doctor in question was a handsome, single man with a large fortune, a dead wife, an adorable toddler and a broken heart.

'What?' asked the ghost. 'What's my problem?'

'You think that people like me, wealthy people, should behave like everyone else and be treated like everyone else. We don't, we can't, and we shouldn't be. We've worked hard for our money, we give an inordinate amount back to fund the essential services that keep this country running, and, in doing so, we deserve to have our lives made a little easier. But instead, we're let down at every turn. Let me give you an example. When I fly to America, say, naturally, I go first class and am taken in through the first-class security lane, and a few minutes later I'm in the British Airways first-class lounge. Bliss. The bubble opens and welcomes one inside. But between the two, there's a good ten minutes' walk. And during that time, I am stranded among the economy- and business-class passengers, in their shorts and their too-tight T-shirts, drinking beer at eight o'clock in the morning and already getting into fights with each other. Don't you think there should be a separate area for me to walk through? I'm paying good money, so why should I have to mix with the everyday folk?'

'Like your readers?'

'Like my readers. Exactly. I wrote a letter to *The Times* on this subject last year and, inexplicably, they didn't publish it. I assume it must have got lost in the post.'

The traffic moved forward again and, to Beverley's relief, the little boy's car took a different route to hers, turning left as they approached the Marylebone Road crossing.

'It's not that I dislike the poor,' continued Beverley, warming to her theme. 'Indeed, one is grateful for them. After all, if there were no poor people, then, by extension, there would be no rich people. We'd all be the same. Like in one of your communist countries.' She sighed. 'How is Ustym Karmaliuk, by the way? Is he doing okay?'

The ghost lifted the lid of the shoe box and looked inside. The tortoise was resting its head inside an After Eight wrapper.

'I think he's asleep,' said the ghost.

'Is he breathing?'

'How would I know?'

'Put your finger to his throat.'

The ghost did as instructed.

'He's breathing,' she confirmed.

'Good. Let's not wake him. He'll only be cranky later if we do. Anyway, what was I saying?'

'Something about how disappointing it is that, in 2021, there's a spoilt, privileged and entitled upper class who, because they've somehow stumbled into money despite lacking intelligence, compassion or any sense of decency, think they're superior to hard-working men and women.'

'I don't think that was quite it,' said Beverley, after a lengthy pause. 'Really, I've told you before that you should be taking notes when I talk. This is an invaluable education that I'm giving you. But what about you anyway? You've never told me, do your people have much?'

'We do fine,' said the ghost.

'Oh good,' replied Beverley cheerfully. 'One must never want too much from life. Want is what makes us unhappy. It's better to know one's station and remain there. I had a friend once, married a poor man because she loved him, and was she happy?'

'I don't know,' said the ghost. 'Was she?'

'Well, she claimed she was, but who's to know? I expect he drank. And beat her. So many of the poor do, of course. Read your D. H. Lawrence. It's in the blood. It will take generations to breed out. Oh look, there's a spot.'

They had arrived at the veterinary clinic and, to their good fortune, a car was pulling out directly across from the front door. Beverley swept in and breathed a heavy sigh of relief.

'Thank goodness for that,' she said. 'I feel quite done in. Shall we find a little wine bar somewhere and have a drink? I could do with a pick-me-up.'

'It's not even lunchtime,' said the ghost. 'And we're supposed to be taking Ustym Karmaliuk to the vet, remember?'

'Oh yes!' cried Beverley, bursting out laughing. 'I'd almost forgotten. See what the roads do to one? Never again, I promise you that. Never again!'

THE PEDICURE

Elizabeth was at the spa when Wilkes texted her.

Wilkes Maguire
Hey, where are you?

Since her arrival a couple of hours earlier, she'd drunk a half-litre of a colon-cleansing blend of mango, broccoli and goat's urine, completed twenty minutes of Jivamukti yoga, meditated while a triangle sounded quietly behind her head, barked like a dog to clear the toxins from her spirit animal, which, according to the on-site shaman, was suffering a trauma from a previous life when it had been caught in a bear trap, and wept like a baby while an elderly Chinese lady screamed in her face, telling her what a worthless human being she was, in order to release the impurities from her chakras. Afterwards, she'd indulged in a Swedish massage, a hydro-facial and was now in the middle of a pedicure. She waited for a few minutes before replying, irritated that he was killing her buzz.

Elizabeth Cleverley
At the British Library, reading about leprosy. It's really horrible, isn't it?

She set the phone aside and looked down at Hernán, the young Brazilian boy who was using a pumice stone to clear the hard skin from her heels. He attacked her feet as one might pursue a fly that was hovering around one's face, brushing it away in strange, spasmodic movements.

'You're new, aren't you?' she asked, looking down and feeling an urge to run her fingers through his thick black hair. He was about twenty-one, the same age as her, and rather short and undersized, but what he lacked in build he more than made up for in enthusiasm, having greeted her in the reception area like a sister he had not seen for many years, going so far as to kiss her cheeks multiple times and comment on how sexy she was, an intimacy that she allowed, since he clearly offered no sexual threat.

'You're right, you clever bitch,' he replied, just about getting away with the phrase, due to his flamboyant nature. She got the impression that he called everyone 'bitch', 'sister', or 'Queen'. 'Today is only Hernán's third day. And yours are only his second feet. His first, they make him vomit.'

'They make who vomit?'

'Hernán.'

'Aren't you Hernán?'

'Yes.'

'Oh, you talk about yourself in the third person. That's not annoying in the slightest.'

'He learns English this way. It's easier. First feet are horrible. Disgusting old man. Six toes.'

'What happened to the other four?'

Hernán frowned. 'Six toes on one foot,' he clarified. 'Five on the other. One too many toes for Hernán.'

'Did he give you ten per cent extra?' she asked. 'To compensate for the extra work?'

Hernán threw his head back and burst into laughter. 'You nasty,' he said. 'Hernán like that. He like the nasty sluts.'

Elizabeth giggled. Normally, she wouldn't have accepted this kind of abuse from anyone, but there was something about this boy that endeared him to her.

'Well, I'm glad mine are more aesthetically pleasing,' she said, glancing across the room towards an occasional table, on top of which some incense sticks were burning. In general, Elizabeth didn't like getting pedicures, but maintenance of her extremities was something to which she was fully committed, knowing that if she didn't come here twice a month, her feet would end up looking as if they'd been stitched together by someone who didn't have even the slightest understanding of his craft, like Brooklyn Beckham with his photography book.

'Hernán is happy to work with the pretty feet,' said Hernán. 'But not the ugly ones.' He pulled a vomit face.

'You remind me of an old lover of mine,' said Elizabeth. 'A dancer. His English was also a little . . . idiosyncratic.'

'What is this?' asked Hernán, looking up. 'What is this idiosyncratic?'

'Unique,' she explained. 'Distinctive.'

Hernán shrugged and began clipping her nails.

'Is nice,' he said, apropos of nothing.

'All right.'

'Tell me of this lover,' he continued. 'He is big man or small man?'

'Big man. Big man all over. Ukrainian.'

'I know of this place. In Russia.'

'Well, near it, I think.'

'You do the bad-girl shit with him?'

'A lot of the bad-girl shit.'

He exploded in laughter again and slapped her ankle lightly. 'You filthy whore!' he declared. 'Hernán likes this!'

'Well,' she said, a little taken aback. 'I wouldn't go that far.'

'He is boyfriend of you?'

'Oh God, no. It was, like, a year ago. I barely even think of him any more. And how about you? Do you have a boyfriend?'

'Hernán has nine boyfriends,' he replied proudly.

'That's impressive.'

'He has only been in London six weeks,' he said apologetically. 'He hopes for many more yet.'

'And why not? Fill your boots, as they say.'

He looked up, not understanding, but she didn't bother to explain.

'Have you always enjoyed feet?' she asked. 'It's a strange part of the anatomy to work with, don't you think?'

'Since he was small boy in the favelas of Rio de Janeiro,' he told her, as if he was narrating the opening chapter of an audiobook, 'Hernán would take all his friends to his bedroom and tell them to take their shoes and socks off. They had the horrible feet, smelly with the nasty nails, but he would soak them tenderly in the salted water, like the women who wash the feet of Jesus, before clearing all their fungus away. Then he would try to sex them.'

'To sex the feet?'

'To sex the boys.'

She shrugged and examined her fingernails. He was very good at giving pedicures, she'd give him that, very tender but also completely committed to getting the job done in a professional manner, much like she'd always imagined Harry Styles would be in bed. She wondered what Hernán might be like as a lover and spent a pleasant few minutes daydreaming about this, only snapping out of her reverie when her phone buzzed again.

Wilkes Maguire

Well, yes, of course it is.

She stared at the message for a moment, uncertain what Wilkes was talking about, but then remembered her reply. She thought about sending him another text, but didn't bother.

'I don't suppose you know much about leprosy, do you?' she asked, and Hernán looked up at her with a curious expression on his face.

'What is this?' he asked.

'It's a disease of some sort. It's pretty awful, to be honest.'

He pulled his hands away from her feet.

'A disease that you have?' he asked.

'No, not me,' she replied quickly. 'I'm totally disease free. No, there's an island off Indonesia, apparently, and quite a few people have it there, I'm told. Well, at least ten. My boyfriend wants us to go and help them.'

'You are doctors?' asked Hernán, returning to his work, albeit a little more apprehensively.

'No, neither of us is.'

'Then how you can help them?'

'Your guess is as good as mine. Perhaps just by being there and showing them what healthy people look like, it will give them hope. Or will it just make them bitter and envious? It's hard to know, really, isn't it?'

'And this disease you like, does it have cure?'

'I don't really know, to be honest. I'm supposed to be doing some research on it, but I don't even know where to start.'

'If you are going to live among these people,' said Hernán, 'you must learn something about them first, yes?'

'I suppose so,' she agreed. 'Did you learn anything about the British before you came to London?'

'Hernán, he reads many books,' he replied, sounding a little smug. 'He reads novels about the King Henry Eight Times.'

'He lived a very long time ago.'

'Yes, but all the English novels are about the King Henry Eight Times. And his sixteen wives. Is rule, no?'

'Well, I don't know if it's a rule as such,' she agreed, 'but I can see why you might think so.'

'And then he reads the book about the Victorian people by the Jacob Rees-Mogg.'

'Oh dear,' said Elizabeth. 'What on earth made you do that?'

'He is contemporary of them, Hernán thinks. He is oldest man in England. Maybe in world.'

'I'm not sure that's true,' she said.

'He is very handsome man,' said Hernán, sighing a little.

'Who, Jacob Rees-Mogg?' she asked, frowning.

'Yes.'

'Good God. Don't go around telling people that. You'll get deported.'

'You think him not handsome?'

'I mean, he's not the Elephant Man, but it's hard to imagine anyone getting too worked up over him. He is very polite, though; I'll give him that.'

'One day, I hope the Jacob Rees-Mogg will be Hernán's boyfriend.'

'I think it's unlikely. I don't think he bats for your team.'

'Even the spaghetti is straight until you put it in the hot water,' replied Hernán. 'You have heard of this, yes?'

She nodded. 'Well, I wish you luck in your quest. The Jacob Rees-Mogg would be a very lucky man indeed. What else have you read?'

'Hernán reads three books by the Beverley Cleverley that makes him hard.'

Elizabeth shook her head, uncertain that she'd heard him correctly. 'What did you say?' she asked.

'That her books make him hard.'

'That's what I thought you said. How do you mean?'

He set her feet on a fresh towel and stood up, clutching his groin and jerking forward in an unnatural movement, much like Michael Jackson, and uttering a few yelps that might have been some form of Brazilian mating call before kneeling down again and resuming his work.

'Yes, that's what I thought you meant,' said Elizabeth. 'Only I didn't think it possible. Why did they . . . you know . . . arouse you?'

'Handsome doctors,' said Hernán. 'Always with their shirts off.'

'You're very forthright,' said Elizabeth. 'Are you always like this?'

'He says what he feels,' said Hernán. 'In the favelas of Rio de Janeiro, he learns that it is better to be honest with people. Otherwise, they find out that you lie and cut your throat while you sleep, washing their hands in your blood.'

'Actually, I was in Rio de Janeiro once,' said Elizabeth. 'With my father. He'd gone there to interview Pelé.'

Hernán stopped what he was doing and blessed himself.

'You met the Pelé?' he asked.

'No, I stayed at the hotel that day and had a massage. I didn't really know who he was. I mean, I knew the name but that was about it. My father, he's a sort of journalist. He met him.'

'You have the chance to meet the Pelé and you do not take it?' asked Hernán, looking at her as if she'd just discovered she'd won the lottery but had torn up the ticket because she couldn't be bothered to make the phone call.

'That's right. Why, was that terrible of me?'

Hernán shook his head. 'Tell him someone you admire,' he said.

Elizabeth thought about it. 'Kylie Jenner,' she said.

Hernán laughed. 'No, Hernán is serious now. Tell him someone you admire.'

'I am being serious,' said Elizabeth. 'She's probably the person I most admire in the world. She's done so much for lips. Probably more than anyone else, ever.'

'She is the girl with the father who becomes the mother, yes?'

'Well, in a manner of speaking. But I wouldn't advise you to say something like that outside of these four walls. People might take it the wrong way.'

'Take it what way you mean?'

'Saying something like that can make you sound a bit . . . you know . . . transphobic.'

'Yes, but this is what Hernán is.'

'He's transphobic?'

'Very much so. But is okay. He confesses this to his priest and priest, he say, "Do not worry, Hernán, you go to the hell anyway because you sex the boys."'

'Charming,' said Elizabeth.

'So Hernán thinks, is okay to be hater,' he added, reaching for a moisturizer and beginning to massage the creamy liquid into her feet, which felt instantly cool.

'I didn't see any of the fajitas, though,' continued Elizabeth. 'When I was in Rio, I mean. Although we stayed at the Four Seasons, so it's possible there weren't any near by.'

'Fajitas?' asked Hernán, looking up. 'Fajita is Mexican dish.'

'But you said you grew up in the fajitas?'

'No, he didn't.'

'Liar.'

Before they could debate the point further, her phone buzzed again.

Wilkes Maguire

Shall I come around to yours tonight? We can tell your parents. Also, I have great news for you!

She typed a reply.

Elizabeth Cleverley

Tell them what? And what's the great news?

'Fajitas,' muttered Hernán under his breath as he shook his head contemptuously.

Wilkes Maguire
About the leper colony, of course! And I'll tell you when I see you.

She rolled her eyes. This whole humanitarian thing was really getting out of hand. Still, she didn't want to let him down and figured it would be easier for George or Beverley to tell him that it was a non-starter rather than her.

Elizabeth Cleverley
Sure. Say 7.30. I really want to help the lepers.

The pedicure continued silently for a few more minutes and Elizabeth wondered whether she had said something to offend Hernán.

'Your feet are finished,' he said finally, stepping back and admiring his handiwork. She looked down and wiggled her toes and, when she reached down to touch the skin, it felt uncommonly smooth and clean.

'Very professional,' she said. 'Thank you.'

'It is Hernán's job, you silly tart, you don't have to thank him.'

'I know, I'm just being polite. I don't really mean it.'

He went over to the sink to wash his hands and she stepped into her flip-flops. She liked to stay off her feet after one of these sessions and decided that she'd hail a black cab to take her home, then lie on her bed for a few hours until Wilkes arrived, abusing strangers on Twitter. A perfect day!

'Depression?'

'Severe depression.'

'But when this starts? And how this can happen?'

Beverley was in what she inexplicably called her writing room, talking to Pylyp through Skype, while he was seated in the same position he had been in during their last conversation. He'd chosen not to wear a shirt and, while she appreciated the view, she made sure to keep a wary eye on the background in case any more scantily clad young women appeared from what she assumed was the bedroom area.

'Well, I don't quite know, darling,' she replied. 'Yesterday afternoon, I suppose. I've done everything you asked me to do. I've paid more attention to him than I have to either my husband or my children. I've massaged his undercarriage and played the Celine Dion albums he enjoys. I've taken him with me whenever I've left the house, including to a screening at BAFTA last night, and let me tell you, Ian McKellen was *not* happy when he found that there was a tortoise seated between us, so I don't think any of this is my fault. Dr Cavarlio said it's probably separation anxiety. To put it simply, Ustym Karmaliuk misses you.'

'I miss him too,' replied Pylyp, looking gloomy. 'Is he there now?'

'No, he's in the living room. I propped him up in front of *Politics Live.*'

'But how you knew he was sick?'

'The vomit. There was a lot of it and, speaking as a mother, I know what it means when someone throws up all the time. No matter what treats I lay out for him now, he turns his nose up at them.'

'Treats? What is this treats? You feed him the crickets, like we agree?'

'Believe me, that tortoise has seen more cricket action than a crowd at Lord's,' lied Beverley, who had spent ten minutes arguing on the phone with a sales assistant at Fortnum & Mason over why they didn't stock the delicacy. The young woman had suggested Lidl or Aldi – premises that Beverley had never entered in her life – but a quick Google search had put her in contact with a man in Ealing who offered to provide five hundred in a polystyrene box, with the warning that it would only take a couple of escapees to leave her house over-run with the insects. And so, she'd stuck to the After Eights. Which, after all, he seemed to enjoy.

'And the green leaves?'

'So many green leaves,' she replied. 'I pick them myself. From, you know, the trees.'

'From *trees*?'

'I'm kidding,' she said, seeing the horror on his face and assuming she'd said something genocidal. 'I meant spinach leaves. And rocket. And kale.'

'And he say no to eating this?'

'Not only that, but he stopped following me around. Dr Cavarlio asked whether he'd ever behaved like this in the past and I said I didn't think so. Did he have any sort of trauma in his younger years?'

'Of course, but I am not there to see it,' said Pylyp. 'He is alive to see First Big War. He is alive to watch Soviets invade

Ukraine. He is alive throughout Holodomor, when the people, they have no food and must eat their own socks. He is alive to see Second Big War. He is alive when Chernobyl, it goes boom. He is alive for Orange Revolution. He sees everything, just as you see the Queen Victoria and the Simpson and Mrs Edward and the Charlie Chaplin. There is big age difference between Ustym Karmaliuk and me. But I do not care about this. I like big age difference. Is why things work so well between you and me.'

Beverley's lip curled in distaste.

'I wasn't in my nineties when we met, Pylyp,' she protested. 'I'm not even two-thirds of the way there yet.'

'Fifty, sixty, ninety,' said Pylyp with a shrug. 'Is all same.'

'Is very much not all same.'

'To my eyes, is all same. I love everyone. The wrinkles and the lines and the purple veins on the legs that look like they will go pop. Is all beauty to me.'

'I know you mean these things as compliments,' replied Beverley, 'but I don't think you fully appreciate how they come out. Can we get back to talking about your tortoise?'

'Yes. I worried, this is all.'

'At least you know that he's in safe hands,' said Beverley. 'Aren't you at least going to thank me for taking him to the vet?'

'Thank you,' said Pylyp.

'Well, it's no good if I have to drag it out of you. Now, when are you coming home?'

'I am home.'

'I mean back to London.'

'Oh. Soon. My mother, she starts to feel better now that she can visit grave where my father, he rots into the earth. No more is she pulling the hair from the head and running down the street tearing at the clothes.'

'Is that something she did?'

'Yes. But people understand. Many women, they gather the ripped skirts and blouses and soon they will make a cover for the bed with them and present it to her as offering.'

'Waste not, want not,' said Beverley.

'Is tradition,' said Pylyp.

'Well, I'm glad to hear that she's feeling a little more positive about the future. Have you considered setting up an account for her on Tinder? There might be any number of men who would be interested in her. An older divorcé, for example. Or a widower.'

'I do not like this idea,' said Pylyp, shaking his head. 'My mother respected brain surgeon. She must not bring home the young men to sex.'

'I meant the occasional dinner date,' said Beverley. 'Or a glass of wine down her local beer hall.'

'I understand what the women of this age are like. They want to find the young man and get him to bang, bang, bang like the stallion all day and all night. Is not what I want for my mother.'

'I hope you're not referring to me when you say such things,' said Beverley, feeling wounded by the insinuation.

'No, you still have the husband, but there is no bang, bang, bang. I not talk about you. I talk about the Ukrainian women. And the Moldovan women, these are worse again. They look for the boys in the short trousers who still have not the hair on the chests.'

'I feel like we're drifting into uncomfortable territory,' said Beverley. 'Of course, I don't know what the women are like in your part of the world, but they're certainly not like that here. Which is where you belong.'

Pylyp said nothing, his face darkening so much through the

screen that Beverley wondered whether she needed to adjust her brightness settings.

'Is that your suitcase in the corner?' she asked, narrowing her eyes and looking over his shoulder. He turned and looked at the item in question, which appeared to be fully packed, its handle extended, his coat hanging off it. 'Are you coming home today? Please tell me you are.'

'Is sitting there since Monday,' he replied, not sounding particularly convincing. 'I must move it.'

Beverley sighed. 'The truth is, I'm having a terrible time of it,' she continued, when the silence became uncomfortable. 'I've hired a new ghost and I'm not sure I made the right choice, George has caused some sort of kerfuffle at work and the children are causing no end of drama. I miss your touch, Pylyp.'

'And I miss Ustym Karmaliuk,' said Pylyp plaintively.

'You do know how to make a girl feel special,' she said with a sigh. 'I'll give you that. Did I ever tell you that I had a pet when I was young?'

'This must be during the wartime blitzes, yes?'

'No,' said Beverley. 'Because the war had already been over for almost twenty years by the time I was born. It was during the early seventies. I had a gerbil, but John Lennon killed it.'

'Who is this John Lennon?' asked Pylyp. 'You want that I should punch him in face for what he does?'

'John Lennon,' she repeated, but louder now. And slower. 'As in John Lennon.'

Pylyp shrugged. 'I know not who this is,' he said. 'He is man on your street? Or different writer, maybe? One who says your books are the trash?'

'The Beatles.'

'You had a gerbil and some beetles?'

224

'What is wrong with you today, Pylyp?' cried Beverley. 'Can't you just listen to what I'm saying? John Lennon. From The Beatles. The band. You must have heard of The Beatles?'

'Of course,' said Pylyp. 'The music band, yes? From olden days. "Hey Jude",' he chirped, tunelessly. 'You must take the sad song and then you must make it better.'

'Yes, something like that.'

'I am finding myself in the times of trouble and the Mother Mary, she comes on me.'

'Comes with me,' corrected Beverley. 'Comes *to* me.'

'I know all of this. But why we talk of The Beatles? Is crickets you must give Ustym Karmaliuk, not beetles.'

'Oh, for God's sake,' said Beverley, beginning to understand what might lead an otherwise sane, professional woman to run down the street, ripping her clothes off so they could later be fashioned into the Bedspread of the Damned. Just tell me this, Pylyp, when are you coming back? You're not staying in Ukraine for good?'

'Yes, I am coming back. I would never desert Ustym Karmaliuk. And when I do, I bring big surprise for you.'

'The only big surprise I want from you is – wait! Who's that? It's that girl again! Pylyp, why is that girl in your apartment? Pylyp? Answer me! Pylyp?'

But it was too late. The line had gone dead, the screen had gone black, and Beverley was left on her own in the room. She looked around to see Ustym Karmaliuk, who had abandoned *Politics Live* and somehow made his way into her writing room but got himself into difficulties and overturned. He was lying on his shell, his little legs cycling pointlessly in the air, and Beverley felt a sense of grief as she righted him.

'This is what it's come to,' she muttered under her breath.

AN 'UMBLE MAN

When George exited the lift on the fourth floor of Broadcasting House, Ben Bimbaum was waiting for him, wearing a T-shirt that displayed a man's groin area from navel to just above the knees, the genitals mercifully covered in a pair of black Calvin Klein boxer shorts. He was old enough to remember when everyone at the BBC wore a suit and tie and a person was suspected of being a communist sympathizer if he so much as removed his jacket or rolled his sleeves up.

'Is that entirely appropriate?' he asked, grateful that the producer's lanyard was covering the bulge at the heart of the image.

'What?'

'Your T-shirt. Do I really have to look at that for the rest of the day?'

'It's Justin Bieber's crotch,' said Ben, sounding offended. 'This cost me two hundred pounds.'

'Christ alive,' replied George, walking in the direction of his office. 'Why would you wear such a monstrosity? Remember when we had him on the show?'

'Vividly.'

'And you still liked him afterwards?'

'More than words can say.'

George shook his head. He'd tried to put that particular Saturday night, one of the most exasperating *Cleverley* interviews he'd ever been forced to conduct, from his mind.

'Well, that's the closest you'll ever get to that particular hot spot, my old son,' he said. 'Anyway, speaking of cocks, I suppose I'm in for a bollocking, am I?'

'I'm afraid so,' said Ben, picking up his pace, for George was walking in the *West Wing* style that he favoured, keeping the flow of conversation going as he slipped around corners, water dispensers and those uncomfortable red pods where the young creatives met to interface and dialogue, and to discuss cross-platform activity and millennial branding.

'And who will be delivering this rebuke? You or Margaret? Please God, say it's you. At least then I won't have to pretend to be paying any attention.'

'I'm afraid not. It's Margaret.'

'Fuck.'

'Indeed.'

'How's her mood?'

'I don't know. I haven't seen her yet. Apparently, I'm in for one too.'

'But you have nothing to do with any of this,' protested George, who preferred not to let innocent people take the fall for any of his blunders. 'I posted the tweet. It wasn't as if you were looking over my shoulder as I typed it.'

'Upstairs seems to think that we producers have some power over our talent,' said Ben.

George laughed. 'Bless their hearts,' he said.

'I honestly don't know if I'll even be able to get through the day,' he continued. 'I was so worked up last night that I ended up having an argument with Pancake in a chatroom and it lasted till, like, 3 a.m.'

'I'm sorry,' said George, pausing at the door to his office. 'You did what with who now?'

'Pancake. He's one of the Flat Earthers in my group chat.

He was talking about how there are dragons on the outer edges of the world that eat anyone who falls off – and people *do* fall off, you know, but the government keeps it quiet – and I told him he was crazy, that there's no such thing as dragons.'

'Yes, he's the crazy one,' muttered George. 'Good job you set him straight.'

'So, in the end, I didn't get my seven hours and I started the day with three doughnuts and a Red Bull so my blood sugar's spiking. I'll crash in about an hour, I imagine, and fall asleep on the floor.'

George hung his coat up, left his bag in its usual place and was about to sit down behind his desk when he noticed, to his immense dissatisfaction, that Ben was still standing there.

'You're hovering,' he said.

'She wants us now,' said Ben.

'Who does?'

'Margaret.'

'What, right now? I don't even have time for a coffee and an extended period of inactivity?'

'The moment you arrived, that's what I was told. And I daresay Security was told to alert her when you came through the door. She's probably waiting for us as we speak.'

George sighed and stood up with the air of a man who's been told to negotiate a settlement to the Middle East conflict in the next five minutes, before leading the way back towards the lifts.

'You know the funny thing about Margaret, don't you?' he asked as the doors opened. 'No one ever remarks on it, but Mrs Thatcher's maiden name was Roberts. Just like our Margaret.'

'Our Margaret is married,' said Ben.

'Yes, but was she originally a Roberts or did she marry a Roberts? Beverley changed her name when we got spliced, of course, but it might have been illegal not to back then. Simpler times. She was actually a Quint by birth. Beverley, I mean. One of the Cornish Quints. *Not* the Penzance Quints, but the Port Isaac Quints. The Penzance Quints were a bit . . .' Here he allowed his left hand to tremble, which signified nothing to Ben. 'Although the Port Isaac Quints were also a bit . . .' And here he held both hands out before him and moved them up and down in alternate motions, rather like feet on an elliptical machine. 'So, who's to say, in the end, am I right? Who's to say?'

Ben nodded and looked completely bewildered.

'I have no idea,' he said.

'My point is that they share a name. And there is something a little Thatcherite about our Margaret, don't you think? The hair, the eyes, the way she looks at you as if you haven't laid off enough miners today and need to be spanked on the bottom until you make up the quota.'

'She frightens me,' said Ben quietly.

'Does she? I can see where you're coming from, but I rather like that aspect of her character. But then I've always enjoyed an intimidating woman. I felt the same way towards Mrs Thatcher herself.' The lift doors opened again and they made their way down the corridor.

'Dead men walking,' whispered Ben.

'I had her on the show several times, of course,' continued George. 'Mrs T, I mean. You'd have been just a boy back then, discovering your nascent sexuality and holding tea parties in your back garden.'

'I never—'

'Anyway, we knew each other a little socially, Margaret and me. Beverley and I had her over to dinner a few times. She was always terribly good with the children, which surprised me, and insisted on helping with the washing-up afterwards too, which was really unnecessary. She didn't want to leave, particularly on that final occasion. She just wanted to drink whisky and growl about how all these terribly wet men had stabbed her in the back. I told her that she could probably have her own political show if she wanted, and she shook her head, placed a hand on my arm, and said, "But George, one shall never leave office. One must go on and on and on." Of course, this was ten years into her retirement, when she was starting to go a bit doolally. She didn't even remember that she'd been put out to pasture a long time before.'

'Well, here we are,' said Ben as they approached the receptionist's desk, glad that this particular trot down memory lane would be forced to come to an end.

'I always felt a little sorry for her afterwards, to be honest,' continued George with a sigh. 'After all, without work, without an audience, what is there?'

'George Cleverley and Ben Bimbaum for Margaret Roberts,' said Ben, addressing the receptionist, who barely looked up before reaching for the phone.

'Good morning, young man,' said George in an unnecessarily loud voice.

'Good morning,' he replied, looking a little shaken by the exuberance of the greeting.

'And just to be clear, you are a young man, aren't you?'

'My name is Dennis,' he said uncertainly, turning to Ben, who smiled reassuringly.

'Dennis, Denise, you tell me what you want me to say,' said George, 'and I will most cheerfully say it.'

He offered a half-bow from the waist and went over to sit on a sofa while Dennis, bewildered, made the call.

'There's no one in there with her, of course,' said George when Ben joined him after checking that the boy wasn't going to call Human Resources to issue a complaint. 'But she'll keep us waiting for a few minutes, just to prove a point.'

'What point is that?'

'That she's more important than us.'

'She is more important than us,' said Ben.

'Than you, yes,' admitted George. 'But not me. She is senior in the organization, certainly. She outranks me. But Heads of Entertainment come and go. The talent, on the other hand, stays. We go on and on and on.'

'You certainly do,' agreed Ben.

A ping went off on Dennis's desk and he looked up and told them that they could go in now. George led the way, opening the door without knocking and offering a hearty 'Good morning, Margaret!' to the fifty-something woman seated behind the desk by the window, who looked up and smiled wearily before ushering them into seats.

'George,' she said, nodding at them both. 'Bob.'

'Ben,' said Ben.

'I thought your name was Bob?'

'No,' said Ben. 'It's Ben.'

Margaret frowned, her eyes narrowing a little.

'I'm not trying to be difficult,' he said, his voice growing quieter by the syllable. 'It really is.'

'If you say so,' she replied. 'So, we seem to have got ourselves into a little bit of a mess, don't we?'

'We?' asked George, raising an eyebrow. 'Why, what have you done? Or are you using the royal "we"?'

'All right, let's be clear,' said Margaret. '*You* have got yourself into a little bit of a mess. I am perfectly innocent in this matter and my hands are clean.'

'As are Bob's,' said George. 'So there's really no need for him to be here. He has nothing to do with any of this.'

'Ben,' said Margaret.

'Sorry, yes, Ben.'

'Shall I go, then?' asked Ben, rising from his seat, but Margaret shook her head and pointed her index finger at the chair.

'Stay where you are,' she said. 'You're the producer. Ultimately, all of this falls under your purview.'

'Does it, though?' asked George, sceptically.

'I'm extremely sorry,' said Ben, sitting up straight now and clearing his throat. 'It was never my intention to offend and I apologize unreservedly to anyone whose feelings have been hurt by my tweet. My words were intended as a show of support for all my transgender brothers and sisters, but I realize now how damaging and hurtful they were. Please understand that I am still learning and that I will work hard to do better from now on. I want to hashtag be kind. I beg your forgiveness. To make amends, I have made a donation to—'

'What on earth are you blathering on about?' asked George, turning to look at him. 'You haven't posted something too, have you?'

'No, this is the kind of statement that I think you should put out,' said Ben. 'An apology.'

'An apology for what?'

'An apology for the offence you've caused,' said Margaret.

George rolled his eyes and looked out the window in the direction of the Langham hotel, where he wished he was now, drinking a large glass of red wine and enjoying a lobster roll.

'Look,' he said. 'This whole thing has been blown out of all proportion. I've known the chap in question for some years.

Always got along fine with him. The fact is, I was wishing him well on his journey. How that has been interpreted as some form of hate speech is completely beyond me.'

'But you're doing it again right now,' said Margaret.

'Doing what?'

'Causing offence.'

'How?'

'He's not a chap. He's a young woman.'

'*She's* a young woman,' said Ben, correcting her.

'Sorry, yes, that's what I meant.'

'Was that hate speech on your part?' asked George. 'Misgendering her?'

'No, of course not,' said Margaret. 'It was simply a mistake.'

'But so was mine. The thing is, I've always known him – her – as Aidan. And she didn't have the courtesy to tell me that she was, you know, transitioning. From a caterpillar to a beautiful butterfly. Which, if memory serves, is what the serial killer thinks he's doing in *The Silence of the Lambs*. Not that I'm drawing any connection between the two. Honestly, Margaret, you should have seen her. Really quite stunning. You'd be hard pushed to tell the difference. In some ways, you might say it was a compliment. If I'd, you know, screamed or something when I saw him—'

'Her.'

'If I'd screamed when I saw her, then that would have been tremendously impolite. But no, I naturally assumed that this was just a new receptionist, so I introduced myself and was making small talk, and honestly, it was like getting blood from a stone. You know, just because you're going through some sort of personal rite of passage doesn't give you the automatic right to be rude, does it?'

'Be that as it may,' said Margaret, 'your words have caused offence.'

'But that's like complimenting someone on losing weight and then they complain that you're suggesting they were fat before.'

Margaret frowned. 'I'm not sure that's quite the same thing,' she said. 'And I would steer clear of referring to women's weight, if I was you. Especially in the workplace.'

'I never mentioned women,' he replied huffily. 'It could have been a man I was talking about.'

'Be that as it may,' she repeated, 'we live in strange times—'

'You just assumed that it was a woman, which says more about your prejudices than it does about mine.'

'When people are not only liable to take exception at any perceived slight but are actively looking for reasons to do so. You may have meant well, George, but intentions no longer matter. Social media has changed all that.'

'Because, ironically, when it comes to social media, anything is acceptable and nothing is acceptable.'

'Exactly.'

'You agree with that?'

'I agree with your interpretation of that. The patriarchy are—'

'Oh, please,' he said, rolling his eyes. 'Just . . . let's not. Also, *the patriarchy* is a single collective noun so whatever you were going to say, it should have been *is*, not *are*.'

'The patriarchy are being held to account,' she continued, speaking over him.

'It is, is it?' he asked.

'It are.'

'You see?'

'Let's not play semantics. You hold a position of responsibility here. The BBC itself holds a unique place in the life of this nation. People like you and I are held to a higher standard.'

'Me, yes. You, no. No one knows who you are.'

'I assure you that if I tweeted something transphobic from this office, people would be very aware of my existence before I even had a chance to clear out my desk.'

George opened his mouth to protest further but found that he was lacking the energy to bother, so closed it again.

'You see what I'm saying?' she asked.

'I do,' he said. 'I think it's idiotic and it feels like the obsession of narcissistic morons with far too much time on their hands, but I accept that the culture exists in the world. Just like National Socialism did in the thirties. And McCarthyism in the fifties.'

'Please don't say anything like that on social media, George. Those are both very powerful lobbies.'

'Not the Nazis. They got defeated.'

'Well, they're back. And, this time, they've all got Twitter accounts.'

'Fine. But I just want you to admit that it is not so appalling that I got it wrong in the first place. If you got married tomorrow, Margaret, say you married Tom Thatcher over in Accounting—'

'There's nothing going on between me and Tom,' said Margaret, rearing up in her chair and looking appalled. 'What on earth would make you suggest such a thing?'

'I'm just using it as a for instance,' said George. 'Say you and Tom got married and I was invited to give a speech at the reception, and in that speech I said that of all the Heads of Entertainment under whom I have worked in my long and illustrious career at the BBC, Margaret Roberts is by far the most recent, would you be offended that I had called you by the name by which I have always known you, rather than by your married name?'

'No,' admitted Margaret. 'But you have to appreciate that we're not talking about normal people here. We're talking about people on Twitter. There's an enormous difference. It's like comparing house cats to lions that have only ever lived in the wild, ripping the heads off young gazelles and feasting on their bodies.'

George threw his head back and laughed. 'I'll have to remember that one,' he said.

'I love those shows,' said Ben, eager to get back into a conversation from which he felt he had been excluded for too long. 'When you see animals ripping each other apart.' He made a tiger face and presented his hands as claws. 'Grrrr,' he said.

'My point is,' said Margaret, ignoring him. 'While the average man or woman on the street is smart enough to know that you meant no offence, the Twitterati is not. Are not. Is not. And they want your head.'

'Well, they can't have it.'

'Then we must do something to keep it attached to your shoulders.'

'I'm extremely sorry,' said Ben, sitting up straight again and repeating his earlier mantra. 'It was never my intention to offend and I apologize unreservedly—'

George interrupted him. 'Do you know how long I've been at the BBC?' he asked.

'I do, of course,' replied Margaret. 'And I have nothing but respect for you and all that you've—'

'I am the man who called Enoch Powell a racist to his face on live television, causing him to rip off his microphone and storm off the set. I am the man who got Ronald Reagan to re-enact his "Where's the rest of me?" scene from *Kings Row* in front of a studio audience while he was still President of the United States, making him look like a complete buffoon. I am the man who handed a condom to Pope John Paul the Second and asked him did he know what it was.'

'An unwrapped condom at that,' added Ben, nodding in support.

'Unused, in fairness,' added George.

'I know all that,' said Margaret. 'But—'

'But me no buts!' cried George cheerfully. 'I am the man who did all those things and more. Hundreds more. I have met everyone, interviewed everyone, fought with everyone, fallen out with everyone, written obituaries for everyone and, as dear Elton so memorably sang, I'm still standing.'

'Yeah, yeah, yeah,' sang Ben, sotto voce, while doing a little bit with his hands.

'The trick is not to add fuel to this fire, Margaret. If we give it oxygen, it will continue to roar and the flames will engulf us all. The best thing to do is just sit it out and wait for someone else to cock up. And they will, rest assured. Lineker or Hislop or Norton or one of that lot. They'll say something untoward, they'll be the villains of the week, all this will be forgotten, and I will return to my place on the stage as a national treasure, along with my dear friends David, Judi and Maggie.'

'Dear Maggie,' said Ben with a sigh.

George leaned back in his chair and adopted his reminiscing pose. 'I remember I had her on the show once. Well, many times, of course, but on this particular occasion—'

'George, please,' said Margaret. 'Can we stay on topic?'

'Just a moment,' he replied. 'You'll like this. Not a lot, as darling Paul used to say.'

'Darling Paul,' said Ben. 'He once made me disappear.'

'Enough!' shouted Margaret.

The two men fell silent and looked down at their hands, momentarily chastened.

'Now, I've had a word with the Director-General,' she continued, 'and obviously, we'll support you a hundred per cent while publicly disassociating ourselves from everything you've said. But it would be very helpful if you could make some sort of statement in the meantime to express your regret. Nothing as flowery as what Bob suggested. Just something to take the heat off you.'

'Ben,' said Ben.

'Something simple and uncontroversial.'

'Fine,' said George, throwing his hands in the air. 'I give in. I am Napoleon surrendering to Wellington after the Battle of Waterloo.'

'At least you don't have delusions of grandeur,' replied Margaret.

'Very true. I am an 'umble man. Ever so 'umble. And if it will put this whole nonsense to bed and mean that I can get back to work, I'm willing to say a few conciliatory words. When do you want me to do it?'

Margaret glanced at the clock on the wall. 'This evening on the *Six O'Clock News*,' she said. 'Sophie will ask you a few questions and then you'll say whatever needs to be said and we can put the entire matter behind us, all right? Which gives you a few hours to prepare. Bob, I'm trusting you on this.'

'Of course, Mildred, said Ben.

THE LAST NIGHT OF YOUR LIFE

An awkward silence fell upon the hall when Nelson stepped inside, and he stood up straight, pulling on his belt, while appreciating the attention that was coming his way. If there had ever been a time when he needed to exude confidence, then this was it. Walking towards the cash desk, he could feel the eyes of everyone in the room turn towards him, while a middle-aged man wearing a shell-suit picked up his bag and made his way quickly out of the door.

Seated behind the desk was a woman in her late thirties with badly dyed hair. As Nelson approached her, she glanced up from her copy of *Grazia* and looked him up and down appreciatively.

'One ticket, please,' said Nelson, handing across a ten-pound note, and she rooted in her cash box to give him his change, along with a sticker with a number on it, Number 37, which he attached to his tunic.

A few dozen people were gathered in the hall, most standing awkwardly on their own, staring at their phones, and Nelson glanced at his watch. He'd timed his arrival thinking that proceedings would begin soon after he walked through the door and, perhaps because his clothing brought an air of authority into the room, a woman made her way towards the microphone stand and leaned into it, obeying the constitutional obligation to ask 'Is this thing on?' so close to the grille that she sent a stab of reverb around the room, causing everyone to rear back and cover their ears.

'Can you hear me?' she asked.

'They can hear you, Alice,' shouted the cashier, whose own name tag read *Belinda*. 'So get on with it, you daft cow.'

'Oh good,' said Alice, beaming with joy. 'Well, you're all very welcome here tonight. Some of you have been here before – yes, I recognize you desperate people! – but some of you are new. All of you, I expect, are a little nervous, but I hope you're excited too because' – and here she raised her voice again – 'tonight might be THE LAST NIGHT OF YOUR LIFE!'

Her face exploded in happiness and she broke into applause as the people gathered before her turned to look at each other in confusion, uncertain whether they had heard her correctly.

'Dozy mare,' muttered Belinda, who had sidled up beside Nelson now and was getting perilously close to touching him. In fact, he was certain that he could feel one of her hands stroking his left buttock.

'No, I got that wrong, didn't I?' said Alice, frowning. 'It's not the last night of your life. I mean, it might be, but who's to say? Anything could happen. No, what I meant was' – voice raising again – 'tonight might be the last night of the rest of your life!'

A groan from the audience.

'No, that's not it either, is it? Oh dear, I'm so sorry, it's—'

'The first night of the rest of your life!' roared Belinda, definitely cupping him now, and he stepped forward, out of her reach. 'For Christ's sake, Alice, you get it wrong every time! It's like handing a microphone to Mel Gibson when he's six hours into a bachelor party and asking him whether he'd like to go to Israel on his summer holidays.'

'Yes, that's it,' replied Alice, looking apologetic, her face turning beetroot red. 'The rest night of the first of your life. I do apologize. Now, let me begin by thanking you all for coming to our sixth speed-dating night of 2021. It's such a pleasure to see so many lonely, miserable people, all hoping to find someone who might give their lives some meaning. It matters so much to Belinda and me—'

'Doesn't matter to me,' muttered the cashier in Nelson's ear. 'But I love a man in uniform, I do.'

'—that you've come here tonight. You are the dreamers, and we are the dreamers of your dreams. Love, love is strange. Many people take it for a game. Lonely, you might be Mr Lonely, or Miss Lonely, but you've gotta have faith. You've gotta have a-faith-a-faith-a-faith. I say you've gotta have a-faith if you wanna dance with somebody who loves you and have sweet dreams till sunbeams find you. Can you feel the love tonight? It's a little bit funny, but I can—'

'She does this whole fucking routine every time,' said Belinda, shaking her head in exasperation. 'Honestly, there are times I'd like to press a pillow over her face.'

'This feeling inside. Now, don't be worried if you say something stupid like I love you, although you may not want to say that as you've all only just met, but remember that each of you is beautiful, it's true, in every single way, and you need to open your hearts to each other, because one of you holds the lock and the other holds the key.'

'I think you'd better leave right now,' shouted a man at the back of the room, and Nelson looked in his direction. He was big, bald and burly, and had the number 22 on his sticker.

'Don't feel under pressure, that's all I ask,' continued Alice. 'And you might end the night flying without wings!'

'Which would leave you crashing to the earth and exploding like a watermelon,' roared Number 22.

'All right,' said Alice, who had evidently reached the end of her speech and looked almost as relieved about that as everyone else. Nelson felt his heart sinking, wondering whether he'd not only wasted £9 on a ticket to this shambles, but also £142.50 on his policeman's uniform.

'Now, in the olden days,' continued Alice, 'back when men did all the DIY and women knew how to make a perfect Victoria sponge, we used to have two lines of seats, women on one side and men on the other. We're not allowed to do that any more, of course, as it would contravene equality laws and, for all I know, some of you might be straight, some of you might be gay, and some of you might be homosexual. Which is fine.

There's room for all sorts, no matter what your perversion. Some of you might not even know what you are! I ran one of these events recently in Battersea and a man told me he was pansexual and I had to go home and google what that meant! But that was Battersea so, you know, you're up against it there. Anything goes. I should add that I feel no prejudice towards those women who do not ride on my side of the bus, none whatsoever. Or the men who . . . also ride on the . . . maybe sit downstairs. On the bus. Or even walk! Or use their bicycles, who knows?'

She beamed out at the audience, most of whom were now shifting uncomfortably and wondering whether they could just make a break for it.

'For what it's worth,' she added, 'my best friend's neighbour has a daughter who's a lesbian and she's a pretty little thing, so it's very sad, but she's getting married later this year, so to speak, to a woman, so to speak, and I'm delighted for her, so to speak. It just goes to show, there's hope for everyone! Every old sock meets an old shoe! Or, in their case, a pair of old boots!'

Nelson watched as two people ripped off their badges and left the hall, and he considered doing the same thing, but he felt like he was driving slowly past the scene of a car crash. He didn't want to stare, but he just couldn't help it.

'Right,' said Alice, leaning in to the microphone again and sighing deeply. 'So here's the way we do things now since equality came in.' She made inverted comma symbols in the air when she said the word *equality*. 'You sit down wherever you like and you talk to the person seated opposite you.' Again, inexplicably, she signed inverted commas around *opposite*. 'Some will be people of the gender to which you are attracted, and some will not. But no matter who's facing you, just have a chat! Talk as if you're normal, well-adjusted people. And when I ring the bell, which will be every three minutes, everyone moves one space to their left and starts talking to whoever's sitting opposite them then. Is that clear? Of course it is. Clear as mud, I hear you say! Ahahaha! Anyway, it'll all become clear once we get started. So now, without any further ado, and unaccustomed as I am to speaking aloud, let me invite you all to take a seat, and when I ring the bell, just talk, just *talk*—'

'Just fucking *talk*,' implored Belinda.

'Now, let the games begin, may the odds be ever in your favour, and to those about to die, we salute you!'

And then she picked up a bell and rang it so loudly into the microphone that Nelson thought blood might pour from his ears.

'Well, go on then, Inspector Gadget,' said Belinda, detaching herself from his body. 'Give it your best shot. I'll be watching.'

SUGAR BABIES

Achilles had put a lot of time into his outfit this morning and was wearing his favourite Calvin Klein jeans, a snow-white V-necked tee that sunk low enough to reveal the tight pads of his pectoral muscles, a blue short-sleeved shirt that he left completely unbuttoned and the replacement trainers he'd bought online, adding a touch of Paco Rabanne fragrance to his neck, wrists and crotch. As he came downstairs, he caught a whiff of something ghastly and gave his armpits a quick sniff to make sure that it wasn't him, but a moment later Elizabeth and her boyfriend emerged from the living room.

'Forgot to put your deodorant on today, Catweazle?' he asked, maintaining a safe distance in order to avoid being infected by any vengeful aromas that might attach themselves to him.

'Shut up, Achilles,' snapped Elizabeth.

'You shut up,' replied Achilles, ever the wit, as he left the house.

Boarding the District Line Tube in the direction of Whitechapel, he appreciated the admiring glances he was receiving from men, women, boys and girls alike but pretended to be completely oblivious to them. Usually, he kept his eyes on his phone, ignoring the attention, but he sensed someone standing up further down the carriage and making their way in his direction, before sitting down on the empty seat next to him.

'Ghost!' he said, turning to look at her and breaking into a wide grin. 'You don't mind if I call you that, do you?'

'I'd prefer if you didn't,' she said. 'I'm more than just a job title, you know.'

'All right. But I don't think I've gone so far as to learn your name yet.'

'You've been told it.'

'Have I?'

'Several times. But perhaps you didn't feel it was worth remembering.'

He thought about this before shrugging his shoulders. 'That does sound like me,' he admitted. 'You're all dressed up,' he added, looking her up and down. 'Going somewhere special?'

'I'm meeting a friend later,' she said.

'A male friend.'

'Yes. And you?'

'The same. I bet you're going on one of those *Guardian* blind-date things that they publish on Saturdays, aren't you?'

'I'm not, actually,' she said. 'And that's a pretty random assumption to make, don't you think?'

'I didn't mean it to sound rude,' he replied.

'I don't think you're rude so much as lost,' continued the ghost. 'Were you always like this or is it something that's grown progressively worse as you've got older?'

Achilles was not someone who typically found himself stuck for words, but he did now.

'You couldn't be any further off the mark,' he said, hating how plaintive the words sounded as they left his mouth. 'I'm neither of those things.'

'Perhaps I'm wrong,' she replied. 'But you give off this sense of constant amusement at the world, as if it exists purely for your pleasure while you hover above it, rolling your eyes. Beneath all that charming disdain, though, I feel like you're bristling with rage. Those snarky comments of yours, that sense of superiority. They're not attractive traits.'

Achilles looked straight ahead of him at a woman seated on the opposite side of the carriage who was nodding her head in time with the music playing through her earphones, although something in her expression and movements made him think that she'd put it on mute and was listening in to their conversation.

'You don't know me,' he said quietly, his tone laced with petulance as his earlier confidence began to slip away.

'I know your type,' she said. 'The truth is, boys like you are two a penny. Popular teenagers who lose just a little of their status when they go to university and realize that others aren't so impressed by them any more. And then, when that comes to an end and everyone is struggling for work and trying to make ends meet and you're not quite as young as you used to be?' She shook her head. 'Believe me, things can change very quickly. I wonder is there a decent little boy in there some-where, behind all your bluster?'

'Stop calling me a little boy,' he said. 'I might be short for my age but—'

'Oh Christ, if you say that you make up for it in other departments, I'll be so disappointed in you. Nothing you've said since I've met you has been a cliché. It's been smug and obnoxious but never a cliché. So please don't fall into that trap now.'

'I wasn't going to say that,' he replied, even though that's exactly what he had been about to say. 'And I'm not so insecure that anything you say can affect me in the slightest.'

'But you are,' she said with a smile. 'You're exactly that insecure.'

He swallowed and looked away. The train passed through Westminster and then Embankment before he spoke again.

'Fine,' he said. 'I'll stop behaving like a douche around you if you stop saying mean things to me. I'm not made of stone, you know.'

'That would be lovely, thanks.'

'No problem. I hope you've got all that out of your system anyway. Otherwise, your date's in for a rough time of it. So how are you enjoying the new job? Getting on okay with my mother?'

'It's more complicated than I expected,' said the ghost. 'She doesn't give a lot of direction.'

'No? Does that help or hinder your creativity?'

The ghost considered this. 'I suppose it helps,' she replied.

'But I don't know if Beverley will be happy with what I'm writing. Assuming she even reads it, that is.'

'Of course she'll read it,' said Achilles defensively. 'Why wouldn't she?'

'It's just that I've been around your family for a couple of days now and the only thing any of you seem to read is the screens of your phones. Well, not you, to be fair. But the others. Were you always like this?'

'I don't think so,' he replied. 'But . . . yes, they do seem to have an unhealthy regard for the opinions of complete strangers. Although they're in the public eye, so perhaps it's only natural.'

'Your sister isn't. And she's surgically attached to her phone. Social media is not reality, you know. It's a mirage.'

Achilles frowned. He didn't like the direction the conversation was taking. Anything that upset his perfect view of the Cleverleys upset him.

'Who is he anyway?' he asked.

'Who is who?'

'This chap you're meeting.'

'It doesn't matter who he is. You wouldn't know him.'

'Well, no, of course not. It's not like we move in the same circles.'

'You're doing it again.'

'I'm not!' he protested, laughing a little. 'But we don't, do we? I'm seventeen and you're an adult. It's not like we have a connected group of friends.'

'Fine,' she said, rolling her eyes.

'So, tell me about him. Is it a first date?'

'Yes. It's all happened rather unexpectedly.'

'Do you think you'll have sex with him?'

'I have no intention of telling you anything about my sex life.'

'Where's he from, then?'

'Ukraine.'

He frowned. 'So, do you and this guy just sit around and talk Ukrainian politics together?'

'Of course,' she replied. 'What else could we possibly discuss but that?'

'I suppose you look into each other's eyes and talk about great Ukrainian folk heroes and sing ballads of war-torn Odessa.'

'Look at you, knowing where Odessa is,' she said.

'Lucky guess. You know when people say that they're not just a pretty face? My problem is, that's exactly what I am. I just want to live each day the way I want to live it, answering to no one. Getting up when I want, seeing who I want, coming home when I want.'

'You need money to do that.'

'I'm working on that. So, tell me about him. This boyfriend of yours. What's he like?'

'He's not my boyfriend,' she said. 'I told you, it's a first date.'

'Did someone set you up with him?'

'No, I answered a phone,' she said. 'And he was on the other end of it.'

'Just a random phone?'

'Something like that.'

'Okay.'

'As we spoke, I heard his accent and I told him that I was Ukrainian too, or at least my grandparents were. And we kept talking. Then, when I got home, we talked again. For hours. One thing led to another and he booked a flight to London for today. He should have landed about thirty minutes ago.'

'That's very romantic,' said Achilles, smiling. 'The stuff of a Hollywood movie. Of course, another thing that often happens in Hollywood movies is the naïve girl who falls for the handsome man gets murdered by him and he wears her skin as a coat. You don't think that's going to happen, do you?'

'I hope not,' admitted the ghost.

'I could come with you, if you like. Keep you safe.'

She smiled. 'It's a generous offer. But no.'

'Well, don't say I didn't offer. Anyway, he's a lucky man,' he added, bowing his head chivalrously. 'And whoever left their phone in your care should feel happy that he or she set this great romance in motion.'

The ghost pulled a face. 'I'm not sure that she'd be completely thrilled,' she said. 'It belonged to a woman he was dating. Well, I say dating, but she was actually paying him for sex.'

Achilles frowned. 'You're dating a rent boy?' he asked.

'No, it's not like that. They were seeing each other and, apparently, she liked to give him financial gifts afterwards.'

'I like the sound of this guy more and more. I could probably learn a lot from him. So, the other woman doesn't know yet?'

'She doesn't even know that he's coming back to London this evening, and she's been calling him relentlessly.'

Achilles looked up at the Tube map as the train started to slow down.

'This is me,' he said. 'Which stop are you?'

'The next one,' she replied. 'And I didn't even get a chance to hear about where you're going.'

'Oh, it's far less interesting,' he said. 'I wouldn't worry about it.'

He stood up and looked down at her.

'I have this overwhelming urge to kiss you,' he said.

'Resist it,' she replied. 'I'd hate to see a young boy like you embarrassed in front of a Tube full of strangers.'

He grinned and nodded as the train pulled to a stop.

'I'd better get off,' he said. 'But I'll look forward to our next encounter.'

'I'm sure you will.'

'Have fun with the sugar baby.'

'Have fun with whoever you're meeting.'

He made his way to the doors and stepped out, minding the gap. Just before they closed again, he turned around and shouted back in to her.

'Hey!' he shouted. 'You still haven't told me your name!'

EFF TWITTER

Beverley was busy preparing dinner by scanning the different options on a food-delivery app while Elizabeth was seated on the sofa, barefoot, tweeting as @TruthIsASword. During this particular session, she'd exchanged insults with the wife of a Premiership football player who'd been accused of impregnating two different women in recent months, with a consultant at a London abortion clinic and with a *Big Brother* housemate from 2007, all of whom were now threatening legal action. She had also sent abusive tweets to @jk_rowling ✅, @OwenJones84 ✅ and @ElonMusk ✅, and was hoping that one of them might take the bait but, to her disappointment, none of them were biting as yet. She knew that a response from a blue-ticked person was so much more powerful than a reply from a civilian, for the moment someone famous engaged with her, her followers would grow exponentially. It didn't matter in the slightest what any of them said, they could be as rude as they liked, as long as her numbers kept increasing. @JohnCleese ✅ had snapped at her once, calling her a 'stupid woman' and that had been good for an extra five hundred.

'Have you noticed anything strange about Achilles lately?' asked Beverley, putting the phone down, having ordered something wholesome and overpriced.

Elizabeth shook her head. 'I try to avoid Achilles most of the time. He's an idiot.'

'Do you think so? I've always found him the most companionable of my children. No offence.'

'How could I possibly be offended?'

A thought occurred to her and she posted the following tweet:

@TruthIsASword @AchillesCleverley u know there's a rumour going round yr school that u have a tiny cock? And that u have 3 nipples?

She waited a minute to see whether he would reply and, to her surprise, it only took a few moments for him to simply block her account. She frowned, wondering whether he might not be such an idiot after all.

'It's not that I love him any more than you or Nelson,' continued Beverley, pouring herself a glass of white wine. 'Although, in a way, I do. It's just that, speaking as a mother, he's always had a certain . . . how shall I put this? A certain *je ne sais quoi*. Nelson is so furtive and you're so angry all the time. But Achilles—'

'I'm not angry all the time!'

'Oh, darling, you're permanently furious. You're like a

Labour backbencher at Prime Minister's Questions. Achilles, on the other hand, just larks around and brightens everyone's day. Every house should have an Achilles, don't you think?'

'We could send him out on work experience,' suggested Elizabeth, tweeting a nineties pop star who'd recently announced that she needed a liver transplant to suggest that she'd got herself into this mess by spending most of her adult life as a dipsomaniac. When the pop star replied, threatening a lawsuit, Elizabeth responded by telling her to 'finish off that bottle of wine in your fridge, love' before laying bare her hypocrisy by adding that 'kindness will be the fixing of this'. 'Why do you ask anyway?' she said, putting her phone down for a moment and massaging the fingers of her right hand with those of her left. She was starting to worry that she might be developing carpal tunnel syndrome in her thumb, as it ached constantly. 'What's he done?'

'He hasn't *done* anything as such,' said Beverley. 'But he's being very secretive, that's all. Coming and going at the strangest times and behaving in a shifty fashion. And I don't know where he gets the money to buy himself all these fancy toys. You don't think he's dealing drugs, do you?'

Elizabeth thought about it and shook her head. 'No,' she said. 'He's not the type. I think he'd find it a bit grubby, to be honest.'

'Perhaps he has a girlfriend. An older woman. And he's nervous about introducing her to us.'

'The last I heard, he was having a fling with some boy.'

'No, that was just an experiment on his part, and he told me it wasn't for him. I think we should pretend it never happened. Don't get me wrong, I have nothing against the gays per se, but it would be a lot simpler if he was, well, you know—'

'Normal?'

'I didn't want to use that word, but since you say it.'

'You realize that's quite homophobic of you, right?'

'I didn't say it!' protested Beverley. 'You did!'

'Still. You agreed.'

Beverley let out a long groan. 'Is it wrong of me to hope that my son is a heterosexual?' she asked. 'I mean, let's face it, life is hard enough without throwing another difficulty into the mix.'

'I don't think gay people see it quite like that, Mother. Most of them are perfectly content with their sexuality. If anything, many feel it enhances their lives.'

'And good for them. I'm absolutely *delighted* for them! Put out the bunting! You know, I'm not going to continue with this conversation because I just know that whatever I say, you'll take it the wrong way and accuse me of all sorts.'

'Did you ever have sex with a woman?' asked Elizabeth, the thought crossing her mind that her mother might want to reveal a long-held secret.

'Good Lord, no,' said Beverley, shivering a little. 'Although a well-known lady novelist once invited me to her room when we were both attending the Hay Festival, but I declined. And when I was a girl, one of my closest friends told me that she dreamed of us swimming naked together in the Lake District and would I like to try that sometime, but I said no, that I couldn't imagine anything worse than holidaying in one's own country. Why, have you?'

'Have I what?'

'Ever . . . you know . . . with a woman?'

Elizabeth shook her head. 'Not my bag,' she said.

Beverley considered this. 'I sometimes wonder whether lesbians are just making a point,' she said.

'A point about what?'

'Oh, who knows? The patriarchy, I imagine. It's usually the patriarchy, isn't it? Oh, look! Ustym Karmaliuk is nibbling on an After Eight. He's getting his appetite back.'

Elizabeth stood up and walked over to examine the tortoise, who stopped eating and turned its head to look at her, blinking multiple times.

'I told you,' continued Beverley in triumph. 'No one can resist an After Eight. They're sublime. Now, if he finishes that one, we'll give him another. We need to build his strength back up. I am worried about him, though. I hope he's not getting himself into any trouble.'

'There's not a lot of trouble he can get himself into,' said Elizabeth. 'It takes him about an hour to leave the room.'

'Not Ustym Karmaliuk. Achilles. Seventeen-year-old boys are prone to rebellion and you never know what they're going to do next. Nelson wasn't like that, of course. He was more—'

'Dad's on TV,' said Elizabeth, and Beverley turned to see her husband staring back at her from the wall-mounted television. 'Shall I turn it up?'

'But that's the *Six O'Clock News*,' said Beverley. 'What's he doing on there? Yes, let's hear what he has to say. But rewind it to the start, will you?'

Elizabeth did as instructed, pressing 'Play' just as the programme returned to Sophie Raworth sitting behind her desk, explaining to the country how the beloved chat-show host George Cleverley had yesterday found himself in some online trouble regarding a tweet that had been considered transphobic. Happily, she said, George was with her now to discuss this. The camera pulled out to a two-shot and there he was, looking both pissed off and elated simultaneously.

'Good evening, George,' said Sophie.

'And good evening to *you*, Sophie,' he replied cheerfully. 'I'm thrilled to be here.'

'And we're glad to have you. It's been a strange twenty-four hours for you, wouldn't you agree?'

'Oh terrible, terrible,' he agreed, nodding his head. 'Very upsetting.'

'Would you like to tell us what happened?'

'I'd be *delighted* to. Well, really, it was all a lot of nonsense, but most of it was of my own making. The truth is, I've been a very naughty boy!' And here he slapped one hand with the other, much as he had done on that fateful afternoon at Arlo, Quill, Fitzgerald & Connolly. 'A naughty, naughty boy, and I need to do my penance or there'll be no jelly and ice-cream for George after dinner!'

Sophie appeared unimpressed. Five minutes earlier, she'd been interviewing the American Secretary of State live from Baghdad, and now there was this.

'No, but seriously,' continued George, adopting a serious tone now. 'The thing is, I happen to be friendly with a young man, no, I'm sorry, a young woman, who works in my solicitor's office, and I used the Twitter machine to offer my support on her transition to womanhood, only it seems that I committed the most terrible offence when I referred to her as "he" rather than "she".' He turned to the camera now and addressed the audience directly. 'And let me say from the bottom of my heart how grateful I am that so many of you made me realize what a terrible human being I am. I thank you. I thank you all.'

Sophie paused, looking uncertain about where to take the interview next.

'You've received some online criticism, then?' she said finally.

'Indeed I have,' he continued. 'And rightly so! When so many deeply caring and compassionate people call one to account for such an appalling moral transgression, it does make one sit up and think, wouldn't you agree? As hundreds of strangers abused me and expressed their collective desire that I would soon pass from this world to the next, I realized that they alone knew how to live good, decent lives and that I could learn from them. From that moment on, Sophie, I determined to "be better", as they exhorted me to be, and to let strangers know that I have no business breathing the same air as decent, kind-hearted folk. Only that way will scoundrels like me see the error of our ways!'

Sophie nodded and shuffled her papers. 'Social media can be a murky place at times,' she remarked.

'*Au contraire*, Sophie,' said George, his face breaking into a broad smile. '*Au contraire!* What I have come to recognize is the sheer courage of these tireless crusaders, so brave that they dare not use their real names, and who cry tears of frustration as they tap-tap-tap away on the Twitter and the Facebook and the what-have-you, blaming me for making them feel unsafe.' He leaned forward in the chair and pointed a finger at his host. 'These audacious souls, these titans of fortitude, these paragons of virtue, they have held up a mirror to me, Sophie, and I have not liked what I have seen.' He lowered his voice now and shook his head sadly, pulling a handkerchief from his pocket and dabbing at his eyes. 'I have not liked it one little bit.'

'He's being sarcastic, isn't he?' asked Beverley, turning to her daughter. 'He doesn't mean a word of this.'

'You think?' she replied.

'I understand you have a message that you want to impart to the transgender community,' continued Sophie, who appeared to be getting an instruction in her earpiece, because her attention wasn't fully on her guest now.

'I do,' agreed George. 'I certainly do.' He turned towards

the camera again with a smile, as if he was about to welcome Barbra Streisand on his chat show. 'I want to say that I extended the hand of support to one of your number, I wished her well on her journey and encouraged others to be empathetic, considerate and kind. I tried to do something positive in a cruel, cruel world. But I see now that this was an outrageous act on my part and I fully accept that I was in the wrong. I think my producer, Ben Bimbaum, a homosexual of this parish, said it best when he said that I'm extremely sorry, that it was never my intention to offend and—'

'George,' said Sophie, butting in. 'If you don't mind me saying so, you don't sound as if you really mean any of this.'

'Don't I?' he asked, sitting back in his chair and looking shocked.

'No, it sounds a bit . . . well, mocking.'

George smiled and nodded his head. 'There's no getting one past you, is there, Sophie? That's why you're here in News and an old bigot like me is stuck in Light Entertainment! No, of course I don't mean a word of it.'

'Uh-oh,' said Elizabeth, leaning forward now and setting her phone down on the arm of her chair.

'Might I ask why not?' asked Sophie.

'Because it's all a load of old nonsense, isn't it?' he said, rolling his eyes. 'Look, everyone who has criticized me, both online and off, has claimed to be offended by what I said. But let me take you as an example. Were you offended, Sophie?'

'Well, having read your original tweet, I can see that you meant it in a kindly way.'

'But do you think that anyone was *actually* offended? Or are people just getting off on pretending to be?'

'Well, I—'

'Don't you think that most of these people who feign umbrage spend most of their time just *looking* for something or someone to be offended by? They wake up, scavenge for a few half-eaten slices of last night's take-away pizza, and then they're on to their smartphones, scrolling through the news headlines to decide who's upset them today. Perhaps it's an airline executive who's been rude to a flight attendant. Or a film actress who's dared to put on weight. Or a television interviewer who's offered encouragement to a person going through what one assumes is a traumatic but hopefully positive experience. They identify the criminal who most meets their needs and they start tweeting about it. Oh, the pain, they cry! The hurt! The offence! I'm so upset that I can't get out of bed today! I'm so wounded that tears are rolling down my cheeks and I'll have to cancel my plans to help out at the local homeless shelter! It's all offence, offence, offence, these days, isn't it? Every person vying with everyone else to see who can be the most affronted, who can show that they're the most Woke – that's the word, isn't it? – and each one desperate to prove that they're morally superior to the poor unfortunate idiot who's been dragged into their cauldron of pain. Frankly, the whole thing sickens me. These people are morons, Sophie, every one of them, with their fake names and their fake profiles, screaming into the wind for no other reason than that no one is listening to them in the real world. But Twitter will listen to me, they think! Twitter will hear my pain! Well, eff Twitter, Sophie! Eff Twitter! I won't say the full word, as this is the *Six O'Clock News* and there might be children watching, but if this was *Newsnight*, then I most certainly would. Eff Twitter! How do you like that? I've spent my life, my entire life, supporting people who are victims – my own son is named after Nelson Mandela, for Christ's sake – and these idiots dare to criticize me? There isn't a prejudiced bone in my body, but they don't want to hear that because that's not the narrative they want to project.

I'm just an old straight white man, so I must be the enemy, right? If I was young, they wouldn't go after me. If I was a poof, they wouldn't go after me. If I was coloured, they wouldn't go—'

The screen suddenly flashed to the test signal and Beverley and Elizabeth turned to each other, their mouths hanging open in shock.

'Did he say *poof*?' asked Beverley.

'Did he say *coloured*?' asked Elizabeth.

The screen changed again and now there was just Sophie Raworth on her own in the studio, looking perfectly poised, while in the background a muffled sound of protest could be heard, as if someone was being pulled out of a chair while having a hand forcibly placed across his mouth.

'Apologies for that,' said Sophie, 'we appear to be having some technical difficulties. Now let's move on to the sport.'

'Let's not,' said Beverley, pressing the remote control to switch the television off. She turned to her daughter and shook her head. 'That wasn't good, was it?' she asked.

'Oh no,' said Elizabeth, laughing as she picked up her phone and pressed the blue app with the cheerful little bird icon. 'No, he's completely fucked now.'

SPEED DATING

Everyone moved carefully towards the centre of the hall, circling the seats slowly like children playing musical chairs at a birthday party, and Nelson found himself in the centre of the group, facing a perfectly nice-looking woman only a few years older than him. The bell rang and they stared at each other and smiled.

'Apparently, I'm Number 16,' said the woman in an aggressive tone, pointing towards her sticker. 'I'm not even worthy of a name, it seems. Typical.'

'I'm Number 37,' replied Nelson.

'Lucky you.'

'Actually, Number 16 is one of my favourite numbers. It's a perfect square.'

'A what?'

'You know, two times two is four. Four times four is sixteen. You can't do anything with thirty-seven. It's a prime. I've always felt a little uncomfortable with primes.'

The woman snorted and shook her head. 'Nerd,' she said.

'I'm sorry?'

'I said you're a nerd.'

'Oh. Okay.'

'I bet you keep lists, don't you? To-do lists, and so on.'

'I do, as it happens,' admitted Nelson. 'They can be very helpful.'

The woman laughed and placed her hands on her lap, each one positioned perfectly on a different knee. 'Christ, how has it come to this?' she muttered to no one in particular.

'It's been quite fine out for this time of year, hasn't it?' asked Nelson.

'My father was a maths teacher,' she said, ignoring his question. 'He was a nerd too. And a prick.'

'Really?' he replied. A silence fell. 'I had a maths teacher when I was in school,' he added eventually. 'It's a small world, isn't it?'

'Yes,' she said. 'But I wouldn't want to be the one who had to clean it.'

He frowned. 'What?' he asked.

'I said I wouldn't want to be the one who had to clean it,' she repeated. 'The world, I mean.'

'Why would you clean the world? How could someone do that?'

'No, it's a . . . it's a joke. When someone says . . . actually, you know what, forget it, it doesn't matter.'

'Are you a cleaner?' asked Nelson. 'It's fine if you are.'

'Oh, I'm *so* glad I have your approval. Thank *Christ* that a *man* is telling me that it's okay to be a cleaner.'

'So you are, then?'

'No, I'm a paediatrician.'

'I don't know how anyone does that job,' he said with a shudder. 'Don't you find them kind of disgusting? And smelly?'

'Children?'

'No, feet.'

'What have feet got to do with anything?'

'I thought you said you were a paediatrician. Isn't that a foot doctor?'

'No.'

'Oh. Sorry, I'm not very good at this. It's my first time.'

'I can tell.'

'Are you enjoying it so far?'

'Well, it's not been a great start. But Number 18 should be opposite me in a while and he's drop-dead gorgeous.'

'Oh, right,' said Nelson, looking down the line, but there were too many heads bobbing back and forth for him to locate Number 18.

'I'm not really enjoying it either,' he said finally.

'I suppose that's my fault, is it? Fucking men.'

Nelson opened his mouth, then closed it again. He started to think about his quiet room at home and how nice it would be to be there right now, lying on his bed, listening to some music and reading the latest Hilary Mantel. 'I didn't mean that,' he said.

'My ex-husband, my first one, he always blamed me for everything too. He'd take me out to a restaurant and sit there, saying nothing, then blame me for the silence. He said I have no personality. That the only people I can talk to are children.'

'He sounds quite unpleasant,' said Nelson. 'You were right to break up with him.'

'I didn't. He broke up with me. And, needless to say, he got married to someone ten years younger before the ink was even dry on the divorce papers. I suppose you'll say that I was asking for it.'

'I wasn't going to say anything of the sort,' said Nelson.

'Pfft. Men always side with other men.'

'I don't.'

She sighed and looked away.

'So are you going to ask for my number or what?'

'I know your number,' said Nelson, pointing towards her right breast. 'You're Number 16. A perfect square.'

'My *phone* number.'

'Oh. No, I don't think so.'

She laughed bitterly. 'See?'

'Well, it's just that we've only just started talking and—'

'I could do a lot better than you anyway.'

'Yes, of course.'

'Copper or not.'

'I mean, if you want to give it to me—'

'I don't.'

'All right, then.'

Fortunately, just as the perspiration began to break out on Nelson's back, the bell rang and they all moved down a seat.

Now Nelson was faced with Number 22, the man who'd been shouting at Alice when she was making her introductory remarks.

'Don't get any ideas, Romeo,' he said immediately, holding up a hand. 'I'm as straight as they come. I've had more women than you've had hot dinners.'

'I am too,' replied Nelson. 'I'm here to meet a nice lady.'

'Then you've come to the wrong place. I've got bigger tits than some of this lot,' he added, looking around. 'So we've got three minutes and nothing much to do. What do you want to talk about?'

Nelson drummed his fingers on his knee. He liked the way they sounded against his polyester policeman's trousers. 'I don't know,' he said. 'Perhaps we could discuss politics.'

'Bollocks to that,' replied Number 22.

'Books?'

'I don't read books. What's the point? None of it ever happened, people! It's all made up!'

'Do you watch television?'

'Nah, fifty thousand channels and nothing on, know what I mean?'

'Do you travel much?' asked Nelson.

'I go to Norwich once a month,' he conceded. 'To visit my Aunt Ida. She had a fall a while back. Broke her hip.'

'Oh, I'm sorry to hear that,' said Nelson. 'Is she recovering?'

'No. It'll see her off in the end, fingers crossed. Save me the train fare every month. She says she's leaving the house to me in her will, so I'll play friendly until she pops off, but if she doesn't, then I'll feel like a right mug. You watch the footie?'

'I'm not much of a sports fan,' said Nelson. 'Although I do enjoy Wimbledon when it's on.'

'Wimbledon's for poofs,' said Number 22. 'All that mincing

around with royalty and strawberries and cream and pints of Pimm's. Can't be doing with it. I used to follow the England football team on their away matches, but I'm not allowed any more. I got banned.'

'Oh dear,' said Nelson, not sure that he wanted to know why.

'Do you want to know why?' asked Number 22.

'I'm not sure,' replied Nelson.

'Because of your lot.'

'My lot?'

'The police. Well, the German police anyway. They stitched me up. They still haven't got over the war, have they? Any chance to throw an Englishman in jail overnight and they take it. You know what I'd like to do to them? I'd like to line each and every one of them up against a wall and—'

'I don't think that's a very healthy attitude to take, if you don't mind my saying so,' said Nelson.

'You what?'

'It's just, when I see riots on television after international football matches, I always feel sorry for the police who have to try to keep the peace. And people like to criticize them, but if your sister was walking home alone one night and a man jumped out at her from behind the bushes and, you know, tried to attack her, then you'd be very happy if a police car went by, wouldn't you?'

'Are you having a laugh?' asked Number 22, leaning forward now.

'Or if your house was broken into,' continued Nelson, warming to his theme. 'Who's the first person you'd call? Your local social worker? The parish priest? Ghostbusters? No, it's the police, isn't it? They provide . . . *we* provide an invaluable service, and yet people like you criticize us and call us names.'

'Fuck me,' said the man, shaking his head. 'And I don't mean that literally, Romeo. But I'll tell you this, I respect you for standing up for your profession. I do. We'll have to agree to disagree, but you're not a bad fella, are you, Number 37?'

'I hope not,' said Nelson.

'When'd you last get some, then?'

Nelson frowned. 'When did I last get some what?' he asked.

'You know.'

'Oh. Right. Of course. Some . . . a romantic . . . moment. Well, it's been a while.'

'How long? Two days? Three?'

'A little longer,' said Nelson.

'I haven't had any in about three years,' said the man, sitting back again and crossing his arms.

'I thought you said you'd had more women than I'd had hot dinners?'

The man looked offended. 'Well, I have, haven't I?' he said. 'When I was younger. It's a lot of hassle now, that's the truth. Women want you to respect them and some of them don't even want to go home once you're finished. Bollocks to that. I only come here for the biscuits, if I'm honest. I stock up, you see.' He opened his bag and showed Nelson the contents and, true to his word, it was full of biscuits. 'Gets me through the week. Last Thursday, I went to a meeting in Colliers Wood and—'

Fortunately, Nelson never found out how the meeting in Colliers Wood went, as the bell rang again and he moved to the next seat. Now he was seated opposite a woman old enough to be his grandmother, who, somewhat cheerfully, had brought her knitting with her. He looked at her, trying to remember who she reminded him of. And then it came to him: the Queen Mother. Who'd been dead for years, of course, but still. The resemblance was uncanny.

'I'm Nelson,' he said, raising his voice a little, assuming she was deaf.

'No need to shout, dear,' said the woman. 'And no names. It's all anonymous here, remember? Like AA. Which I'm also a member of, as it happens.'

'Of course. Nice to meet you, Number 1. Oh, you must have been the first one here.'

'I always am,' she said, click-clacking away with her needles. 'I try to come early so I can look at all the men as they arrive. I rate them in my head on a scale of one to ten and then I make sure to put extra effort in when I'm sitting opposite the ones who scored high. It saves a lot of time, I find.'

'I see,' said Nelson. 'And what number did I get?'

'You're a five, dear. Maybe a six. A sort of any-port-in-a-storm type. You're no Number 18, that's for sure, but you're a damn sight better than Number 26.'

'Thank you, I suppose,' he said. Number 18 again. Whoever he was, he was proving very popular among women of all ages.

'Still, a policeman! That's impressive. Brought your truncheon, have you?' She giggled like a manic pixie.

'Ahahaha,' said Nelson, to be polite.

'I would have thought a policeman could have his pick of the women.'

'No, sadly no. We're very manly, of course. And fearless. But no.'

'When did you last arrest someone?'

'Yesterday,' he lied. 'Down Bridge End.'

She winked at him. 'I'd bet you'd like to put me in handcuffs, wouldn't you?'

'Ahahaha,' he said again.

'Don't blush, dear. You don't stand a chance. Do you know, I once had sex with a royal?'

'I didn't know that, no,' said Nelson. 'But then, we've only just met.'

'It was Lord Lucan,' she said with a knowing smile.

'Strictly speaking, Lord Lucan wasn't a member of the royal family,' said Nelson. 'He was a member of the House of Lords.'

'Oh, but it's all the same thing, isn't it? This was before he murdered the nanny, of course, and disappeared up the Swanee.'

'Of course,' said Nelson. 'What was he like?'

'In bed?'

'No, just in general.'

'He didn't have much of a sense of humour. But they don't tend to, do they?'

'Lords?'

'No, murderers.'

'I suppose not.'

'But he was quite the tiger in bed, since you've asked. He enjoyed water sports, but then so do I. You know what they say? Wild women do, and they don't regret it. Do you like water sports?'

'My parents took me to Euro Disney when I was a child,' replied Nelson. 'And I enjoyed the slide. You know, the one that goes around and around and then you land in the swimming pool with a big splash?'

The old woman stared at him and shook her head. 'Oh my,' she said. 'You're quite the innocent, aren't you?'

'I don't know,' he said with a shrug. 'Perhaps.'

'Did you have a Bourbon earlier?'

'A what?'

'A Bourbon biscuit.'

'Oh, no,' he said. 'I got here at the last minute. There does seem to be a lot of attention given to the biscuits, though. You're the second person to mention them to me.'

'I can't eat them,' she replied, lowering her voice. 'I have an intolerant bowel – it's basically Nigel Farage in organ form – so I have to be careful what I introduce to it. My doctor tries to keep me away from sweet things for the most part, but I used to love a Bourbon back in the day. When I was being naughty.'

'And are you still naughty?' he asked, attempting a flirtation, but she sat back now and looked affronted.

'Cheek,' she said.

'I do apologize.'

'Don't. I like cheek.'

'Ahahaha,' said Nelson, never so happy to hear a bell ring in all his life as he moved to the next chair.

'Hello,' said the woman sitting opposite him, who was in her late thirties and looked as if she'd just chewed a wasp. 'Go on, then. Give it your best shot.'

'I'm sorry?'

'We're about fifteen seconds in and already I can tell you're a no-hoper. Come on, try harder. Give it some welly.'

Nelson felt like he might burst into tears. 'It's awkward, isn't it?' he asked. 'Talking to strangers like this. The pressure is very intense.'

'Do you want to know what I hated most about my ex-husband?' she asked.

'Not really, no.'

'He was a bastard. And a cliché. He had an affair with his secretary, if you can believe it. It's like something out of a Beverley Cleverley novel.'

'Oh,' said Nelson, brightening up. 'Do you enjoy her work?'

'It's fine. I mean, I might read one when I'm on the bus or if

I'm waiting for a smear test. They're easy and you don't have to think. She's not exactly Maude Avery, is she?'

'Well, she's very popular, I know that much,' said Nelson, feeling on safer ground. 'I thought *The Surgeon's Broken Heart* was particularly good. Although, no, perhaps not quite at the level of *Like to the Lark*.'

'I read that when I was at university,' said the woman, folding her arms tightly around her own body as if she was trying to wrap herself up in a cocoon. 'It changed my life.'

'In what way?'

'Mind your own business,' said the woman, looking infuriated by the question. 'I did read the latest Sarah Waters, though, and that was very good. Have you read her?'

'I haven't, I'm afraid,' admitted Nelson.

'Oh, let me guess,' said the woman, sneering at him. 'You're one of those men who say they don't read women.'

'Not at all,' said Nelson. 'Like I said, I read Beverley Cleverley's most recent one. And I've read books by . . .' He racked his brain for names. 'Anne Brontë. Anne Enright. Anne Griffin. Anne Tyler.'

'All you're doing is naming writers called Anne. Have you really read them or are you making this up?'

'I've really read them,' he said.

'And is it a fetish, all these Annes? Might you move on to a Rose, perhaps? Or a Claire? Or a Zadie?'

'I expect I will,' he said. 'Do you read a lot of novels, then?'

'Not really,' she said, turning away. 'I always say, if a book's any good, then they'll make it into a film. Like *Captain Corelli's Mandolin*. Or *The Bonfire of the Vanities*.'

'Three of Beverley Cleverley's novels have been made into films, you know. One won an Oscar.'

'For what?'

'Best Make-up and Hairstyling.'

The woman snorted. 'Anyone would think you're her publicist, the way you're carrying on. Christ, is that bell going to ring anytime soon? BONG!' she roared at the top of her voice, making everyone else in the room turn to stare at her. 'BONG!'

And then the bell did go off and on they moved.

Nelson now found himself seated opposite a young man of around his own age. His sticker said Number 18 – the famed Number 18! – and he had to admit, the two women had been right earlier, for he was very good-looking, with a boyish face, thick brown hair, kind eyes and excellent stubble. He was wearing scrubs, the same type that Nelson himself had been wearing on the day that Dr Oristo told him that she was retiring, but he knew better than to trust that this meant anything. It was entirely possible that he worked in H&M, or was the Foreign Secretary.

'Nice to meet you,' said the man. 'My name's Shane.'

'Nelson,' said Nelson. 'Names are easier than numbers, aren't they?'

'I don't know why they don't let us use them,' replied Shane, lowering his voice. He had an Irish accent, which Nelson had always been drawn to. He'd read somewhere that Irishmen made the best lovers. 'It's awkward enough without adding to it. How are you getting on so far? I don't mean to be too personal, but are you interested in men or women? Or both?'

'Women,' said Nelson. 'You?'

'Men.'

'Right.'

'Shame. I had high hopes when I looked down the line.'

Nelson smiled and stared down at the floor, feeling a little embarrassed but also hugely flattered. This was probably the nicest thing that anyone had said to him in years.

'Thank you,' he said.

'No bother.'

'I liked a girl once, but she got eaten by a lion.'

Shane burst out laughing and Nelson looked at him, appalled. 'Oh, I'm sorry,' said Shane. 'I thought that was a joke.'

'No, it really happened.'

'Shit. Sorry. My bad.'

'It's okay.'

'I feel like a right twat now.'

'Don't. It's an easy mistake to make.'

'So how about you? Any luck so far?'

'Not really. I've been sexually assaulted by the cashier, talked to a woman who refused to give me her phone number even though I didn't ask for it, a football hooligan, a woman who accused me of fetishizing female writers who share a Christian name, and an elderly lady who, now that I think about it, might be into a rather unhygienic sexual practice.'

'Impressive,' said Shane. 'I've been asked what my favourite Gilbert O'Sullivan song is, whether I'd be interested in being a sperm donor and, if so, do I know what the motility rate of my sperm is. Also, which *Game of Thrones* character I most relate to and how often I work out.'

'I'm surprised you're here at all,' said Nelson. 'You're . . . well, if you don't mind me saying so, you're very good-looking.'

'I don't mind you saying it at all. Say it again if you want.'

'You're very good-looking.'

Shane smiled and cocked his head a little to the side, as if he wasn't sure whether Nelson was messing with him or not.

'Well, thank you,' he said. 'Anyway. Yeah. I don't seem to have a lot of success in love. Not sure what I'm doing wrong, to be honest. I have a good job. I'm kind, I'm considerate. At least, I try to be. I have a family who loves me.'

'That's a nice thing to be able to say,' said Nelson, feeling an unexpected urge to take Shane's hands in his own.

'But, I don't know, I'm just not great at talking to guys and I don't feel comfortable in clubs. You've probably never been to a gay club, but they're full of totally ripped guys with perfect skin and hair, and if you don't impress them instantly, then they're on to the next one. And my problem is, I get nervous and start saying stupid things.'

'I once asked a girl in a pub whether she preferred bras that went over the shoulder or around the back,' said Nelson.

'I took a guy to a funfair and threw up on his face while we were on the roller-coaster.'

'I asked out a nun.'

'I told a guy that he looked like Donald Trump Jr.'

'Oh, that's bad,' said Nelson.

'Tip of the iceberg,' said Shane.

They remained silent for a few moments and then Shane leaned forward. 'Listen,' he said. 'Assuming we both crash and burn at this, do you fancy a pint after? We could compare notes on our mutual disasters. I could do with a drink, if you could. And I'm off tomorrow so . . .'

Nelson thought about it and nodded. 'Sure,' he said. 'That sounds good. It's a date. I mean, not a date, but—'

'I get it,' said Shane, laughing and, before things could get any more awkward, the bell rang.

They moved on again and, over the next twenty minutes, Nelson chatted with a female wrestler, a card sharp and a man who twisted balloons into animals at children's parties. Time was getting on and he could see that there was only one person left to talk to and, as the bell rang, a middle-aged man moved into place opposite him. He glanced back down the line and saw Shane talking to the water-sports enthusiast and hoped that he'd meant it when he said that he'd like to go for a drink. It wasn't often that Nelson made new friends and he felt that they might get along well.

'Looks like we're stuck with each other,' said the man, who seemed friendly enough, extending a hand. 'My name's Jeremy.'

'Nelson,' said Nelson.

'Last of the night.'

'So it would seem.'

'I hope this isn't a rude thing to say, I certainly don't mean it to sound that way, but I happen to be straight.'

'Oh,' said Nelson. 'That's fine.'

'I just didn't want to give the wrong impression. Although it's not like I'm much of a catch anyway.'

'Oh, I don't know about that,' said Nelson, warming to the man's obvious discomfort. 'We're all here for the same reason. That we find it hard to meet people.'

'True.'

'And have you been single for long?'

'Since my wife died three years ago,' said Jeremy. 'It's not been easy. She was a wonderful woman.' He rotated the wedding ring on his finger. 'It was my niece who suggested I try an evening like this. She looks out for me.'

'She must be very kind.'

'She is,' said the man, smiling proudly. 'It must be interesting being a policeman,' he added after a moment.

'It is, yes.'

'Did you always want to be one?'

'Not always, no,' admitted Nelson, feeling a little guilty for deceiving the man. 'Can I ask what you do?'

'I'm a solicitor. I'm surprised to see a young lad like yourself in a place like this,' said Jeremy. 'I always assume young people just fall in and out of each other's beds with gay abandon, as they say.'

'If only,' said Nelson with a sigh.

'Him down there,' said Jeremy, nodding in Shane's direction. 'You can see all the women want to sit opposite him.'

'Well, he *is* gay, as it happens,' said Nelson.

'I know, yes. I was talking to him earlier. Nice chap, I thought. Very personable.'

'Yes, I thought so.'

'When I was your age, people were very rude about the gays, but no one minds any more, do they? It's a better world. I met a young lad recently, also gay, I assume. A very unfortunate boy. I probably shouldn't tell you this, but—'

The bell rang before Jeremy could reveal anything more and everyone stood up as Alice took to the stage again, thanking them for coming and asking whether they would mind stacking their seats at the side of the room before leaving. As he took his over, Shane caught up with him.

'Well, that was a waste of nine pounds,' he said. 'And, you know, a shower.'

'No luck?'

'None. Still on for that pint? I hope it wasn't weird of me asking you like that. If you've changed your mind—'

'No, I'd like to,' said Nelson. 'Let's do it. Actually, I know a nice place quite close to here with a beer garden outside. And it's quite warm out, isn't it?'

'Sounds perfect,' said Shane. 'It's good to be able to go to pubs again, isn't it? Not that I'm an alcoholic or anything but, you know. There's only so much sitting in your own flat you can do. I'd have become a scientist myself if it would have made the vaccine come along a bit sooner.'

They started to walk down the street together and, as they passed a newsagent's, Nelson's eye was caught by a sign outside listing the headline from the *Evening Standard*.

TELLY FELLA LOSES HIS MIND ON AIR

'I wonder what that's all about?' asked Nelson, pointing towards it.

THE TEETH

'You're late.'

Rebecca was seated at a table outside the pub, reading a novel. She put it back in her bag and Achilles looked at her approvingly. It was their second date, if their initial encounter in the coffee shop could be counted as their first.

'I am,' he admitted, offering a half-bow. 'By all of twelve minutes. You have my apologies. But I'm glad to see that you were early.'

'Actually, I only got here five minutes ago,' she said. 'So, in fact, I was seven minutes late. I ordered drinks because I'm the only one of legal age.'

'Thank you,' he said, sitting down opposite her and lifting the pint she'd bought him. She'd made an effort, too, and, the weather being good, was wearing a light summer dress. 'And thank you, too, for the snapchat of your breasts last night. They're very impressive.'

She stared at him. 'What are you talking about?' she asked. 'I didn't send you any such thing.'

'Oh, then that must have been some other girl. Sorry, I'm very popular.'

She didn't even blink and Achilles realized that this line, which he had used to good effect in the past, was not having its usual effect.

'I'm kidding,' he said. 'A bad joke.'

'Don't be a twat, okay?' she replied.

He glanced around at the other customers seated outside, all older than him, and felt a strange sensation at the pit of his stomach. At first, he wondered whether he'd eaten something that didn't agree with him, but then it dawned on him that no, whatever was going on inside his body was connected to the fact that he actually quite liked this girl and he would have to abandon his usual techniques if he wanted to impress her. He might even have to be himself, if he even knew who that person was.

'What's wrong?' asked Rebecca. 'You look as if you're having an epiphany.'

He shook his head. 'Is it just me or is it a bit chilly out here?' he asked.

'It's just you. It's twenty-two degrees.'

'Okay.'

Rebecca sat forward and touched his arm lightly. 'Relax, Achilles,' she said.

'I am relaxed.'

'You seem nervous.'

'Perhaps I am. A little bit. I don't want to mess this up.'

'You know, I wouldn't be here if I didn't like you,' she told him. 'And believe me, you're giving me plenty of reasons not to. And yet, inexplicably, here I am.'

He smiled. 'Basically, I need to just take it down a notch, right?'

'That would be good.'

'Okay. And for the record, I like you, too. And when I say *like*, I mean that I'm interested in you. And I'm not usually all that interested in other people. I don't know if it comes across or not, but sometimes I can be a selfish, narcissistic little brat who only thinks about his own feelings.'

'I'm absolutely shocked to hear that,' she said, smiling a little.

'But from the moment we met—'

'All of twenty-four hours ago.'

'All of twenty-four hours ago, I've found that I want to get to know you better. And not just because I want to have sex with you. Although I do. But it seems to run deeper than that.' He stopped and thought about it for a moment, frowning. 'Oh Christ, I'm not growing up, am I?'

'It's possible. Have you thought about seeing a doctor?'

'Let's see how long it goes on for. A couple of Nurofen might sort me out. This is too deep a conversation for me.'

'Well, it's better than small talk.'

'True. The funny thing is, I feel so desperate to impress you that I don't want to do anything that looks like I'm trying to impress you. Does that make any sense?'

She took a sip of her drink and nodded. 'I think so,' she said.

'What were you reading anyway?' he asked. 'When I arrived, I mean. Do you read a lot? What kind of books do you like? Which authors? That's a lot of questions, isn't it? I'm not sure why I'm asking so many. I feel like one of those wind-up toys that keep chattering away. Like the teeth. You know the teeth? The ones that keep rattling when you put them on the table?'

'I know the teeth,' she said. 'I love the teeth.'

'I feel like the teeth.'

'You're behaving like the teeth. But in answer to your many questions, I was reading one of your mother's novels, an early one. I've never read her before and thought I'd give her a go to see whether it might tell me something about you.'

'And does it?'

'Well, the heroes of her books do tend to live entitled, extravagant lifestyles, and I figure either that's how you live or how you want to live.'

'Sort of true and very true, in that order.'

'But it would seem very strange if your mother based these romantic, slightly dumb but highly sexualized leading men on her son.'

'In normal circumstances, yes. But you haven't met my mother. It's very much the sort of thing she might do. She likes to tell people that she taught me how to masturbate, just because she thinks it makes her sound hip.'

'And did she?'

'If she did, she did an excellent job, since I'm thinking of turning professional.'

Rebecca smiled.

'We have thousands of books in our house, of course, because of my parents' jobs, but I can't remember the last time I saw either of them reading one. Someone told me earlier that she thinks everyone in my family just stares at their phones.'

'And is that true?'

'I'm afraid it might be.'

Rebecca nodded. 'Have you ever heard of the word *tsundoku*?' she asked.

'Like that puzzle in the papers?'

'No, that's Sudoku.'

'Then no, I haven't.'

'It's a Japanese word. The constant act of buying books but never reading them.'

'Right. Well, that's what they've got, then. My father bought this massive biography a couple of days ago and seemed very excited about it, but I know for a fact that it's been sitting on his bedside table ever since, unopened, just gathering dust. Both my parents used to be massive readers. But not so much any more, for some reason.'

'Do you like your mum?' asked Rebecca, and Achilles frowned.

'Of course I do,' he said, surprised by the question. 'I love her.'

'No, I meant do you like her books?'

'Oh, I don't read them.'

'What, you've never read any of them?'

'Well, I read her first two, and they weren't bad, actually. But ever since then, she's hired a ghost and I just can't be bothered. She's had a few over the years. Ghosts, I mean. The last one got eaten by a lion, if you can believe it. I preferred it when she wrote them herself.'

'Still,' said Rebecca, as she raised a hand only slightly and a waiter came over in an instant, a skill among beautiful women that Achilles had long envied. 'If my mother was a novelist, or had her name on the front of novels, at least, I'd want to read them.'

'What does your mother do?' he asked, as he finished his first beer and the second was placed before him. He didn't normally drink lager, preferring rum and Coke, but he didn't want to make any suggestion that she'd ordered wrong.

'She's a minister,' said Rebecca.

'A minister? Like a priest?'

'Yes.'

'Gosh!'

'I don't think I've heard anyone say *gosh* before outside of an Enid Blyton book.'

'I don't think I've ever said it,' admitted Achilles. 'I don't know where it came from. I feel embarrassed now. I should have said *fuck me*.'

'Don't be embarrassed, I thought it was cute.'

'Really? Gosh!'

'Don't milk it. Anyway, yes, she's a minister, and I think I told you that Dad is a chiropodist.'

'Cool.'

'Is it?'

'I don't know,' he said. 'I'm afraid to say anything now. Are they still together?'

'No, they split up last year.'

'That must have been difficult for you.'

'It was vile.'

He nodded. The conversation was becoming quite personal and he wasn't accustomed to such talk.

'I suppose I'm lucky that my parents are still together,' he said. 'I'd hate it if they broke up.'

'You have a tendency to do that, you know,' said Rebecca.

'To do what?'

'To take something that somebody is telling you about themselves and then turn it around so the conversation returns to you.'

'That's because I'm an asshole,' he said, lifting his drink and taking a large draught. His phone beeped in his pocket with a text message, but he ignored it for now.

'It could be that,' replied Rebecca. 'Or it could be that you're uncomfortable learning too much about other people. Delving too much into their lives. Because if you know they're hurting, then maybe you'll feel obliged to help in some way.'

'That makes me sound like a better person than I think I am.'

She leaned forward and held his eyes with hers. 'You don't think you're a good person, Achilles?'

He swallowed, feeling the blood inexplicably rush to his face. He never blushed, especially not in front of girls, and didn't know quite what to do. He leaned forward now too, hoping that they might kiss, but instead she sat back and looked away, glancing at another boy, almost as handsome as Achilles, who was passing by.

'I think I'm okay,' he said, trying to reclaim her attention. 'But I could be a lot better. I don't cheat on my girlfriends, for one thing. If I don't want to be with someone, then I'm not.'

His phone beeped again but he still ignored it.

'Will you excuse me?' asked Rebecca. 'I need the loo. And someone's clearly keen to get your attention. Maybe it's who-ever sent you the snaps of her tits last night.'

'I told you I was kidding,' he said, but she'd already walked away and disappeared inside the pub. He took his phone from his pocket, tapped in his code and read the message:

Jeremy Arlo
Still ok for tomorrow night?

He stared at it for a few moments, weighing up his options. He wasn't sure why, but his confidence wasn't as high as it usually was.

Achilles Cleverley
Of course!

He watched as the blue dots indicated Jeremy was typing and waited for the reply.

Jeremy Arlo
Great, looking forward to it.

Achilles experienced something approaching shame. He'd never before cared about the feelings of the men whose money he extorted, they were just casual marks to him, but something about the idea of Jeremy sitting at home alone, planning dinner or drinks for the following night, made him feel bad. He considered typing something kind in reply, but Rebecca reappeared at that moment and stood by her chair.

'I'm really sorry,' she said. 'But my mum just called me while I was in there. She's in a bad way.'

'She's sick?'

'She's depressed. I should probably go home to her.'

'Oh.'

'I'm sorry. Can we do this another time? I have to be there for her.' She took her coat from the back of her chair. 'You do understand, don't you?'

'This isn't just a ruse to leave, is it?' he asked. 'Because if you're not interested in me, you can just say so and—'

'It's not a ruse,' she said. 'Honestly, things have just been really difficult at home. Look, text me, okay? We'll do this again, I promise.'

He nodded and stood up, moving closer towards her, hoping for a kiss, but she turned her head, offering only her cheek. And then, a moment later, she was gone.

Disappointed, he watched her disappear into the night and wondered whether this was what falling in love felt like. And then, after a few moments, he began to feel angry. It was night time, after all, he looked great and had nowhere to go. Sure, he could go to a club and pick up a girl easily enough, but he didn't want to do that. No one had ever walked out on him before. Add that to the things the ghost had said to him earlier on the Tube, and the evening was turning into a disaster. He took his phone from his pocket and tapped out a quick message.

Achilles Cleverley
Actually, you don't fancy meeting this evening, do you?
Don't think I want to wait until tomorrow!

And it only took a minute or two before Jeremy's reply arrived:

Jeremy Arlo
Absolutely! Where are you?

WE

The atmosphere in the living room was strained when Elizabeth came downstairs to open the front door to Wilkes and, as they walked inside to join her parents, she could tell they'd been discussing the reaction to her father's latest antics on television. Husband and wife sat facing each other on opposite sofas while Ustym Karmaliuk stood silently on the glass table between the two, his small head moving back and forth, as if he was an umpire on the court of play.

'I was just telling your father,' announced Beverley in a regal tone, without so much as a hello, 'that he's a moron.'

'Well, of course he's a moron,' said Elizabeth. 'That's old news.'

'Do you know, it's such a joy to have a supportive family,' replied George, walking over to the drinks cabinet, where he poured himself a large whisky and made a point of ignoring everyone else's needs. 'At a time like this, when it feels as if the entire world is turning on me, at least I know I can return home to the warm embrace of my nearest and dearest and they will tell me how loved and respected I am. Hello, Wilkes. What's that on your head? Is it a small fox? And would it be terribly rude if I remarked that I can smell you from here? I have a horrible feeling that you might be decomposing.'

'It's a man bun,' replied Wilkes, putting a hand to the tiny dark hillock at the back of his head. 'And I'm not surprised. I haven't had a wash in eight days.'

Beverley turned to look at him, wrinkling her nose.

'I beg your pardon?' she said.

'It's a new regime that I've started,' he said, sitting down on the sofa next to her, which immediately made her stand up and move to the window seat. 'Do you know, the human body is actually self-cleaning?'

'Like our new oven,' added Elizabeth helpfully.

'What on earth are you talking about?' asked George.

'It's true. We spend so much of our time taking baths and showers, scrubbing layers off our epidermis, then adding pollutants to our skin, but in reality, after a couple of weeks, the body releases its own natural purifiers and cleans itself. In fact, the more soap you use, the more your skin dries out.'

'I've never heard anything so ridiculous in all my life,' said

Beverley. 'And I speak as someone who once heard Jeffrey Archer delivering a lecture to the Royal Society of Literature.'

'In fact, it's only in the last century or so that people have started to use shampoo,' continued Wilkes, warming to his theme. 'And in the last few decades we've become inundated with hand soaps, shower gels and bath salts which, yes, might make us smell nice for a couple of hours, but they're not natural, are they? Why should a person smell of pomegranate seeds and cassis, after all? A person should smell of person.'

'Well, you certainly do,' said George. 'You smell like all the people of the world, since the dawn of time, put together into one big blender. Are we going to be forced to put up with this unholy stench until our daughter comes to her senses and breaks up with you?'

'Not for too long, no,' said Wilkes. 'Another few weeks and you won't even notice it. By then, I'll have become entirely self-cleaning. Look at the turtle, after all,' he added, nodding towards Ustym Karmaliuk, who turned his head at the mention of him but wore a disgusted expression, as if even he found the man repulsive. 'You don't see him lathering up with Jo Malone Geranium and Walnut shower scrub, do you? Or washing his paws with Molton Brown Lime and Patchouli handwash?'

'I have three comments to make and then a question to ask,' declared Beverley, clearing her throat. 'First, he's a tortoise, not a turtle. Second, they are not paws, they are feet. And third, for someone who is opposed to personal cleaning products, you certainly seem to know the names of a lot of luxury brands, not to mention the various lines they produce. Finally, my question. Speaking as a mother, what about, you know, when you use the bathroom? Do you not wash your hands afterwards?'

'I rinse them, yes,' he admitted. 'In cold water. But I don't use any unnatural detergents.'

'I shall never touch you again,' said Beverley, shivering.

'You've never touched me before.'

'Well, I shall never touch you for the first time, then. Anyway, I don't think I can deal with any of this right now. Can't you both go somewhere else? Your father and I are discussing his idiocy.'

'We have opposing points of view, I might add,' said George.

'Actually,' said Elizabeth, sitting down next to her boyfriend, before reconsidering and moving to the other sofa. 'There's something we wanted to talk to you about.'

'Please don't tell me he's proposed,' said George.

'No, I don't believe in traditional marriage,' said Wilkes. 'It only encourages outdated notions of a woman's place in society.'

'Hear, hear,' agreed Elizabeth. 'Although I would like a nice day out at some point in the future. I've always imagined having my wedding reception at the Savoy. What do you think, Daddy?'

'It depends on who's waiting for you at the other end of the aisle, my love. And whether or not he's run a wet flannel over his face that morning.'

'Actually, before we get into our *big* news,' said Wilkes, 'there is something else I'd just like to clarify. Going forward, I mean.'

'Have we become a commercial business?' asked George. 'Are you going to give us directives and goals, then drill down to incentivize our core competency?'

'This is the great news I mentioned earlier,' he said, turning to Elizabeth.

'Oh yes, I forgot about that. Is it to do with the lepers?'

'The leopards?' asked Beverley, frowning. 'What leopards? If you think you're bringing a leopard into this house, then you have another think coming. It would eat Ustym Karma-liuk on sight, and who knows what it might do to Achilles? It would be such a shame to spoil that beautiful face. He's the only one of my children who one might call conventionally attractive. No offence.'

'What's your great news?' asked Elizabeth, choosing to set this latest insult aside as she turned to her boyfriend. Wilkes broke into a proud, self-satisfied smile.

'The thing is,' he said, 'from now on, I would appreciate it if you would stop referring to me as *he*.'

'I'm sorry?' said George.

'That's all right. No need to apologize. You weren't to know.'

'I wasn't apologizing. I was expressing the fact that I haven't the slightest clue what you're talking about.'

'Whatever this is,' said Elizabeth, 'perhaps it can wait until another time? When we don't have our other news to impart?'

'If you're pregnant—' began Beverley.

'I'm not. Wilkes doesn't believe in ejaculating inside a woman. He calls it a form of colonial ingress.'

'The other news is important, yes,' said Wilkes. 'But so is this. It would just mean the world to us if, from now on, every-one could make an effort to get our pronouns right.'

'What's he talking about now?' asked Beverley, turning to her husband and making the hand signal that she always employed when she wanted a large glass of wine. He opened a new bottle, suspecting that she'd need a lot of it before the night was over, and poured an extremely healthy measure.

'As of today,' continued Wilkes, 'we are officially non-binary.'

'Non-whattary?' asked George.

'Non-binary. We no longer identify as male or female.'

'Oh, Christ on a bike,' muttered George, filling a second glass with whisky.

'If it's helpful at all,' said Beverley, 'I've always had trouble identifying you as either. I've never been entirely sure that you're even human.'

'We do love your sense of humour, Bev,' said Wilkes, sitting back on the sofa and placing a cushion behind his back. George, watching, made a mental note to have the cushion incinerated later. 'But you see—'

Before he could continue his sentence, Beverley had leapt from her seat, charged across the room and, ignoring the foul odour that wrapped itself around her like an Edwardian great-coat, pointed her index finger in his face. 'Do not ever – *ever* – call me Bev,' she shouted. 'My name is Beverley Cleverley. You can call me Mrs Cleverley, or Beverley, if you must, but never Bev. And, all being well, after the new year, it will be Lady Cleverley, if my husband hasn't managed to mess that up too.'

'Beverley,' said Wilkes, holding his filthy hands in the air in an act of surrender. 'We only meant that we no longer wish to be associated with the heteronormative constraints of trad-itional male and female identities. We don't want to be labelled.'

'I labelled you as a complete moron from the moment I met you,' said George.

'So, it would be great if you could bear this in mind from now on. That's all we're asking.'

'I don't care what you call yourself,' replied Beverley, sitting down again, confident that she'd got her point across. 'You can call yourself Ozymandias, King of Kings, if it makes you happy. Just don't ever call me Bev.'

'Non-binary,' mused George. 'When you think about it, isn't that a label in itself?'

'No,' said Wilkes. 'On the contrary.'

'Well, what is it, then?'

'It's a . . . it's a term we use to express who we are.'

'So, a label, then.'

'No, it's less labellic, you see.'

'It can't be, since *labellic* is not actually a word.'

'Non-binary is like being gender fluid. It—'

'I didn't ask for synonyms. I asked whether it's also a label.'

'Well, perhaps,' admitted Wilkes, sounding a little crest-fallen, as if he'd been told that the Tooth Fairy didn't exist just after he'd lost a particularly impressive molar. 'But either way, it doesn't have the societal or sociological implications that other phrases have.'

'I don't even know what that means,' said George with a shrug. 'I suspect it means nothing at all.'

'Actually, I've read about this,' said Beverley. 'So, you're saying that, from now on, if we find ourselves in the unfortunate position of having to refer to you in conversation, then we should say *they* rather than *he*, as if there are two of you.'

'We're not suggesting that there are two of us,' said Wilkes.

'Good,' said George. 'Because one is bad enough. Two would be insupportable.'

'You don't want to be labelled with a conventional pronoun that has been in common usage since the English tongue was first established,' continued Beverley. 'And so, instead, you'd like to be labelled with an equally conventional pronoun that has been in common usage since the English tongue was first established. Simply the pluralized version. That's it, isn't it?'

Wilkes frowned, the tiny mind in that vast Grand Canyon of a head scrambling to think of an answer. On the table, sensing that this conversation was going to continue for some time, Ustym Karmaliuk allowed his own head to retreat a little further into his shell, giving him the appearance of Anne Boleyn or King Charles I in their latter moments.

'He's changed his Twitter profile to *they/their*,' said Elizabeth, who had been tapping away at her phone for the last minute or two.

'They have,' said Wilkes, correcting her.

'What?'

'You said, "He's changed his Twitter profile." You meant, "They've changed their Twitter profile." '

'Oh yes. Sorry.'

'It's fine. We totally forgive you. And we still appreciate you.'

'And we appreciate you too. I mean, I do. I'm staying binary for the time being.'

'I have a question,' said Beverley. 'What do you do when you're in France?'

Wilkes stared at her, wondering why she was asking such a thing. 'We don't . . . we're sorry, we don't understand what you mean.'

'Well, here in England, we employ just one form of the third person plural. *They*. But in France, of course, they employ two. *Ils* and *elles*, the former for men and the latter for women. So, what do you do when you're in France? How do you define yourself there? Do you pretend that you're two men or two women?'

Wilkes looked down at the ground, his forehead crinkling so deeply in confusion that Beverley was sure that she could see some of the filth squeezing its way out of his pores, like the last globules from a tube of murky russet oil-based paint.

'Actually, we don't know the answer to that,' he replied. 'We haven't been to France since the pandemic, so the issue hasn't arisen. But we'll look into it and get back to you.'

'Oh, please do,' said Beverley, placing her hands together as if in prayer. 'I'll be on tenterhooks until I know. Honestly, I don't think I'll get a wink of sleep.'

For a few moments, no one in the room spoke. George found that he quite enjoyed the silence, and if it hadn't been for the stench of his daughter's boyfriend wafting through the air like the waste pipe of a sewage works, it would have been the most enjoyable part of his day so far.

'Anyway,' said Elizabeth finally. 'If we can move on—'

'I'd be delighted if you did,' said George.

'We wanted to discuss something with you.'

'Oh yes,' replied Beverley. 'What was it? Are you going to find your own flat? That's fine. We totally support your move towards independence, don't we, George?'

'Absolutely. I'll even pay for the Uber.'

'We're planning a trip to Indonesia,' said Wilkes.

'Now, when you say *we*,' replied George, 'are you referring to yourself as a non-binary identity or to you and my daughter?'

'To both of us.'

'To both of who?'

'To Elizabeth and us.'

'Ah, good. I'm not trying to be difficult, you understand. It's just that it makes it very confusing. If you're a plural, how is someone to know when you're referring to yourself alone and when you're referring to yourself in company with others?'

'Context will probably be all.'

'Ah, context. I see. Good to know.'

'The point is, we're hoping to go there quite soon.'

'I must admit, I've never actually been to Indonesia,' declared Beverley, looking up at the ceiling. 'But I have a friend who went there a couple of years ago – I think she stayed in the Bulgari Resort – and she raved about it. I'm sure you'll have a lovely time. How long will you be gone? No need to rush back.'

'We won't be staying in the Bulgari Resort, Mother,' said Elizabeth. 'We're going to a leper colony.'

Another brief silence before George and Beverley turned to each other and burst out laughing. They laughed for a long time, tears streaming down their cheeks, and when they had finally finished, George remarked on how much he'd needed that.

'It's been a rotten couple of days,' he added.

'It's not a joke,' said Wilkes. 'We really are going to a leper colony.'

'But there are no leper colonies any more,' said Beverley, looking utterly bewildered. 'And even if there were, why on earth—'

'There's a few.'

'Nonsense.'

'It's true. And they need our help.'

'Again,' said George, 'when you say *our*—'

'I mean Elizabeth's and our help.'

Beverley turned to her daughter, looking at her as if she couldn't quite understand what was going on.

'Wilkes wants us to go,' said Elizabeth, hoping that something in her tone might make her parents realize that she was hoping they would forbid it, a prohibition that, in normal circumstances, she would not tolerate but which, on this occasion, would prove perfectly acceptable.

'But why?' asked George.

'Because if we don't help them, then who will?' asked Wilkes.

'Other people?' suggested Beverley. 'The Red Cross? Judah Ben-Hur?'

'It's out of the question,' said George. 'You're not dragging our daughter halfway around the world so she can catch leprosy. What would happen when she came back? I can't imagine the NHS have a lot of experience with that sort of thing, even if we didn't go private.'

'It's important to us,' insisted Wilkes.

'Again—'

'To *us*! To Elizabeth and me. Us. We. What is the point of life if we don't do everything we can to help other people, people in need, people in depressed areas—'

'Like Glasgow?' asked George.

'And then share all our work on social media. Do you know how many new followers we get every time we help out at the soup kitchen?'

'But what does that matter?'

'Oh my God,' said Elizabeth, looking at her father as if he'd just sprouted horns. 'It matters enormously. A few weeks ago, I took a selfie with a homeless man eating a ham sandwich and I got over a thousand likes.'

'People are that interested in seeing pictures of a homeless man eating a ham sandwich?' asked George, dumbfounded.

'Well, no, I was the one eating the ham sandwich,' said Elizabeth. 'He was just in the frame. Although he did look a little hungry, now that you mention it.'

'And how long would you intend on staying in this oasis of tranquillity?' asked Beverley. 'A week? A month? All the way to monsoon season?'

'As long as they need us,' said Wilkes.

'You'll fit in very well with the whole not-washing thing,' remarked George. 'And just for the record, I was using the word *you* in the plural form there, not the singular. You and your many personalities will all fit in very well.'

'Wilkes,' said Beverley in a calm voice, as if she was trying to reason with a four-year-old. 'Let me ask you a question. In the unlikely event that a woman allowed you to impregnate her, and then you inflicted a daughter upon the world, would you agree to letting someone you barely knew take her to a leper colony? Is that the kind of parent you would be?'

'We'd like to think that we would, yes.'

'And you don't think that Social Services would have anything to say about it?'

He frowned again, as if his brain, such as it was, was going into overdrive.

'We can't deal with hypotheticals,' he said eventually. 'We don't have a daughter so we can't answer that.'

'Well, do you have a sister?'

'We did,' he replied in a sorrowful tone, looking down at the carpet.

'You did?'

'When we were growing up, yes,' he said. 'But not any more.'

'Oh shit,' said George, looking momentarily humbled.

'What do you mean?' asked Beverley. 'Did she . . . did she die? Oh, I'm sorry, Wilkes. That was insensitive of me. I didn't know. Elizabeth never said.'

'No, she didn't die,' replied Wilkes, shaking his head.

'Then what happened to her?'

'She got cancelled,' said Elizabeth.

Beverley blinked. 'I'm sorry?'

'I said, she got cancelled.'

'I heard what you said. It just didn't seem to be a collection of words that, placed together in an otherwise reasonable sequence, made any sense.'

'Our sister was cancelled late last year,' explained Wilkes. 'So, naturally, we haven't spoken since. It's sad, but there's really nothing we can do about it.'

'Your sister was cancelled,' said George, trying out the phrase on his tongue. 'I'm sorry, but is she a television programme, perhaps? Or a train timetable? A subscription service of some kind?'

'No, she's a human being. Well, she was.'

'And how does one go about cancelling a human being, if you don't mind my asking?'

'Well, what happened was, late last year Frances tweeted something about Greta Thunberg that caused a bit of an uproar.'

'The little Swedish girl?' asked Beverley. 'I don't know why, but she gives me the heebie-jeebies.'

'Frances tweeted that she thought Greta should be in school completing her education,' explained Elizabeth. 'Not travelling around the world shouting at grown-ups. And that was that.'

'That was what?'

'That was how she got cancelled,' said Wilkes.

'But I still don't—'

'Oh, Mother,' said Elizabeth, throwing her hands in the air. 'It means that she lost all her followers, no one talks to her any more and she's considered a pariah. Like, in your day, when someone was sent to Coventry. Her friends have all abandoned her and she's not welcome in polite society. Like Harvey Weinstein, say. Or members of the European Research Group.'

'And all of this because she expressed an opinion?'

'The wrong opinion,' said Wilkes.

'The wrong opinion,' repeated George, laughing again as he

opened another bottle of whisky. 'The powers that be, the Great Unelected Consciences of the World, didn't approve of what she said and that was the end of her. How Orwellian. Have you ever heard of "civil death", any of you?'

All three shook their heads.

'Of course not. So much for the expensive education I put you through, Elizabeth. Back in medieval Europe, the moment a person was convicted of a crime they lost all their civil rights. And this was known as civil death. More often than not, it meant that anyone could simply kill them without consequence because, officially, they no longer existed. Sounds fair, doesn't it?'

'Sounds awful,' said Wilkes.

'I was being sarcastic, you cretin.'

'Oh.'

'And this is effectively what you're doing to people who don't agree with you, is it? Including your own sister?'

'There's nothing we can do about it,' protested Wilkes. 'She got cancelled. It was decided.'

'By *who*?' roared George.

'By social media!'

'Oh, fuck social media! And fuck all the morons who spend their time on it. That bloody tortoise has more insight into the world than any of those miserable trolls do.'

'George, your blood pressure,' said Beverley.

'Well, I mean to say,' he replied, sounding utterly fed up now, 'I've heard some stupid things in recent times, but this one takes the biscuit, it really does. I don't know which is worse, that you think you either have the power or the moral right to, in your words, *cancel* another human being, or that you think that normal, sensible people would play along with your idiocy? *Cancelled!* It's actually offensive to the ear even hearing such a word spoken aloud. The . . . the . . . the . . .' He struggled to complete his sentence, but with each utterance of the word *the*, the other occupants of the room sat forward a little, waiting to see where he went with it. 'The . . . the . . . the insufferable *arrogance*,' he spat out finally. 'The unspeakable *superciliousness*! The grotesque sense of *moral superiority*!'

'All right, George,' said Beverley, sitting back again and sipping her wine. 'You've made your point. Chillax, darling.'

'I will not *chillax*, whatever that means. And I don't think I have made my point. Not if this pair of numbskulls fail to recognize the truth of what I'm saying.'

'Your father's right,' said Beverley. 'The whole idea is ridiculous.'

'So you think I shouldn't go?' asked Elizabeth, hopefully.

'Of course I think that. And, while we're on the subject, I think you should stop associating with this . . . this creature,' she said, nodding in the direction of Wilkes. 'You can do far better for yourself.'

'We are in the room, you know,' said Wilkes, looking across at her with a wounded expression on his face.

'I know. I can smell you.'

'But I appreciate him,' insisted Elizabeth. 'Them.'

'And I appreciate a glass of wine after a hard day of reviewing my ghost's writing, but I don't want to set up home with one. You've had much nicer boyfriends in the past. And you'll have much nicer ones in the future too.'

'No, I haven't,' said Elizabeth. 'Gareth was too insecure. David had too much of a temper. Nick was too bisexual. Conor was only after my money. Tuscany was too self-centred. Pylyp was too boring. Will was—'

'I'm sorry,' said Beverley, sitting up, fully alert now. 'Philip? You said Philip, yes? I don't remember a Philip.'

'No, Pylyp,' said Elizabeth. 'That guy you danced with when you were on *Strictly*, remember? Oh, I never told you about him and me, did I? We had a bit of a thing.'

Beverley shook her head slowly, unable to speak.

'Oh, don't look so shocked. It hardly matters now. It was ages ago. And it didn't last long. It was purely physical.'

'I really don't want to hear that,' said George. 'I live in a fantasy world where you're all virgins.'

'Even me?' asked Wilkes, momentarily forgetting his correct pronoun.

'Especially you.'

'How long?' asked Beverley.

'How long what?'

'How long did it go on for? You and Pylyp.'

Elizabeth scrunched up her face, trying to remember. 'I don't know,' she said. 'A few weeks? Until just before I met Wilkes.'

Beverley said nothing, simply sat back and finished her glass of wine in one gulp.

'What does any of this matter?' asked George, his face still red with anger. 'The point is, you are not going to Indonesia. I'm putting my foot down.'

'Daddy—'

'No, I'm sorry, but this is an absurd conversation. I'm under a great deal of stress at the moment and I simply won't listen to another word of your nonsense. Beverley, Elizabeth, Ustym Karmaliuk, Wilkes's multiple personalities and Wilkes himself – and I list you in order of how seriously I take you all – I'm picking up my whisky and I'm going upstairs to read a book. One printed on paper and that has no comments at the end of each page.'

'But Daddy,' protested Elizabeth as he made his way towards

the door, 'what about Indonesia? What about our trip to the leper colony? What do you think we should do?'

'Isn't it obvious?' he asked, turning back to pick up the bottle before leaving the room. 'Cancel it.'

PART 4

16 September 2011

They're seated outside a restaurant in Newport, Rhode Island, on the second-to-last afternoon of their trip. Since arriving a month earlier, they've spent time in Massachussetts, New York and Washington, DC but have decided to end their trip here, in a town where Beverley spent a summer when she was a student, working in the Newport Creamery.

It's been a hugely enjoyable holiday. Nelson has been fascinated by every city they've visited, wanting to explore every museum, every architectural site, and have his photograph taken in front of the Liberty Bell. Achilles, too, although only seven, has kept them entertained with an endless stream of jokes and performance pieces. Although the last to join the family, he is, both George and Beverley agree, the glue that holds them all together, the one around whose antics they all revolve.

President Bush, the first President Bush, has been in the north-east over the last few weeks and, as an old friend of George's, having appeared on his chat show several times over the years, had invited them all out to Walker's Point Estate in Kennebunkport for a weekend.

But their holiday is drawing to a close now. Their flights are booked for home and George is due back at the BBC the following Monday. There's an air of dissatisfaction around the table; they would all like to stay longer. Really, none of them wants to leave.

'Can't we just cancel our flights?' asks Nelson, popping the head off a grilled shrimp and tossing its torso into his mouth.

'If only,' replies Beverley with a sigh. 'It has been magical, hasn't it?'

'Let's just move here!' suggests Achilles.

'Our lives are in London,' says George. 'But don't worry, we'll do this again. It's been tremendous fun.' He glances across at his eleven-year-old daughter, who, while generally quite vivacious, has seemed rather quiet over the last half-hour. 'Are you all right?' he asks.

'Yes,' she replies, looking down at the table, unable to meet his eye.

'We're lucky, aren't we?' says Beverley. 'To have such experiences. Well . . .' And here her voice cracks a little. 'I feel lucky anyway. To be with you, George. And you children. You're all rather wonderful.'

'Don't get soppy, Mum,' says Nelson.

'Well, I mean it.'

'You're not all right,' says George, frowning and leaning forward, noticing how his daughter is trembling slightly. 'What's the matter? What's happened?'

All eyes turn towards Elizabeth and, in a moment, tears begin to roll down her cheeks. Her parents, her brothers, all stare at her. They've never seen her behave like this before. In a moment, both Nelson and Achilles each take her by a hand and pull her from her seat, dragging her towards the beach front, where George and Beverley can't see them any more.

'What on earth . . . ?' asks George, ready to stand up and follow them, but Beverley places a hand on his, telling him to stay where he is.

'Let's just wait,' she says, her voice also filled with anxiety. 'Let's see what the boys do.'

It takes almost ten minutes but, eventually, all three children reappear. Elizabeth's eyes are red, but she returns to her food without a word. Achilles looks confused and uncertain. Nelson looks furious. He's the only one who doesn't sit down and, when he walks back towards the bar area, both George and Beverley stand up and follow him, knowing that he's waiting for them. Their eldest son. The responsible one.

'That man over there,' says Nelson, pointing to a table about fifty yards from their own, where a man in his early thirties is sitting alone, drinking beer. 'He said something to her. When she went to the toilet.'

George and Beverley stare at their eldest son, taking his words in.

'He said something to her,' repeats Nelson, not meeting their eyes, clearly hoping that he won't have to reveal what the man has said. It's too embarrassing.

His parents turn around and look in the direction that the boy has indicated. George's hands twist into fists and he takes a step forward but, before he can move, Beverley grips his forearm.

'Oh no,' she says, her face filled with contained rage, as she shakes her head. 'I'll handle this, thank you very much.'

And although what takes place over the next five minutes lands Beverley in a jail cell overnight on a charge of assault and battery, as far as she and everyone else is concerned, it's worth every minute.

And at that precise moment, a group of former Stanford University students agree that 'Ghostface Chillah', a black-and-white shape centred in a yellow background, will become the image to represent their new multimedia messaging application, called Snapchat.

Thursday

SON OF ADOLF

Four groups of protestors, some carrying placards, were gathered outside the BBC and, when his taxi pulled up, George glared out of the window with barely concealed contempt before asking the driver whether he could remain in the safety of the back seat for a few minutes.

'You can stay as long as you like, mate,' replied the man, reaching for a copy of the *Daily Mail* from the passenger seat. 'Just tell me when you're ready to leave and I'll turn the meter off. Here,' he added, pointing towards the front page. 'I see you're in the wars.'

George peered through the glass screen and saw a particularly bad photograph of himself on the front page, looking both angry and double-chinned.

'What have you done, then?'

'It turns out I'm a horrible old bigot.'

'I am too, as it happens,' admitted the driver. 'But they don't stick me on the front page of the papers over it. That lot waiting for you, are they?'

'I suspect so, yes. Have you ever read *Frankenstein*?'

'I've seen the film.'

'That's what this reminds me of. An angry mob waving

pitchforks and hurling abuse, ready to drag me off to the river and hurl me in.'

'I don't see any pitchforks.'

'Trust me, they're all carrying them. Metaphorical ones anyway.'

'Well, it'd be a lot better to get poked in the arse by a metaphorical pitchfork than a real one, I imagine. Hello, we're in trouble now.'

A security guard was walking towards them and he tapped on the driver's window. The driver rolled it down and smiled politely.

'Yes, guv'nor,' he said.

'You can't park here,' said the guard. 'You have to go around the side if you're waiting for someone.'

'My passenger won't leave,' said the driver.

The security guard glanced into the back seat.

'Oh, Mr Cleverley,' he said in surprise. 'I didn't realize it was you.'

'Hello, Samir,' replied George, offering a half-wave. 'Climb in. I could do with the company.'

Samir opened the back door and stepped inside.

'You don't have to ask me twice,' he said as he shut the door. 'As it happens, I have a passion for black cabs. I've often dreamed of owning one.'

'You can have this one, if you like,' said the driver, turning the pages of his newspaper. 'Quarter of a million quid and I'll give you the keys right now.'

'I'm afraid my BBC salary wouldn't stretch that far,' said Samir.

'Then we'll stay as we are, shall we?'

'I suppose they're all here for me, are they?' asked George, nodding towards the crowd.

'Most of them, yes,' admitted the security guard. 'I split them into groups so I could keep track of them. Over there on the left are the ones who think you're a racist.'

'You know I'm not a racist, don't you, Samir? I'd hate it if you thought otherwise.'

'Of course, Mr Cleverley.'

'As it happens, I'm particularly fond of your people. Always have been.'

'My people?'

'Moroccans. That's where my wife and I went on our honeymoon, you know. Casablanca.'

'Actually, I'm Lebanese,' said Samir.

'Not Moroccan?'

'No.'

'Well, how do you like that? Anyway, as long as you know that I'm not racist. So, who else is out there?'

'The next group are the people who think you're transphobic.'

'Ah, them,' said George, frowning.

'They seem particularly energized.'

'Indeed. They're furious at me for doing something to support their cause. My bad, as the young people say. And the next lot?'

'The Friends of Israel. They say you're anti-Semitic.'

'Anti-Semitic?' asked George, surprised. 'That's a new one. What on earth have I done to upset the Jews? I don't recall saying anything about them.'

'I think they just assume that you hate them too,' said Samir.

'That's a bit presumptuous, isn't it?'

'They're very insistent.'

'The truth is, I don't hate anyone,' protested George. 'Except all those morons with nothing better to do than stand around here on a Thursday morning waving idiotic signs in the air. I despise them.'

'Perhaps it would be best not to say that to their faces.'

'They wouldn't understand anyway. The cheese fell off their crackers a long time ago. Anyway, that's three groups. What about the group hanging around outside Wogan House? Those six overweight white men who look like they've never been laid in their lives? What am I supposed to have done to them?'

'Actually, they're not here for you, Mr Cleverley,' said Samir. 'They're *Doctor Who* fans and they show up every week to protest the fact that the Doctor is being played by a woman.'

'Oh, for God's sake,' replied George, rolling his eyes. 'They can't still be upset about that, surely? It must be three years by now, and she's leaving anyway.'

'They take the Time Lord very seriously.'

'There's not one of them would even fit inside the Tardis. I don't care how big it is. But look, how am I supposed to get inside the building with all those fools screaming for my blood? I have a meeting with the top brass, and I don't want to get murdered before I get fired. I'd lose out on my pay-off.'

Samir sucked in his breath and shook his head. 'There's not much for it, I'm afraid,' he said. 'You'll just have to make a run for it, that's all. I'll come with you, to keep you safe. And maybe the driver . . . ?'

'You can leave me out of it,' came the reply from the front seat. 'I drive. I don't walk.'

'Then just the two of us,' said Samir. 'Come on, Mr Cleverley. We'll go quickly so you won't get hurt.'

'All right,' said George with a sigh, paying the cab driver his fare and adding a five-pound tip. 'Let's do it.'

Samir opened the door and all heads turned in their

direction as they made their way across the concourse, although George kept his bowed, hoping that the protestors might not recognize him. But, within a few seconds, a cry went up and they rushed in his direction, surrounding him with animalistic expressions on their faces. Once they had him trapped within a circle, he stared around anxiously but offered them his most ingratiating smile. They might all be pretending to hate him, he knew, but they'd also love the opportunity to spend a few minutes in the warm glow of celebrity.

'Please, everyone,' shouted Samir. 'You need to step away. If you don't—'

'No, it's all right, honestly,' said George, touching his arm and turning to the mob. 'Actually, I think what you're all doing here is commendable and I'm happy to answer your questions. This whole thing, you see, has been an enormous misunderstanding. Let's cool the temperature a little, though and, oh, by the way,' he added, looking at one of the placards that a young woman was holding, 'there's an e before the last letter of my surname. Your sign says *Fuck George Cleverly*, but it should say *Fuck George Cleverley*.'

The woman looked up at the sign that she'd painted earlier.

'Oh, I'm terribly sorry,' she said. 'You don't have a Sharpie on you, do you?'

'I don't, I'm afraid,' replied George. 'And it's perfectly fine. No apology needed. It's actually quite a common mistake. Joan Plowright gets it wrong on her Christmas-card envelope every year and we've known each other for decades. Funny story, as it happens. It was Larry Olivier who—'

'Do you feel no shame?' shouted a man who was dressed a bit like Joseph from *Joseph and the Amazing Technicolor Dreamcoat* but lacked the athletic body that actors in that role usually displayed.

'I feel a great deal of shame,' said George. 'But perhaps you could narrow down what I'm supposed to feel ashamed about?'

'Your racism, man!'

'But I'm not a racist! I'm genuinely not. I have plenty of black friends.'

'That's *such* a racist thing to say!'

'Well, what would you have me say?' asked George. 'That I don't have any? That I exclude them from my social circle? The fact is, I do. And I see them regularly. If I was a racist, I wouldn't do that, would I? I'd . . . I don't know . . . I'd poison them when they came for dinner. I'd put arsenic in the bouillabaisse.'

'Name some!' asked a woman standing to his left.

'Well, there's Trevor McDonald,' he said, thinking about it. 'And Moira Stuart. She's a lovely woman. Lenny Henry. Ian Wright. I'm quite friendly with James Cleverly, the Conservative Party chairman, although he's no relation. And, interestingly, he *doesn't* have a third e in his surname.'

'They're all *famous* black people,' said Joseph. 'Don't you have any not-famous black friends?'

'Alan Gillingham,' said George. 'And his wife, Rose. Deborah Carlyle. Steven MacDaid.'

'Who are they? No one's ever heard of them!'

'Well, you wouldn't have, would you? You asked for not-famous black people.'

'At least you're saying *black*,' said a woman with a rich Trinidadian accent. 'And not *coloured*. Who say *coloured* these days? You think God take the white canvas and Him break out the crayons before putting us in our mothers' bellies?'

'I admit, it was a poor choice of word,' said George. 'But it was in the heat of the moment. You have no idea how warm it can be under the lights in a television studio.'

'You're a big fat racist bastard!' shouted someone from the back of the crowd.

'Well, really,' protested George, turning to look in the direction of the voice. 'I do think that's a little unfair. I may have put on a few pounds lately, but I'm hardly—'

'Trans rights are human rights!' cried a person of indeterminate gender, pushing his, her or their way towards the front of the crowd, and George nodded his head, even as he took a step back in fright.

'They are,' he agreed. 'They most certainly are.'

'You want to put us all in concentration camps, don't you? To be ethnically cleansed!'

'I don't want anything of the sort!' said George. 'When have I ever said such a thing? Although it's worth pointing out that, if that were to happen, it wouldn't be considered ethnic cleansing. That term relates specifically to the eradication of racial or religious groups.'

'Oh my God, that's *such* a transphobic comment!' roared someone else.

'But it's not! It's simply a statement of fact. Ethnic cleansing has nothing to do with transgender people. You might as well connect homophobia to a fear of horses!'

'Why you think the gay men hate the horses?' asked the Trinidadian woman, hands firmly on hips.

'The Doctor has always been played by a man and he should still be played by a man!' shouted someone else over the throng. 'It's political correctness gone mad!'

'Now, I take exception to that,' said George, turning around. 'Jodie Whittaker is a very fine actress who, in my opinion, has embodied the role with élan and—'

An egg flew in his direction, hitting his shoulder, and he stared at it as it fell to the ground before breaking open. It appeared to be hard-boiled, which seemed to defeat the purpose of the exercise. But a moment later, another soared through the air, a fresh one this time, and smashed against his shirt, just to the left of his tie.

'Oh, really, this is too much,' shouted George. 'I'm not some sort of monster, you know. I'm a beloved BBC personality! You've got it wrong, all of you.'

Now, two tomatoes came his way, along with an onion, but before he could assemble the raw ingredients for a tasty omelette, Samir had taken him by the arm and dragged him towards the revolving doors and they made their way inside, away from the rabble, while George examined the damage the protestors had done to his suit.

'What a bunch of absolute fuckers,' he said, taking his handkerchief from his pocket and trying to remove the egg detritus from his clothing. The yolk proved impervious to his efforts, leaving a yellow stain along his shirt. 'I try to be polite and understanding, and this is what I get for my troubles. We should keep a set of fire hoses down here and turn them on people like that. What gives them the right?'

'The law,' said Samir. 'The right to protest peacefully.'

'You call that peaceful?' snapped George. 'They're about as peaceful as a recently divorced couple taking a holiday together in the Gaza Strip. Can't we call the police?'

'I don't recommend it, sir,' said Samir. 'The best thing is to allow them to let off steam, get their photos and videos for social media, and then they usually disperse. They probably think you'll be in the building for the rest of the day anyway, so they won't wait around for no reason.'

'And why wouldn't I be here for the rest of the day?' asked George, frowning. 'Do you know something I don't know?'

'Only that you're in a great deal of trouble.'

'Well, the dogs on the street know that. So, thanks for the insight.'

Samir gritted his teeth. 'There's no need to take out your frustrations on me, Mr Cleverley,' he said. 'I'm simply trying to help.'

George nodded. 'You're quite right,' he said. 'I apologize, Samir. None of this is your fault. It's just been an incredibly stressful week, that's all.'

'George.'

A voice from his left made him turn around, and his heart sank as a woman appeared from the waiting area and made her way slowly towards him.

'Oh, Jesus wept,' he said, pressing his hand to his forehead. 'Who the hell let her in?'

'She said she was your sister,' said Samir. 'And that she'd come to offer her support.'

'She's not my bloody sister,' snapped George. 'My sister lives in Los Angeles with a woman old enough to be her mother and she hasn't spoken to me in years due to a misunderstanding entirely unrelated to my current troubles.'

'I can ask her to leave, if you like,' said Samir.

'No, it's fine. She's a . . . a friend. Thank you, Samir. If you could just give us a moment.'

The security guard nodded and made his way back outside, where the crowds had put down their banners and were taking selfies with a remarkably friendly Gordon Brown, who had shown up to pre-record an episode of *Celebrity Mastermind*.

'Angela,' said George, smiling broadly as he greeted his visitor.

'You've been ignoring my text messages,' she replied.

'Not deliberately,' he said. 'Responding has been on my

to-do list, along with saving my job and trying to stop my daughter from contracting leprosy.'

'We have to talk,' said Angela. 'This baby isn't going away.'

'Of course we do,' he said. 'Now, I've forgotten, how far along are you now?'

'Four months.'

'Right, so we're anticipating a Christmas miracle. That's another present I'll have to buy.' He laughed to himself and looked at his erstwhile lover, hoping that perhaps she would laugh, too, but her face remained rigid.

'I told you before,' she said. 'If you don't want anything to do with the baby or with me, then you just need to say so. I don't want to be left in limbo, that's all.'

'I believe the last pope got rid of limbo,' said George. 'Or cancelled it, as they say. Or maybe it was the present pope. One of them anyway. Was it the one who lives in the bed and breakfast or the one who lives in the garden shed? Honestly, you'd think one of them would just move into the papal suite, wouldn't you? It's got to be a lot more comfortable.'

'Why are you rambling like this?' asked Angela. 'Are you just trying to fob me off?'

'No, I think it's because I'm about two steps away from having a massive coronary. The truth is, I can't think straight right now, Angela, I'm sorry. I'm honestly not trying to be a cad. Everything is just up in the air and, until some of those things, you know, fall and land on me, crushing me to death and leaving my body to be scraped off the street, I don't think I can make any big decisions.'

'So, in the meantime, I'm left to worry about my future. And Basil's future.'

'Who on earth is Basil?' asked George, frowning.

'Basil,' she insisted, pointing at her stomach.

'Oh, it's a boy, then?'

'I think so, yes. I told you before. A mother can tell.'

'I rather hoped it would be a girl. So I'd have two of each. Like Abba.'

'Well, I'm sorry to disappoint you. Should I send it back and we can try again?'

'Christ, no,' said George. 'And what do you mean by Basil? Who calls their child Basil these days? It's a terrible name.'

'It was my father's name.'

'So what? My father's name was Adolf, but I didn't call any of my sons after him.'

'No it wasn't,' said Angela.

'It was, actually. It's not something I've told very many people, so don't spread it around. Hang on, maybe that's why the third group out there think I'm anti-Semitic? Perhaps someone found out and told them? It doesn't show up on my Wikipedia page. At least, it wasn't there last time I checked.'

'George, can we just agree a time and place to—'

'Anyway, don't I have a say in the name?'

'Not if you're abdicating all responsibility for the child, no.'

'I'm not abdicating anything. I promise you, Angela, there's more chance of the Queen abdicating than me. But you can't call him Basil. The first thing everyone will think of is *Fawlty Towers*. He'll be plagued by people shouting, "Don't mention the war!"'

'Says the son of Adolf.'

'Shush,' he said, looking around to make sure that she hadn't been overheard. 'Please, Angela! God, I don't know why I even told you that.' He glanced at his watch. 'Forget I said anything, all right? Look, I'm sorry, I have to go. As you probably know, I'm in a spot of bother, and I have a meeting shortly with a bunch of people who want to push me gently off the roof. Can I call you later?'

'You can,' agreed Angela, looking momentarily appeased. 'But if you don't, George, I won't be contacting you again, is that understood? Call me today, or that's the end of it. I'll take matters into my own hands.'

'You were always rather good at that, as I recall,' replied George with a smile and a wink.

'Oh, for God's sake,' she said, turning around and leaving.

Perhaps not the best time for a bit of cheeky innuendo, he told himself as he made his way towards the lift. But honestly, he needed a little levity in his life right now.

ECONOMY CLASS

Beverley's flight to Odessa involved an early start, departing Heathrow for Vienna at 6 a.m. before making a quick transfer in a crowded airport for the next leg of her journey. She did her best to sleep on the first plane, but images of her daughter locked in bouts of passion with Pylyp kept dragging her back to consciousness, so by the time she boarded the second, which, to her horror, did not offer business class, she was feeling grouchy and tired, emotions that were only exacerbated when she saw that her neighbours were an elderly man and a seven-year-old boy.

The boy remained mostly silent at the start of the flight, content with reading his comics and listening to music through his headphones, but the man seemed starved of adult companionship and tried unsuccessfully a number of times to strike up a conversation.

'Are you Ukrainian?' he asked, breathing coffee fumes over her.

'I most certainly am not,' she replied. 'I'm British.'

'I used to be British,' he said wistfully. 'But when I married my wife, I gave up my citizenship and became Ukrainian.'

'And is this your son?' she asked, unimpressed by the idea of a man his age procreating with some unfortunate young woman.

'Oh no,' he said, laughing a little. 'My grandson.'

She nodded, relieved.

'Do you have grandchildren?' he asked. 'Or great-grandchildren?'

She gave him her chilliest expression, wondering whether he was being deliberately rude, before shaking her head.

'My children are aged between seventeen and twenty-two,' she said. 'So I hardly think it likely that a new generation would have appeared just yet. Let alone the one to follow that. Now, if you don't mind, I must get some work done.'

She removed a set of pages from her bag and, pulling the tabletop down from the seat back in front of her, placed her folder on it and began to read the chapters that the ghost had delivered overnight. To her relief, the story was progressing rather well, although the woman had an infuriating habit of doing what Beverley called 'writing up'. On one page, for example, a character had fallen asleep 'counting sheep, but, in her dreams, clouds drifted across the arid landscape of her reveries like inscrutable posies of wool'. On another, a gynaecologist's surgery was 'steeped in the blood of lost foeti', which, frankly, was a phrase that turned Beverley's stomach. And the heroine appeared to be developing a Sapphic element to her character, too, that none of Beverley's readers would understand, let alone appreciate. Also, there was a new experimental sequence, five pages of words thrown randomly on the page, like paint splattered across a Jackson Pollock canvas, none of which seemed to connect to each other in any way but which were clearly intended to mirror the confused mind of the protagonist.

She made notes beside each of these and more.

No gynaecologists! she scrawled. *And stop talking about her angry cervix!*

'So, what brings you to Odessa?' asked Beverley's neighbour, refusing to accept her rebuff.

'Personal business,' she replied.

'Oh yes,' he said. 'A lot of women do that. I'm told that it's a lot cheaper over there than at home.'

She frowned and turned to look at him.

'What are you talking about?' she asked.

He raised his index finger and tickled it along the flabby skin that hung beneath his chin. 'You're getting a little procedure done, I assume? And why not? We all like to make the best of ourselves. Odessa is well known for the skill of its plastic surgeons.'

'I'm doing nothing of the sort,' replied Beverley, outraged. She placed the palm of her hand beneath her own chin, concerned that something might have collapsed in the hours since she'd left London, but nothing there seemed untoward. 'That's very rude of you, if you don't mind me saying so.'

'I don't mind in the least,' he said. 'No offence.'

'Well, I *am* offended.'

'Touchy,' said the man under his breath. 'As it happens, I had a hair transplant there a couple of years ago. You'd never know it, but all of this' – and here he pointed towards

322

a thin thatch sitting atop his head that made Bobby Charlton look like Bob Marley – 'is fake. It's taken years off me, though.'

'And did you pay a lot for that?' she asked.

'About five thousand pounds.'

'So about two hundred and fifty pounds per strand then. No offence.'

He looked a little wounded by the remark and the boy took his headphones off and glanced at them both, as if he was worried that something interesting might be going on and he was missing out on it.

'Hello,' he said, leaning forward.

'Hello,' replied Beverley, who was always pleased to see a child reading. 'Are you enjoying your comic?'

'No. It's boring.'

'Oh. Well, I'm sorry to hear that.'

'You look like the Queen.'

'I think you mean Princess Diana.'

The boy frowned. 'Who's Princess Diana?' he asked.

'Long before your time,' said his grandfather, and the boy shrugged and put his headphones back on.

'If you don't mind my asking,' said Beverley, 'why are you travelling with your grandson?'

'I went to visit him in Vienna,' explained the man. 'His mother is my daughter. And his father . . . well, who knows? Anyway, she's not a great mother – not my fault, I left all the parenting to my wife, and it turned out that she was no good at it – so I decided to take him back to Odessa with me. I can give him a good home there.'

'And his mother agreed to this?'

'I left her a note,' he said.

'She doesn't know you've taken him?'

'No. And it'll probably be days before she even discovers that he's gone. Anyway, he's perfectly content. Look at him.'

'So, are we all going to be trapped on this plane when we land while the police come on board to arrest you?'

'It's a definite possibility,' he admitted. 'But I really don't think so. Honestly, if anything, she'll be dancing for joy. Actually, would you mind watching him for a few minutes? I need to go to the toilet. To do a number one.'

'I don't need the details,' said Beverley. 'But yes, I'll keep an eye on him. Although it's hard to imagine him going missing. This isn't *Flightplan*, after all.'

The man nodded and clambered over his grandson. The boy removed his headphones again and stared at Beverley, as if he was worried that not only had he been taken away from his mother, but now his grandfather was about to disappear on him too, perhaps parachuting out somewhere over Romania.

'What were you listening to?' asked Beverley, nodding towards his iPod.

'Brahms,' said the boy. 'I find his music soothing.'

'I do too,' replied Beverley. 'I once heard Lang Lang perform the *Paganini Variations* at the Royal Albert Hall.'

'I prefer the waltzes for piano,' said the boy.

'It's unusual for a boy of your age to enjoy classical music,' said Beverley. 'How old are you anyway? Seven?'

'And three-quarters. But I also enjoy Judy Garland, Supertramp and The Prodigy.'

'An eclectic selection.'

'Have you ever heard "Smack My Bitch Up"?' asked the boy.

'I must admit I haven't. Is it any good?'

'It's my favourite song of all time. The lyrics are outstanding.'

'Really? How do they go?'

The boy took a breath and then started singing, shaking his

body as if he was having some sort of fit while punching his arms in the air.

'*Smack my bitch up,*' he shouted. '*Change my pitch up. Aaahaaa-haaaaaaaaaaaahha. Eaaaheeyheeaheyyyee. Aaahaaahaaaaaaaaaaahha. Eaaaheeyheeaheyyyee.*'

'Good Lord,' said Beverley, putting a hand to her throat. 'That's appalling!'

A stewardess ran along the aisle and crouched down beside the seats, her cheeks flushed red. 'I'm sorry, madam,' she said. 'Could I ask you to have a word with your grandson? He's upsetting some of the other passengers.'

'He's not my grandson,' replied Beverley. 'We've only just met. His grandfather is using the facilities and asked me to keep an eye on him. But yes, I'll keep him quiet, don't worry.'

'I'd smack that bitch up,' remarked the little boy, glaring at the stewardess as she made her way back towards the galley area.

'That's a very rude remark,' said Beverley. 'Has no one taught you manners?'

The boy shrugged.

'What's your name?' he asked, not looking even slightly bothered by his chastisement.

'Mrs Cleverley,' she replied.

'No, what's your *name* name?'

Beverley rolled her eyes. 'Beverley,' she said.

'Beverley Cleverley?'

'That's right.'

The boy stared at her for a few seconds before bursting into uncontrollable laughter and rolling around on his seat while keeping a firm hold of his crotch area with his right hand, presumably to stop himself from urinating in his underpants.

'That's the funniest thing I've ever heard,' he said finally.

'I don't see why. What's your name?'

'Joe.'

'Joe what?'

'Joe Smith.'

'Well, frankly, that's the most boring name I've ever heard. Your mother must have had very little imagination.'

'Smack my bitch up,' repeated the boy, apropos of nothing.

'Your grandfather's taking a very long time,' said Beverley, looking up towards the toilet area.

'He's not my grandfather,' said the boy.

'But he said that he was.'

'I only met him today. I was at the airport with Mummy and Daddy and he asked me would I like some sweets and I said yes, and I ran off with him and then he took me on to this plane.'

Beverley stared at him, her mouth falling open in surprise.

'Are you lying to me right now?' she asked.

'No.'

'So you're being abducted?'

'I don't know what that word means.'

Beverley noticed two passports in the seat pocket in front of the man's chair and took them out, turning to the picture pages.

'Well, you have the same surname,' she said. 'So I assume you're just making all this up.'

'All right, I am,' he admitted.

'You're very naughty.'

'I don't know what that word means either.'

At that moment, the boy's grandfather reappeared and took his seat again.

'All better,' he said with a sigh.

'I'm delighted to hear it,' replied Beverley.

'Although, once I start, I'm ruined. I'll be in and out of that toilet from now until we land.'

'Perhaps you should remain up there?' she suggested. 'To save you popping back and forth. You could take the child with you to stretch his legs.'

He shook his head. 'No, I prefer sitting,' he said. 'Anyway, you never told me what you're going to Odessa for. If it isn't for . . .' And here he tapped his chin again.

'If you must know, I'm going to see a friend,' she said.

'A gentleman friend or a lady friend? Because, if you're new to the city, I'd be happy to show you around. You're a little older than the ladies I usually go for, but you're still a fine figure of a woman.'

Beverley's mouth fell open in a mixture of disgust and outrage. 'You must be twenty years older than me,' she said. 'Old enough to be my father, in fact. And you say that *I'm* too old for *you*?'

'I'm just being honest. There's life in the old dog yet. And not just in the old dog.' He winked at her lasciviously and she felt the Krispy Kreme doughnut she had unwisely consumed at Vienna Airport turning in her stomach.

'Well, as flattered as I am by such a delightful offer, I think I'll pass. As it happens, I'm going to Odessa to be reunited with my lover. Who, I'll have you know, is twenty-four years old.'

'That's disgusting,' said the man, pulling a face.

'But it's all right for you to hit on women young enough to be your granddaughter?'

'Totally different thing,' he said, waving a hand in the air. 'You must be a bit desperate if you're giving it away to a boy that age. You want a man, not a child. Look, the offer's there if you want it. If you don't, it's no skin off my nose.'

'Thank you, but I'll pass,' said Beverley, turning her attention back to her pages and hoping that he would leave her alone. But something in his words had stung her. Was she desperate? Possibly. But a young man like Pylyp didn't come along that often, and she missed him terribly.

Although, she had to admit to herself, she missed George terribly too.

THE REAL DEAL

'The thing is,' said Nelson, lying in bed with one hand behind his head and the other stretched across his chest. 'I'm not entirely sure that I am gay.'

'Oh, you are,' said Shane, propping up the pillows behind him as he sat up to light a post-coital cigarette. 'You most definitely are.'

'But how can you be sure? How can any of us be sure?'

'Well, the fact that we had sex three times last night and twice already this morning is a bit of a giveaway,' he replied. 'Not to mention that you really, really, *really* seemed to enjoy it.'

'Yes, I admit there's a certain logic to that,' said Nelson, waving away the cigarette smoke, which, so far, was the only thing that he didn't like about Shane. Other than that, he found him to be like Mary Poppins: practically perfect in every way.

'I have this theory,' continued Shane. 'If you like vagina-type things' – and here he gave a theatrical shudder – 'then you're probably straight. And if you like cock, then the chances are you're gay.'

'I suppose. My brother, Achilles, has been telling me for years that I'm into guys, and I've always denied it.'

'He sounds like a smart puppy.'

'I don't know how he knew it if I didn't.'

'Perhaps he's just very intuitive?'

'Achilles?' Nelson laughed. 'Oh no. Achilles is a complete idiot. He's fun to be around, but he's a total moron. Don't get me wrong. We love him. We just don't take him seriously, that's all.'

'And yet . . .'

'And yet,' admitted Nelson. 'Perhaps I need to give him more credit.'

'You've never had sex with a woman, then?' asked Shane, turning his head to blow the cigarette smoke away from Nelson's face.

'God, no,' he replied, shivering slightly. 'Although I once had drinks with my mother's late ghost and—'

'Her what?'

'Her ghost-writer.'

'Oh.'

'And I thought that perhaps we might be about to start dating each other. I got the impression that she liked me. She said as much, in fact. She said I wasn't the most boring man she'd ever met, and I was touched by that, although I didn't want to lead her on if I wasn't absolutely sure that she was right for me. Mother always told me be careful who I loved. Not to go around breaking young girls' hearts.'

'That's "Billie Jean".'

'What is?'

'Those song lyrics.'

'Really? Mother has been saying that to me since I turned thirteen. I thought it was something that she came up with.'

'No, Michael Jackson came up with it. And you know things are bad when you're taking romantic advice from Michael Jackson.'

'True. But she says that women can be very calculating when it comes to finding a rich husband.'

'If they're living in a Regency novel, perhaps,' admitted Shane. 'But in today's world, I'm not so sure. So did you arrange to meet this ghost for another drink? What was her name anyway?'

'The ghost's? I don't know. I don't think I ever asked.'

'You do know my name, don't you?'

'Of course I do. It's Shane.'

'That's a relief.'

'We said we'd see each other when she returned from her safari. But the lion put an end to those plans. I wasn't particularly looking forward to it anyway, I must admit, so it all worked out for the best, I suppose.'

They lay there in silence for a few minutes, until Shane put his cigarette out in the ashtray on his bedside table and turned to look at Nelson with a cheeky smile on his face.

'I have,' he said.

'You have what?'

'Had sex with a woman.'

Nelson's eyes opened wide in a mixture of fascination and horror. 'Have you really?' he asked. 'Why?'

'I thought it might be a bit like sprouts,' he said. 'My mother always said that sprouts were good for me, but I couldn't stand the taste of them. They made me gag. But she insisted that I eat them. And, in the end, they sort of grew on me.'

Nelson lay back down and looked up at the ceiling. It was a very different ceiling to the one he looked up at in his own bedroom, which was perfectly white. Shane's, on the other hand, was a little cracked and had some damp spots across it. And his flat wasn't the last word in luxury either, although he owned a lot of books and had a framed poster of *The Talented Mr Ripley* on the living-room wall, which, by coincidence, both had said was their favourite film. Still, Nelson felt that he could spend the rest of his life lying in that bed, staring up at that murky white ceiling, with Shane lying next to him, and be perfectly content.

'I have a very strange family,' he said finally. 'I should probably tell you that before this goes any further. I don't know if it's fair to inflict them on you.'

'Well, obviously, I know who they are. Your parents, I mean.'

'And we seem to be in the middle of some very turbulent times.'

'I've been reading about it. Is your father having some sort of nervous breakdown, do you think?'

'I don't know,' said Nelson. 'I hope not. Perhaps I should introduce him to my therapist. He's actually nothing like what the papers make him out to be, you know. He's been a real leftie all his life. A total liberal. He once said that he was a little disappointed that none of his children had turned out to be gay.'

'Well, now you know what to give him for Christmas.'

Nelson smiled.

'When I went to that speed-dating session,' he said, 'I really was intent on meeting a woman.'

'I don't doubt it. But you got lucky.'

'I did.'

'How quickly did you realize you liked me?'

Nelson thought about it. 'The moment we started talking,' he said. 'And when you asked me whether I wanted to go to the pub afterwards, I felt really excited and wasn't sure why. I was hoping you wouldn't ask anyone else to join us.'

'I had no intention of asking anyone else.'

'Could you guess?'

Shane moved his head back and forth, scrunching up his eyes as he did so. 'I had my suspicions,' he said. 'But I noticed you from the moment you walked into the room. There was just something about you. That air of sexy authority, perhaps. I was hoping we'd end up opposite each other at some point. What do you think the other policemen will think of it?'

'What other policemen?'

'At your station. I'm probably living in the past, but I imagine them being very macho and unaccepting.'

'Ah,' said Nelson, biting his lip and feeling a surge of anxiety coursing through his body. He'd forgotten the policeman's uniform that was strewn on the bedroom floor. 'Here's the thing,' he said. 'I'm not actually a policeman.'

'Oh,' said Shane, frowning. 'What, you're in training?'

Nelson turned to look at him, and the expression of disappointment on his lover's face made him realize that he didn't want to tell him the truth.

'Yes, that's it,' he agreed. 'I'm in training. So I'm not supposed to call myself an actual policeman yet. I'm a trainee policeman.'

'Semantics,' said Shane, kissing him on the forehead. 'As far as I'm concerned, you're the real deal.'

BLUE TICK

From the privacy of her bedroom, Elizabeth passed a very pleasant hour abusing complete strangers on Twitter.

She started with some easy targets – vegans, cat owners, Joe Wicks – before moving on to contestants from the quiz show

Pointless. An actress who'd been nominated for an Academy Award in the mid-nineties was castigated for her weight gain, while representatives of charities devoted to helping sufferers of anorexia were chastised for their own trim figures, which, she told them, was giving out entirely the wrong message. She trolled a few footballers and their wives, along with pop stars, backbench politicians and lesser-known members of the US Congress. Her own father was subjected to a string of insults, as was her aunt in Los Angeles. Pope Francis's fashion sense was criticized, as was Rami Malek's face and Heather Mills's one remaining leg.

With no one of any interest taking her bait, she grew bored and decided to pick on herself.

@ElizCleverley Got hit on today by a woman who thought I might bat for her team. It's actually quite flattering! She said I had beautiful skin.

Switching back, she tweeted an instant reply:

@TruthIsASword What a disgusting thing to post! Some women like men. Some women like women. Get over it! It's not worth tweeting about.

Outraged by her own response, she countered with:

@ElizCleverley Just remember, it's Adam and Eve. Not Adam and Steve.

There was simply no way that she was going to allow such a Neanderthal comeback to go unchallenged, however, and so quickly responded:

@TruthIsASword The Bible? Seriously? It's 2021, bi-atch. If you feel such antagonism towards lesbians, maybe you're in the closet yourself? Ever thought of that?

And that was when the shit really hit the fan. Elizabeth did not allow anyone, not even herself, to call her names.

@ElizCleverley I don't feel antagonism, it was just a light-hearted tweet, that's all. (Although I am str8.)

@TruthIsASword Protesting too much? Threatened mebbe?

@ElizCleverley Not threatened. Just don't like being accused of something that's not true.

@TruthIsASword Don't knock it till you've tried it.

@ElizCleverley Sounds like you've tried it enough for both of us.

@TruthIsASword No, I like guys, actually. I just don't choose to spend my time condemning others for the choices they've made in their lives.

@ElizCleverley Choices? CHOICES? It's not a choice, it's how you were born!!

@TruthIsASword That was just a mistake. You know what I meant.

@ElizCleverley You're the one who said it. You think lesbianism is a CHOICE? Hate crime hate crime hate crime.

@TruthIsASword I'm not even going to waste my time replying to that. Grow up. Be better. Do better.

@ElizCleverley You just did reply, bitch.

@TruthIsASword Only to say that I won't.

@ElizCleverley Seriously, have you nothing better to do with your time than argue with me on Twitter?

@TruthIsASword Lots. But this was such a wonderful opportunity for you to learn, and yet you're not willing to. Why is that? Calm down, btw.

@ElizCleverley You have no emotional effect on me whatsoever so there's no need to tell me to calm down.

@TruthIsASword Oh, please. I can hear you crying from here. You ok, hun?

@ElizCleverley What you hear is the sound of me laughing. AT YOU. Cos you're so pathetic.

@TruthIsASword And yet I have more than 100k followers and you have . . . oh wait . . . 6,329.

@ElizCleverley Anyone can get followers by being hateful. That's why Donald Trump had so many.

@TruthIsASword I blocked Donald Trump even before Twitter cancelled him. I told him that I wouldn't engage with someone who has such a history of misogyny.

@ElizCleverley I'm sure he hasn't got over the trauma.

@TruthIsASword It's called speaking TRUTH to POWER.

@ElizCleverley Oh, fuck off.

@TruthIsASword You fuck off.

@ElizCleverley No, you fuck off.

At which point she threw the phone down on the bed, infuriated with the conversation. Some people, she realized, were just too stupid to argue with.

Later, washed, dressed and pleasingly scented, she ate breakfast alongside Ustym Karmaliuk, who was digging into his morning supply of After Eights, and glanced at the replies that were flowing in, and noticed, for the first time, that her account @ElizCleverley had been granted a much-desired blue tick, indicating that she was now considered a person of importance, someone to whom the world should pay attention. Both her parents had received blue ticks years ago, and she'd been longing for one ever since. Indeed, back in the days of her failed sex tape, it had been one of her goals, but it had never materialized. Somehow, without even letting her know, a random person in Twitter headquarters had decided that she was at last worthy.

She let out a scream of delight, entranced by the changes that appeared on her dashboard. Not only could she see her regular notifications but there was now an extra panel alongside it revealing messages and replies sent only by other blue-ticked people. She was in. She had made it. In celebration, she took two After Eights from their slip cases and popped them in her mouth, ignoring the outraged expression on the tortoise's face.

From the newly established @ElizCleverley ✅ she wrote the following:

@ElizCleverley ✅ Wow, just realized that I have a blue tick! How long has that been there? Didn't even notice until now!

She watched as the congratulatory tweets began to pour in. There was nothing like a little #HumbleBrag to get the day off to a good start. To celebrate, she switched back to @TruthIsASword and tweeted:

> **@TruthIsASword** There's something about @BorisJohnson ✅'s face that makes me want to attack it with a machete.

And, within a few minutes, this latest post had been liked almost eight thousand times. Perhaps, she thought, it wouldn't be long before @TruthIsASword got a blue tick too. Now that would be a real triumph.

THE THIN END OF THE WEDGE

The Director-General of the BBC, Lord Wilfred Husbery, arrived in a wheelchair, having broken his ankle in a skiing accident in Hintertux over the previous weekend, where he'd been holidaying with a minor Kennedy, a Spice Girl and a former adviser to Vladimir Putin.

'I'm actually an excellent skier,' he declared as he wheeled himself behind his desk, which sounded unlikely, as he must have weighed more than 300 pounds and looked more likely to sink through the snow than glide across it. 'I might have been an Olympian if my father hadn't insisted that I go into the House of Lords. It was a rogue piece of ice that took me down.'

'And how does that happen exactly?' asked George, looking around at the artwork on the walls of the office, which included the incongruous juxtaposition of a Jeff Koons with a

Gainsborough, along with a portrait of the Two Ronnies in the style of Andy Warhol's *Marilyn Monroe*. To his left sat Ben Birnbaum, wearing a shirt and tie for the first time since his confirmation twelve years earlier, while to his right, Margaret Roberts was hovering slightly above her chair, as if she hoped to make a quick exit.

'Snow can be surprisingly deceptive,' replied Lord Husbery. 'It gives off an air of courteous serenity but, underneath, it's just waiting to rip the throat out of its next victim.'

'A bit like Emily Maitlis,' suggested George.

'Although, in my case, it was an ankle, not a throat.'

'Are you on painkillers?' asked Margaret.

'I am,' he replied. 'A glass of Macallan Estate single malt Scotch, administered orally, every hour on the hour. And the occasional Nurofen Plus. Together, they do the job quite nicely. Now,' he said, pressing his palms down on the desk before him, and George noticed how his wedding ring appeared to be fused deeply into the skin on the fourth finger of his left hand. 'It appears that we have a situation on our hands, yes? I've been reading about it in the papers, of course, but I thought I should hear your version of events before deciding what to do. That's what HR insisted on anyway.'

'This really has nothing to do with me,' said Margaret. 'So, if you'd like me to go back to my office, then that's perfectly fine. After all, I didn't post the original tweet, nor did I approve of its sentiments. I'm afraid that Mr Cleverley went rogue on me.'

Lord Husbery narrowed his eyes and stared at her. Approaching eighty years of age, he had long deplored the presence of women in the workplace. Women, he believed, were best kept in the home, like a budgerigar or a vacuum cleaner.

'And yet, Miss Roberts,' he declared, 'were you not the person who encouraged him to take part in an interview on the *Six O'Clock News* with a lady journalist?'

Margaret hesitated for a moment as the wheels in her head rotated. 'That's true,' she replied. 'But I assumed that with so many decades of experience in broadcasting, George would know better than to say something that would only make matters worse. I didn't for a moment think that one of our longest-serving presenters—'

'Some might say a national treasure,' interrupted George.

'Would have to be physically lifted from his chair and held down with a grip's hand over his mouth while we dragged him from the studio. I was under the impression that I was dealing with a professional.'

'If you don't mind me saying so, Miss Roberts,' said Ben Bimbaum, leaning forward, 'that's a little unfair to George, who at the time was under great duress and probably should have either pre-recorded the interview or been better prepped for it. Although, that said, I agree with everything you say and think you acted completely correctly.'

George turned his head to look at his producer with respectful awe.

'Personally, I don't see what all the fuss is about,' said Lord Husbery, sitting back in his wheelchair now and extending his arms wide. 'So, you don't like nancy boys. A man has a right not to like nancy boys. Of course, here at the BBC, we've always loved them. They're tremendous fun on gameshows, for example, or charitable endeavours like Children in Need. As it happens, my loader is a nancy boy.'

'Your loader?' asked Margaret.

'Yes. On shooting weekends.'

'I think many of my antagonists would like me to take

part in one of those,' said George. 'They'd wait for me to enter the woods, then take aim.'

'You really can't use the term *nancy boy* any more,' said Ben, tentatively.

'It's my office,' replied Lord Husbery.

'Yes, but it's offensive.'

'To whom? To you?'

'Yes, actually.'

'But you can't possibly imagine that I care about your opinion, surely?' he asked, looking genuinely baffled. 'You're a low-level producer of working-class stock and I'm the Director-General of the BBC.'

'It's a new world, Your Eminence,' said Margaret. 'Such phrases are considered outdated.'

'It's Your Lordship. And don't get me wrong, what a chap gets up to with another chap after lights out is entirely his own affair. I went to Eton, after all, so I do know something of these matters. What term would you prefer me to use, then?'

'You could just say *gay people*,' suggested Ben.

'Fine. Gay people. So, you don't like gay people. A man has a right not to—'

'I have absolutely no issue with gay people,' insisted George, sitting up in his chair, offended by the allegation. 'And while I despise people who pretend to take offence over the slightest blunder, I do find that an unfair suggestion. Some of my best enemies are homosexuals. And, of course, Ben here is married to a man named Mark—'

'Matthew.'

'Let them do what they like in the privacy of their own homes,' said Lord Husbery. 'But not where others have to watch. Wouldn't want to scare the horses, and all that. I make a point of never showing any affection towards my wife in public. Or in private, for that matter. And I don't hear her complaining about it.'

'If I may say,' said Ben, sounding annoyed by the direction the conversation had taken. 'If I may just say . . .' He paused for a long time. 'If I may say—' he repeated.

'Look, the issue here isn't about what George may or may not have said,' interrupted Margaret. 'It's what we're going to do about it.'

'No, you're wrong there,' said George. 'The issue is very much about what I said. Firstly, Lord Husbery, it was not homosexuals who I didn't attack, it was men and women of the transgender persuasion. But, as I say, I *did not* attack them. I offered support and encouragement to one of their number. But because I used the wrong pronoun, all hell broke loose. I was actually trying to *help* but, in their wisdom, the great collective minds of social media decided that I wasn't helping in the right way. And so, with nothing else to fill their morning, having already spent half an hour checking that all their fingers and toes were present and correct, they took their anger out on me. But, you know, just because you're part of a minority does not automatically qualify you for sainthood. You can still be small-minded, you can still be narcissistic and you can still be a bully.'

'But it's not just that, George,' said Margaret, shaking her head. 'It was also your use of the word *coloured*.'

'I admit, I got that very wrong,' said George, looking genuinely remorseful. 'And I feel terrible about it. But the terms keep changing and it gets increasingly difficult to keep up. I would never intentionally say something racist, because I'm *not* racist. Nor, for that matter, would I deliberately insult a transgender person, because I'm *not* transphobic. But people don't want to believe that because if they can put these labels on me, then they have a living, breathing human being upon whom they can take out their anger about inequality and injustice. But they've chosen the wrong person and it's deeply unfair. I remember being both criticized and praised for going on the Black Lives Matter march and—'

'Oh, please,' muttered Lord Husbery, rolling his eyes. '*All* lives matter.'

'No!' shouted George, standing up suddenly and kicking his chair from beneath him in a fit of spontaneous fury. 'It is simply wrong to say that!'

'Good heavens, George,' said the Director-General, rearing back in his wheelchair. 'What on earth—'

'I'm sorry, but there is nothing – *nothing* – that squeezes my lemons more than people saying that. It is the ultimate way of diminishing the experience of black people and the manner in which they've been treated over the years. The Black Lives Matter movement is not suggesting for a *moment* that their lives are of more intrinsic value than anyone else's. It is pointing out that, historically, black lives have *not* mattered to so many people around the world.'

'All right, George,' said Lord Husbery. 'Sit down. You've made your point.'

'I don't think I have,' replied George, reclaiming his seat but incandescent with rage. 'Saying "All Lives Matter" is like going to a cancer benefit and storming the stage to declare that Alzheimer's Matters. No one is suggesting otherwise! It's intentionally taking away from the fact that black people have suffered extraordinary hardship throughout history, from slavery in the States to the Stolen Generation in Australia to the Windrush scandal here in England. Black Lives Matter is saying to people "Stop killing us for no reason"; All Lives Matter is pretending that this doesn't happen. It's a nefarious attempt to stall any conversation about systemic racism. Remember, no one ever used that phrase until the BLM campaign came along, so it was invented and is being employed purely as a direct contradiction of these three simple words. And it's thrown out by pasty-faced, posh-boy, D-list actors of minimal talent who've grown up in such a cocoon of privilege that they think, if they haven't experienced prejudice themselves, then it doesn't exist. Trust me. I know. I've had far too many of them on the show over the years and, in the future, I'd rather not give airtime to people who, quite frankly, are too stupid to recognize their own biases and their lack of intellectual resources.'

There was silence in the room for a few moments as George calmed down.

'I'm sorry,' he said finally, nodding his head firmly, feeling a great sense of relief at having got that out. 'But I'm not just here for the comic relief, you know. I've lived my life with a very clear set of beliefs, entirely untroubled by bigotry, so to be accused of it by people who do not know me at all is simply too much. Now. Let me ask.' He took a deep breath and looked at Ben, the youngest person in the room. 'My daughter tells me that the phrase in current usage is *person of colour*. Is she correct in this?'

'Yes,' said Ben.

'Fine,' he replied. 'Then, naturally, I am happy to employ that term and will do so from now on.'

'What I don't understand,' said Lord Husbery, scratching his chin, 'is what's the difference. Why is it politically correct to use the phrase *person of colour*, but a racist insult to use the phrase *coloured person*? Surely they're the same words, just turned around?'

'It's completely different,' said Margaret.

'But how?'

'We should ask @TruthIsASword,' said Ben.

'What's that?' asked Lord Husbery.

'A Twitter account that's gone viral,' he explained. 'Whoever runs it is calling out any public figure who says the wrong thing. Naming, shaming and cancelling. He, she, it or they have built an enormous following over the last few days.'

'Sounds like a wonderful use of that person's time,' replied George, rolling his eyes. 'I feel sorry for the parents who put that particular moron through school and university. They may as well have pissed their money up against a wall.'

'Still,' said Lord Husbery, leaning forward. 'Can no one answer my question?'

An eerie quiet descended on the room and George looked from person to person, waiting to see whether any of them might be able to explain.

'The reason is this,' he declared finally in an authoritative voice, and all eyes turned to him nervously. 'The main difference between *coloured people* and *people of colour* has to do with context and ownership. *Coloured* originates in the American South, starting with signs on buses, in restaurants and toilets, but always in the context of exclusion and racism. *No Coloreds Allowed*, for example. In the seventies, the term *people of colour* was reclaimed in the US, but it took many years for it to find widespread usage in Europe. One of the reasons *people of colour* came to be used was that it encompassed all non-white people. For example, Latinos in the US are not considered white, but are they black? They often suffer the same racism and exclusion, but to call them black is not accurate. Although, that said, *people of colour* has its own problems and is not universally welcomed. It assumes, of course, that *white* is the default and that any other skin tone diverges from the norm. It homogenizes the non-white experience, which is anything but homogeneous.'

A long silence ensued and the prisoners at the dock stared at George in total bewilderment.

'Now,' he said. 'To move on to the charges of anti-Semitism. They're even more ridiculous. As it happens, I've always been a great supporter of the Jews. After all, Woody Allen is my favourite film-maker and remains a dear friend. Followed closely by Roman Polanski.'

'Oh Lord,' said Ben, bowing his head, as if in prayer. 'It's like we take one step forward, then two steps back.'

'Look,' said Lord Husbery, raising his hands in the air to indicate that he'd heard enough. 'If you ask me, the whole thing is a storm in a D-cup, as the actress said to the bishop. It'll blow over in a week or so, as the bishop said in reply. Some other idiot will say something that people pretend to be out-raged by and George here will resume his place as a popular figure—'

'A national treasure.'

'A popular figure in the broadcasting schedules. But I'm sure you all understand that heads will have to roll. The BBC simply cannot be seen to condone this sort of thing and so, regret-fully, I have no choice but to terminate both of your contracts with immediate effect.'

The three people seated opposite him looked at each other nervously.

'Both?' asked Ben. 'Which two do you mean?'

'You pair,' replied Lord Husbery, nodding towards Ben and Margaret. 'We can't get rid of the talent, so George stays, but you're both eminently replaceable. I'd be enormously grateful if you could both hand in your passes to the security guard who's waiting outside my office, and he will escort you from the building. Your personal effects will be sent on in due course.'

'What?' cried Ben.

'Me?' roared Margaret. 'I get the boot while this cantankerous old dinosaur gets to keep his job?'

'Oh, that's very unfair,' said George, turning to look at her with a disappointed expression on his face. 'My feelings are wounded by such ageist remarks. Be better, Margaret. *Do* better.'

'Oh, fuck off, you stupid old twat,' she snapped.

'There is nothing more offensive to my ears than the sound of a woman swearing,' said Lord Husbery, shaking his head and looking aggrieved.

'It's the thin end of the wedge,' agreed George.

'If you think that I'm going to take this lying down—'

'Don't worry,' said Lord Husbery. 'We don't want any unpleasantness. I'm happy to offer you a year or two's salary to ease your way back into civilian life. Perhaps you could buy a little tea shop somewhere? That's a lovely job for a woman.'

'Two years,' she replied. 'Two years and no gardening leave.'

'Fine, fine.'

Margaret nodded. This was an excellent deal for her, after all, as she'd recently been offered a job with a film production company and had been planning on accepting it.

'And what about me?' asked Ben Bimbaum, looking distraught. 'Do I get two years' salary?'

'Of course not,' said Lord Husbery. 'You're not important enough. But we won't charge you for the expense of sending your effects on. How does that sound?'

'This is all your fault,' said Ben, turning to George.

'I mean . . .' George shrugged, conceding the truth of this. 'I suppose it is. But there we are. What can I do?'

'You could resign in solidarity with me.'

After a respectful pause, George, Lord Husbery and even Margaret burst out laughing in unison, and it seemed as if they weren't going to stop for a long time, which led Ben to stand up and march out in a huff, directly into the welcoming arms of the burly security guard, followed soon after by Margaret.

'Well,' said George, looking at Lord Husbery with a satisfied expression on his face. 'On the whole, I think that went rather well, don't you?'

THE BOUNCY-BOUNCY

The address was located outside central Odessa, near Horkoho Park, and Beverley took a taxi there, stepping out on to the almost deserted street and looking around with a growing sense of unease. A strong wind was blowing and she pulled her coat around her, staring up at the tall buildings that stood on either side of the road as she walked along in search of Number 15. When she located the imposing grey doors, she was confronted by a series of bells and checked her notes again before pressing the intercom for Apartment 4. A voice answered, speaking quickly in Ukrainian, and Beverley frowned.

'Hello,' she said, enunciating her words loudly and slowly, employing the unusual syntax that she often used when confronted by a foreigner. 'I have come here . . . to your beautiful city . . . in search of the man . . . Pylyp.'

The woman replied by shouting something completely unintelligible into the intercom, and Beverley experienced a sinking sensation at the pit of her stomach.

'Pylyp Tataryn,' she said, turning back to the intercom. 'I

look for Pylyp Tataryn. Where is the man Pylyp Tataryn? Bring him to me!'

A long silence ensued, and just as she began to think that her entire journey might have been in vain, a buzzer sounded at the door, and she pushed it open with a sigh of relief.

Inside, she was surprised to discover a very pleasant court-yard, furnished with comfortable benches and with a circular pond in the centre, at the front of which stood a statue of an imposing-looking man wearing a Robin Hood hat on his head and a constipated expression on his face. She leaned forward to read the plaque that stood before it and, although she could not translate the words, she recognized the capitalized name at its heart and turned back to the stone appreciatively.

'So, Ustym Karmaliuk,' she said, smiling a little. 'We meet at last.'

She took a quick selfie on her iPhone and posted it to her Instagram account before turning in the direction of the marble staircase and ascending to the third floor, where she paused outside Apartment 4, taking a deep breath to steady herself, before knocking. She heard the sound of footsteps coming slowly down the hallway inside and, when the door opened, a small woman appeared, looking as if she was fully prepared to engage in a wrestling match, should she be so challenged.

'Hello,' Beverley said, speaking more loudly than necessary. 'Me: British woman.' She tapped the space between her breasts. 'You: Ukrainian woman.' And here she pointed towards her new acquaintance.

'I know I Ukrainian woman,' she replied. 'Why you tell me this?'

'Oh, you speak English,' said Beverley, breaking into a broad smile. 'Thank God!'

'I speak a little, yes,' said the woman with a shrug of her

shoulders. 'Also, some French, German, Italian and Norwegian. I learn all this from schoolman teacher. You not speak Ukrainian?'

'I'm afraid not,' replied Beverley, shaking her head. 'Does anyone?'

'Ukrainians do. And some Russians and Moldovans.'

'Still, one might call it a niche language.'

The woman narrowed her eyes. 'Here, in Ukraine, is many Ukrainians. All speak our own language.'

'Well, that makes sense, I suppose. Anyway, might I ask who you are? You're not Mrs Tataryn, I assume?'

'No, I not Mrs Tataryn. I *Dr* Tataryn.'

'Oh, of course,' said Beverley, thrown off her stride.

'I work hard for this title.'

'I'm sure you did. I did too.'

'You are doctor?'

'Well, after a fashion.'

'What you doctor of? You look like doctor of the facelifts.'

'Actually, I was awarded an Honorary Doctorate of Letters by my old university,' said Beverley proudly.

'You not real doctor?'

'I'm allowed to call myself Dr Cleverley on official correspondence.'

'But you not real doctor, no? Doctor with hands in the blood? You pretend doctor?'

'I suppose so, yes.'

'Then don't say you doctor. You just end up looking like slut.'

Beverley frowned. The woman's grasp of English was obviously poor so she decided to let that remark pass.

'Who are you anyway?' continued the woman. 'Your name this time. No doctor.'

'My name is Beverley Cleverley,' replied Beverley. 'I'm an English lady of good birth and breeding. I come in peace and mean you no harm.'

The woman stared at her and blinked several times.

'What you want here?' she asked. 'You sell the cabbage?'

'I sell the what?' asked Beverley.

'The cabbage. You sell the cabbage? I have woman who sell me the cabbage. I no need another.'

'I don't sell cabbage,' said Beverley, astonished by the accusation. 'Do I look like someone who sells cabbage door to door? This is a Hermès bag. It cost me eight thousand pounds.'

She held up her handbag, but the woman didn't even look at it. She was too intent on staring at Beverley's face.

'Then why you here?' she asked. 'I busy. Is day when I scrub dead skin from heels of feet.'

'Might I come in?' asked Beverley, not wishing to continue this conversation on the doorstep.

'To my home?'

'If that's all right.'

'But why?'

'Just to talk. I can explain better if I'm inside. I don't like standing out here like a Jehovah's Witness.'

'Who is this Jehovah's Witness? You are on trial?'

'No, it's a . . . it's a religion. Or a cult. I'm not sure. Forget it. It's neither here nor there. Please, if I could just come inside, then I can explain.'

The woman considered this for a moment before stepping aside, directing Beverley in with all the grace of Donald Trump greeting a gathering of black female Nobel Prize-winners.

'I have gun, so you know,' said Dr Tataryn. 'Any trouble, I shoot you in vagina.'

'What a bizarre target,' said Beverley. 'Although I'm sure it won't come to that. I only want to talk, that's all.'

She made her way down the hallway, which opened up into a large living room, and was immediately impressed by what she found. It was bright and well appointed, one wall holding a full library of books with broken spines, while the occasional tables and shelves all held interesting *objets d'art*.

'You keep a very nice home, Dr Tataryn,' said Beverley approvingly, running a finger along one of the bookshelves and examining it for dust. It came back spotless. 'It's a pity you don't live in London. You could do very well as a cleaner.'

'Why I want to clean in London?' asked the woman. 'I brain surgeon. I no clean for anyone. I have slut who comes clean for me.'

Beverley smiled. Perhaps, she decided, Dr Tataryn thought *slut* was a term of endearment.

'Oh yes,' she said. 'Pylyp did mention that.'

'You know Pylyp? He tell you of my slut?'

'No, he tell me that you are brain surgeon.'

'I best brain surgeon in Ukraine. Ask dogs on the street. They all know this.'

'I don't doubt it,' said Beverley. 'And many congratulations on rising to such an important position.'

Dr Tataryn shrugged her shoulders and sat down. 'Is brain surgery,' she said. 'Is not rocket science.'

'Indeed. May I take a look at your books?'

'Please,' said Dr Tataryn, looking a little baffled as to why this complete stranger had entered her home and was now examining her library.

'All very highbrow,' she said. 'Tolstoy, Dickens, Virginia Woolf. I have a Ukrainian publisher, as it happens. I don't suppose you've read any of my books?'

'You are writer?' asked Dr Tataryn.

Beverley reared back in horror, as if she'd been accused of doing her weekly shop at Lidl. 'I'm Beverley Cleverley,' she declared. 'I'm a very popular writer.'

Dr Tataryn frowned and thought about it before nodding. 'I hear of you, I think,' she said. 'You write the romances, yes? With the sluts and the doctors who want to save them from life as slut.'

'Well, I'm not sure I'd describe them in those exact terms,' said Beverley. 'But yes, you're probably on the right track.'

'Young pretty slut, she meets the doctor when she has the incurable disease, then he saves her life and reveals himself to be secret billionaire, yes? Then they do the bouncy-bouncy together.'

'The what?'

'The bouncy-bouncy.' Dr Tataryn, from a sedentary position, pushed her hips forward in an aggressive and come-hither fashion, like Madonna might do when encountering a twenty-two-year-old Moroccan dancer. 'The bouncy-bouncy.'

'If you mean what I think you mean, then not quite,' said Beverley. 'They do occasionally make love, it's true. But usually towards the end of the novel, and not until she has a ring on her finger.'

'Is all bullshit,' said Dr Tataryn, dismissing this with a wave of her hand. 'Doctors in my hospital, most of them fat pigs. Stinky stinky. Most of them whores at night, when shift over.'

'The doctors in your hospital are prostitutes?' asked Beverley, frowning. 'That doesn't seem likely.'

'Not prostitutes, no. Men who go to prostitutes. Men who pay the women for the bouncy-bouncy.'

'Oh yes, of course.'

'No secret billionaires in hospital.'

'Of course, what I write is a sort of fantasy,' said Beverley, sitting down on the sofa opposite Dr Tataryn and using the tone she employed when on stage at the Edinburgh Festival. 'It's not supposed to represent real life.'

'Is all bullshit,' repeated Dr Tataryn.

'Perhaps, but is very popular bullshit,' countered Beverley, feeling stung by the criticism.

A silence fell for a few moments while the two women sized each other up.

'So why you here?' asked Dr Tataryn. 'You are writing the trashy book set in Ukraine, yes? I have story for you. Story of poor girl who grows up without mother or father, but girl determines to make something of life. She work five jobs to put herself through medical school then becomes great brain surgeon in her country. She eats the beef steak every day with eggs and never shaves legs. No man wants to do bouncy-bouncy with her but she smart and she rich. Is good story. Is real story. Is true story.'

'Is your story?' asked Beverley.

'No, friend of mine.'

'Oh, I just assumed.'

'Do I look like I eat beef steak every day with eggs?'

'You do, as it happens. But no, I'm not writing about Ukraine. I actually came in search of Pylyp. Your son. He's a friend of mine.'

Dr Tataryn's eyes opened wide in suspicion. 'How you know Pylyp?' she asked.

'We met when I was a contestant on *Strictly*. He was my dance partner.'

Dr Tataryn rolled her eyes. 'Ever since he is little boy he is liking the dancing and the fancy clothes and the make-up,' she said. 'I want him to be important man. Doctor. Lawyer.

Television weather reporter. But no, he spends his days putting the mascara on dolls. His father, he beats him soundly when he is boy to take the evil spirit from him, but it grows, like a fungus between the toes. He says no son of mine is being fudge-packer who sexes the other boys. He would rather die than sit in room and watch him sex the other boys. But I say no, Pylyp is good boy, is nice boy, is just different boy.'

'Well, he's not gay, if that's what you're implying.'

'I don't know this gay,' said Dr Tataryn.

'He's not a homosexual,' she clarified. 'Pylyp is quite the ladies' man, as it turns out. Too much of one, as I've recently discovered.'

'He has many girlfriends, all his life. He is fourteen years old and he is bringing girls back here for bouncy-bouncy. Each day I come home, blood still under my fingernails from brain of some slut, and new girl walking out with love hearts in eyes.'

'A young man has an appetite, I suppose,' said Beverley, feeling a little miserable at the idea that she was only the latest in a long line of Pylyp's conquests.

'Young girls, women, older girls, older women, grandmothers. He is not caring who he sexes,' said Dr Tataryn. 'How old you?'

'I'm fifty-eight,' said Beverley. 'Although most people find that hard to believe.'

'You fifty-eight? I fifty-two.'

'You're kidding!'

'I never kid. I tell only truth, all the time. Liars must spend their many years in jail, I think.'

'Well, I suppose I have access to better skincare ranges in London.'

Dr Tataryn frowned. 'I think I know why you here,' she said. 'Pylyp, he sexes your daughter and gives her baby in the belly, yes? And now you say, come back, Pylyp, come marry my slut daughter. Or maybe you want him horsewhipped? You are right to be angry. I provide you with horsewhip, if you like. I keep one in closet for moments like this.'

'No, that's not it,' said Beverley, shaking her head. 'Although, speaking as a mother, I do have some strong words for him regarding my daughter, with whom he had an inappropriate relationship that he never revealed to me. Look, is he here? As much as I'm enjoying this conversation, I really need to talk to him.'

Dr Tataryn shook her head. 'He not here,' she said.

'Where is he?'

'Why I should tell you this? Maybe you want to hunt him down and shoot him?'

'I assure you that I don't,' said Beverley. 'And you were the one offering me a horsewhip a moment ago.'

'Man put baby in my belly when I am girl,' said Dr Tataryn. 'My father, he horsewhip him. Man marry me, though.'

'I see.'

Beverley looked around, hoping that the front door might open and her erstwhile lover would appear, but there was only silence from the staircase outside.

'The thing is,' said Beverley, turning back to her host, 'when Pylyp left London . . . oh, I'm so sorry. I haven't even offered my condolences.'

'Condolences? What are these?'

'Expressions of sadness. On your recent loss.'

'What loss?'

'Your husband.'

Dr Tataryn stared at her in surprise. 'My husband is dead ten years,' she said. 'Killed by tram. I do not cry then and I do not cry now. He free up my life to be better brain surgeon.'

Beverley stared at her, unsure how to take this news. 'But

Pylyp said he died only recently,' she said. 'That's why he came home, isn't it? To bury him and comfort you.'

'If Pylyp say this, then Pylyp lie. Unless he dig father up and bury him again someplace else. But I do not think this likely.'

'I don't think this likely either,' said Beverley, looking down at the floor in despair. 'But he is staying with you, isn't he?'

'He was staying with me,' admitted Dr Tataryn. 'But not now. He leave.'

'Where did he go?'

'He go back to London.'

'But that's impossible,' cried Beverley. 'I've been calling and messaging and emailing and have heard nothing in return. I thought he was dead. Or off fighting the Russians.'

Dr Tataryn laughed. 'Yes,' she said. 'Boy who spends life dancing is off fighting the Russians. This seem idea for comedy show. Or film with the Eddie Murphys. Say again how you know my son?'

'As I told you, we met on *Strictly Come Dancing*.'

'What is this *Strictly Come Dancing*?'

'It's a television programme where celebrities dance with professional dancers and a team of judges rates their performances.'

'Why?'

'Why what?'

'Why they do this?'

'Well, to entertain an audience. And to raise their public profile, I suppose. Most of them are washed-up soap stars or retired politicians. I was brought in to appeal to the intellectuals.'

Dr Tataryn considered this. 'People are entertained by watching other people dance?' she asked.

'I know it sounds odd, but it's actually very enjoyable. There are some lovely costumes. And a lot of sequins. Thousands of sequins, in fact. Millions, probably. And a glitterball for the winner.'

Dr Tataryn shook her head.

'And you were on this programme?'

'I was, yes.'

'So you celebrity?'

'Of a sort.'

'I thought you say you write books?'

'I do. But they're very popular books. And my husband is quite famous too. People know our name. We're what's called a power couple.'

'What is this power couple?'

'It's a husband and wife, high achievers both, who are in the public eye.'

'Like the Prince William and the Kate Middletons?'

'Well, I'm not sure they'd describe themselves in that way,' said Beverley. 'More like the Beckhams, really.'

'Who is this Beckhams?'

'David and Victoria. You must have heard of them? He was a footballer and she was a Spice Girl. Now, they're basically like Maria and Captain von Trapp from *The Sound of Music*, pimping out their children in order to keep the brand alive.'

'And what they do, these children?'

'Nothing, as far as I can tell. But they take a lot of pictures of themselves doing it. I'm not sure their ambitions stretch any further than that.'

'They sound like sluts.'

'Indeed.'

'And Pylyp, he dances with you?'

'We danced many dances.'

'And then you sex him?'

Beverley's mouth opened and closed a few times in surprise. 'Well, yes. I sexed him. I mean, we sexed each other. I mean, we had sex with each other. That is to say, we made love.'

'You old woman, but still you sex boy like Pylyp?'

'I'm not an old woman,' insisted Beverley. 'I'm a lady of a certain age. And Pylyp is not a boy. He's a man.'

'He is boy. And you sex him. You like sexing the little boys?'

'He's not little.'

'He is little where it matters,' said Dr Tataryn, tapping her forehead. 'Up here. Up here in brain. I never perform surgery on him up here because is nothing to work on.'

'I think you're being very unfair, if you don't mind me saying so.'

'I do mind you saying so. I don't need you to tell me about my stupid son. And I do not like you sexing him. Bouncy-bouncy is not right for woman as old as you.'

'Well, I enjoyed sexing him and I'd like to go on doing it, so perhaps we can put an end to this inane conversation and you can tell me where he's gone.'

'I tell you already. He go back to London.'

'But that's impossible!'

'Why is impossible? Is very possible. Plane brings you here. Plane sends him there. He like London. Many women there to dance with and sex.'

Beverley looked down at her hands, which were trembling slightly, and for the first time she noticed how thin her fingers had grown. Blue veins had appeared under her skin too. These were not the hands that had attracted so many admirers in her youth. A thought occurred to her.

'Do you know a young woman?' she asked. 'With frizzy black hair, big bosoms and long legs?'

'You mean Karabina?'

'Do I?'

'I don't know, do you?'

'I saw her. Here. In this apartment. When I was Skyping Pylyp. She kept appearing in the background. He said she was his cousin.'

Dr Tataryn laughed. 'She not his cousin. He sex her. He sex her all the time when he is here. You very stupid woman. Maybe you perfect for my son.'

'He said he loved me.'

'He say that to every girl he sex. Every woman, too. Every grandmother. Pylyp sex everyone. Except me. He never sex me.'

Beverley looked up in disgust. 'Well, I should hope not,' he said. 'You're his mother.'

'I know. I just say.'

'Well, it's a bit of a peculiar thing to say.'

'Oh no,' said Dr Tataryn, putting a hand to her face. 'Writer of silly stories think brain surgeon say peculiar thing! How will I get over hurt? Is shame too great to live with. I go now, take gun, and blow head from shoulders.'

'I loathe sarcasm,' said Beverley, gathering up her coat and bag and standing up. 'You're a very rude woman, Dr Tataryn.'

'Boo hoo,' she replied, pretending to cry. 'Stupid writer who like sexing the little boys, she call me rude. I hang myself from nearest lamp-post.'

'How childish.'

'Moment you leave, I gather all pills in house and swallow them with whisky.'

'This is not a conversation that I want to continue.'

'Police come later and they find wrists sliced open with scalpel.'

'Oh, shut up.'

Beverley made her way towards the front door before turning around and offering one final salvo.

'You can tell your son that if he thinks he can make a fool of me, he's got another think coming,' she said. 'After all, I still have his tortoise!'

OVER THE RAINBOW

'I'm sorry, you did what now?'

Dr Angela Gosebourne placed her pen and notebook in her lap and stared across at Nelson, uncertain whether she'd heard him right. Her eyes were red-rimmed from crying, something he'd noticed when he'd entered her office.

'I quit my job,' he said. 'At the school. I told them I didn't want to work there any more.'

'I see,' she replied, nodding her head as she considered this. 'And when did all this happen?'

'A few hours ago,' he said. 'I was waiting for Mr Pepford outside his office when he arrived. The funny thing is, it was exactly the same seat that I used to sit in when I was a boy and being blamed for being bullied. When he showed up, he gave me his usual look of disdain before saying that he didn't have time to talk to me as he'd been out with Martin Rice the night before and had a rotten hangover. I told him that I didn't much care, that I had something to say and he could listen or not listen, just as he pleased, but I was going to say it anyway. That shocked him, I don't mind telling you.'

'The worm has turned, it seems.'

'I'm not a worm,' said Nelson, frowning.

'No, I didn't mean that you are. It's just a saying, that's all. A *bon mot*.'

'I know it's a saying. I'm not an idiot. I just don't like being compared to a worm, that's all.'

Angela said nothing for a few moments, uncertain whether she should congratulate herself on instilling some much-needed confidence into her patient or whether she should throw him out for his rudeness. She really wasn't in the mood for this today. Not after what she'd just discovered.

'My apologies,' she said finally. 'So what happened then?'

'Well, I told him that I no longer wanted to be a teacher. That I loathed the children and thought he was a total twat.'

'You said that?'

'I said exactly that.'

'Gosh. An *ad hominem* attack. Okay. Go on.'

'Then I said that it had been a mistake for me ever to seek employment at the same school where I had been a student and that I no longer wanted to be cloistered in an institution where favouritism and bullying ran riot and we had a special code word for every time one of the girls got knocked up by one of the boys. His face went puce – I doubt anyone had ever spoken to him like this before – and he just stared at me as if I'd gone mad, before bursting out laughing and sitting down behind his desk. *You've obviously had a bad night's sleep, Cleverley,* he told me. *I suggest that you get back to work and we forget this conversation ever happened or you might find yourself in detention.*'

'Detention?'

'I know! I'm a teacher, I told him, not a student. You can't put me in detention. But he was right about one thing, I said. It wasn't just that I'd had a bad night's sleep. I'd barely had any sleep at all. In fact, I'd been shagging all night long and only got about two hours.'

'Good Lord!' said Angela, astonished. 'And is that true?'

'Oh yes. I barely got a wink.'

'I can't imagine he liked that very much.'

'He didn't. He told me that if I said one more word, then he'd fire me. And I told him that he must be as deaf as he is stupid because – hello! – I'd already resigned. Things went rather downhill from there.'

'In what way?'

'He took off his shoe and threw it at me.'

Angela sat back in surprise. 'He did what?'

'He took off his shoe and threw it at me. His right shoe. Then he took off his left and threw that one too. I was only standing about twelve feet away, but he missed both times, which I thought was a bit lame. It reminded me of that time a journalist in Baghdad threw his shoes at President Bush.'

'I remember that. He actually dodged them very well.'

'He did. Lightning-quick reactions.'

'Still, an extraordinary thing for a headmaster to do.'

'That's what I thought.'

'And what happened then?'

'He sort of sank back into his chair and repeated that he had a terrible hangover and wasn't even sure this conversation was taking place. I told him it definitely was. And I had meant every word. That's when things started to get strange. He went very quiet, then turned around in his chair and looked out the window and began singing "Somewhere Over The Rainbow".'

' "Somewhere Over The Rainbow"?'

'Yes. From *The Wizard of Oz*.'

Angela stared at him, utterly bewildered now. 'But . . . why?' she asked.

'I wondered that too. I asked him whether he was all right and he spun back and, in a rather good soprano, sang of how someday he'd wish upon a star and wake up where the clouds were far behind him. Then his face went a strange colour, sort of lavender I'd call it, and I asked whether he needed some water. There was a bottle on a side table and I turned around to pour some into a glass and, when I turned back, he'd taken his trousers off. He'd gone quite mad, you see.'

Angela frowned. 'As a clinical psychologist, you must understand that I don't much care for the word *mad*.'

'No, but there's really no other way to put it. He stood up and danced around for a little, then sat back down again, in his shirt and underwear.'

'Good heavens. It sounds like quite the *cri de cœur*.'

'Then he started calling me Roger, for some inexplicable reason, and said that he'd fought with T. E. Lawrence in the Battle of Aqaba. A man of peculiar tastes, he said of Lawrence. I pointed out that, as far as I was aware, Lawrence had died in the thirties while he himself could not have been born until the late sixties, and he stood up and told me I was a fool to believe all the rubbish that's written in the newspapers, that Lawrence was alive and well and living in a commune in Milton Keynes. At that point, I called one of the school secretaries and she came in and found him lying on the sofa, weeping like a baby. An ambulance was called, and that, as they say, was pretty much that.'

'What an extraordinary start to your day,' said Angela.

'It was. And it was annoying too, because it meant I had to repeat my resignation to the school secretary. *What about today's classes?* she asked. Bugger today's classes, I told her. Bugger the classes, bugger the students, and bugger you! You should have seen her face! And then Martin Rice came out of his classroom, I suppose he must have heard the commotion, and asked what was going on, so I said I'd resigned and I knew full well that he was the person who'd got Sarah Wilmot from Year 10 pregnant, that he was responsible for the Code Purple.'

'And was he?' asked Angela. 'If so, it's a matter for the police.'

'I have no idea. But I've had my suspicions, and he didn't deny it, just went a little pale, and said that if I repeated that to anyone, then I'd be eating my dinner through a straw for the next six months, so I marched right up to him and punched him in the nose, and I think I must have broken it because there was blood everywhere. He doubled over and didn't even fight back! That's what you have to do with bullies, isn't it? Beat them at their own game. The boys were delighted, of course. They all stood up on their desks and started shouting encouragement at me, like we were in the last scene of *Dead Poets Society*.'

'Nelson,' said Angela, sitting back in her chair and looking a little exhausted by the drama that he had related. 'I do think this is something you might have discussed with me first. Major life decisions can have consequences that you wouldn't imagine. You might wake up tomorrow and regret it.'

'I won't regret it,' said Nelson confidently. 'I knew exactly what I was doing and I'm glad that I saw it through. I'm only sorry that I can't do it again. I hated that place. I hated the teachers, the pupils, the desks and the chairs. I hated the smell of disinfectant and sweat. I hated the fact that I'd spent so much of my life there.' He thought about it for a moment. 'And I hated the food. I really hated the food.'

'Well, it's a school, Nelson,' replied Angela. 'What did you expect, cordon bleu?'

'Something digestible,' he said. 'No, I'm better off out of the place. I would have done someone an injury if I'd stayed any longer. Most likely myself.'

Angela sighed and scribbled a few things in her notebook.

'What are you writing?' asked Nelson.

'Nothing for you to worry about.'

'Still, I'd like to know. Is it about me?'

She looked up at him with a derisive expression on her face. 'No, Nelson, it's a reminder for me to pick up laundry detergent on the way home. Of course it's about you. This is your session.'

'There's no need to be sarcastic,' he said, feeling a little miffed. 'That's not very professional.'

'I'm sorry,' she said. 'You're quite right. I have to admit that I'm not feeling myself today.'

'Is there anything you'd like to talk about? You do look a bit peaky, if you don't mind my saying.'

'Plenty of things,' she replied. 'Only not with you.'

'I'm a good listener.'

'You're also my patient. And I'm your therapist. We don't want to go down the transference and counter-transference route. So let's stay on track, shall we? All right, you've quit your career. It's an extreme action, but sometimes a person can just walk away from their job on the spur of the moment and it can prove to be the best decision of their life. But staying at home on your own every day isn't going to fix your problems with women. Especially when you're still living with your parents. One thing I wanted to talk to you about, in fact, is the possibility of you moving out. And perhaps persuading all your siblings to move out too. Letting your father live his own life without having to take care of you all.'

'My parents, you mean,' said Nelson. 'My mother and my father.'

'Well, sure,' she said. 'If that's the way things go.'

'It's certainly on my agenda,' he agreed. 'And as for my

problems with women, they're completely fixed.' He waved a hand in the air. 'Nothing to worry about there at all.'

Angela tried not to laugh. 'Just like that?' she asked.

'Just like that,' he repeated, giving her his best Tommy Cooper impression.

'So,' said Angela. 'You said that you enjoyed intimate relations last night?'

'I did.'

'And where did you meet your partner?'

'At a speed-dating session. We struck up a conversation, went for a drink afterwards and there we are. Smash bang.'

Angela stared at him and had to admit to herself that he seemed to be both telling the truth and very happy about it.

'Again, very sudden,' she said. 'Although, as we've said, that's not necessarily a bad thing. May I ask what the girl's name is?'

'Shane,' said Nelson.

'Shane is a boy's name.'

'Yes, he's a boy. Well, a man. I mean, he's my age. Twenty-two.'

'Right.' Angela nodded and thought about this. 'So you're in a gay relationship?'

'Labels, labels, labels,' replied Nelson with a sigh. 'Must we label everything? I'm in a relationship with someone I like and yes, he happens to be a man. I had sex with a man and really enjoyed it. Does that make me gay?'

'It probably does, yes.'

'Fine. Then yes. I guess I'm gay.'

'Congratulations.'

'Why are you congratulating me?'

'On being gay.'

'Is that something that's worthy of congratulation?'

'Well, on coming out, then.'

'Right,' he said. 'Thanks, I suppose. Only I don't know if I have literally *come out*, as you say, which is such an old-fashioned term, when you think about it.'

'Quite. Well, you seem very happy. And that's a positive thing.'

'I'm a new man. So much so that when I was travelling here on the Tube, I struck up a conversation with a pretty girl and it went very smoothly. Had I wanted to ask her out, I'm sure I could have done so.'

'And did you want to?'

'Of course not. I'm gay now, remember?'

'Yes. Sorry.'

'Also, you may have noticed that I'm dressed as myself.'

'I had noticed that, yes. And I'm very pleased.'

'I feel like I'm cured.'

'You certainly seem . . . altered,' she admitted. 'Meeting this Shane fellow has clearly done you the world of good. But I'd hesitate to say that you're cured. Let's just say that you've had a breakthrough. I'm glad that I've been helpful to you.'

'Oh, it's had nothing to do with you,' said Nelson with a shrug. 'No offence, but we barely know each other.'

'Still. The breakthrough came on my watch, so to speak.'

He nodded. 'If you need the validation, that's fine. Take it.'

Angela pursed her lips and began to re-evaluate who was currently her least favourite Cleverley.

'So what will you do now?' she asked. 'For work, I mean?'

'As it happens, I've already got another job.'

'You have? That was quick.'

'Well, I have to pass a physical and take a written examination. But I think I'll be fine. I'm quite healthy, really.'

'And what are you going to be?'

'A policeman.'

'And why a policeman, if I might ask?'

'Because I was dressed as one when I met Shane, and he thinks I'm in training. So I have no choice but to put in an application.'

Angela poured herself a glass of water, which she drank slowly as she thought this through.

'Have you ever wanted to be a policeman?' she asked.

'Oh no. I don't like fights and I imagine there's an awful lot of pulling people to the ground and shouting at them to put their hands behind their backs.'

'So let me see if I have this right, then. You've met a man and fallen in love—'

'Well, I wouldn't go so far as to say that I'm in love. But I daresay it's only a matter of time. I've definitely fallen in like, if that helps.'

'And because he thinks you're a policeman, you've quit your job and are signing up to a career that frightens you, just so he won't realize that you only wore the uniform to feel confident around women, a sex that you say no longer interests you.'

Nelson considered this for a moment before nodding his head. 'Yes, that's about the long and the short of it. What do you think, are you proud of me?'

DELETE CONTACT

After Nelson left, Angela rose from her seat and walked towards the window, watching through the net curtains as he exited the building and turned right in the direction of the

Tube station. She looked utterly miserable, like Melania Trump on date night, and put a hand to her stomach, holding it there for a few moments, feeling tearful for the baby that she'd believed herself to be carrying but which her doctor had told her that morning was nothing more than a phantom pregnancy, brought on by stress, depression and an unhealthy diet. Her periods had stopped, her stomach had grown bloated, and she needed to change her lifestyle entirely if she was not to fall seriously ill.

It wasn't that she had particularly wanted a child – in fact, motherhood wasn't something she'd ever felt a great pull towards – but now that the possibility had been taken away from her, she felt the loss of what might have been. And, she had to admit, she'd hoped that a baby might induce George to leave Beverley and start a new life with her.

She picked up her phone and scrolled through her contacts, stopping at C, before picking out his name. Then, taking a deep breath, she pressed 'Delete Contact'.

AND THIS WILL MAKE YOU MISERABLE

Although the day had started well, it went downhill quickly after breakfast when Elizabeth learned something so deeply upsetting that by the time she met Wilkes in his favourite coffee shop, the Fair Trade Equality Place for All Love, she was in a state of heightened anxiety. Understanding the need to remain calm at such a troubling moment, however, she did her best to take comfort from the nettle-grass tea she ordered, and when he eventually arrived, her disquiet was not eased by his shambolic appearance.

'Good God, Wilkes,' she said as he sat down. 'You look terrible.'

'I'm on the turn,' he said, ordering a goat's-urine banana smoothie from a passing waiter whose nametag read *I Don't Believe in Names (they/their).*

'You're going through the menopause?'

Wilkes shook his head. 'I wish,' he said. 'It's so discriminatory that only women get to experience that. Women are really lucky, when you think about it. Cis women, I mean. It's part of their privilege.'

'I suppose you'll have to blame God for that,' said Elizabeth.

He frowned. 'You know I don't believe in God,' he said.

'I know. Sorry. I just meant that, if there was a God, then it would be His fault.'

'If there was a God,' he replied with a deep sigh. 'I very much doubt that He would be a He anyway. Speaking of which, I woke up feeling binary again this morning, so, for now, will be referring to myself as I.'

'That didn't last long,' she said, rolling her eyes. She really wasn't in the mood for his nonsense today. 'So when you say you're on the turn,' she asked, sitting as far back in her chair as she could in order to avoid the stench of effluent that was seeping from his person; it was at moments like this that she missed the days of social distancing. 'What are you referring to, exactly?'

'The hygiene turn. It's now been ten days since I last washed, so my body is starting to release its own essential oils. I'm incredibly sticky all over, my boxer shorts are practically stuck to my crotch, and the strange thing is, I find it really arousing. You don't fancy coming back to mine to peel them off me, do you?'

'I don't,' she said slowly as I Don't Believe in Names (they/their) left Wilkes's smoothie on the table. 'It's a lovely offer, but no.'

'Thank you,' said Wilkes, looking up with a smile. 'I appreciate you.'

'I appreciate you too,' replied I Don't Believe in Names (they/their). 'And I appreciate your appreciation.'

'I appreciate your appreciation of my appreciation.'

They walked away wearing a serene expression on their face and Elizabeth stared into her boyfriend's face. There was something not quite right going on there.

'You look . . .' She hesitated, not wishing to sound rude. 'I don't quite know how to describe it, but it's almost as if you sprayed yourself with suntan lotion and then went for a ten-mile run in the blistering heat.'

'It's my pores,' he explained. 'All the poisons in my bloodstream are escaping.'

'Through your face?'

'Well, not just through my face, no. Through my hands, my legs, my feet, my back. Everywhere.'

She bit her lip, wondering whether it would be wrong to go into the ladies' toilets, light a match and hold it up to the smoke detector in the hope that the sprinkler system might activate and give him, at the very least, a rudimentary wash.

'Are you sure what you're doing is healthy?' she asked.

'Joaquin Phoenix did it for seven months.'

'Is he really who you want to model yourself on?'

Wilkes shrugged and reached for his smoothie but, in his

desperate attempts to get a firm grip on the glass, it slipped from between his sweaty fingers and Elizabeth had to reach out to grab it before it spilled mushed banana and goat's piss all over them both.

'Probably best just to use the straw,' she suggested, and he did so, bobbing his head up and down as he filled his body with bacteria derived from animal waste.

'God, that's absolutely disgusting,' he said happily. 'What's up with you anyway? You look upset about something.'

'I am. I have some really bad news.'

'Oh?'

'You need to remain calm when I tell you. We can fix this; I know we can.'

'Okay, you're scaring me now,' he said, taking another mouthful of his drink and gagging visibly. 'What is it? Just tell me.'

She reached for her phone and, to his surprise, took a quick selfie of the two of them, before opening her Instagram feed and posting the picture with the following caption:

@ElizCleverley Spending time with @Wilkes4Love

'Look!' she said, turning the screen around for him to see.

'What am I supposed to be looking at?'

'Your Instagram account has disappeared. There's no link coming up to your name. And the same thing is happening on Twitter. I tried to tweet earlier that I was meeting you and there was no sign of your feed.'

Wilkes laughed and shook his head. 'Is that all?' he asked, sounding relieved. 'Honestly, I thought it was something serious.'

'This *is* serious,' she insisted, surprised by his nonchalance. 'It's about as serious as things can get. Has someone hacked you, do you think? Was it the Russians?'

'No,' he replied with a self-satisfied smile, his favourite type. 'The thing is, I deleted all my social media accounts last night.'

Elizabeth did her best to remain steady as these simple and yet utterly inexplicable words filtered through the complex ecosystem of her mind, but soon reared back in her seat as if she'd been shot.

'You did what?' she shouted, the words emerging in a tone that neither she nor Wilkes had ever heard before, but that reminded I Don't Believe in Names (they/their), who was passing by at that moment, of the little girl in *The Exorcist*, when the devil's got a hold of her and expresses its strongly held belief that Father Merrin's mother is most likely engaging in fellatio with strangers while drifting unaccompanied through the underworld.

'I deleted them,' he repeated. 'Last night. Before I went to bed. Actually, I'm not sleeping in a bed at the moment. I'm sleeping on the floor. To get in touch with the woodwork. Apparently, if you sleep with your ear to wood, you can hear the screams of the trees as the chainsaws ripped through them.'

'But why?' she asked in disbelief. 'Why would you do such a thing?'

'To share their pain.'

'Not that; why would you delete your accounts? Have you gone insane?'

'I just realized that I'd prefer not to be part of the social media world any more,' he explained. 'From now on, I simply want to enjoy my life instead of constantly documenting it. To exist in the moment and allow my memories to live up here' – he tapped the place where his brain might have been in a more forgiving biosphere – 'instead of in one of these.' He pointed now towards Elizabeth's iPhone. 'We live on these devices now but, in reality, they're a total waste of time. Think about it. You spent however many minutes telling strangers that you were meeting me for coffee, minutes that you could have spent doing something more productive.'

'Like what? Lying on the floor listening to what our kitchen tiles might have to say?'

'And ultimately,' he said, ignoring this, 'you achieved nothing. In the end, who cares?'

'My followers care!'

'No, they don't. Look, show me that thing.'

He grabbed her phone off the table, his greasy fingers skating across the screen, leaving a slimy residue behind, and pointed towards the tweet in question. 'Ninety-four likes and eight retweets. That's all you got. So ninety-four people who don't know either of us have now been given the information that you're meeting me for coffee. And they'll already have forgotten.'

'But I have a blue tick!' she cried. 'The common people want to know how blue-ticked people fill their days. Otherwise, how can they have aspirations?'

'Come on, Elizabeth,' he said calmly. 'It's all bullshit. I had an epiphany and I'm responding to it, that's all. Like Dylan, when he went electric.'

'This is deeply shocking,' she said.

'Tell me this,' he said. 'Does getting likes make you happy?'

'Of course it does! It's like sex. Only better.'

'If you think that, then you're having sex with the wrong people.'

'I'm having sex with *you*.'

'Oh yes,' he said, laughing. 'Own goal there.'

'Look,' she said, reaching across to take his hand before thinking better of it. She hadn't carried any hand sanitizer since getting the vaccination. 'It's not too late to fix this. You have thirty days to reactivate your account after you've closed it. You won't lose any of your followers and no one will be any the wiser.'

'But I don't want to reactivate my account,' he protested. 'And anyway, I didn't choose that option. I just deleted the entire thing. It's over for me. I'm no longer on social media.'

'Oh, sweet mother of Jesus,' she cried, putting her hands to her mouth. 'What have you done? IN THE NAME OF ALL THAT IS GOOD AND HOLY, WHAT HAVE YOU DONE?'

'I've become free,' he said. 'I've reclaimed my privacy. Social media is over anyway. It's so last year. The fact is, when you sign up for an account and accept the terms and conditions, there should also be a warning attached: *And this will make you miserable*. Actually, you should tweet that, that's some solid wisdom there.'

'But you've—'

'Seriously, have you ever heard someone say: *my life is so much better now that I'm on Twitter*? Invisibility is a good thing.'

'Who has *ever* found invisibility to be a good thing?'

He thought about it. 'Lord Lucan,' he said. 'Salman Rushdie, for many years. The Invisible Man himself was very big on it.'

'The Invisible Man wasn't *real*!' she shouted.

'Wasn't he, Elizabeth? Wasn't he? Just because people couldn't see him doesn't mean he should be denied an identity. I'm disappointed in you for saying that. Be better.'

'Are you being serious with me right now? Are you *actually* being completely fucking serious?'

'Yes. I've changed. I've evolved.'

'Overnight?'

'Overnight. I think it has something to do with all the toxins that are draining out of me. All I want now is to do good without other people needing to know about it. I want to be virtuous rather than signal my virtue. Isn't that a good thing? Honestly, Elizabeth, you should try it.'

He reached for her iPhone again, but before he could grasp

it between his oleaginous digits, she swiped it off the table and returned it to the safety of her pocket.

'Don't even think about it,' she snapped.

'Just give it some thought,' he said. 'You could deactivate just one platform and see how you get on.'

'I would rather show up at an open-mic poetry night,' she insisted, raising her voice again. 'I would rather be stuck in a lift for three hours with Harry and Meghan while they tell me how to live my best life.'

'Ah, Harry and Meghan,' said Wilkes, putting his hands together, as if in prayer. 'Their weekly press interviews complaining about press intrusion really force the media to take a long hard look at itself.'

'I'm not deleting anything.'

Wilkes frowned. 'I don't feel that you're appreciating me right now,' he said.

'Well, I don't feel very appreciative.'

'Why not?'

'Gouge out my eyes, Wilkes. Rip off my toes. Pull the ears from my head. But don't ever come between me and my followers.'

'It's that kind of talk that makes me wonder whether you might have a problem.'

'Me? Look in the mirror, if you can stand it. If anyone has a problem, it's you.'

He offered her his most insufferable expression. 'If you say so. But look, it's only been twelve hours and I already feel better. I feel cleansed.'

'That's because your body is literally leaking ectoplasm from every orifice. Where's your phone anyway?'

'I smashed it up with a hammer.'

'What the fuck?'

'Look, just trust me, Elizabeth, when we're in Indonesia you won't even be thinking about social media. Your fingers will be exactly where they should be. Cleaning the festering wounds of lepers.'

A long pause ensued and Elizabeth shook her head, more in sorrow than in despair. In order for him to truly understand the importance of her words, she spoke very, very slowly.

'But what . . . on earth . . . would be the point . . . of going to a leper colony,' she asked, 'if I couldn't . . . tell people . . . about it?'

Wilkes laughed. 'Are you being serious?'

'I'm being completely, one hundred per cent serious.'

'You can just do good for its own sake. Pro bono, as they say. And God knows, Bono knows a thing or two about philanthropy.'

She stared at him as if he'd gone entirely mad.

'I'm worried about you, Wilkes,' she said. 'Do you think you might be having some sort of breakdown?'

'Why, because I suddenly have clarity of purpose?'

'I wonder whether all of this is happening because you need a good wash. And a shave. And to cut your nails. And to put on some deodorant and some moisturizer. My God, you haven't even put on any moisturizer, have you!' She looked around and appealed to I Don't Believe in Names (they/their), who was standing behind the counter now, performing a salutation to the sun, raising her voice to a pitch of hysteria. 'HE'S NOT EVEN WEARING ANY MOISTURIZER!' she screeched.

'Jesus, Elizabeth,' said Wilkes, reaching for her hand. 'Calm down, will you?'

'Don't touch me,' she said, pulling back from him. 'I don't know what kind of bacteria you're covered in. I don't want to be Patient Zero for Covid-21.'

He sat back, looking both disappointed and hurt. 'Perhaps I've thrown all of this at you too quickly,' he said. 'Maybe when we're in Indonesia—'

'I don't think I can go,' she said, shaking her head. 'I don't appreciate this new Wilkes.'

'You can't fall out of appreciation just like that!' he protested. 'I'm still the same man I was yesterday, Elizabeth. Just without social media. I might be a little more pungent but—'

She threw her hands in the air.

'I don't know who you are any more. Or what you are.'

'I'm Wilkes,' said Wilkes. 'The same Wilkes you fell in appreciation with. I've just disconnected from the grid, that's all. Like Keanu, when he slipped out of the matrix.'

Elizabeth stared at him as if she'd never heard such nonsense in all her life and stood up, gathering her coat and bag.

'You don't get it, do you?' she asked as she hovered over him, looking down at his greasy hair and dripping complexion. 'The grid is life, Wilkes! THE GRID IS LIFE!'

I HAVE TAKEN A LOVER

Achilles was not accustomed to girls ignoring his messages, which made Rebecca's infrequent responses all the more bewildering. He had thought they were getting on well, even welcoming the fact that she was proving to be more of a challenge than his usual conquests. And so, when he woke to discover a message from her at last, he felt considerable relief to learn that he was not, at the ripe old age of seventeen, losing his touch.

Rebecca Jones

Sorry for late replies. Been really busy. Want to meet up tomorrow night? My place? I'm alone for the weekend.

Although he immediately got a hard-on, there was a part of him that felt a little disappointed. He'd wanted to sleep with her from the moment they met in Schuh, of course, but he'd been rather enjoying the chase. Still, he wasn't going to look a gift horse in the mouth.

Achilles Cleverley

Yeah, I think I can make that. Eight o'clock? Text me the address and I'll see you then.

He got out of bed and went to his wardrobe, opened the bottom drawer and removed the tin box that he kept inside. Ensuring the door was locked, and trying his best not to feel like Fagin in *Oliver Twist*, he indulged in one of his favourite pastimes: counting his money.

There was almost £35,000 in hundreds, fifties and twenties, all taken from lonely men who'd fallen for his tricks, and with any luck he'd have another £5,000 by the end of the weekend. He'd been stringing Jeremy Arlo along long enough, he decided. It was time to go in for the kill. He'd meet him tonight and put the squeeze on him, and get him to pay up tomorrow, which would set him up nicely for his date with Rebecca.

A knock came on the door and someone tried the handle.

'Achilles?' said a voice that he recognized as his brother Nelson's. 'Why is the door locked?'

'I'm busy,' he shouted, locking the box again and putting it back in its hiding place.

'Can I talk to you?'

He sighed and unlocked the door.

'What do you want?' he asked.

'Why are you still in bed at this time of the day?' asked Nelson. 'Why aren't you in school?'

'I had free periods this afternoon, if it's any of your business, and I fancied a nap. What do you care?'

'Just because I'm not a teacher any more doesn't mean that I don't care about the education of our young people. You're our greatest natural resource, you know.'

'What do you mean, you're not a teacher? You were yesterday.'

'I quit this morning.'

Achilles rolled his eyes and turned around, climbed back into bed and pulled the covers up to his neck.

'Come in if you want,' he said. 'But close the door behind you. I wasn't planning on being at home to visitors.'

Nelson did as instructed and stepped into the bedroom, looking around at the books, games, magazines and teenage paraphernalia that surrounded him.

'What are you doing here anyway?' asked Achilles, opening one eye. 'If you're planning on molesting me, just get on with it so I can go back to sleep.'

Nelson sat down on the bed and let out a dramatic sigh.

'This isn't just a social visit, is it?' asked Achilles. 'I feel you want to tell me something.'

'I do, yes.'

'Or perhaps you want to ask me for advice?'

Nelson frowned. 'Why on earth would I ask you for advice?' he asked. 'No offence, Achilles, but you're an idiot.'

'At least I'm not a virgin.'

'I'm not either, as it happens,' said Nelson.

'Really?' said Achilles, sitting up now and propping a pair of pillows behind him, his face lighting up at this unexpected development. 'You finally popped your cherry?'

'I did,' said Nelson, blushing a little. 'It's quite good fun, isn't it? Shagging.'

'Well, yes,' said Achilles. 'I mean, you must have heard rumours to that effect.'

'I'd heard something,' said Nelson. 'But it's even better than I expected. And it turns out I'm quite good at it.'

'Don't be ridiculous,' replied Achilles. 'I can just about believe that you finally lost it, but that would be going too far.'

'If I'd known that I'd enjoy it this much, and that I'd be so brilliant at it, I'd have started long ago. Where's Mother and Father anyway? And Elizabeth? Why is no one else home?'

'I have no idea. Why, are you planning on telling them the good news too? Please don't do it until I'm in the room, okay? I want to see their reactions.'

'Of course not. I just wondered, that's all. There's something else I want to tell you.'

'What is it, are you a secret MI5 agent? Oh wait, you're not going on *Bake Off*, are you? That's just the kind of thing you'd do.'

'No, it's nothing like that. I want to prepare you for a shock, though. This will come as a surprise, but I hope that nothing between us will change.'

'You mean we'll be as close as ever?' asked Achilles. 'You'll take me to football matches and down the pub for my first pint?'

'You know, you don't always have to be so sarcastic,' said Nelson. 'You could take a day off from being Achilles.' He made inverted comma symbols in the air when he said his brother's name. 'I'm trying to tell you something important here. And you're the first family member I've told. So a little respect would be nice.'

'Sorry,' said Achilles, feeling chastened. 'Go on, then. I'm all ears.'

Nelson took a deep breath.

'Circumstances in my life have changed in recent days,' he announced. 'Rather unexpectedly, I have taken a lover and—'

'Please,' said Achilles, holding up a hand. 'Do one thing for me. Never, ever refer to anyone as *your lover*. I can't handle it. The images it conjures up.' He shivered. 'Just say *my boyfriend*.'

'Rather unexpectedly,' repeated Nelson. 'I have taken a . . . wait, what? What did you say? What do you mean, *my boy-friend*? Why would you think I have a boyfriend?'

'You said you're getting laid, so what else am I meant to assume?'

'I just—'

'Oh, come on, Nelson, just spit it out, whatever it is.'

Nelson swallowed and looked a little confused. 'Well, the thing is that I was going to tell you that I've realized that I am . . . you know . . . a gentleman who enjoys the company of other gentlemen.'

'Don't most gentlemen enjoy the company of other gentlemen?'

'Yes, but I enjoy it in a more sensual way than most. It is time for me to admit to the world that I am—'

'Gay,' said Achilles. 'And I, for one, am shocked! Shocked, I say! You! A gay! Who would ever have thought it?'

'You don't sound surprised.'

'I'm not. So if that's your big revelation, I'm sorry, but it's about as thrilling as an episode of *Emmerdale*.'

'Right,' said Nelson. 'And you're okay with it?'

'Why should I care? Put your pecker where you want. Stick it in a box of Haribo, for all I care.'

Nelson smiled and stood up. He'd hoped for a little more but was willing to take what he could get.

'What's his name anyway?' asked Achilles as he made his way towards the door.

'Shane.'

'Do you like him?'

Nelson nodded. 'I like him a lot.'

Achilles smiled and, to his astonishment, felt tears forming behind his eyes. 'Fuck me,' he said. 'I'm getting all weepy.'

Nelson looked away. He felt a little emotional too.

'There's something I need to tell you too,' said Achilles, 'but if you ever repeat this to anyone, I'll deny having ever said it. Understand? I might even sue you for slander.'

Nelson nodded.

'I love you. Now get out.'

FACEPALM

Returning to his office, George collapsed into his chair in exhaustion and took out his phone, then tapped on the blue Twitter icon. Despite the sacking of Ben Bimbaum and Margaret Roberts, the morning had gone much better than he'd anticipated, and he decided it was time to put this whole unpleasant business to bed once and for all by sharing his relief with the world.

He began to type.

@GeorgeCleverley ✓ A great meeting with @LordHusbery this morning who's confirmed the new series of @CleverleyTV for the autumn. Get well soon, LH! Goes to show that crippled people are just as wise as normal people. Let's get more cripples on to the boards of our national institutions!

He read it several times, searching for anything that could possibly cause offence, decided there was nothing problematic there, and pressed 'Tweet'.

TOMMY THE TORTOISE

By the time Achilles met Jeremy again on Thursday evening, he was fully prepared to take his scam to endgame, but he also felt a little thirsty, so allowed the older man to buy him a rum and Coke before being so vulgar as to talk money. Usually, at this point in the con, the mark was growing anxious for something sexual to happen between them, suggesting a trip back to his house or flat, but to Achilles' surprise, Jeremy seemed only to be growing in confidence, exhibiting far less anxiety than he had in any of their earlier encounters, and had yet to show any interest in an erotic development.

They were sitting in a fairly run-down pub in Chiswick, where Achilles was spinning his latest hard-luck story, which, surprisingly, had a thread of truth running down its centre.

'I know it was only a tortoise,' he said. 'But he was my grand-father's tortoise, and then my dad's, and when my dad went inside, I was given the responsibility of looking after him.'

'That must have helped you maintain a connection with him,' said Jeremy. 'A pet that both you and your father loved.'

'Yes, and because I was only four years old when Dad got sent away, it really helped me a lot.'

'What exactly did your father do, if you don't mind my asking?'

Achilles adopted a tragic expression and leaned forward, as if he was nervous of being overheard.

'This isn't something I tell a lot of people,' he said. 'Because it could be dangerous, you know? But I trust you, Jeremy. The thing is, there was a drugs cartel operating on our estate and they were supplying to children. To children! And that's just not right, is it? So he ratted them out. And then one of their . . . let's say, associates . . . got their revenge planting drugs on him, and he got ten years.'

'What kind of drugs?' asked Jeremy.

Achilles thought about it. 'I want to say . . . heroin?' he said.

'Are you asking me or telling me?'

'Telling you. Then Dad got killed when he was inside. Some guys who worked for the, you know, for the drug lord, the kingpin, they cut his throat with a toothbrush.'

'How do you cut someone's throat with a toothbrush?' asked Jeremy.

'You take the bristles out, then you melt the plastic and stick a blade in. Then—'

He made a swooshing and slicing motion through the air, his hair falling into his eyes as he did so.

'How awful for you,' said Jeremy, sitting back a little. 'And how old were you when this happened?'

'Like, eight,' said Achilles.

'They kept him alive for four years and then killed him?'

'Yes. Weird, I know, but that's the way it happened.'

Jeremy nodded. 'What prison was he in?'

Achilles looked around the bar while he racked his brain for the names of prisons.

'Holloway,' he said.

'But Holloway was a women's prison,' said Jeremy, frowning. 'He couldn't possibly have been there.'

'Sorry, you're right,' said Achilles, shaking his head. 'Not Holloway. I meant Belmarsh.'

'I thought Belmarsh was used for terror suspects? It's Category-A, as far as I know.'

Achilles stared at him, wishing he had a toothbrush with him right at that moment.

'Wormwood Scrubs,' he said definitively. 'That's where he was.'

'Ah.'

'I don't like to think about it, to be honest.'

'Apparently not.'

'Anyway, as I say, the tortoise went back a few generations in my family. They can live up to about 150 years, you know.'

'Really? I had an aunt who lived to 104.'

'Not quite the same, though, Jeremy, is it?' said Achilles. 'Thirty-six years' difference there.'

'Forty-six,' said Jeremy.

'Either way, the tortoise died. That's my point. So if I seem a bit down, you'll know why.'

'You must be very upset.'

'I am, yeah.'

'What was his name?'

'The tortoise or my dad?'

'The tortoise.'

Achilles opened his mouth to say the name of Ustym Karmaliuk, but he really didn't have the energy to get into a
lengthy conversation about that so he decided to make things
a bit simpler.

'Tommy,' he said.

'Tommy?'

'Yes, Tommy. Tommy the Tortoise.'

'And how did he die, if you don't mind me asking?'

'He overdosed on After Eights. They're not good for tortoises. You don't have one, do you?'

'An After Eight?'

'No, a tortoise.'

'Oh. No. I have a cockapoo, but I never give her chocolate. Or
mints. Although her breath can be terrible. So perhaps I should.'

'Jeremy, haven't you been listening to a word I've been saying?' asked Achilles, raising his voice now. 'Don't give that
cockapoo none of that crap. Or you'll end up suffering like I'm
suffering. It's not right, man! It's not right!'

Jeremy reached across and tapped his hand against Achilles'
on the table. The boy looked at it and smiled inside. He'd
known all along that the moment would come sooner or later.
'I can see how distraught you are,' said Jeremy. 'I wonder, is
there anything I can do to help?'

You're going to suggest some stress relief, aren't you? thought
Achilles. *Back at yours. With my pants around my ankles.*

Achilles shook his head. 'I couldn't ask you to,' he said. 'It
wouldn't be fair. You've been so good to me already.'

'But I'd like to. I would.'

'Is there anything you'd like to suggest?'

Jeremy blinked and thought about it. 'Nothing springs to
mind,' he said. 'But if you can think of something, then—'

'No,' said Achilles. 'No, I couldn't do it.'

'Do what?'

'Ask you for five thousand pounds.'

Jeremy sat back in his seat now and raised an eyebrow. 'I'm sorry,' he said. 'Did you say five thousand pounds?'

'Yes, that's what it will cost.'

'What what will cost?'

Achilles sighed and wiped a non-existent tear from his eye. 'See, the thing is,' he said, 'my family is originally from New Zealand.'

'All right.'

'That's where my grandfather emigrated from. He died in the war.'

'Which war?'

'The First.'

'Could he have even been born then?'

'No, you're right. The Second. He died in the Second World War, at the Battle of . . .' He racked his brain again to remember a name from one of his history classes. 'Ypres,' he said. 'Did I pronounce that right?'

'You pronounced it right, yes,' said Jeremy. 'But it couldn't have been Ypres, because that *was* in the First World War.'

'It must have been the Marne, then.'

'Also the First World War.'

'Verdun?'

'Ditto.'

'Waterloo?'

Jeremy frowned. 'That was during the Napoleonic era.'

'Agincourt?'

'No, that was Henry V. Sometime around 1415, if memory serves.'

Achilles sat back in his seat, losing the will to live.

'Wow,' he said. 'You really know your battles, don't you?'

'I am a bit of a military history buff,' admitted Jeremy.

'So tell me some of the major battles of the Second World War. Maybe one will ring a bell.'

'Well,' said Jeremy, pushing his glasses up his nose. 'I mean, where to start? There was the Battle of Normandy, of course, and the—'

'Normandy,' said Achilles, slapping a hand down on the table. 'That was the one. He died there. In the Battle of Normandy.'

'Right,' said Jeremy, looking a bit confused. 'I got it right first time. How odd.'

'You know your stuff, no question. Anyway, what was I talking about? Oh yeah. So, my grandfather, he died at Normandy and then his body was sent back to New Zealand to be buried in . . . can you guess the city?'

Jeremy glanced up at the ceiling for a moment as if he might find the answer up there. 'Auckland?' he suggested.

'That's the one. And then when my dad was stabbed in the guts in Dartmoor—'

'Slashed across the throat in Wormwood Scrubs.'

'Who's telling this story, Jeremy, you or me?'

'You are. I do apologize.'

'When Dad died, is the point, when he was so brutally murdered by men who had been using him as their sex toy for two years—'

'Four years.'

'His body was sent back to Auckland too. To be buried alongside his own father. And his dying wish, it was in his will, was that his beloved Ustym Karmaliuk would one day be buried in the same grave.'

Jeremy stared at him as if he had gone mad. 'Ustym Karma-liuk?' he asked. 'The famous Ukrainian folk hero?'

'I am constantly impressed by how many people are aware of this man,' replied Achilles, more to himself than anyone else. 'No, not Ustym Karmaliuk. I don't know why I said that name. I might be having a stroke. No, he wanted . . . he wanted . . .'

'Tommy the Tortoise?'

'That's right. He wanted Tommy the Tortoise to be buried with him. And I want to do that for my father. But flying to New Zealand and back costs money.'

'I'm sure it does.'

'It can be very expensive.'

'Let me guess, five thousand pounds?'

'Spot on.'

'That seems quite pricey.'

'Well, you have to factor in hotel costs, and so on. The flights themselves wouldn't cost that much. I could probably get a cheap business class seat for about half that amount if I wanted to slum it. But I'd have to eat while I was there too. And, you know, buy a wreath. All in all, I'd say we're looking at around five grand all in. And I couldn't possibly expect you to give me that.'

'No,' said Jeremy, looking a little relieved. 'No, of course not. But if you wanted to bury him here in London, I could probably help you dig a hole in a park somewhere.'

Achilles smiled. 'Would that be legal, do you think?' he asked.

'We could do it under cover of night.'

'You and me in a London park, in the dead of night, with the moon shining down on us,' said Achilles. 'You wouldn't be trying to get into my pants, would you?'

Jeremy stared at him and his mouth opened and closed a few times, like a goldfish in a bowl.

'I only ask,' continued Achilles, 'because I've started to worry about where this friendship is going. I mean, you are a lot older than me.'

'Well, only by about thirty years,' protested Jeremy. 'That's only a fifth of a lifetime, in tortoise terms.'

'But we're not tortoises, are we, Jeremy?' asked Achilles. 'We're not tortoises. You're a grown man. And I'm a teenage boy.'

'True,' replied Jeremy, looking a little disconcerted now.

'I mean, I know that we're just friends and it's not as if you've tried to get me into bed, is it?'

Jeremy flushed. 'No, of course not,' he said. 'I've never even suggested—'

'But you do take me out for drinks a lot, don't you? And I am underage.'

'You said you were eighteen.'

'I might have exaggerated by about a year.'

Jeremy stared at him for a moment, then looked around, tapping the tip of his thumb against the tips of each of his fingers in a strange, fretful tic, and Achilles watched him, always intrigued by how his victims behaved at this moment.

'Perhaps it's best if we don't see each other again,' said Jeremy, drinking the rest of his pint quickly.

'Probably, yes.'

'I don't know what I've done to give you the impression that I had any . . . nefarious intentions towards you.'

'No idea what that means, to be honest. But if you're asking do I think you want to take me up the Khyber Pass, then yes, that's what I think.'

'But I've never . . . I've never so much as—'

'Doesn't matter what you've said or haven't said, does it, Jeremy? It's what it looks like that matters.'

'And what does it look like?'

'Looks like you're a middle-aged man taking out a teenage boy who he met on a dating app to get him all liquored up and then . . . well, it doesn't take a genius to figure out what comes next, does it?'

Jeremy stared at the boy for a moment before looking around and biting his lip.

'Is that what this has been all about?' he asked, utter disappointment in his tone. 'Extortion?'

'I really don't like that word,' said Achilles, frowning. 'And I'm sure you're a nice guy, other than the obvious paedophiliac tendencies, but let's face it, why would I be interested in you? You're old enough to be my dad. And I barely give him the time of day.'

'Your dad is dead.'

'Oh yeah.'

'Your dad *is* dead, isn't he?'

Achilles shrugged. He hadn't intended to get this deep into things. 'Does it matter?'

'Is anything you've told me the truth? Is your name even Nick?'

Achilles thought about it. 'The tortoise story was true,' he said. 'Most of it. And my advice about the After Eights. They're what killed the little bastard. Keep them away from your cockatoo or whatever it was.'

'Cockapoo.'

'I don't know much about birds, but I do like a cockatoo, am I right?' said Achilles, laughing, and Jeremy's face turned into an angry sneer.

'You little shit,' he said.

'We can sit here trading insults if you want,' said Achilles. 'Or we can just get on with our business. I get my five thousand pounds and you get my silence. After you pay me off, you won't ever hear from me again. I don't go back to the same well twice. What do you say?'

Jeremy looked down at the table and tapped his fingers against the woodwork. 'It doesn't feel as if you're leaving me much choice,' he said.

'Probably not, no.'

'It's a lot of money.'

'It could be a lot more.'

'How soon would you want it?'

Achilles thought about it. 'Tomorrow,' he said. 'Six o'clock.'

'All right,' said Jeremy, sounding defeated. 'And then you won't contact me again?'

Achilles made the shape of a cross over his heart. 'Scout's honour,' he said.

Jeremy shook his head. 'Were you ever a Scout?' he asked.

'Oh, Jeremy,' said Achilles, laughing a little. 'That hurts me. It really does. I'm wounded.'

A DEATH IN THE FAMILY

It was almost 10 p.m. when Beverley returned home, exhausted from her day. The house was in darkness and she went straight into the living room, kicked off her shoes and poured herself a large whisky. On the table in front of her, a copy of that day's

Evening Standard was lying folded in half and she picked it up, only to be confronted by her husband's face.

TV CLEVERLEY IN FRESH SCANDAL!

screamed the headline, and she closed her eyes, wondering whether she would ever be given some respite from her family's dramas. She felt something damp licking at her toes and looked down to see Ustym Karmaliuk standing on the carpet next to her feet, and smiled. Reaching down, she picked him up and placed him on her lap, stroking his shell tenderly.

'You're going to live with me from now on,' she whispered. 'Instead of with that nasty, lying, deceiving piece of shit.'

The tortoise remained silent, expressing no preferences about his accommodation, and, after a moment, she placed him on one end of the table, where he began to make gallant efforts to make his way to the other side, where the promise of an uneaten After Eight lay within its wrapper. As he crawled along, she returned to the newspaper, where the head of Disability Rights UK was calling on the BBC to sack 'the prominent and much-loved television presenter George Cleverley, who referred to those with physical disabilities as "cripples" in a now-deleted tweet'.

'Oh, for Christ's sake,' she said, taking another swig from her glass and, a moment later, her husband plodded into the room with a forlorn expression on his face.

'I see you've fucked up again,' muttered Beverley, nodding towards the newspaper.

'So it would seem.'

'First you're transphobic. Then you're a racist. And now you hate disabled people.'

'Apparently, I'm anti-Semitic too, although there doesn't

seem to be any real evidence for that one. Why are you home anyway? I thought you were going to stay in Ukraine for a few days?'

'My plans changed,' she said. 'There was nothing there for me.'

'Nothing for your novel, you mean?'

'Nothing for my novel. Is this going to blow up even more?'

'I expect so,' he said, collapsing into an armchair. 'They're out to get me and won't be happy until I've been stripped naked, dragged through the streets of London and dumped head first in the Thames.'

'Who?' asked Beverley. 'Who won't be happy?'

'The POOTs.'

'Oh, why do you even pay attention, George?' she asked, frustrated by how personally he took all of this. 'Who cares what they think? These people live in an echo chamber. Well, most of them still live with their parents, but you know what I mean.'

'Because I don't like it when they say terrible things about me. A man's reputation is all he has.'

'You also have this house,' she pointed out. 'And about ten million quid in the bank. None of the POOTs has that.'

'It just frustrates me, since I've been a dyed-in-the-wool liberal my entire life. You of all people know that.'

'I do, yes,' admitted Beverley.

'What's most upsetting is how things seem to have changed. I'm starting to feel that nowadays there's no one more bigoted than a liberal. The right-wingers, at least they own their hatred and don't try to dress it up in anything other than the intolerant, narrow-minded, self-serving bullshit that it is. You know where you are with the Right. But the Left? My God, disagree with them for even a moment, dare to ask a question or deviate from the company line, and they're on you like flies on shit. They won't stand for even an iota of disagreement, pleading for kindness while masking their own intolerance in sanctimony. It's McCarthyism hidden beneath the umbrella of Wokeness.'

'As I understand it,' said Beverley with a sigh, 'Wokeness is about creating a fairer and more equal society.'

'It might have started out like that,' replied George, looking downcast. 'At the beginning, its heart was in the right place. But now it's about nothing more than tearing people down, stalking them on social media and, if they can get away with it, destroying the lives of strangers. Usually *successful* strangers, I might add. I've spent my entire life trying to be a decent, honourable man, and look where it's got me. You know, earlier today, some lunatic posted an eighteen-tweet-thread about what a monster I am. A man who's never even met me and yet presumes to know everything about me.'

'Yes, but someone like that has mental health issues. Why give him the time of day?'

'That doesn't make it any easier. It's cruel, Beverley. It's bullying. Nothing more, nothing less.'

'George, you're not . . . you're not crying, are you?'

He shook his head and wiped his eyes, surprised to find that he was. 'It hurts, that's all. It really fucking hurts. These people have no decency.'

Beverley breathed in heavily through her nose. 'You don't think that you bear some responsibility for all of this, though, do you? You are the common denominator, after all.'

George shrugged. He was too tired to argue. 'I don't know,' he said. 'Perhaps I'm just getting too old to be let loose on the world. Everything I say seems to offend someone. When all I'm actually trying to do is help.'

'But you're helping the wrong way.'

He smiled. 'Someone else said that to me a while ago.'

'Who?'

'Oh, just someone at the Beeb.' He thought about this for a moment and then his face took on a look of horror. 'Oh shit,' he said.

'What's wrong?' asked Beverley.

'What time is it?'

She glanced at her watch. 'Nearly half past ten,' she said.

'Damn.'

'All the blood has drained from your face.'

'I was supposed to make a phone call, that's all. Before close of play. It went completely out of my mind.'

'Something important?'

'Someone important.'

'Who?'

George looked at his wife and considered his answer carefully.

'Nobody,' he said.

They both turned around as they heard the sound of the front door opening and Elizabeth walked into the living room.

'And what's the matter with you?' asked George.

'I broke up with Wilkes.'

George kept his features entirely still. 'How terrible,' he said. 'He seemed like a keeper. I am distraught.'

'Oh, darling,' said Beverley, standing up, giving her a hug and pouring her a glass of wine. 'It really is for the best. How did he take it? Was he terribly upset?'

'Absolutely devastated,' said Elizabeth. 'He turned on the waterworks, of course. It was like Niagara Falls pouring down his cheeks.'

'Well, it's a bit of a wash, at least.'

'But I held firm. I told him that my mind was made up and we shouldn't be sorry that it was over; instead, we should be happy that it happened.'

'Darling, that's beautiful. Did you come up with it?'

'No, I think it was Dr Seuss.'

'Well, good for you anyway.'

'I've washed my hands of him, Mother. Both literally and metaphorically.'

'You did the right thing,' agreed Beverley. 'As it happens, I've sworn off men for the time being too. All they do is deceive you.'

'What do you mean, you've sworn off men?' asked Elizabeth, turning to her mother with a frown on her face. 'You're married!'

'Tell me about it,' said Beverley, rolling her eyes. 'And just look how much trouble your father is causing.'

'Oh, that's just Dad. He'll sort himself out.'

'I might not,' grunted George. 'Where are the boys anyway?' he asked, reaching for a bowl of olives that he studied for a moment before pushing away in distaste.

'Achilles is out,' said Beverley. 'And I don't know where Nelson is. Do you, Elizabeth?'

'No, but I did receive a strange text from him earlier to say that he'd quit his job and had taken a lover, but I assumed that was some sort of auto-correct mistake.'

'Nelson? Taken a lover?' asked George. 'Have we slipped into an alternate universe?'

'I'll call him tomorrow and see what's going on,' said Beverley. 'Make sure he hasn't got himself into any trouble. The apple doesn't fall far from the tree, after all,' she added, glaring at her husband.

'Ah. Back to me. Wonderful.'

'Will all of this blow over in time, do you think?' asked Elizabeth, trying her best to look concerned.

'Who knows? Right now, my popularity level's on a par with Laurence Fox's. I'm pretty sure my cards are marked.'

'You think you'll end up getting fired?' asked Beverley, sitting upright.

'I think there's an excellent chance of that happening, yes.'

'But what will we do? For money, I mean,' asked Elizabeth.

'That's hardly an issue. We own the house. And the other houses. We're financially secure. And I daresay I'll be able to sell my memoirs. I'll be in the doghouse for a year or so, then I'll do an interview with one of the Sundays saying how much I've listened, and grown, and learned—'

'Do you plan on listening, growing and learning?'

'Not a chance. But I'll be happy to say so if it shuts the POOTs up. And after that, I might get an offer from ITV.'

'Oh, George!' cried Beverley, putting her glass down. 'It hasn't come to that, surely?'

'You could go into the jungle,' suggested Elizabeth. 'Or the *Celebrity Big Brother* house. They like nothing more than someone who's publicly disgraced himself. It's a chance for redemption.'

'Yes to the former. No to the latter.'

'Well, you have always loved Australia,' said Beverley. 'And they say you lose about ten kilos if you make it to the end. It could be the making of you. I'd be happy to come along. I believe they put the spouses up in a luxury hotel. You don't think I'd have to socialize with Ant and Dec, though, do you? There are limits.'

George looked down at his protruding belly, which had expanded noticeably in recent years. 'It would be cheaper than a gym, I suppose,' he said. 'In fact, they'd probably pay me a small fortune. We'll see what happens tomorrow, and I'll decide then.'

The door opened again and Achilles threw himself energetically into the room, as if he'd been despatched from a cannon, looking around at his parents and sister cheerfully.

'Good to see you're all keeping your blood alcohol levels up,' he said, nodding towards their glasses.

'Oh, shut up,' they all replied in unison.

'And at least it doesn't make you cranky,' he replied. 'What's everyone talking about in here anyway? You all look so gloomy.'

'I've broken up with Wilkes,' said Elizabeth.

'Catweazle? Oh no,' he said. 'How awful. He was like the brother I never wanted. I hope he stays in touch.'

'And I'm probably going to be fired,' said George.

'Will that affect my allowance?'

'It's conceivable, yes.' And then, realizing the word he had just used, he felt a stab of pain in his stomach.

'And what about you, Mother darling?' asked Achilles. 'What has you so blue?'

'I don't want to talk about it,' she said. 'I've been let down by someone I trusted.'

'The ghost?'

'No, I never trusted the ghost to begin with. There's something in the way she speaks to me that makes me think she doesn't respect my writing.'

'Her writing, you mean.'

'MY WRITING! THEY'RE MY IDEAS!'

'So who has let you down, then? Tell Achilles. He's wiser than he looks.'

'You're a very annoying boy,' she replied, pouring another glass of wine and handing it to her son before tousling his hair. 'I don't know how you're related to any of us, I really don't.'

From behind them, a faint scraping came at the half-open door and they all turned to look in its direction. Slowly, almost imperceptibly, the door began to open wider. But, to their astonishment, there was no one there.

'It's the ghost!' cried Achilles, delighted with himself.

'No, it's the fucking turtle,' said George, pointing down at the ground. 'What's wrong with him anyway?'

'He's a tortoise, not a turtle,' said Beverley as all eyes turned to the reptile, who appeared exhausted by his long journey down the hallway and all the effort that had gone into pushing the door open with his tiny head. Having secured the attention of eighty per cent of the Cleverley family, however, he pulled himself upright, or as upright as a tortoise can, before opening his mouth and despatching a stream of green-and-white tortoise vomit across the floor.

'Jesus fucking Christ,' said George.

'Poor baby, he's sick,' said Beverley, standing up to help him, then thinking better of it and resuming her seat. 'It must be something he ate.' She sniffed the air. The stream of puke was moving in her direction at the same glacial rate that its former host generally employed. 'Why does it smell so minty?' she asked.

'It's the After Eights,' said Elizabeth. 'He's addicted.'

'Has that little bastard been eating my After Eights?' asked George, sitting up in annoyance. 'As if things aren't bad enough. You know I look forward to them of an evening.'

Ustym Karmaliuk gathered all his energy and began to make his way towards the pool of sick with the clear intention of ingesting the constituents for a second time, but as he trudged along, he suddenly froze in the most dramatic fashion, looked around at each member of the family in turn, before narrowing his eyes in an attitude of accusation and allowing his head to slump forward.

'What just happened?' asked Elizabeth.

'I think he might have died,' said Achilles, reaching down and picking the tortoise up. He felt a momentary pang of remorse for having prophesied the tortoise's death in this exact way earlier in the evening, although he had no intention of using Jeremy's remuneration to return him to his ancestral home for a hero's funeral. 'Where do you find a tortoise's pulse?'

'In his neck,' said Beverley. 'It always throbbed in a rather erotic fashion, I thought.'

'Well, it's not throbbing now,' said Achilles. 'And look, his eyes have gone all black. Fuck me, we've killed the tortoise.'

The Cleverleys stood up and gathered around, staring down at the non-responsive vertebrate in Achilles' hands.

'Well, now,' said George after a suitable pause. 'That's that, then. What do we do now, throw him in the bin?'

'He won't flush down the toilet, that's for sure,' said Elizabeth.

'We could just chuck him in the bushes and let the foxes carry him off,' suggested Achilles.

'You'll do nothing of the sort,' said Beverley, who, to her family's surprise, had started weeping. 'I'll put him back in his box and sort him out tomorrow. He was happy there.'

'How can you tell?' asked Elizabeth.

'A mother knows.'

'But you weren't his mother.'

'Oh, shut up,' she snapped. 'He was a lovely tortoise and should be treated with respect at this tragic moment.'

'He was,' agreed George, seeing how upset his wife was and not wishing to cause her any further pain.

'The best of us all,' said Beverley.

'Well, I wouldn't go quite that far.'

'He was 115 years old, wasn't he?' asked Achilles, falling to his knees and raising his hands to the heavens, replicating the image on the poster for *Platoon*. 'Why are the good ones always taken so young? Why? Oh, sweet Jesus, WHY?'

'Shut up, Achilles,' said George. 'You're an idiot.'

'I'd started to grow very fond of that tortoise,' said Beverley. 'There was something dignified about him, I thought. He reminded me of Ted Heath in his last years in the Commons. Just sitting there, observing, keeping his own counsel. Occasionally going to the bathroom in an inappropriate place. Achilles, clean this floor up. I'm going to bed.'

And with that, she took hold of the dead reptile, placed him carefully back into his shoe box, before covering it with a lid and going upstairs, where she fell quickly asleep.

PART 5

27 September 2016

For several years, the Cleverleys would joke that Achilles had damaged his tendon when he stumbled into the door drunk but, in reality, it was three toes that he broke on his left foot as he stumbled down the corridor and slipped on one of the hallway mats. The fact that he was inebriated at only twelve years old shocked both George and Beverley and, after putting him to bed and leaving a basin on his bedroom floor in case he needed to throw up, they gathered in the kitchen with the seventeen-year-old Nelson and the sixteen-year-old Elizabeth, demanding explanations.

'What is going on in this family anyway?' asked George, looking at his wife and elder children in turn. 'Did anyone know that Achilles was drinking?'

'Not a clue,' replied Nelson and Elizabeth in unison.

'I certainly didn't,' added Beverley.

'He's just a child!' continued George. 'Not even a teenager yet. Who are his friends? Who does he play with?'

'Play with?' asked Elizabeth, smirking. 'He doesn't "play with" anyone. Other than himself.'

'Don't be vulgar,' said Beverley.

'Who gave him the alcohol, then?' asked George. 'One of you must know.'

'Why should we know?' asked Nelson, who was annoyed to be drawn into this interrogation when he'd been busy watching a television documentary about Mykonos and was thinking it might be a nice place to visit one day.

'Because you're his brother and sister!'

'And you're his father,' said Elizabeth. 'And you're his mother,' she added, turning to Beverley.

'We can't be expected to know everything that goes on in our children's lives,' replied Beverley. 'We're busy people. With busy lives.'

'Some might say that your children should come first.'

'Are any of those people in this room?' asked George, before calming down a little and dismissing them both. He poured two glasses of wine from the fridge and sat down at the island. 'She has a point, you know,' he said quietly.

'I know she does,' admitted Beverley.

'Are we a bit . . . distant, do you think?'

'We are a bit preoccupied at times,' she admitted. 'Me with my books. You with your television show.'

'It's not just that, though, is it?' asked George.

'What is it, then?' asked Beverley, looking up from her phone.

George raised an eyebrow and nodded at what she was holding in her hand.

'Oh, please,' she said, laughing. 'You think our phones are to blame for this?'

'I don't think they help,' he replied. 'We're on them all the time, aren't we? And not just us, Nelson and Elizabeth too. And we gave Achilles one for his birthday. It's possible that he's met some . . . undesirables . . . through the various . . .' He waved a hand in the air, uncertain of the correct terminology. 'Applications.'

Beverley shook her head. 'Phones have existed since the dawn of time.'

'Well, they haven't, actually.'

'For a century anyway.'

'Landlines. But no one ever came in and stood in their hallway and stared at their landline, did they?'

'When they became push button, that was quite exciting.'

'I wonder if . . .'

'If what?'

'If we should take them off the children. Until they're eighteen. Or twenty-one.'

Beverley laughed. 'Good luck with that,' she said.

'I mean it. What I worry about is that we all get so addicted to them that—'

Before he could say anything more, the door to the kitchen opened and a scrawny little boy in a pair of bright pink underpants stood before them, looking deeply sorry for himself. Beverley placed her phone on the island and turned to him.

'Darling,' she said. 'You look awful!'

Achilles opened his mouth to answer but, before he could say a word, he lurched forward and a stream of vomit poured from his mouth, covering his mother's brand-new iPhone.

And at that precise moment, in Beijing, a man named Zhang Yiming turned to his high-school girlfriend and said, 'I think I'll call it TikTok.'

Friday

George was sitting in the kitchen, drinking his morning cup of coffee, staring at the sealed box containing the dead body of Ustym Karmaliuk. For some inexplicable reason, Beverley had elevated it to the top of a pile of six thick hardback books, the uppermost one being the eight-hundred-page biography that George had bought on Monday and still hadn't opened. It gave the sarcophagus a faintly deified air.

'He's still here, then,' he muttered, looking across at Elizabeth, who glanced up from her phone for a moment. She didn't like being distracted from her Twitter arguments.

'I'm sure Mum has a plan,' she replied. 'I'm not going anywhere near him.'

'He was definitely male, then?'

Elizabeth shrugged. 'Well, I didn't turn him over to look, but the real-life Ustym Karmaliuk was a man, so I would assume so.'

'Actually, the way to tell the gender of a tortoise is not how you might expect. The females have shorter tails than the males, and they also have a U-shape notch on their underside, unlike the males, who have a V.'

'How do you know that?'

'I've interviewed thousands of people over the years,' he

said. 'I'm a fount of useless information. I hope your mother isn't going through some sort of mid-life crisis. God only knows what she might bring home next. A starving child from Malawi, for example. Didn't Madonna do that? And she liked her so much that she went back for more?'

'That,' said Elizabeth, fixing him with a sharp look, 'is exactly the kind of comment that gets you into such deep trouble.'

'Oh, there's no one else here,' he said, waving her criticism aside. 'Just you, me and a dead tortoise. It's not as if that @TruthIsASword bastard is going to hear any of it.'

'Still,' replied Elizabeth, avoiding his eye, 'you need to be more careful from now on if you want to make people like you again.'

Before he could reply, his phone rang. He glanced at the screen.

'Oh Christ, this can't be good. It's my agent. Hello, Denise,' said George cheerfully as he answered it. 'How are you, darling?'

'I'm wonderful, darling,' she replied. 'And how are you, darling?'

'Smashing, darling. And what can I do for you? I suppose you're calling to let me know that the BBC wants to renegotiate my contract a year early and give me a substantial salary bump?'

'If only wishing made it so,' she said, laughing joylessly. 'What are you doing right now, darling?'

'Talking to you, darling.'

'I mean, are you at home, darling?'

'I am, darling.'

'And are you busy?'

'Not especially.'

'Fabulous. Could we meet? Shall we say Soho House in an hour?'

'Is it good news or bad news?'

Denise laughed properly now. 'Now, you know I don't

believe in such terms,' she said. 'All news is good news. Even bad news leads to new opportunities so ultimately becomes good news.'

'Fine,' he said. 'So is it good news or new opportunities?'

'Have you seen today's *Daily Mail*?'

'No, I've given up reading the papers.'

'Then just meet me at twelve,' she said. 'Dean Street, all right? The last time I was in Greek Street, James Corden was there. Never again, I swore after that. Never again.'

'All right,' he said. 'You can't give me a little clue, though, as to whether I'm going to come away in a good mood or not?'

'Afraid not, darling. I'll tell you all at twelve. Until then.'

He nodded and hung up.

'Well?' asked Elizabeth.

'I don't know. She likes to deliver good news in person so she can receive my gratitude face to face. But she also likes to deliver bad news in person so she can talk me out of firing her.'

'Something tells me that, of the two of you, she's the one in more stable employment right now.'

THE SKI INSTRUCTOR OF VERBIER

Sometime before George exited his taxi on Dean Street, Beverley was seated not far away, across the street in Barrafina, enjoying a latte and an early-morning Bellini while awaiting the arrival of her ghost. Before her lay a print-out of the latest chapter of what was now officially titled *The Ski Instructor of*

Verbier, each page scarred red where Beverley had made increasingly furious corrections.

A copy of that morning's *Daily Mail* lay on the table, and Beverley unfurled it, reading the lead article once again. She was angry with George, of course, but she also felt deeply upset by how their once happy marriage had reached this place of mutual infidelity and distrust. There was a time when they had loved each other, been kind to each other, when they had been desperate to be in each other's company. They had thrown themselves into parenthood and, even if their children had so far failed to build lives independent of them, she had plenty of friends who never even saw their offspring, while hers would barely leave the house. There was something positive there, surely? When and how had their passion fallen away?

The article itself only added to her frustrations, describing the romantic entanglement George had found himself in with a therapist. It referred to Beverley as 'the ageing romantic novelist Beverley Cleverley, last seen batting her eyelash extensions in the direction of handsome Ukrainian dancer Pylyp Tataryn on *Strictly Come Dancing*', and the woman who George had cheated on her with as 'a lithe and still-attractive woman, despite being thirty-eight years old'.

The door to the café opened and as the ghost stepped inside, something about the way she was carrying herself irritated Beverley. She looked more confident than usual, filled with a certain *joie de vivre*. She was even wearing make-up, which she normally eschewed. She waved across the room, then pointed to the sign leading towards the toilets, and Beverley nodded. In the meantime, she ordered two coffees and another Bellini and, when the waitress brought them over, Beverley asked her to take the newspaper away and shred it.

'Don't put it in the recycling,' she insisted. 'It has no further business in this world.'

'So sorry I've kept you waiting,' said the ghost when she reappeared, making a great show of removing her jacket and scarf. 'I had a bit of a late start this morning. I stayed in bed longer than expected, if you know what I mean.' She giggled and Beverley frowned. Was this the ghost's way of telling her that she had had sex that morning? Why on earth did she think that she would care? It was obvious, anyway, from the glow in her cheeks and the faraway look in her eyes.

'I've been waiting ten minutes,' said Beverley, taking a sip of her coffee. 'I do have other things to do, you know.'

'Oh, you got me a coffee,' said the ghost. 'You're a super-star. I need this. I don't suppose you ordered any food, did you?'

'No, I did not,' said Beverley. 'I'm not your personal assistant.'

'No, of course not. I just wondered, that's all.' She reached forward and, to Beverley's horror, took her hand in her own. 'How are you?' she asked, pulling a sympathetic face.

'I'm absolutely fine,' Beverley replied, rearing back and wiping her hand on her skirt. 'Why wouldn't I be?'

'Only I saw the article in this morning's newspaper. About George.'

'You mean Mr Cleverley.'

'If you like.'

Beverley looked away and did her best to maintain a calm demeanour. 'If you think the hacks can upset me, then you're wrong,' she said. 'I know my husband, and I'm sure the entire thing is a massive exaggeration. Also, the woman in question is obviously a tart.'

'Oh,' said the ghost, shocked. 'That's really not the way that women should talk about each other, is it? Sisterly solidarity and all that.'

'Spare me,' said Beverley, waving this away. 'She's not my "sister". She's a person of low morals who thought nothing of sleeping with another woman's husband, pretending to get pregnant by him and then, when scorned, selling her story to the *Daily Mail*. She's no more my sister than you are.'

'Well, we do share a sort of bond, don't we?' asked the ghost. 'Given that we're both writers.'

'Only one of us is a writer, dear,' said Beverley, with a patronizing smile.

'True. But your name is on the covers of your books so people think of you as one.'

Beverley gritted her teeth, feeling an urge to throw the coffee in the ghost's face, an urge she resisted for now.

'It hasn't been the best week for George, has it?' asked the ghost.

'Mr Cleverley has been going through a difficult time,' said Beverley. 'Which is not uncommon among men of a certain age. I'd prefer not to discuss it, if you don't mind. It's a private family matter.'

'Of course. But if you want to talk—'

'I don't.'

'But if you do—'

'I don't.'

'Then I hope you know that I'm—'

'But I *don't*.'

'All right.'

'So,' said Beverley, not wishing to continue this part of the conversation any further and placing her hands on the manuscript before her. 'I've read the chapters you submitted.'

'Oh good!'

'And I have to say that I'm very disappointed.'

The ghost raised an eyebrow. 'Really?' she said. 'I thought they were some of your best work.'

'It's as if you've entirely ignored all the parameters I set out for you. Carolyn, our heroine, is supposed to fall deeply in love with Marcel, the ski instructor, while only *pretending* to despise him. Instead, you have her *actually* despising him.'

'Yes, but I thought your idea was a bit Jane Austen so—'

'And what's wrong with Jane Austen, might I ask? Her books have lasted for, what, four, five hundred years?'

'There's nothing at all wrong with Jane Austen, if you are Jane Austen. But if you're not, then perhaps it can seem a bit silly to recycle one of her standard plot devices. Can't we leave that sort of thing to Hollywood?'

'But the way you write him goes against the whole spirit of the novel. Marcel is, for want of a better word, a complete dick.'

'He is, isn't he?' said the ghost, looking delighted by this description.

'But that's not a good thing! He's supposed to be gruff and unapproachable, wounded by a terrible secret from his past, but underneath . . . underneath, there is a kind, sexy billionaire – possibly with a neglected child in boarding school who only wants him to notice her – just waiting to get out. What he needs is the love of a good woman to strip away the dark exterior.'

'Yes,' said the ghost, taking a sip of her coffee. 'But don't you think that's been done to death?'

'Everything's been done to death, my dear,' said Beverley. 'Life has been done to death. But we keep on breathing, don't we?'

'It's just . . . and I don't mean any offence here—'

'I hate it when anyone starts a sentence in that way,' said Beverley, finishing her Bellini and ordering another with a quick point to the waitress. 'You can always guarantee that they're about to offend you.'

'It's just that I feel your novels have a certain *Groundhog Day* feel to them.'

Beverley blinked. 'I have no idea what that's supposed to mean,' she said.

'They're repetitive. The same stories, the same characters, repeated over and over. Don't you want your books to surprise people?'

'I most certainly do not,' said Beverley, picking up the new drink and swallowing a third of it. 'Nobody likes surprises.'

'I do.'

'Then you're abnormal. My readers want to be comforted by my books. They want to open one and know that they can sink into it as they might their favourite armchair. And when they're finished, they don't want to remember a word of it.'

The ghost nodded, considering this. 'Perhaps we have different expectations of what a book should be,' she said.

'Perhaps we do,' agreed Beverley. 'In your mind, it's perfectly fine to write Marcel as a total bastard with no redeeming features at all—'

'But there's plenty of men out there with no redeeming features at all! Plenty of women too, for that matter!'

'Yes, in real life! But is that what you want from a novel? Real life?'

'Well, some semblance of it, yes.'

'Then go read one of Maude Avery's miserable dirges. But don't bother with any of mine.'

'In general, I don't.'

'In general you don't what?'

'Bother with any of yours. No offence.'

Beverley laughed. 'How could that possibly be offensive?' She closed her eyes for a moment and breathed in through her nose, trying to maintain some sort of equilibrium. 'You're quite the sly boots, aren't you?'

'I don't think so.'

'I do. I wonder what goes on inside your mind.'

'Quite a lot, actually.'

'Well, you'll never find a husband if you insist on proving that to everyone. Nobody likes a clever woman. But look, I'm not here to discuss your inadequacies as a person or your oh-so-highbrow taste in literature. I'm here to discuss my novel. The novel that will have my name on the cover and my name on the spine and that I will end up defending on *Woman's Hour* while Emma Barnett takes pot-shots at me. Now look at this here.' She lifted a page that was so full of red marks that it looked as if it had been leeched. 'This flashback scene. Where Marcel is remembering his first romantic encounter with his late wife.'

'Yes? What about it?'

'I mean . . . have you read it?'

'Yes. I wrote it.'

'This line. This outrageous line. *Reader, he raped her.*'

'I thought that was rather good.'

'And you're the one who says you don't want it to be all Jane Austen!'

'That was Charlotte Brontë.'

'Same difference. How on earth is Carolyn supposed to fall in love and marry a man who is a rapist? Do you honestly think the reader is going to want that to happen?'

'No, but that's the point. She's not going to fall in love with him and she's not going to marry him.'

Beverley looked utterly bewildered now.

'Then who is she going to marry?' she asked.

'No one.'

'What do you mean, no one?'

'I mean, no one. She's not going to marry at all. She's going to remain single.'

'My dear,' said Beverley in a careful voice. 'All my novels end with a marriage. They have to.'

'But why?' asked the ghost. 'Why do they have to?'

'Because they're the rules!'

'So break the rules! What if, rather than having your heroine find fulfilment only through marrying a man, she ditched that man as being beneath her and went off to find it in another way? Through her work, for example? Or, perhaps, with another woman? Or with a non-binary—'

'DON'T!' shouted Beverley. 'Just don't. I've had quite enough of that for one week. And it's not as if anything like that happens in Jane Austen anyway, is it?'

'No, but you're not Jane Austen.'

'Jane Austen wasn't Jane Austen during her lifetime either,' countered Beverley. 'It took time.'

'Yes, well, I don't think that's something we have to worry about here,' said the ghost sniffily as she drank her coffee.

'You're very cocky for such an inexperienced young woman,' said Beverley. 'I don't approve of confidence in an employee. It gives them notions.'

'I'm not actually your employee, Beverley,' said the ghost with a sigh. 'I'm paid by the publishing house.'

'You are my employee,' insisted Beverley.

'Am not.'

'Are too. Look, I'm not going to play this game with you. It's beneath my dignity and above yours. The fact is, this just isn't going to work out. I'm sorry, but there it is. I don't think I can continue to allow you to be my ghost.'

'Oh dear,' replied the ghost, not sounding particularly concerned. 'What a shame.'

'Please don't take it personally—'

'I won't.'

'And don't let it affect your new-found confidence—'

'You don't need to worry about that.'

'It's not that you don't have some talent—'

'I'm aware of that.'

'It's just that we're not a great fit.'

'I couldn't agree more.'

Beverley sat back, feeling a growing sense of irritation. She'd never fired a ghost before, but she'd sacked the occasional cleaner and had always rather enjoyed the experience. It wasn't that she wanted the ghost to grab the nearest butter knife and make a play for her wrists, but surely a few tears, perhaps even a little gentle begging, wouldn't go astray?

'I must say you're taking this awfully well,' said Beverley. 'You do realize that I'm dismissing you, yes?'

'Well, as much as it's in your power to do so, yes, I get it,' said the ghost. 'And that's fine. I mean, my contract says that I get paid for every submitted page, so it doesn't make a huge amount of difference to me either way. It just means that I don't have to spend any more of my time on this. Although, it has been a positive experience.'

'Has it?' asked Beverley, resisting the urge to scratch her eyes out. 'In what way?'

'Well, as I told you when we met, I originally wanted to go into journalism,' said the ghost. 'But this week, spending time on *The Ski Instructor of Verbier*, I've come to realize that my true calling might be fiction.'

'Then perhaps you should go into journalism after all? The tabloids would find you indispensable.'

'Taking rather mundane plots and stereotypical characters and then breathing some actual life into them has proved rather interesting to me. I've started to think, well, what if I didn't have to start with a bunch of clichés and do everything I can to make them sound a bit less ridiculous? What if I could start with authentic characters who do things that people actually do in the twenty-first century? And perhaps play with the language a little. I even have an exciting idea about page layout that—'

'I'm not interested.'

'To shape prose on the page to mirror the emotions of the—'

'I don't care, dear.'

'Even to find a way to blend poetry with prose and—'

'Is this monologue going to continue much longer? I don't know if you're mistaking me for the Publishing Director of Faber & Faber, but that sort of thing doesn't interest me in the slightest.'

The ghost shrugged her shoulders, looking a little disappointed by the lack of encouragement.

'Well, it was just a thought,' she said.

'Some thoughts are best kept to oneself,' replied Beverley, making a distinct effort to stop gritting her teeth, worried that she might pare them down to stubs in anger. 'During the whole Brexit drama, I found myself erotically drawn to John Bercow, but I didn't go around telling people.'

'I feel that I've offended you,' said the ghost after a slight pause.

'It's just that you have such little respect for what I do,' replied Beverley. 'Speaking as a mother, you do realize that, having sold twenty million books around the world, there are some who might say that my work actually appeals to readers?'

'Well, it's not really your work, though, is it? It's the work of your ghosts.'

'They're *my* ideas!' insisted Beverley, finishing her Bellini now and wishing she had four more lined up, before throwing a quick, imperious look towards the waitress, who scampered off to pour another. Waiting for it to arrive, Beverley decided that she'd wasted enough of her morning on this smug little creature and wasn't going to indulge her any longer. 'I'm glad you're not upset,' she said. 'And, naturally, I wish you all the best with your literary endeavours.'

'Thank you. As it happens, I have an idea for a historical novel set in Ukraine during the Cossack uprising of 1648.'

'Sounds utterly tedious,' said Beverley.

'Sort of a *Doctor Zhivago* tale. Only set in Odessa. My new boyfriend, Pylyp, has been telling me some stories and—'

'I'm sorry,' said Beverley, feeling as if someone had just placed her left hand in a bucket of water and her right in a toaster before pressing the 'on' switch on the wall socket. 'Did you say Pylyp?'

'Yes, that's right.' The ghost sat back and feigned surprise. 'Of course, you know him a little, don't you? He worked with you on *Strictly*.'

A lengthy,

     lengthy,

          lengthy,

               silence.

'How on earth do you know Pylyp?' asked Beverley, her words coming out in a voice that even she didn't fully recognize. Somehow, it reminded her of Kermit the Frog.

'Well, it's the funniest thing,' said the ghost. 'I was in your house the other day when the phone rang. I answered it, and it was him. Well, we got talking because I recognized his accent and I told him about my own family history, and one thing led to another and he asked me to meet him for a drink. To talk about the old country, you know. He was in Odessa breaking up with an old girlfriend at the time, but he came back the next day and we met up. And that was it. Love at first sight. For both of us.'

An

            even

                    lengthier

                            silence.

'You're in a relationship with Pylyp?' asked Beverley eventually. 'Yes.'

'And you're in love with him?'

'Well, I mean it's only been twenty-four hours, but I feel it might be the real thing. We're like a couple of Lego pieces that just click. Perhaps it has something to do with our shared heritage.'

'And your big speech about a woman not needing a man but finding fulfilment through her work and so on?'

The ghost laughed. 'Well, yes, I believe that in general. And it's important to write about such characters. But, come on. You've seen him. He's gorgeous. He's opened me up in ways I never thought possible. His skills as a lover are—'

Beverley stood up and slammed her hands on the table, making the cups rattle. She gathered up her pages and threw them in the ghost's face. The ghost sat there, looking utterly bewildered.

'I have only one thing to say to you,' she hissed. 'And it isn't even for you. It's for Pylyp. You can tell him from me that he will never see Ustym Karmaliuk again.'

And with that, she collected up her belongings, charged through the doors, out on to Dean Street, and hailed the first black cab that passed by, leaving the ghost with the bill.

THE IMPORTANCE OF BEING IN UNIFORM

Nelson and Shane were still in the first flush of excitement about their new romance when Shane remarked on how flexible the Metropolitan Police were with their working hours.

'How do you mean?' asked Nelson.

'Well, the fact that we get to spend so much time together,' replied Shane, who was alphabetizing Nelson's bookcases at the time. It was his first visit to the Cleverley household and Nelson had snuck him upstairs without running into any members of his family. 'We're lucky in that, aren't we?'

'Very lucky,' agreed Nelson.

'So how do they organize it, then? The hours, I mean?'

'Well, when you finish at the . . . you know . . . the police academy, you fill in a form saying the hours you're available and basically . . . well, they just work around you.'

'Really?' asked Shane, turning around with an incredulous expression on his face. 'That seems very accommodating of them.'

'They need all the police they can get, you see.'

'That makes having a social life easy. Anyone would think there's no crime after 5 p.m.'

'There isn't, really,' said Nelson. 'Most criminals go home to their families at the end of the day, just like everyone else. Or down the local pub to catch up with friends. Maybe out to a show in the West End.'

'Right,' said Shane. 'Back in Ireland, there's rotas, I think. My cousin is a garda in Newbridge and he's run ragged half the time.'

'Perhaps the Irish have more criminal tendencies?' suggested Nelson.

'Hmm,' said Shane, returning to the books and deciding not to pull at this particular thread. 'Anyway, my point is that we'd find it a lot more difficult to get to know each other if you were working twelve-hour days at unsociable times.'

'I definitely chose the right uniform,' agreed Nelson, checking the emails on his phone to see whether he'd received any more information from the Met. He'd got confirmation of his application and was now just waiting for a date for the interview. It might be a tricky year ahead, he reasoned, keeping his training secret from Shane. He was glad that he hadn't shown up to the speed-dating night in his scrubs or he'd now have seven years of medical school ahead of him.

'Oh, I forgot to tell you,' said Shane, turning around and bouncing over to the bed. 'My sister messaged earlier. She's in London for the day and suggested meeting for lunch.'

'That's nice,' said Nelson. 'You should go.'

'I meant we could go together. I could introduce you to her.'

'Ah,' said Nelson, who wasn't quite ready to meet his boyfriend's family yet. 'I can't today. It's one of those rare Fridays when I have to go in.'

'Oh no!' said Shane. 'Can't you get out of it?'

'No, sorry. We're going after some . . .' He racked his brain.

'Some bad drugs people. Supplying half the schools in the city. We're going in hard. It's a 747.'

'What's a 747?' asked Shane.

'I can't tell you. It's top-secret police talk.'

Shane grinned. 'That's such a turn-on,' he said. 'Tell me another one.'

'Um . . .' Nelson thought about it. 'An A-380.'

'Jesus, that's hot.'

'A 777-300.'

'Okay, stop it, sexy, or I'll never be able to finish these books. What time do you have to be in at?'

'Two o'clock,' said Nelson.

'Oh, that's fine, then,' said Shane. 'I told Susan I'd meet her at one. Why don't you just stop by and say hello first? You'd probably have time for a quick sandwich.'

'I don't know if I should,' said Nelson. 'I need my brain to be in the zone. For the drug cartel. I really want to take them down, you know? They're poisoning our kids with their filthy crack heroin.'

'Isn't it crack cocaine?'

'It's a new blend. A sort of shandy.'

'Please. It would mean a lot to me.' Shane put his arms around Nelson. 'I've told her all about you and she's excited to meet you. And she'll be really impressed if you wear your uniform. In fact, I suppose you'll have to if you're going into work immediately afterwards.'

Nelson thought about it. The uniform did give him confidence, after all, and it meant that he'd probably be able to talk to her without completely falling apart.

'Well, all right, then,' he said, giving in. 'But I won't be able to stay long.'

'Brilliant! She'll be delighted.' Shane leaned in for a kiss. 'I feel so lucky that I met you, Nelson.'

'And I you,' he replied, a warm sensation filling his entire body. 'I was honestly convinced that I was going to spend my life alone, that no one would ever be interested in me.'

'How could you have thought such a thing?' asked Shane. 'You're handsome, you're clever, you're funny. You have a great job and you look so sexy when you're all dressed up for it.'

Nelson smiled. He had to admit this was true.

NEGATIVE TWITTER RATIO

@TruthIsASword's followers count was climbing due to the endless stream of vitriol Elizabeth was pushing into the world but, to her disappointment, @ElizCleverley ✅ seemed to have plateaued and had even lost followers in the wake of George's imbroglios. In fact, she'd received quite a few abusive messages from strangers on Twitter, condemning her for even being related to the disgraced chat-show host. She hadn't dared to respond to any of them, fearing a greater backlash, but had to admit that she was beginning to dread tapping on the little blue app on her iPhone. It wasn't easy being on the receiving end of such nastiness. Why did people do it, she wondered?

In an attempt to reverse the slide, however, she'd arranged a meeting with her former social media creativity director, Trevé, who she hadn't spoken to since the disappointing leak of her sex tape. As she sat in the waiting area, staring at him through the glass walls of his office, she could see him talking to a young woman who had recently appeared on a reality-television show where all she did was sit in a laundromat, inexplicably wearing a bikini, while handsome young men came in to express how deeply in love they were with her. Elizabeth narrowed her eyes as she watched the girl, whose name was Sofiii, with three i's, throw her head back and laugh uproariously at whatever Trevé had just said before taking her phone from her pocket and pointing it in their direction. This would be good for a few hundred Instagram likes.

'I'm sorry, there's no photographs in here,' said the boy behind the reception desk, who couldn't have been more than nineteen, and whose chiselled features and blistering blue eyes guaranteed that he would not be stationed there for long.

'I'm not taking a picture,' she lied. 'I'm just checking my make-up.'

The boy raised one perfect eyebrow, unconvinced, but returned to his own phone while she took a snap of the scene that was playing out before her and posted it under her @TruthIsASword identity.

@TruthIsASword Fake boobs Sofiii looking for panto work this Christmas? #desperate #gorgeous #slut #lipfiller #tragic #sisters #talentless #freakshow #heroinaddict #dearfriend #nohateplease #whore #girlpower

This quick burst of nastiness did for her temper what a glass of fresh orange juice might do for a diabetic whose blood sugar had run dangerously low. Still, she resented being kept waiting and tapped her foot on the ground impatiently, incurring the irritated stare of the receptionist.

'Problem?' she asked.

'It's hard to concentrate when you're tapping your foot like that.'

'Do you really need to concentrate when you're playing Candy Crush?'

The boy laughed and shook his head. 'Candy Crush?' he asked disdainfully. 'I'm sorry, did 2017 call? Does it want its games back?'

Elizabeth's face grew red at the slight. It was one thing to ask her to quieten down, but another entirely to accuse her of being off-trend.

'Do you always speak to your clients in such a rude fashion?' she asked.

'You're not a client.'

'I used to be.'

He smiled. 'Ah, the worst words in the English language,' he said. '*I used to be*. We get a lot of used-to-bes showing up here, hoping to reclaim their relevance.'

'It was my choice to move on,' she said, cut to the quick. 'Trevé is a dear, but he wasn't doing all that I needed.'

'And yet here you are. Back again.'

'Yes, but . . . but . . .' She scrambled to think of something cutting to say, but nothing sprang to mind.

'What did you say your name was again?'

'Elizabeth Cleverley,' she said. 'She/her,' she added, hoping this might win her a few points in his eyes.

'Oh, please,' he said, laughing contemptuously. 'Seriously, that's beyond cringe.'

'I was being ironic,' she said, chastened.

'No you weren't,' he replied, tapping something into his phone and snorting. 'Fuck me,' he said.

'I'd rather not, thanks.'

'You've got less than 7,000 followers.'

'Have I?' she asked, feigning ignorance. 'I never look, to be honest. I have a blue tick,' she added, sitting upright.

'Six thousand eight hundred and sixty-seven, to be precise. No, wait, you just lost two – 6,865. And yet you've tweeted almost 70,000 times. That's an NTR of . . .' He tapped something quickly into his phone. 'About 10.2. You're literally a Negative 10.2. No wonder you're here. You hear about people with high NTRs, but you don't ever expect to meet one in real life.'

Elizabeth glared at him. NTR? What the fuck? 'I literally have no clue what you're talking about,' she said.

'NTR,' he repeated, putting his phone down on the desk and leaning back to stretch out, ensuring that his too-short T-shirt rose up above the waistband of his jeans, revealing a perfectly sculpted six-pack. She stared at it, willing herself to look away. 'Negative Twitter Ratio. It's a basic rule on social media. The number of your tweets should *never* exceed the number of your followers. If you've got, say, a hundred followers but have tweeted ten thousand times, then you're just screaming into a void.' He scrolled through the app. 'Look at this guy, for example. Says he's one half of a podcast. But he's tweeted 120,000 times to about 5,000 followers. That's a NTR of 24! You'd wonder how the poor guy still has a fingerprint on his thumb after so much tweeting. Someone needs to tell him that not every random thought that goes through his head needs to be immortalized for the sake of four likes. Don't worry, Elizabeth, your account is nowhere near as embarrassing as that, but still, you have a NTR of 10.2. I, on the other hand, have around 430,000 followers, but I've only tweeted 7,000 times. That's the way it should be. So I have a *Positive* Twitter Ratio of 62. Hashtag winning.'

'Four hundred and thirty thousand followers?' she asked, trying to keep the envy and disbelief out of her voice. 'Who are you? What have you done?'

'A bit of everything,' he said with a shrug. 'Some runway. Some commercial. Some magazine. A little reality. I did a stint on *Hollyoaks* when I was younger, but it wasn't the place for me to develop, you know? It's one thing to be on a soap but another to show up at the Soap Awards and act like it's the Oscars. Plus, I've got some really great stuff in the pipeline, but I'm not at liberty to talk about that right now. Sorry.'

'Of course you're not,' she said, rolling her eyes. 'How convenient.'

'I've also got some important followers.'

'Really?' she asked, intrigued now. 'Who?'

'Dermot O'Leary. Ed Sheeran. Mabel. Some of the writers at *GQ* and *Esquire*. Oh, and Haz, of course.'

'Haz?'

'Harry.'

'Harry who?' she asked, her eyes opening wide. 'Prince Harry?'

'Christ, no. That would be mortifying. Harry Styles.'

'What . . . ?' she asked, putting her hands on the sides of the chair to settle herself. He couldn't possibly be telling the truth. 'No . . . you can't have . . .'

'We're, like, mates,' said the boy, as if it was neither here nor there. 'Honestly, I can't talk about him, though, so please don't ask. He really values his privacy and I respect that. He's the same about me.'

She looked around the waiting area, hoping to see a water dispenser because she was beginning to feel dehydrated.

'Harry Styles follows you,' she said, more of a bewildered statement than a question.

'Yeah, but we mostly talk over text. I don't even check his tweets most of the time. They're, like, more for the public, you know?'

'You have his number?'

'Sure.'

She felt sick.

'God, sometimes I forget that he's so famous,' said the boy, laughing. 'To me, he's just Haz, you know? He's just a mate.'

'Of course,' said Elizabeth, trying to play it cool and not feel utterly resentful that this boy, this receptionist, this *nobody*, had hit the social media motherlode. 'He's such a great guy.'

'Oh, do you know him, then?'

'Well, not personally, no.'

'Then, can I ask that you don't talk about him as if you do? He's not public property, even though so many of you think he is. Just give the guy some space, yeah? Anyway, my point is, you've got an NTR of 10.2. You need to stop tweeting and concentrate on building your followers.'

Elizabeth stared at him. As much as she was torn between wanting to rip him limb from limb and have sex with him on the desk, she began to feel that she was in the presence of a social media Yoda and it was best to learn what she could from him before he kicked her out of Dagobah.

'But if I stop tweeting,' she asked, 'then how will my followers build?'

'It's not that you stop entirely,' he explained with a sigh. 'You just need to give it more thought, that's all. You slow it down and ask yourself, is this something that people are going to be interested in? Will they like it, retweet it? Will others follow you because of it? Or will it just attract trolls?' He picked up his phone and started scrolling. 'Like, there's way too much virtue signalling on your timeline. No one's interested in that shit. Not any more. People picking a topic and tweeting about it all day, every day. Total waste of time. What's all this bullshit about a leper colony, for example?'

435

Elizabeth looked down at the ground, feeling a little embarrassed by the question.

'My boyfriend and I – well, he's not my boyfriend any more,' she added, glancing up to see whether he might react in some way to this, but nothing. 'We were thinking about going to Indonesia to help out in a leper colony.'

'Why?' he asked.

She shrugged and, honestly, felt too exhausted even to try dressing it up. 'Oh, I have no fucking idea,' she said, throwing her arms in the air. 'He wanted to go and I wanted to be with him so I said sure, whatever.'

'And did you go?'

'Christ, no. I ended up dumping him. So that was the end of that.'

'Then why are you posting this shit? No one wants to read about lepers. Do you honestly think Kendall is interested in lepers? Or Billie? Or Harry – actually, he probably is. He's such a caring guy, but don't spread that around, please. It's a private thing. Anyway, what I'm saying is that this kind of polish-my-halo tweeting is the absolute worst. It's olden days, man. It's got fleas. It's on a Zimmer frame.'

Elizabeth nodded, impressed by his wisdom. She started to picture him wearing a slim-fit suit, waiting at the top of an aisle for her, while Harry Styles stood at the altar in a Stella McCartney dress, long earrings and a pair of Doc Martens as he prepared to officiate. 'What's your name anyway?' she asked.

He tapped something on his phone and hers immediately beeped. Picking it up she saw her new follower. He had a blue tick too, the fucker.

'@WillBuchanModel ✓,' she said, following him back.

'Take a look at my timeline,' he said. 'I post once every few days at most. And I keep it minimal.'

She scrolled through his recent posts. Most of them were pictures of him having just emerged from the shower, wearing a low-slung towel, looking deeply concerned, as if someone had just informed him that the Spanish flu had wiped out three per cent of the world's population in the early twenties and he was devastated by the pointless loss of life.

'You're ripped,' she said.

'Am I? Oh, thanks. I basically eat whatever I want. I don't even go to the gym more than five or six times a week.'

She looked over at him and waited for his eyes to meet hers, feeling a sudden conviction that this conversation was one they would recall months from now, when they were lying in bed together, and laugh at how cute their first encounter was. He didn't look back, though. In fact, he was focussed on something on his MacBook and seemed to have forgotten her presence entirely.

'You can just ask, you know,' she said finally.

'I can what?' he replied, finally looking up at her.

'You can just ask.'

'Ask what?'

'For my number.'

'Why would I do that?' he asked, baffled.

'I think we both know why,' she said, laughing a little.

He stared at her, his beautiful face as blank as his beautiful mind.

'So you can ask me out.'

'Oh,' he said, leaning back in his chair, as if this was something that happened to him a lot. 'Oh, right. I'm flattered. Honestly, that's just so nice of you. But no. That's okay.'

She stared at him. 'Excuse me?' she said.

'It's okay,' he said. 'I don't need your number.'

'Oh, of course. You have it on your system already.'

'Do we? Oh, right.'

'So?' she asked.

'So what?'

'So I'll wait to hear from you?'

'You've lost me.'

'For drinks.'

'Oh, I don't drink,' he said.

'Dinner, then.'

'You want me to take you to dinner?'

'Well, don't you?'

'Not really, no. Sorry. I think you've got the wrong idea.'

She felt her breakfast beginning to make its way from her stomach in the opposite direction than nature had originally intended.

'I was kidding. Obviously,' she said.

'Were you, though?'

'Yes.'

'I don't think you were. And like I say, I'm flattered. But no, sorry. No offence.'

'Oh, sweetie,' she said, trying to hold back the tears that were unexpectedly building behind her eyes. This was turning into a rotten day, a rotten week, a rotten month, a rotten life. 'You couldn't offend me if you tried.'

'It's just, you're not really my type, that's all.'

'Oh, I get it,' she said, breathing a sigh of relief. 'You're gay. Sorry, I should have realized. My mistake.'

'No, I'm not gay,' he said, frowning. 'I don't have to be gay for you not to be my type and, quite frankly, it's incredibly homophobic for you even to think that way. What is *wrong* with you?'

She swallowed and looked away. This entire encounter was turning into a disaster. Thankfully, beyond the glass wall, Sofiii seemed to be finishing up with Trevé, for she was on her feet now and they were beginning what would no doubt be a lengthy series of cheek kisses before releasing each other on to an unsuspecting public.

'There's no need to be a prick,' she said.

'I'm not being a prick,' he replied. 'I'm just being honest.'

She sat there, seething, wondering what she could possibly say to get her revenge on him, but nothing sprang to mind. What *was* wrong with her, she wondered? She was young, she was pretty, she was stylish. She'd nearly gone to a leper colony but hadn't, so had no infectious diseases.

'I get it,' she said finally. 'You're playing hard to get.'

'I'm honestly not.'

'You must be,' she replied, feeling her mortification grow and wondering how strong the windows were and whether, if she were to throw a chair at one, it would break and she could simply jump out. 'There's no reason why you wouldn't be interested in me. I'm hot.'

'You're okay,' he said with a shrug.

'I'm *hot*.'

'If you say so.'

'All right, then,' she said. 'Tell me. What is it? Give me one simple reason why you don't want to go out with me.'

He looked at her and sighed. 'It's not obvious?' he asked.

'Not to me.'

He picked up his phone and held it in the air. 'Six thousand, eight hundred and sixty-five followers,' he said. 'I don't date below six figures, let alone five. Sorry, sweetheart, but the fact is, you just don't matter.'

WAGES DAY

Achilles was pleased that Friday had finally arrived. He'd grown bored of Jeremy and anxious for Rebecca and prepared carefully for the evening ahead, shaving, showering, plucking and trimming, and applying manly scents to various parts of his body. He wore his smartest jeans and a blue satin shirt, opening the top two buttons to offer a preview of his smooth, hairless chest. Looking at his reflection in the mirror, he felt an almost erotic attraction to himself.

He'd arranged to meet Jeremy in Covent Garden and planned on arriving at Rebecca's house a couple of hours later £5,000 better off. Entering the pub, he was surprised that his mark was not already waiting for him but chose a table in a corner and passed his fake ID to the barmaid as he ordered a rum and Coke.

Sitting alone, he began to think about the £35,000 locked away in his bedroom, feeling rather smug at his own ingenuity. No one in his class at school was as wealthy as him. Their families were, yes, but they weren't. In fact, most of his friends were still existing off handouts from their parents and, while he too accepted George and Beverley's weekly stipend, he rarely needed to dip into it. He wondered whether Rebecca might be impressed if he was to whisk her away, first class, to Paris for the weekend, staying in the George V or Le Meurice. Or would that be too flashy, too gauche? He didn't know her well enough yet to be sure whether conspicuous consumption might diminish him in her estimation. Still, there was plenty of time to find out, and Jeremy's five grand alone would cover the cost of the trip if she wanted to go.

Glancing at his watch, he frowned when he saw that it was almost ten past the hour. He hated being kept waiting, and most of his previous victims had never dared, particularly on what he thought of as Wages Day.

The only time that he'd ever felt a little guilty about what he was doing was with the chiropodist. The poor man had grown pale and started crying when Achilles explained that their entire relationship had been a con. He'd tried to make Achilles feel guilty by telling him stories about the horrendous things that had happened to him in his childhood and how they had led him to this place, sitting in a bar with a boy young enough to be his son, flirting tragically. In the end, he took eight grand off him, one of his most financially successful deceptions yet.

The barmaid came over and handed him a newspaper. 'Been stood up?' she asked.

'Hardly,' he said. 'I'm early, that's all.'

'Something for you to read,' she said, leaving the paper on the table and, although he never really bothered with the news, he opened it now for something to do and was met with the face of his father on the front page, along with that of a woman he didn't recognize.

CLEVERLEY GOT ME PREGGERS AND THEN DIDN'T WANT ANYTHING TO DO WITH ME

the woman was quoted as saying.

'Fuck me,' he said under his breath, reading it slowly, his heart sinking, uncertain whether or not his father had actually got this woman pregnant or not. By the time he reached the end, his excitement about the night had diminished somewhat as he wondered whether he'd even have a family to go home to in the morning. It was gone six twenty now and still no sign of Jeremy, so he took out his phone and sent a message:

Achilles Cleverley
You on the way?

He stared at the screen, waiting for the dance of the little blue dots that would signify a reply was forthcoming, but nothing appeared. Perhaps Jeremy was underground, he decided, on a Tube with no signal.

He flicked through the rest of the newspaper, dreading the hell that would surely break loose at home while feeling grateful that he would not be there to witness it. His parents used to be happy – he could remember plenty of happy years – but that seemed to be in the past now. His family had changed. All of them. And not for the better. When had that happened? And why?

Achilles Cleverley
Dude, you're nearly 30 mins late. Don't let me down.
Wouldn't be a good idea.

How long could he keep this scam going, he wondered as he ordered another rum and Coke and tried to forget about his parents' difficulties. He would be eighteen soon and, before he knew it, he'd be in his twenties. At what age did one's looks start to fade? Twenty-seven? Twenty-eight? Nelson was twenty-two, but he'd never been that good-looking to begin with. Although, in fairness, his brother seemed to be getting more handsome now that he was getting laid. Perhaps it was a confidence thing. Perhaps that was all he'd ever needed, to feel that he was worthy of someone's love.

To his surprise, he felt tears forming in his eyes and wiped them away. What the fuck, he wondered? What am I crying over?

This burst of humanity made him feel good about himself, and he would have revelled in his own innate decency if he hadn't been growing increasingly annoyed about the fact that the middle-aged man who he was ripping off for £5,000 had still not arrived.

Achilles Cleverley

5 more minutes, then I leave. And it's bad news for you if I do.

'Another drink, love?' asked the barmaid, coming over, and he shook his head.

'Better not,' he said, not wanting to have too much alcohol in his system when he met Rebecca. They'd probably have a couple of drinks before hitting the bedroom, and the last thing he needed was to incapacitate himself.

'Big plans for the night? Handsome boy like you, all dressed up.'

He looked up at her, wondering whether she was flirting with him. She was old enough to be his grandmother, but the idea intrigued him. Perhaps he didn't just have to go after men. Perhaps he could go after women too. Once he hit his twenties, he could be a high-class gigolo. He'd seen it in movies, the busy, middle-aged career woman, too exhausted to focus on a personal life, but who wanted a hot young guy to be waiting in her apartment when she got home.

'Something like that,' he muttered, and she wandered off. He took one last look at his watch and then his phone. Jeremy clearly wasn't coming, the fucker. Chickened out at the last minute when it came to handing over the money. Well, he wasn't going to hang around any longer; he had better things to do tonight.

Achilles Cleverley
Leaving now

he messaged.

> You'll be hearing from me tomorrow and it won't just be 5k I need then. You messed up, Jeremy. Big time.

THE HOMEBODY

Beverley was on her sixth glass of white wine when an extraordinary hammering came on the front door. She startled, wondering whether someone was trying to break in. Gathering herself together, she made her way slowly into the hallway, where the banging was growing more insistent by the second.

'Who's there?' she asked, leaning a little unsteadily against the woodwork.

'Is me!' called a voice from outside. 'Is Pylyp!'

She gasped. She'd been waiting to hear from that lying,

cheating son of a bitch, and now here he was at last. And he didn't sound best pleased.

'Pylyp who?' she asked, playing for time.

'How many Pylyp you know? Open door before I kick it down with big Ukrainian foot!'

'What do you want?' she cried.

'I want tortoise of mine!'

'Well, you can't have him. You abandoned him. He lives with me now! We've grown very close.'

'Open door!' he shouted and, anxious that her neighbours might hear the fuss, she did as instructed, standing in the doorway while he remained on the step outside with a furious expression on his face. He'd cut his hair a little shorter since last she'd seen him, and it suited him. Also, he was a little more pumped, his arms and chest bulging in his too-small T-shirt. Taking him in with a hungry stare, she wanted nothing more than to rip his clothes off and commit an act of public indecency on the street. Still, ever the lady, she restrained herself.

'Well, look who it is,' she said, swirling the wine around the glass she was holding. 'I assumed you were dead. Killed fighting those pesky Russian invaders.'

Pylyp had the grace to look a little shame-faced.

'Was bad of me,' he admitted. 'I should have called.'

'Or texted. Or emailed. Or Skyped. Or Facebooked. Or Tweeted. Or Snapped. Or Insta'd. We live in a world where it's basically become more difficult *not* to contact someone than it is to contact them. So yes, you should have called.'

'I terrible man. I very sorry.'

'How sorry?'

He shrugged his shoulders, clearly uncertain how apologetic he needed to be. Beverley sighed and opened the door further.

'Fine. Come in,' she said, the wine and the earlier Bellinis working their way through her system so enthusiastically that she felt that, even if she was furious with him, one last shag for the road wouldn't go amiss. And, as an added bonus, it would put that ungrateful ghost in her place.

'I no come in. I no fight with husband.'

'My husband is elsewhere.'

'Where he is?'

'I don't know and I don't care. Out offending people, I assume.'

Pylyp stepped inside and she led him into the living room, where she sat down on an armchair, leaving him standing. She felt a bit like Blofeld staring at James Bond, preparing to reveal her dastardly plan before killing him.

'So,' she said. 'I gather you're in a new relationship. I'm so happy for you.'

'Was wrong of me not to say. I thought you go crazy shit-bag if you find out, so I say nothing.'

'Me?' she asked, adopting an innocent expression. 'Go crazy shitbag? Oh, please. Speaking as a mother, you can't possibly imagine that you meant that much to me.'

'You send me hundreds of messages,' he replied. 'Is too much. It makes me think you mad woman.'

'How dare you!'

'Is not strange thing to be. So many women go crazy shit-bag and become mad woman over me. I very sexy.'

'If you'd just replied,' she said plaintively.

'I sorry for that. I know how much you like sexing me.'

'Don't flatter yourself. I can barely remember what it was like.'

'But you always go big bang and say, Pylyp, you are best lover ever.'

'I think you're mixing me up with someone else.'

'No, is true story. You ride me like cowgirl at funfair.'

'Oh, shut up! Just shut up!'

'But is true story.'

'It doesn't matter now anyway,' said Beverley, finishing her glass of wine but staring inside it, as if she hoped some more might magically appear. 'As it happens, I've moved on too. I met a lovely . . .' She ran through countries in her mind, trying to decide which would be the most offensive to him. '*Moldovan* boy. Vladimir.'

Pylyp had the rudeness to look relieved. 'Is good news,' he said. 'Now I no longer feel so guilty.'

'But you should feel guilty, you fucker!' she shouted. 'The last time I saw you, we were at Heathrow Airport and you were swearing lifelong devotion to me. Then you shag your way around Odessa before coming back here and falling for a nobody just because she has a little Ukrainian blood in her veins. The whole thing is ridiculous. And insulting.'

'Sometimes,' he said, sitting down now and scrunching up his face as if he was about to offer words of profound wisdom. 'Sometimes the heart, it is wanting what it is wanting. And we must follow it like the dog after the smell in the grass. We had many happy times together. This we must remember.'

'And we could have had many more,' she replied. 'But now my happy times will be with . . . Dimitri.'

'I think his name is Vladimir?'

'It is. Dimitri is my pet name for him.'

'Yes, I see,' he said, and the expression on his face so infuriated Beverley that she threw the contents of her glass in his face.

'Is more effective when you haven't drunk it all already,' he said, remaining bone dry.

She let out a scream, then stood up, reached for the bottle and poured herself another.

'You go to Odessa, I hear,' he said.

'Not for you,' she replied. 'It was a research trip for my novel. In fact, I barely thought about you when I was there.'

'But you call on my mother to say hello and how are you.'

'I happened to be passing, yes.'

'This, you should not have done. She piss in my ear for sleeping with old woman like you.'

'She did what?' asked Beverley, uncertain that she'd heard him correctly. 'She pissed in your ear?'

'Is expression,' said Pylyp. 'It means—'

'I can guess what it means. Unless you Ukrainians do things literally.'

'You say the racist things now,' said Pylyp, growing annoyed. 'Like your husband. Is the way with all the Englanders, yes? You all hate the foreigners. You think you still have the empire but you no have this any more.'

'My husband isn't a racist!' shouted Beverley, forgetting for a moment that he was on her shit list too. 'Don't you dare say a bad word against him.'

'Your husband is the phobic.'

'That's not even a word!'

'Is word.'

'Isn't.'

'Is.'

'Is not!'

She let out a scream of frustration. It seemed that today was a day when her conversations were only going to go around in circles.

'What are you doing here, Pylyp?' she said eventually. 'What do you want? If it's to try to get back together with me—'

'Is not that,' he said. 'I no want that.'

'Oh,' she replied, feeling deflated. 'How stupid of me.'

'I come for best friend of my life, Ustym Karmaliuk.'

'He's out.'

'How he is out? Where he go?'

'He had a date.'

Pylyp frowned, looking like he almost believed this for a moment.

'With other tortoise?' he asked.

'No, with a local Labrador. They've become very close. They went to the cinema together to watch the new Marvel movie. I imagine they're doing some heavy petting in the back row now.'

Pylyp shook his head and wagged his finger at her.

'Tortoise no go on date with dog,' he said. 'And Marvel not real cinema. The Scorsese man, he say this. I think you are making fun of me.'

'You do that quite well enough by yourself,' she replied. 'You don't need any help from me.'

'Come. You give me Ustym Karmaliuk, we kiss on cheek, I pat your bottom if you like, we say goodbye. You regret my loss and I forget you for ever. Is proper way.'

'I told you, he's out.'

'He not out. Is crazy idea. Ustym Karmaliuk never go out. He is . . . how you say . . . the homebody.'

'Just leave, Pylyp, all right? I don't want you here. You've hurt me terribly.'

He stood up and his expression turned darker. 'I not leave this house without Ustym Karmaliuk,' he declared. 'Ustym Karmaliuk!' he shouted, raising his voice, as if the poor unfortunate tortoise would hear him and come running. 'Ustym Karmaliuk! You are where?'

'Out!' insisted Beverley, ushering him into the hallway and

towards the door. She opened it and pushed him on to the street. Across the road, a small group of cyclists were taking a break from what appeared to be a lengthy ride, for they had parked their bikes and were drinking from water bottles while looking rather dishevelled. Each one wore a vest displaying the logo of the Royal Society for the Prevention of Cruelty to Animals. 'Get out and don't come back.'

'I no leave without Ustym Karmaliuk,' he protested. 'He 115 years old and part of Tataryn family. I no leave him with crazy shitbag woman!'

'You've left him here all week with crazy shitbag woman!' she shouted.

The cyclists across the street were looking over now, clearly enjoying the little drama playing out before them. One took out his phone and started filming it.

'Is not right!' insisted Pylyp. 'You steal my tortoise. You steal Ustym Karmaliuk. Is family to me.'

'Oh, for Christ's sake,' she said, eager to bring this entire conversation to an end. 'If he means that much to you, I'll get him. Just stay where you are and don't move. I'll bring him out. Do *not* come back inside.'

'Is good solution to vexatious problem,' replied Pylyp, looking relieved. 'I wait here.'

Beverley marched into the kitchen and looked around. Someone had taken the shoe box down from atop the pile of books and relocated it to the garden door. She picked it up and opened it carefully, hoping that she would not be presented with a horrendous spectacle, but, happily, Ustym Karmaliuk looked much the same in death as he had in life.

She marched back towards the front door and opened it with an embittered smile on her face.

'You want the tortoise?' she asked.

'I want tortoise,' agreed Pylyp.

'Then here! Have him!'

And then, with all the determination of a US president throwing out the first pitch on the opening day of the World Series, she drew her arm back and flung Ustym Karmaliuk through the air as if he was a frisbee. He soared high above the street, his body displaying extraordinary aerodynamism, landing only a few feet from the RSPCA cyclists, where his shell smashed into a dozen pieces. Most of the riders screamed. Two threw up. One passed out.

Pylyp placed his hands to his cheeks and let out a roar of horror, but she didn't care.

'We're done,' she said, slamming the door in his face. 'Don't come back!'

IT STARTED WITH A PUPPY

So bruised did Elizabeth feel by her unexpectedly wounding encounter that she didn't even stay for her appointment with Trevé – there was no advice he could give her that would be better than that of @WillBuchanModel ✔ – marching out of his office and making her way down the street, wiping tears from her eyes. Entering the first pub she came across, she ordered a large glass of white wine and sat at a corner table, the only person present at this hour of the day, feeling a strong urge to get completely wasted.

The boy's words had struck her like a hammer-blow and she

took out her phone, staring at it for a moment before placing it on the table before her. When, she wondered, had the success of her life become predicated on the number of strangers willing to read about the minutiae of her day? How had all this madness begun? She'd signed up for Twitter when she was in sixth form without really thinking about it, because most of her friends were embracing the platform, but she hadn't committed much time or energy to it until a sunny afternoon a couple of years ago when she found herself sitting in Hyde Park and a cute puppy had come over to stare at her. She'd taken a photograph and posted a humorous comment alongside it, and the tweet had received a rapturous response. Watching the numbers of likes shoot up had given her a sense of achievement that she'd never quite felt before. She'd never seen herself as someone who might succeed on her own merits. Her parents, after all, were the high achievers. Their children didn't seem destined for any great fame. Nelson was painfully shy, Achilles was an idiot, and she didn't even know what she was or what she wanted to be. But something about that picture of the puppy had changed things for her, making her feel that she could have a voice in the world too.

Once, she recalled, she used to read books. And listen to music. She'd even written some songs that weren't terrible, but she couldn't remember the last time she'd picked up her guitar or read a novel from cover to cover. Whenever she tried, she could barely get through a few paragraphs before reaching for her phone to document the fact that she was reading it in the first place, and by the time she'd posted that and tagged all the relevant people, she'd lost interest in the book itself and would toss it aside. It had served its function, after all. It had given her something to tell people about. To let them know that she was alive.

Why, she asked herself, did she not feel validated as a human being unless strangers were listening to her, commenting on her, liking her? This small piece of plastic and computer circuitry sitting before her had taken control over her life. Would she even exist if it didn't?

She stood up, ordered another glass of wine, and deliberately left her phone on the bar as she made her way back to her seat, waiting to see how she might feel. Her hand started to tremble a little. She held it up and yes, her fingers were noticeably shaking. A newspaper sat on the next table, folded in half, and she saw a picture of an attractive woman on the front, with the words *then didn't want anything to do with me* underneath, and she wondered whether she might get her news from the print media in future. What would that be like? She frowned. It didn't make a lot of sense. Surely, by the time the newspapers were printed, brought to the shops, purchased and taken home again, all that news would be old news?

The barman came over, handed her phone back, and she muttered a quick thank you, feeling a surge of relief to have these six crucial ounces back in her possession. There were some notifications on her home screen, a few messages from her father, her mother and from Nelson, but she ignored them all and switched it to mute as she continued to drink her wine.

Imagine, she thought to herself, just imagine what it would be like to delete your account, like Wilkes had done. Would it be like cutting off your oxygen supply? Now that he wasn't on any social media, she had absolutely no idea where her former boyfriend might be or what he might be doing. He could be still planning his trip to Indonesia, for all she knew.

She made a quick grab for the phone and pressed the Twitter app, turned to the settings and found the red button at the end of the screen that said 'Delete Account'. Her index finger hovered over it for a moment, but she knew it was impossible and returned it to the table. She couldn't do it, she could never do it. The truth was that the phone was as much a part of her as her hands, her feet, her nose, her mouth. She couldn't possibly live without it.

FUCKITY BYE

As George pushed open the door on Dean Street, he reached into his wallet to remove the black member's card before handing it across to the young woman behind the reception desk. Usually, the greeters didn't even glance at it, welcoming him warmly and asking whether he would be joined by any non-members. Today, however, he sensed a distinct *froideur* from the body language presented to him and, when the receptionist scanned the card into her computer, she did an excellent impression of a person who did not believe that he really belonged there.

'I'm not seeing you,' she said after a moment.

'Really?' replied George, raising an eyebrow. 'I'm standing right here. Perhaps if you looked in my direction, that would help?'

She turned and glared at him.

'This is a private members' club,' she said. 'Are you a member?'

'Well, let me see.' He looked up for a moment and put a hand on his chin. 'I remember joining when it first opened in

1995, and I don't believe my membership has ever lapsed in the quarter-century since then. And I've been here, I would imagine, on . . . oh . . . several thousand occasions. My wife went into labour with our third child, a delightful boy named Achilles, a complete idiot, of course, but delightful nevertheless, on the second floor during a dinner with Michael Winner. And, of course, you're holding my membership card in your hand. So I have a strong feeling that if you just continue to tap away on your keyboard, or perhaps consult one of your colleagues, then there's a good chance that I'll be granted access to the sacred area beyond.'

The woman continued to peruse her screen before, barely concealing her disdain, she handed the card back.

'Of course, Mr Cleverley,' she said. 'I should have recognized you.'

'Most people do.'

'It's wonderful to have you back with us.'

'Isn't it, though?' he said, returning the card to his wallet. 'Thank you so much.' He offered a courtly bow at the waist. 'I shall leave you to get on with your lawful business and I shall get on with mine.'

He turned and entered the ground-floor bar area, stepping out into the courtyard, where, he knew from many years' experience, Denise would be waiting for him, as she was, seated at her usual table and wearing an ill-advised scarlet jumpsuit. He glanced around, as everyone always did, trying not to make it obvious that he was looking to see who else was present. A special BAFTA Fellowship ceremony honouring an ageing film director was due to take place the following night, and several Hollywood stars had descended on London to join in the festivities. He smiled and waved at a couple of actors and actresses who he'd interviewed over the years but chose not to approach any of them, not just because it was considered bad form in a place like this, but because it was obvious they were employing all their best RADA or Juilliard skills to pretend that they hadn't seen him arrive.

'Darling,' said Denise as he collapsed into his chair with an exhausted sigh.

'Darling,' he replied.

'You look terrible, darling. Have you been sleeping?'

'Thank you. And no, not very well. It's been a difficult week.'

'The world is a hellish place,' remarked Denise. 'Sometimes I think it would be a lot easier just to put all the tablets in my house into a bowl, grind them up, and swallow the whole mess with a good bottle of Dom. Have you ever thought that?'

'I'm not the type, Denise,' he replied wearily. 'As you know, I have a tremendous lust for life.'

'Indeed. What would you like to drink? A coffee? Or something stronger?'

'What am I likely to need?'

'Something stronger.'

He raised a hand and the most beautiful young man he had ever seen in his life approached, as if from the ether, to take his order.

'So here's what I'd like,' he said, turning to him. 'Write it down so there'll be no mistakes. I want a sparkling mineral water, lots of ice, two slices of lime, and a plastic straw. Not paper, plastic. I want a cold lager in a glass that has been chilling in a fridge. And I want a double Glenfiddich with no water or ice. Just as it comes. Have you got all that?'

The waiter nodded, looking slightly terrified, and made his way quickly back towards the bar.

'I can see you're suffering the ill effects of your recent notoriety,' said Denise with a smile.

'Did I ever tell you that I have a theory about the waiters here?' he asked, happy to put off the inevitable for a few minutes longer.

'No, darling. Tell me now.'

'They're very handsome, yes?'

'Darling, they're works of art.'

'And they look for a job here because, I assume, they're hoping that they'll be spotted and cast in a movie. But the truth is, they're too good-looking. In the olden days, in our day—'

'Your day, darling. I'm a good seven years younger than you.'

'In the olden days – ah, thank you!'

The waiter had returned carrying a silver tray that bore each of George's three drinks, poured to his exact specifications.

'You're welcome, sir,' he said, scurrying away.

'In the olden days, movie stars looked like that. Marlon Brando. Warren Beatty. Robert Redford. But today, it's all changed. The most popular film stars now, as far as I can tell, are all shrivelled up little man-children. Whatever happened to Paul Newman?'

'He died, darling.'

'Yes, I know he died,' said George irritably. 'I mean whatever happened to his type? The waiters here belong to a bygone era, not to the contemporary world. They're simply too attractive to make it in the movies. Beauty, it seems, is no longer in vogue.'

'I don't have a problem with it, myself,' said Denise. 'It's one of the reasons I enjoy coming here so much.'

George grunted and took a sip from his water, then a long draught from his beer.

'It's people like them, however, who have done so much to make my life a misery this week. All of them weeping into their white mocha decafs with ten pumps of raspberry syrup and a chestnut on top over my supposedly transphobic remarks.'

'And the racist ones, don't forget,' said Denise.

'I hadn't forgotten.'

'And the ableist ones.'

'Yes, yes.'

'And the anti-Semitic ones.'

'Now, that's just not fair,' replied George, sitting forward in his chair and taking another drink from the water and the beer, and this time downing half the double whisky. 'I never actually made any anti-Semitic remarks. I hold my hands up to the others but, for the life of me, I don't know where that rumour came from. And now, everyone is sticking pins in voo-doo dolls of me.'

'I'm sure they're not.'

'Well, the girl at the door gave me an awful look when I came in,' he continued.

'Don't let it upset you, darling,' said Denise. 'It's all bullshit. You know it, and I know it. When you respond to these people, all you do is give them oxygen and validate their miserable little existences.'

George simmered down slightly and looked at her with a beseeching look in his eyes. 'You really think that no one pays any attention to them?'

'No one, darling.'

'So shall I assume that the BBC will just be ignoring them? And that they won't be taking any further action against me?'

'Ah,' said Denise, biting her lip. 'Well, not quite.'

'Then they do have a voice.'

'They make a certain amount of noise, it's true. And the problem is, when you're surrounded by noise, when it grows so loud that it becomes deafening, well, what do you do?'

'Turn it down?' suggested George.

'Turn it off,' said Denise.

'And how do they plan on doing that?'

Denise breathed in heavily, like a doctor preparing to tell a patient that the operation for an ingrown toenail has resulted in the amputation of both legs. 'No one can deny that you've had a good run, George,' she said. 'More than thirty years with Auntie.'

'Oh, Christ, they're not firing me, are they?'

'No, no, of course not.'

'They're not?'

'Well, yes. They are.'

'They're firing me?'

'Yes.'

'Then why did you say *of course not*?'

'Well, I didn't want you to get upset.'

'Jesus . . . can we just . . . are they firing me or not?'

'They are, I'm afraid.'

'When?'

She glanced at her watch. 'About seven minutes ago. In fact, your security pass won't work if you try to get back into the building. They're sending your belongings on.'

George sat back in his chair and felt a shooting pain charging through his chest. He gripped his arm, wondering whether he was having a heart attack, and rather hoped that he was, as it would probably force the corporation into giving him his job back.

'Darling, you've gone quite pale,' said Denise.

459

'I've spent my entire adult life at the BBC,' he replied quietly. 'I've given them everything. I thought I'd die there.'

'Well, who would want that? Perhaps you should look at it as early retirement.'

'I'm only sixty! I had another fifteen good years in me. And I haven't been given any lifetime achievement awards yet. And what about my knighthood? I was hoping for a knighthood. Even Anthony Blunt got a knighthood, and he was a Soviet spy!'

'They are giving you a very healthy severance package.'

'It's not about the money,' he snapped, raising his voice now, so some of the stars around him buried their faces in their Eggs Benedict. 'It's the betrayal. The backstabbing. The ingratitude. The shameless capitulation to a generation of morons whose hands are surgically attached to their smartphones.'

'Darling, tell me how to make it better,' said Denise, leaning forward. 'You name it and I'll do it.'

'Get me my job back.'

'No, I can't do that. Sorry.'

'Then what else is there? Christ alive. This is a ... a ... a humiliation. And really, when it comes down to it, what the fuck did I even do? They've created this narrative built around me being some sort of monster, and it doesn't matter what I say or do, they're going to see it their way and damn the consequences. I could withdraw every penny I have from the bank and give it to the homeless and they'd say that I was destabilizing the local economy. I could cure cancer and they'd say I was creating unemployment among oncologists. They want to ruin me – they *have* ruined me – and once they're done they'll start on some other poor unsuspecting bastard and ruin his life too. Bullies, that's all they are. You realize that, don't you? All these brave little souls hiding behind their keyboards, spitting out their venom. I blame Steve Jobs. And that Zuckerberg fellow. All those clever little psychopaths who couldn't get laid in high school but make up for their sexual inadequacy by inventing technology that destroys humanity. They're the Oppenheimers of the twenty-first century.'

'Darling,' said Denise, pressing her hand against his forearm on the table. 'Please. You have to lower your voice. People are staring. You're getting overexcited.'

'Of course I'm getting fucking overexcited!' he shouted, practically hovering over his chair now. 'Thirty-five years of my life, down the drain. My reputation in tatters. Look' – he glanced to his right, where a copy of that morning's *Daily Mail* was sitting on an empty table – 'I bet if I pick up that newspaper, I'll find some story in there saying what a horrible human being I am.'

'Darling, that's not a newspaper,' said Denise. 'It's the *Daily Mail*.'

He reached over and grabbed it. 'How much do you bet?' he asked before unfolding it. 'Come on? How much? Twenty quid? Fifty? One hundred quid that there'll be something about me on the first five pages.'

He let the paper fall open and emitted a cry of horror when he saw that half the front page was, in fact, filled with his face.

'Christ alive,' he said. 'What the hell have I done now?'

And then he saw a second, smaller picture, of a woman sitting on a sofa and looking off into the distance wearing an expression of sadness. He was so surprised to see her there that he didn't even recognize her at first, and it was only when he read the headline that his jaw dropped open in surprise.

CLEVERLEY GOT ME PREGGERS AND THEN DIDN'T WANT ANYTHING TO DO WITH ME

'She went to the papers,' cried George, barely able to get the words out. 'She went to the bloody papers. And all because I forgot to phone her. I said I would be there for her if she wanted me to be. In fact, I told her that I would prefer to be part of the child's life.'

'There is no child,' said Denise, who had read the story shortly before he arrived. In fact, it was her copy of the *Daily Mail* that George was now holding, but she'd tossed it aside quickly when she saw him coming through from the reception area to the bar.

'You don't mean she got rid of it?' he asked, looking remorseful.

'No, it never existed in the first place. It was a phantom pregnancy.'

He stared at her as if she was mad. 'Can that happen?' he asked.

'Occasionally, yes.'

'So I didn't get her pregnant?'

'No.'

'So even the headline is a lie?'

'Well, I suppose so, yes.'

'There's no suppose about it! It says *Cleverley got me preggers*, when I did no such thing.'

Denise looked around, feeling uncomfortable. She didn't like the scene that was being played out. This was Soho House, after all. Not the Groucho.

'You could be accused of splitting hairs there,' she said. 'I mean, you were obviously having an affair with the woman.'

'But I didn't get her pregnant! And I guarantee that if you go on Twitter now, you'll find a load of people all saying that I forced a woman to have an abortion.' He downed the rest of his beer, knocked back the whisky, then ordered seconds of both, which arrived promptly, along with a suggestion by the young Adonis that Sir might want to lower his voice.

'Sir will keep his fucking voice at the exact fucking level that Sir wants it to be,' he shouted, dismissing the boy by shooing him away with both hands. 'Fuckity bye now! Fuckity bye!'

'George, you have to calm down. Everyone is—'

'I tell you what, Denise. I'm not going to take this lying down. I'm going to stand up for myself.'

'I honestly don't know what you can do about it. It might just be better to enter a period of self-isolation.'

'That's what I am now, is it? A virus?'

'No, of course not, but—'

'I can sue Twitter, that's what I can do.'

'For what?'

'For allowing any moron with opposable thumbs to access its service.'

'I'm not sure the courts will entertain something so frivolous.'

'Then I'll sue everyone who made allegations about me online. I'll take every one of them down.'

'I don't think that will work either. There's such a thing as free speech, you know.'

'Free speech doesn't give you the right to lie!'

'It does, actually.'

'Fine, but then there are consequences to lying. I'll make them post apologies, that's what I'll do. I'll get them to admit that they made all this up because they're so bloody deranged.'

'These people will only harass you even further if you provoke them.'

'*People?*' he shouted, spitting the word out as he drank half his beer in one go. 'They're not people. They're thugs! Miscreants! Scoundrels! Villains! Reprobates! Lowlifes!'

'That's just a list of synonyms, darling.'

'Oh, fuck off, Denise.'

'I'm only trying to help,' she said.

'Could we sue the BBC?'

'You could, I suppose. But I don't think it would get you very far. What can they do other than give you more money? They're not going to give you your show back. That's off the table.'

'Do you want to know what my real mistake was here?'

'Of course, darling.'

'Signing up for those ridiculous social media sites in the first place. I said they were created for morons, but Elizabeth said I needed to build my brand. Really, all of this starts with her.'

'Perhaps you could sue her?'

'I'm not going to sue my own daughter,' he replied, rolling his eyes in exasperation. 'If I won, I'd only end up having to pay the compensation myself, since she doesn't have a bean and refuses to get a job. Why doesn't someone put that on Twitter? *George Cleverley is something of a latter-day saint because he takes care of his family, allows all of his children to live at home, and gives them a substantial monthly allowance, even though the oldest boy has a wardrobe full of inappropriate uniforms, his daughter is a sloth and his youngest son is an idiot.*'

'Darling, I really think you need to compose yourself. Your every word is carrying and people are staring.'

'Fuck them.' He turned around and looked at the dozen or so people gathered in the courtyard, three of whom had won Oscars, two of whom were famous musicians, and the rest were unknown to him. 'That's right, you lot!' he shouted. 'You can all fuck off. Did you hear me? Fuck. Right. Off. Go on. Fuckity bye!' he said again. He waved them all away, as if they were pigeons.

As the perspiration began to break out on his forehead, he noticed a young man sitting in the corner dressed in the style of a contemporary hipster and sporting an extravagant moustache, grinning like a Cheshire cat as he tapped away on his phone.

'Hey! Salvador Dalí!' shouted George. 'What are you doing?'

'Excuse me?' said the man, looking up with an innocent expression on his face.

'You heard me, you little shit. I said, what are you doing? Are you posting everything I'm saying online?'

The man shrugged. 'Might be,' he said. 'What's it to you?'

With the speed and agility of a twelve-year-old Russian gymnast running away from her father-slash-coach, George leapt from his chair, charged across the courtyard and grabbed the phone from the man's hand.

'Hey!' he shouted in outrage. 'Give that back!'

'I want to see what you've written.' George stared at the screen before turning around to glare at all the startled faces that surrounded him. 'Every single word!' he roared. 'He's posted every single word I've said in a long thread. And look, the likes and retweets are flowing in.'

'How many am I up to?' asked the man.

'You little prick,' snarled George. 'Hold on.' He started tapping away at the phone himself and, while the younger man tried to grab it back, George spun around in circles, ensuring that he kept a firm hold of it. 'Now,' he said finally in triumph. 'Guess what I've just done? I've deleted your account. No deactivation, a simple deletion. It said *this action cannot be reversed* and I said, good, that's what I want. You are no longer on Twitter. You have no more followers. You are voiceless. So you won't need this, will you?' He raised the phone above his head now and flung it to the ground, where it smashed into a dozen or more pieces. The man screamed and slumped back in his chair, his eyes closed, a faint line of drool seeping from the left corner of his mouth.

'I think he's fainted,' said one of the actresses. 'He has. Look. He's fainted.'

'You're an animal!' cried a man that George had never seen before in his life.

'And who the fuck are you?' George asked, turning on him. 'You're not even famous, so what are you doing here? At least she's famous,' he added, pointing to the actress. 'And he's famous,' he said, pointing to the musician. 'And I'm famous. But who the fuck are you?'

'I'm up and coming,' said the man in a dignified voice. 'If you must know, I had a recurring role in Season Three of *Downton Abbey*.'

'Upstairs or downstairs?'

The man hung his head in shame. 'Downstairs,' he admitted.

'Then you can fuck right off. Up and coming, my arse! Fuckity bye! Go on! Fuckity bye! And you!' he cried, looking over at another of the actresses, who wasn't even a movie star. She was just a regular on *EastEnders*. 'What the hell do you think you're doing?'

Her phone was held aloft and she was pointing it in his direction. 'Filming you,' she said. 'This is classic stuff. Sure to go viral. Also, I want to direct.'

'You don't even know the rules, do you?' he shouted. 'There's no photographs or filming allowed in here.' He looked around, appealing to his audience. 'She's breaking the rules!'

'This will get a million views by this time tomorrow,' she said. 'I think I'll survive.'

'Not if you don't get to post it, you won't,' he said, launching himself at her and, to the consternation of the onlookers, the *EastEnders* actress disappeared beneath George's bulky frame.

'George!' cried Denise, rushing over. 'Someone, help!'

From beneath George, the actress could be heard screaming, while several people, including some of the waiters, waded in to try to drag him off her. When they finally succeeded, he had her phone in his hand too and, like the hipster's, it soon found itself smashed on the ground.

'There!' shouted George. 'Tweet that!'

The atmosphere changed suddenly, and those who were holding him let go. Every head turned in the direction of the entrance, where two policemen had appeared, and they were standing there watching, with bemused expressions upon their faces.

'Some sort of commotion going on here, I see,' said one.

Everyone tried to speak at once and, leaving them to it, George wandered back to his seat, where he buried himself in what was left of his beer and whisky, while the most famous person in the room was given the right to tell the authorities what had just taken place. She explained it all, dramatizing some of the moments and even doing a passable imitation of George's voice.

'*Fuckity bye*, he kept saying,' she told the officers. 'Fuckity bye! What does that even mean? I've never heard it before.'

When she was finished hogging the limelight, the officers made their way over to George.

'Is all this true, sir?' they asked. 'The things this lady has told us?'

'Yes,' he said. 'Why deny it? It'll be all over the Internet by now anyway, so, true or false, it just automatically becomes fact.'

'Then I'm afraid I'm going to have to ask you to accompany us to the station,' replied the younger of the pair. 'I hope you'll come peacefully.'

George shrugged as he stood up. 'Sure,' he said. 'Why not? I've got nothing else to do now anyway.'

He took his Soho House card out of his wallet and threw it on the table.

'It'll save them the hassle of writing to me, asking for it back,' he said, shuffling out towards the lounge.

Denise watched, fifteen years of an agent–client relationship coming to an end, before removing a leather-bound notebook from her bag. On the front page were listed the names of all the people she represented. Taking a fountain pen from the side pocket, she drew a line through George's name. *Cancelled*, she wrote beside it.

TORTOISE KILLER

While George was being bundled into the back of a police car, Beverley was making excellent progress through another bottle of wine, when there was loud knocking at the door again. This time, as she wobbled unsteadily down the hallway, she found herself hoping that it would be her husband. Perhaps he'd forgotten his key. She just wanted to collapse into his arms and have him tell her that he still loved her. To her disappointment, however, she was confronted not by George but by two police officers.

'Mrs Beverley Cleverley?' said one, a young woman with an Audrey Hepburn haircut *circa Roman Holiday*.

'The one and only,' she slurred. 'Nobody I'd rather be.'

'We've had a report of an incident at this address.'

'What sort of an incident?'

'The murder of an animal.'

'The *what*?'

'Specifically, a tortoise who answered to the name of . . .' She consulted her notepad. 'Ustym Karmaliuk.'

'After the great Ukrainian folk hero,' added her colleague.

'Firstly, he didn't answer to any name,' said Beverley, almost falling over. 'He was entirely unresponsive most of the time. Like one's husband becomes after thirty years of marriage.'

She burped and Audrey Hepburn snorted a little.

'And secondly, I didn't murder him. I threw him out, that's all. He's with my ghost. He's having sex with my ghost. And I loved him.'

She started to weep, and the police officers looked at each other in confusion, uncertain what she meant by this.

'The tortoise is having sex with a ghost?' asked the policeman.

'No, of course not. That's idiotic. I didn't say that. Pylyp is.'

'Pylyp Tataryn,' said Audrey. 'The rightful owner of the animal?'

'If any of us can really own animals,' replied Beverley, looking up at the ceiling. 'It's a question for the great philosophers, don't you think?'

'The point is, madam,' said the policeman. 'We've had a report from the RSPCA that you killed a tortoise by throwing him across the road.'

'No, I didn't do that,' she said, drying her eyes. 'He ate too many After Eights, you see, and I was keeping his corpse in the kitchen until I figured out what to do with him. Yes, I threw him across the street, but I assure you he was already dead by then. He wouldn't have felt a thing.'

'We've seen a video, madam,' he continued. 'I'm afraid we'll have to take you in for questioning.'

She burst out laughing. 'You can't be serious,' she said.

'I'm afraid I am. We don't take these matters lightly. Perhaps you'd like to get your things?'

'You're arresting me?'

'Not yet. But we would like you to accompany us to the station, yes.'

She laughed again, hoping that they'd simply leave her alone, but when it became obvious that they weren't going anywhere, she retrieved her coat and keys and phone before following them to the police car, feeling a mixture of horror and excitement when the man put his hand on her head as she climbed inside, just like they did on the television.

Sitting in the back seat, however, as they drove to the station, she began to feel a certain fear building inside her. Her readers were probably animal lovers and the newspapers would surely get a hold of this story. One of the RSPCA cyclists would pass it on. There'd be a scandal. Another scandal.

She felt a sharp pain in her stomach. *I'll be cancelled*, she thought.

LINE OF DUTY

When they arrived at the restaurant, Susan was already seated at a table by the window, and she greeted her brother affectionately before turning her attention to Nelson, looking him up and down as if he was a piece of furniture she was considering buying. He tried to smile but felt his expression made him look rather creepy so executed a half-bow instead, like a knight before an evil queen. Introductions made, they sat down and he tried to figure out who she reminded him of. It came to him after a moment: Wednesday Addams. Only older. And without the charm.

'Shall we order?' asked Susan, summoning a waiter with an imperious click of her fingers, and a boy came over and handed them menus. Shane and Susan decided to share a bottle of wine, and while Nelson would have loved to join them – he felt a strong need for alcohol – he stuck to sparkling water, pointing out that even though he wasn't on duty yet, he would be in an hour.

'Do they give you a breathalyser test when you clock in?' she asked, smiling a little.

'Yes,' he said.

'Really? I was kidding.'

'Then no.'

She stared at him. 'They do or they don't?' she asked, and Nelson could feel himself starting to blush.

'They definitely don't,' he said. 'I was only kidding too.'

'What a pair of kidders!' said Shane, looking from one to the other hopefully.

'I'm very funny,' said Nelson quietly.

'I have to say, you're not my brother's usual type,' said Susan.

'Oh no? What's his usual type?'

'Cockier, I'd say. Like the cat that got the cream. My brother's a catch, don't you think?'

'He is,' agreed Nelson. 'I'm very lucky.'

'You are.'

'Well, I am too,' said Shane.

'Don't be ridiculous,' said Susan. 'You could have any man you wanted. Take a look in the mirror.'

'Susan always sticks up for me,' said Shane, smiling.

'I wasn't aware anyone was putting you down,' said Nelson.

'I'm just saying that I hope you know how lucky you are,' said Susan.

'I do,' replied Nelson, feeling the irritation grow inside him. 'But I hope he feels lucky too.'

'Why, are you a catch? Because he is.'

'Yes, you said.' Nelson swallowed. 'And I think I am, yes. I'm . . . you know . . . nice.'

'Nice?' asked Susan, the expression on her face suggesting that she'd just swallowed sour milk. 'Nice in what way?'

'Oh, just in a general sort of way,' said Nelson. 'I try to be . . .'

'Nice?'

'Yes.'

'Well,' she said, narrowing her eyes, 'I suppose my brother has always liked a man in uniform. When he was fifteen he had a crush on the local curate.'

'No, I didn't!' protested Shane, laughing.

'You did so. The poor man practically had to take out a restraining order against you. And then there was that doctor you dated. And the air steward. Ryanair,' she added, turning to Nelson and practically spitting out the word. 'Not even Aer Lingus.'

'Well, perhaps it's a slight fetish on my part,' admitted Shane. 'Lifeguards, there's another.'

'All they wear is a pair of skimpy red shorts,' said Nelson.

'Exactly.'

Susan laughed heartily and put a hand on Shane's arm, leaving it there much longer than necessary.

'All my friends had crushes on him when we were growing up,' she continued. 'It was such a shame that he batted for the other team. No, not a shame, I don't mean that. But they were disappointed, shall we say. I wouldn't have let them near him anyway. I'm very possessive. Honestly, Nelson, if I wasn't his sister, I'd have gone after him myself.'

'That's an odd thing to say,' said Nelson.

'Is it? I don't see why. He's handsome, funny, he has an amazing body. What more could a woman want?'

'Someone who doesn't share her DNA?'

She brushed this away, as if this was scarcely worth considering.

'Anyway, it's not all about the uniform,' said Shane after a moment. 'It's what's underneath that counts.'

'Oh yes? And does this one' – she nodded violently in Nelson's direction – 'have a lot going on underneath?'

Shane burst out laughing now and Nelson looked from one to the other, wondering what hellish sideshow he'd found himself in.

'Anyway, we should stop talking about my brother,' said Susan, laying a peculiar emphasis on the word. 'I want to know more about you, Nelson. Such a strange name! In Ireland, we blew up Nelson's Column, you know. Or was it Nelson's Pillar? I can never remember. How long have you been with the police force?'

'Three years now,' he replied, hoping this was the same amount of time that he'd told Shane. 'I started in the summer of 2018 and I've been at it ever since. Policing away. With all my policeman friends.'

'And do you enjoy it?'

'The thing about being in law enforcement,' said Nelson, leaning forward, elbows on the table, growing in confidence now, 'is that it isn't so much about enjoying the job as getting a deep sense of fulfilment from it.'

'Isn't that basically the same thing?'

'Not really, no. I don't enjoy shooting people, for example, but if I were to shoot someone – say, because he was kidnapping a puppy or threatening to set an old woman's hair on fire – then that would be very fulfilling.'

Susan frowned.

'But policemen don't carry guns in the UK, do they?' she asked. 'I thought you had to be a specially trained firearms officer for that? That's how it is on *Line of Duty* anyway.'

'You've never shot anyone, have you?' asked Shane, looking at him in alarm.

'No, I haven't,' said Nelson. 'And you're quite right, Susan. I can't actually carry a gun. I was just giving it as a for instance.'

'It sounded like you were speaking from experience.'

'No.'

'So you're fulfilled but not happy?'

'Stop interrogating him, Susan,' said Shane. 'You do have the right to remain silent, you know.'

They ordered some sandwiches while, beneath the table, Nelson reached out his foot to touch Shane's leg. For the first time in his life, he felt safe and loved, although he was uncertain whether he could spend a lifetime with this woman as his sister-in-law, and he was starting to regret having shown up to the speed-dating session in uniform. If he'd just arrived in a pair of jeans, a shirt and a sweater, it would have been so much easier. Then there would have been no need for any of this subterfuge. But, he wondered, would Shane have been drawn to him then? It had never occurred to him that they might share a fetish.

'And what do you do, Susan?' he asked.

'Does it matter?'

'Not really, no. I'm just making conversation.'

'Well, if you must know, since you're practically *grilling* me here, like I'm on *trial*, I'm a professional footballer.'

Nelson laughed.

'Is that funny in some way?'

'Wasn't that a joke?'

'You think the idea of me being a professional footballer is a joke?'

Nelson shrugged. 'Well, yes,' he admitted. 'I mean, I'm not a big football fan but I'm pretty sure they're all men. Cristiano Ronaldo, for example. And . . . who's that other one? Gary Lineker.'

'Oh, I love Gary Lineker,' said Shane enthusiastically. 'The silver fox.'

'I like him too,' said Nelson.

'Although I preferred him in his playing days. When he wore the outfit.'

Nelson frowned.

'Obviously I was talking about *women's* football,' said Susan, rolling her eyes.

'She really is a footballer,' confirmed Shane.

Nelson looked her up and down, as if he wanted to be certain about something. 'But you're a girl,' he said. 'Aren't you? I mean, an actual girl. A real girl. An original girl. As in, born a girl.'

'Yes, I'm a girl,' she replied. 'Why are you rambling?'

'Am I? Am I rambling? It's a funny word, *rambling*, isn't it? Rambling.'

'You are, yes. Does it bother you in some way when women engage in historically male activities?'

475

'Not at all. In fact, my mother has been a career woman her whole life.'

'Career woman!' sneered Susan, shaking her head as the food arrived. 'Oh, I've heard it all now. A career woman. And what are you, a career man?'

'No, but—'

'And why did you seem uncertain that I'm female? Don't I look female?'

'You do, yes. You're very girl-like. It's just, you can never be too certain these days so it's best to be careful. My father got into a lot of trouble recently on this front, as you may have heard.'

'Nelson's father is quite famous,' said Shane, turning to his sister.

'Really?' she asked, intrigued now. 'Who is he? A politician or something?'

'No, a television host.'

'What's his name?'

'George Cleverley.'

'You're kidding!'

'No, I'm serious.'

She whipped out her phone and started tapping away on it.

'But hold on,' she said. 'I'm looking at George Cleverley's Wikipedia page and it says here that he has three children, the oldest of whom, Nelson, is a teacher. It also says that his daughter is an influencer and that his youngest son is an idiot. Why would it say something like that?'

'Because he is an idiot,' said Nelson. 'Although a very nice idiot, to be fair.'

'No, why would it say that you're a teacher?'

'I have no idea,' said Nelson, laughing a little. 'You can't trust Wikipedia. People just go on there and change whatever they want. It could say that I'm a giraffe, but it wouldn't make it true, would it?'

'Why would someone want to pretend that you're a teacher when you're quite clearly a police officer?' asked Shane. 'What's in it for them?'

'I have no idea,' said Nelson, checking the time. 'Nowt as queer as folk, as they say.'

Susan put her phone away but didn't look at all convinced. At a table on the other side of the restaurant, the voices of two men disagreeing with each other began to be heard over the low hum of conversation. The heads of everyone in the room turned in their direction and they watched as a waitress approached them and had a quiet word.

'Anyway,' said Nelson, turning back to Susan, 'you were saying that you're a professional footballer. Are you the only one, or are there others?'

'No, it's just me,' she said. 'I go out on the pitch alone every Saturday and just kick the ball around for ninety minutes, trying both to score and to stop myself from scoring. I almost always win.'

'Right,' said Nelson, looking at Shane. 'Do you have any other sisters?' he asked.

'No, just Susan,' replied Shane.

'Good.'

'Of course there's more of us,' she continued. 'Although most female footballers have day jobs because we don't get paid like the men because of—'

'The patriarchy, I know.'

'Yes,' she said, bristling a little. She looked irritated to have been robbed of her chance to use the word.

'How strange,' said Nelson.

'Is it? Why?'

'No,' he said, shaking his head. 'Maybe that was the wrong word.'

'Maybe,' agreed Shane.

'I meant unusual. The thing is, I've never met a female professional footballer before. And I've met a lot of famous people. Through my father, I mean. Presidents, prime ministers, pop stars. I met Mariah Carey once and she told me to get the fuck out of her way. I still remember that moment. It was my highlight of 2018.'

'As it happens, I don't think I've ever talked to a policeman either,' she said. 'Other than our cousin, but he's a garda and I think he just likes dressing up. He's getting married in a few months, actually, so you'll be able to compare notes with him. If you're still around, that is,' she added, glancing at her brother, who looked down at the table and ate his sandwich. 'It feels a little odd to be sitting here while you're sat opposite me in uniform. I have to say, the Met doesn't exactly put a lot of money into them, does it? It's very tatty material, if you don't mind me saying so.' She reached across and took a fistful of his shirt sleeve in her hand before letting go and glancing at her palm as if she was worried that it might be covered in nuclear waste. 'It's like something a person might buy online for a fancy-dress party.'

Across the room, the men's voices were raised again, this time in fury, and the waitress returned to their table to tell them off. One of the men swore at her, then apologized and promised to keep the noise down. She looked unconvinced but walked away.

'I should be getting off soon,' said Nelson, checking his watch.

'You have some more time yet, surely,' said Shane.

'Well, maybe a few more minutes,' he said reluctantly, not wanting to let his boyfriend down.

'Yes, do stay,' said Susan coldly. 'You're such fun. I can see why my brother likes you. You're the absolute life of the party.'

'Thank you,' muttered Nelson.

'You must have some wonderful stories. About police life, I mean? I'd love to hear them.'

'Oh, not really. Most of it is surprisingly mundane. Drug kingpins, terrorists, flashers, that sort of thing. The really good stuff is top secret, you know. For your eyes only.'

'For my eyes?'

'No, for the eyes of, you know, my superiors.'

'He's being modest, he has lots of good stories,' said Shane. 'Tell her about the time you captured a cat burglar.'

'Oh no,' said Nelson, feeling himself begin to blush again. 'No, she wouldn't want to hear about that.'

'A cat burglar?' said Susan, perking up. 'That sounds fascinating. Oh, go on, tell me!'

'I don't know if I—'

'Tell me!' she insisted. 'Then you can go. Just tell it quickly, the main points.'

'All right, then,' said Nelson, taking a last bite from his sandwich, wiping his lips with a napkin and pushing the plate away. 'Well, it didn't start in London, I should point out. It started in France. On the French Riviera, in fact. It seems that there was a cat burglar working the area, breaking into rich people's houses and the bedrooms of luxury hotels and so on, stealing all the women's jewellery. Really high-priced stuff.'

'Goodness!' said Susan. 'How exciting!'

'The French police had a suspicion about who it was, but they hadn't been able to capture him.'

'And who was he?'

'A fellow named John Robie. They called him *Le Chat*. Which is French for *The Cat*.'

'It's not, is it?'

'It is, yes.'

'And John Robie, you say?'

'That's right.'

'Actually, I think I've heard of him,' said Susan, frowning. 'Perhaps I read about him in the newspapers.'

Nelson looked a little discomfited but carried on.

'Anyway, the gendarmes caught up with him at his hilltop villa but he climbed out on the roof and gave them the slip. Then he made his way to Calais and across the Channel on a boat to England and settled in London, where he took up his old game, breaking into the Mandarin Oriental and the Ritz and the Savoy and all the rest of them. He caused quite a stir.'

Susan's eyes narrowed while Shane's face grew in excitement.

'Go on,' he said. 'Tell her what happened next!'

'Well, this John Robie fellow got caught up with an American heiress and her mother and he fell in love with the younger woman, and she fell in love with him too, and he insisted that he wasn't the one responsible for any of the robberies and he'd only come to London to try to clear his name by catching the real villain in the act.'

'And this is where Nelson came in,' said Shane.

'Yes, I was one of those on the case and—'

'Wouldn't that be a matter for detectives? Not everyday constables?'

'They were short-staffed. They asked for me.'

'Seems odd.'

'And I started to notice a pattern and realized that John Robie couldn't possibly have been The Cat because—'

'Hold on, hold on,' said Susan, shaking her head. 'Correct me if I'm wrong, but isn't this the plot of *To Catch a Thief*?'

'What's that?' asked Shane.

'The Hitchcock film. Cary Grant and Grace Kelly.' She thought about it for a moment, then whipped out her phone once again. 'It *is* the plot of *To Catch a Thief*!' she said triumphantly, turning the screen to show her brother. 'Cary Grant plays John Robie, The Cat. Only he doesn't come to London in the movie. He stays in France. None of this actually happened, did it?' she asked, looking at Nelson. 'You're making it up. What kind of game are you playing here?'

Shane turned to look at Nelson, who wished that the ground would open up and swallow him whole, but before he could say anything in reply, the two men on the opposite side of the room were at it once again, only this time they'd risen from their chairs and were starting to push each other.

'Good Lord,' said Susan, looking over. 'They're really going for it.'

The waitress marched over, but when she tried to separate them, one of the men pushed her and she fell backwards on to the floor, upsetting a trolley of water jugs and glasses. People jumped up and backed away, afraid of getting involved, and as the young woman pulled herself to her feet, she looked over at Nelson with a pleading expression on her face.

'Do something!' she shouted as the men continued brawling.

'What can I do?' he asked, uncertain why she was appealing to him. 'You need to call the police!'

'You *are* the police!'

'Oh yes,' he said, remembering. 'Quite right.'

'Go on, then,' said Susan, pushing him by the elbow. 'They're going to destroy the place.'

Nelson turned to Shane, hoping that he would order him to stay back until help arrived, but his boyfriend looked as if he was terribly excited about what was about to take place.

'You'd better break it up,' he said. 'Do it, Nelson! Go on!'

'Yes,' said Nelson. 'All right, then.'

He stepped forward, feeling a mixture of anxiety and fear in every bone of his body as he approached them.

'Stop that now,' he ordered in what he hoped was an authoritative voice. 'Come on now, gentlemen, that's enough fighting for today!'

The two men stopped for a moment and stared at him, before returning to their quarrel. The taller of the pair punched the other in the face, sending him crashing over another diner's shepherd's pie and into the wall beyond. The shorter man didn't stay down for long, though, and was back on his feet quickly, ready to fight on.

'I must insist that you stop,' protested Nelson, holding out his arms to keep them apart. 'Perhaps your disagreement could be resolved with a calm conversation.'

'Fuck off,' said one of the men, elbowing him in the jaw. Nelson stumbled over and tasted blood from where his lower teeth had collided with the inside of his mouth.

'This is very bad behaviour,' he cried. 'Both of you, stop it now!'

'Arrest them, Nelson!' shouted Shane, rubbing his hands together in glee.

'Oh yes, that's a good idea. Gentlemen, I'm sorry, but I'm going to have to place you both under arrest.'

He pulled a set of handcuffs from the belt around his waist but, the moment he did so, the chain connecting them proved so flimsy that it broke apart in his hands. He noticed a small sticker on the back that said *For children's use only*.

'Oh,' he said, disappointed.

The fight continued and Nelson considered retreating to his seat, but Shane was looking at him with such excitement on his face that he didn't want to let him down. There was only one thing for it, he decided, and that was to throw himself into the mêlée, at which point the two men briefly joined forces, picking him up by his arms and legs and tossing him across the room like a Raggedy Ann before continuing with their fight. Nelson lay on the ground as two police officers – real police officers – charged into the restaurant and made their way quickly towards them, pulling the two men apart and subduing them without difficulty, handcuffing them where they lay on the ground. It was all over with such little fuss that even Nelson felt like applauding.

'You all right?' asked one, reaching down and offering a hand to Nelson, who stood up and nodded, brushing bits of food from his trousers.

'What the hell are you wearing?' asked the other, looking him up and down with a bewildered expression on his face. 'Is it dressing-up day down your manor or something?'

'Jesus, Nelson!' said Shane, rushing forward and throwing his arms around him. 'I thought they were going to kill you. Thanks, Officers,' he said, turning to the two policemen. 'I suppose it's always easier in pairs. Nelson's off duty right now, that's why he's on his own.'

'Who's Nelson?' asked the first officer.

'I'm Nelson,' said Nelson.

'Off duty from what?'

'From, you know, from the police,' said Shane.

The two policemen looked at Nelson, before turning to each other and bursting out laughing.

'You can't be serious,' said one.

'Of course I'm serious,' said Shane.

'Leave it, Shane,' said Nelson.

'That's not even a proper uniform. Look at it! If I threw a match at him, he'd go up in flames.'

Shane turned to his boyfriend, who looked at him

uncertainly. Nelson could practically see the veil falling from his eyes. 'You are a policeman, aren't you?' he asked nervously.

'Of course I am.'

'Are you?'

'Well, no, not quite,' admitted Nelson.

'What does *not quite* mean?'

'Hold on, hold on,' said the second officer. 'Are you going around impersonating an officer? Because if you are, that's a criminal offence.'

'As far as we were aware, he is a policeman,' said Susan, marching over now with all the determination of one of America's Next Top Models out on a go-see at Calvin Klein. 'That's what he told us anyway.'

'What's your name?' asked the officer.

'My name?'

'Yes, your name. You do know it, I assume.'

'My name,' said Nelson, looking back and forth with a smile on his face, 'is Michael Caine.'

Everyone stared at him.

'You're claiming to be Michael Caine?' asked the policeman.

'No, that was . . . that was a joke. It's Nelson Cleverley. That's my name.'

'All right, Nelson Cleverley, so let's clear this up. Are you or are you not a member of Her Majesty's Metropolitan police force?'

'Do I have to answer that?'

'You do, yes.'

'Well, strictly speaking, no, I'm not,' admitted Nelson.

'Then why are you dressed like one?'

'The thing is,' he said, realizing he had no choice but to come clean. 'I went to a speed-dating session earlier in the week. That's where I met Shane.'

'Who's Shane?'

'I'm Shane,' said Shane, raising a hand.

'And I was dressed like a policeman because it made me feel more confident, but then we hit it off and I didn't want to admit that I wasn't a policeman after all, so I stuck with it.'

'Wait,' said Shane, looking aghast. 'Do you mean you've been lying to me from the start?'

'I didn't set out to lie,' he said. 'It just sort of happened.'

'Fuck you!'

'Shane!'

'No, I mean it. Fuck you! What a shitty thing to do!'

'It's not just a shitty thing to do,' said the officer, taking another pair of handcuffs from his belt and snapping them on to Nelson's wrists; this pair, unlike his own, was quite solid, 'it's also illegal. Which means that you, my friend, are under arrest.'

'No!' cried Nelson as his arms were dragged behind his back. 'I'm sorry. I won't do it again. I'll take it off right now, if you like, even though I don't have anything to change into. I'll throw the uniform away when I get home, I promise.'

'Not good enough. You can't go around impersonating an officer. It's a criminal offence.'

'But I've applied!' cried Nelson in a beseeching tone. 'I'm waiting to hear back about the date for my interview. So, in a way, it's only a matter of time.'

'Well, I can assure you that there'll be no interview now,' said the policeman, leading him towards the door. 'We'll look into your application when we get back to the station.'

'And what will happen to it?'

'It's not obvious?' asked Susan, who looked delighted to have her brother back. 'It'll be cancelled.'

Elizabeth's existential crisis continued as she made her way home, only snapping out of it as she turned the corner on to her street, where the sound of a police car's siren dragged her back to the present moment. She glanced to her right as it passed, noticing a woman seated in the back seat, her face pressed up against the window, who bore a surprising resemblance to her mother, Beverley.

Entering the house, she stood in the living room and glanced at the selection of books on display in one of the cabinets and wondered whether she might try to read one after all. That eight-hundred-page biography that her father had bought earlier in the week had now moved to an occasional table by the window, but its spine had yet to be cracked. Breathing slowly, the way she'd seen people do on YouTube videos about mindfulness, she decided to set herself a challenge. From today, she would force herself to put her phone away for a specific amount of time every day. Ten minutes in the home safe now. Fifteen minutes tomorrow. And so on until it was out of her hands for an hour at a time. Perhaps in a month or two she'd hardly be using it at all.

Christ, she thought to herself, an outrageous idea entering her mind, I could even get a job.

Feeling a great wave of contentment as this plan took shape in her mind, she barely had time to think about what sort of job might suit a young woman of her particular skillset, when a noise like an explosion rocked the house. She screamed aloud; it sounded as if the front door was being smashed in. This was followed a moment later by the terrifying noise of men shouting as they stormed into the hallway and spread out, charging up the staircase and into the kitchen and living room, where two of them were confronted by a hysterical Elizabeth. A few more ran in and, to her horror and bewilderment, they were wearing dark blue jackets, bulletproof vests and visors over their faces and were carrying what looked to be loaded machine guns while roaring at her to lie on the floor with her hands behind her head.

She continued to scream, but one of them made a lunge in her direction and, before she knew it, her face was pressed against the carpet while half a dozen rifles were pointed at her head. Someone knelt on her back, fastening what felt like a cable tie around her wrists and ankles before dragging her back to her feet. Looking out to the hallway, she saw more men going upstairs, calling out that they were armed officers and if there was anyone in the house, they needed to come out now with their hands up.

'There's no one here!' she shouted. 'Only me. What are you doing? What's going on?'

Now that the target had been neutralized, a younger man in a sharp suit entered and looked her up and down disdainfully. His clothes and demeanour bore a striking resemblance to Major Toht from *Raiders of the Lost Ark* and she had a sudden image of being locked in an interrogation room with a white light shining in her face.

'Elizabeth Cleverley?' he asked in a casual tone, as if they were great friends and this was just a spontaneous visit.

'Yes, that's right,' she said, tears streaming down her face. 'I don't know what's happening here. I haven't done anything!'

'Haven't you?'

'No! Nothing at all.' She raised her voice now. 'Why are all these guns being pointed at me?'

'Because you're under arrest,' said the man calmly.

She felt herself begin to relax a little; obviously, this was a mistake, and it wouldn't be long before they were begging her forgiveness and settling out of court for the trauma they'd put her through.

'Under arrest?' she asked, laughing. 'On what charge?'

'On suspicion of terrorist behaviour.'

Elizabeth stared at him in disbelief. She tried to move towards the armchair but, because her ankles were tied together, all she could manage was a sort of bunny-hop, and even as she tried that, one of the officers lifted his gun aggressively and pointed it at her head, his finger on the trigger.

'Terrorist behaviour?' she asked. 'That's ridiculous. Don't you know who I am? I'm George Cleverley's daughter! I have absolutely zero interest in politics or ISIS or whatever is popular at the moment. I was going to go to Indonesia, yes, which for all I know might be near Iraq, but that was to help lepers. I'm a philanthropist and an influencer! For pity's sake, I have a blue tick! Now can you please untie me so I can call my father's solicitor and see to it that you're out of a job by evening time?'

The man didn't so much as crack a smile but opened a folder he was carrying and ran his finger down a page.

'*There's something about @BorisJohnson*✓*'s face that makes me want to attack it with a machete,*' he read carefully.

'Me too,' said Elizabeth, attempting to shrug. 'I honestly don't know what people see in him. And honestly, couldn't someone just give him a comb?'

'You wrote this, didn't you?'

'Me? No. Of course not. Why would I write such a thing?'

'@TruthIsASword,' he said. 'You're the administrator of this Twitter account, aren't you?'

She paused for a moment.

'Ah,' she said, swallowing nervously. 'I think I understand now. Right. Okay. I mean, you're making a terrible mistake, but I can see how it got started. How did you even know that I'm @TruthIsASword?'

'In the past six weeks, Miss Cleverley, you've issued threats against the Prime Minister, the Home Secretary, the Leader of the Opposition, President Macron, both Woody Allen *and* Mia Farrow, a backbench MP from Yorkshire, Kate Winslet, Salman Rushdie, Banksy, the wives of three England football players, Delia Smith, Ant and Dec, and Her Majesty the Queen.' He closed his folder now and looked at her with barely disguised contempt on his face. 'Her Majesty the Queen,' he repeated, spitting out the words. 'Elizabeth Regina. Who has served this nation with distinction, while never putting a foot wrong, since coming to the throne at the tender age of twenty-five. Have you no shame?'

'But I didn't mean any of them,' she protested. 'They were just jokes.'

'Threatening to chop the Prime Minister's head off with a machete is a joke, is it?'

'Well, it's not the funniest joke of all time, I'll give you that. But it's just harmless political satire.'

'That contravenes the Terrorism Act of 2018.'

'Well, I haven't read that, so how would I know?'

'Saying that you'd like to see the Duke of York pummelled to within an inch of his life by a kangaroo. That's a joke, is it?'

'Well, we all want that, surely?'

'All right, we could let that one slide. But the rest, Miss Cleverley, the rest—'

Before he could continue, one of the armed officers came downstairs carrying an evidence bag containing a lot of banknotes.

'Thirty-five thousand pounds, boss,' he said, waving it in the air. 'Found it in one of the bedrooms upstairs. Looks like a lad's bedroom by the posters on the wall.'

'Do you know anything about this?' asked the man in charge, turning back to Elizabeth.

'Thirty-five thousand pounds?' she asked, opening her eyes wide. 'I certainly do not. And if you found that in my younger brother's room, then you can take it up with him. The boy's an idiot. He probably sold his brain.'

The man nodded to his colleagues, and they started to lead her outside, which wasn't easy as her ankles were still tied.

'Where are you taking me?' she cried.

'To the station,' he said. 'You've committed some serious criminal offences and it'll be up to the Crown Prosecution Service now to decide what to do with you.'

With that, they put her into the back of a waiting police van and shut the door. She sat there, torn between laughter and shock, uncertain what to do next, before moving her tied hands to her right-hand pocket and nudging it with her elbow until her phone fell out and dropped to the floor. She leaned over it, poking it with her nose, aware of how undignified this must look but not caring, and clicked on the blue Twitter app but, to her horror, the police had obviously got there first.

This account has been suspended due to a violation of our rules, said the message on the homepage.

'Oh my God!' she screamed, looking up at where the heavens would have been, had the roof of the police van not been in the way. 'I've been cancelled!'

THE LUCKIEST BOY IN THE
WHOLE WIDE WORLD

Achilles didn't often come to this part of London and, when the taxi dropped him off in front of Rebecca's house, he felt distinctly outside his comfort zone. He'd grown up around conspicuous wealth and luxury and didn't much care for the cold winds of suburbia. Strolling up the driveway, however, he felt so excited about what lay ahead that he forgot his irritation over Jeremy's no-show. The £5,000 that wasn't burning a hole in his pocket could wait until tomorrow.

He rang the doorbell and, when Rebecca answered, broke into a wide grin. She was wearing an off-the-shoulder dress and her hair was flowing around her shoulders.

'You look amazing,' he said.

'Thank you.'

'Seriously, I just want to throw you down on the staircase right now.'

She offered a half-smile. 'Who says romance is dead?' she asked, before stepping out of the way and ushering him inside.

'I meant to bring you flowers, but I forgot,' said Achilles, glancing around at the narrow hallway. 'And I was planning on buying you some chocolates, but I forgot them too. I thought there was a box of After Eights at home, but someone seems to have eaten them all.'

'It's the thought that counts,' she said, leading him into the living room and turning off the television. He looked around the small room and noticed the same newspaper on the coffee table as he'd been reading in the pub and wondered had she been reading about his father's latest peccadillo.

'So,' he said, rubbing his hands together. 'Here we are.'

'Here we are indeed,' she replied. 'I like your shirt.'

'Thank you. It's new.'

'You look very handsome.'

'I know.'

She laughed.

'Well, I do,' he said. 'There's no need for false modesty, is there?'

'I suppose not,' she replied. 'When you look like you, you might as well use it in any way that you can, right?'

'How do you mean?'

'I mean it exactly as I said it.'

'Right. Well, I mean, you're gorgeous too,' he said. 'Imagine what our children would look like!'

'You're getting a little ahead of yourself there, don't you think?'

'I was only kidding.'

'Sit down,' she said. 'What would you like to drink?'

'A rum and Coke, if you have it.'

'One rum and Coke coming up,' she said, leaving the room, and he watched her as she left. She was absolutely perfect. He sat back and grinned to himself. *I am the luckiest boy in the whole wide world*, he thought.

When she came back in, she was carrying his drink and a glass of wine for herself but, to his disappointment, rather than sitting next to him, she chose an armchair some distance away. He frowned and took a sip before glancing in the direction of some photographs on the mantelpiece.

'Is that your family?' he asked.

'Yes, my mum and dad. And me when I was a kid. But, of course, as I told you, my parents broke up last year.'

'Oh yeah, I remember. I wouldn't be surprised if the same thing happened with mine, to be honest.' He nodded towards the newspaper. 'I guess you read all about it?'

'I did, yes. He seems like a bit of a shit, your father.'

'He can be. But he's okay most of the time.'

'A bit like you, then,' she said.

'You think I'm okay most of the time?'

'Or maybe I think you're a bit of a shit.'

'Ha ha,' he said nervously, feeling a little uncomfortable with how this was going so far. He preferred it when he was more in control of the situation.

'So I came prepared,' he said finally.

'Prepared for what?'

'For . . . you know. For tonight. For us.'

'That was very forward-thinking of you.'

'Not that I think it's just my responsibility. I'm not making decisions for you.'

She smiled. 'You're so Woke,' she said.

'Ha ha,' he said again.

'You seem nervous.'

'Do I?'

'Yes.'

'No, not really.'

'You seem it.'

He shrugged. 'It's just . . . is there something wrong?' he asked. 'You seem like you're . . . I don't know . . . judging me or something.'

'And if I was, what kind of verdict would I come to, do you think?'

'That I'm a charming, funny, good-looking boy who you want to ravage over and over until the sun comes up?'

She laughed and looked away. 'Well, you know what they say,' she replied. 'Hope springs eternal.'

He stood up and made his way over to the photographs, planning on examining them for a few moments before pulling her to her feet and kissing her.

'So what went wrong between your parents?' he asked, looking at a picture of her when she was just a little girl, all pigtails, dimples and happy smile. 'Or would you prefer not to talk about it?'

'I don't mind,' she said. 'My dad cheated on my mum.'

'Fucker.'

'Actually, that's not quite true. He didn't cheat on her. He just planned on doing so.'

'Oh, well, that's not so bad, is it? At least he thought better of it.'

'I don't think it was entirely his choice. The person he was seeing . . . well, my father was being taken advantage of.'

'In what way?'

'In a financial way.'

'Bummer.'

'Mum found out and the marriage ended, just like that. Dad said he was just going through a mid-life crisis but, you know, there was no way back for them afterwards.'

'They didn't go for counselling?'

'The thing is, he wasn't seeing a girl. He was seeing a boy.'

'Ah. Yes, that's hard to come back from.'

Achilles wasn't particularly interested in Rebecca's family dramas but figured he should pretend that he was until he got what he wanted. He continued to glance at the other photographs and saw what appeared to be a happy family gathering of Rebecca with her parents a couple of years earlier. He frowned, narrowing his eyes as he examined it more closely. There was something in the picture that was ringing a bell with him.

'See anyone you recognize?' asked Rebecca.

He turned to look at her, utterly confused, then looked back to the photograph, at which point the penny finally dropped.

'Oh fuck,' he said.

'That's all you have to say?'

He stared at her, then back at the picture, then back at her.

'Your dad,' he said.

'My dad.'

'Shit.'

'You know, I actually told you the very day we met. And you didn't even notice. It was in that coffee shop just after you bought your new trainers. I said that my father was a chiropodist and you said that a chiropodist had bought you a pair of Bang & Olufsen headphones.'

'I did say that,' he said, remembering the conversation.

'And I asked you why he bought them for you, and do you remember what you said?'

Achilles looked down at the ground. 'Because I asked him to,' he said.

'That's right. So you took him for the headphones, but also for another eight grand.'

'Yes.'

'And then you broke up my parents' marriage.'

'In fairness, he contacted me. I didn't go looking for him.'

'But you led him on. And, as far as I understand it, you went out on . . . what was it, four or five dates with him? Got him all confused and excited and then told him that if he didn't pay you off, you'd tell his wife, my mum, about what was going on.'

'You make it sound worse than it really was,' he protested. 'I was just having a laugh.'

'A laugh that earned you eight grand and cost me my family.'

'When you put it like that,' he admitted, 'it doesn't sound great. I don't know what to say to you. I do have a reputation as a bit of an idiot.'

'You could start by apologizing.'

'Right. Yes. Of course. I'm very sorry.' He looked at her, trying his best to look ashamed of himself. 'Does this mean that we won't be having sex tonight?'

She shook her head and turned away.

'That's the very least that it means,' she said.

'Okay,' he said, accepting defeat. 'I guess I should go, then.'

'Oh no,' she said, standing up now and moving towards the door, blocking his way. 'It's not going to be quite as simple as that.'

'You want the money back?' he asked. He thought about it. Yes, he had £35,000 hidden away at home, but £8,000 of that was a big chunk to lose. 'It's not like my returning the cash will sort things out between your parents.'

'True. My mother isn't going to forgive my father for going after a rent-boy just because the money's put back into her account.'

'Strictly speaking, I'm not a rent-boy,' said Achilles. 'I never sleep with any of the guys I meet.'

'You just blackmail them.'

'Yes.'

'Well, that's so much better, isn't it?'

'I guess not, but—'

'How many have there been?'

He shrugged his shoulders. He was growing a little weary of this conversation and was anxious to leave. There were still some friends he could call to make sure that the evening wasn't a total write-off. He had an urge to get riotously drunk and have sex with a random stranger.

'A few,' he said.

'How many?'

'I don't know. A half-dozen or so?'

'Don't you feel any shame?'

He thought about it. 'The funny thing is, I don't really,' he said. 'I think I might be a little deficient on that count. Look, I'm a selfish little twat, okay? I admit it. But it's not like I've murdered anyone, is it?'

'Not yet you haven't,' she countered. 'But it's probably only a matter of time until you do.'

He nodded. That had been something he'd worried about in the past. Threats of suicide. He enjoyed the con, but didn't want anyone's death on his conscience.

'Well, I'm very sorry,' he said, doing his best to sound contrite. 'Truly, I am. I guess I should go.'

'It's not been a good night for you all around, has it?' she asked.

'No,' he admitted, looking down at his shoes before looking up at her again. 'What do you mean?' he asked. 'What do you know about my night?'

'Only that I wasn't the only date you had planned for tonight.'

He stared at her, uncertain what she was getting at. She

moved towards the door and opened it. Standing in the hallway was Jeremy Arlo.

'I think you've met my uncle,' she said.

Achilles stared at him. He was holding an iPhone in his hand, recording their entire conversation.

'Fuck me,' he said slowly.

'Actually, I was never really interested in doing that,' said Jeremy. 'Sorry to string you along.'

'Well played,' said Achilles, nodding his head in appreciation and then giving them a slow handclap. 'Well played, both of you. I'm very impressed.'

'I don't care if you're impressed,' said Rebecca. 'All that matters to me is that you're never going to be able to do this to anyone ever again.'

'Let me guess,' he replied, nodding in the direction of Jeremy's phone. 'You're going to blackmail me now.'

'I've recorded every single conversation since we met,' said Jeremy. 'Up to and including you trying to extort five thousand pounds from me.'

'And now you're going to demand money from me instead? How much do you want? Twenty? Fifty? I don't have that much, so you'll be wasting your time.'

'No,' said Jeremy. 'We need a little more assurance that we've put an end to your ways.'

The sound of a car pulling up outside could be heard and all three looked out of the window. The lights of a police car flashed and, as they watched, two officers climbed out and made their way up the driveway.

'Hurts, doesn't it?' asked Rebecca. 'Thinking someone likes you and realizing they've just been using you all along?'

Achilles nodded. 'Yes,' he told her. 'But you know what they say. The trick is not minding that it hurts.'

He looked around the room despondently, recognizing that his time as a small-time con artist had drawn to an end.

'I'm not even going to get laid, am I?'

'Afraid not,' said Rebecca, smiling at him. 'The sex has been cancelled.'

EPILOGUE: CANCELLING THE CLEVERLEYS

On the veranda of a small wooden house on the Scoraig peninsula of western Scotland, George Cleverley sits looking across the sea in the direction of the Isle of Harris, an eight-hundred-page biography on his lap, through which he is making great progress, and feels an extraordinary sense of calm. It's a warm summer's day and, other than the occasional squawk of a seagull, there's not a sound to be heard. It's the beginning of his third week here and he wonders why more people do not come to such remote spots after periods of crisis. The nearest village is a five-mile walk away, and he has completed this twice daily, an activity that has helped him lose some weight as well as filling his mind and body with a general sense of well-being.

It's been more than three months since his embarrassing arrest for causing total chaos at Soho House and, although charges were eventually dropped, it proved the last straw for the BBC, which made it clear that there would be absolutely no way back for him now. The corporation could not possibly allow itself to be associated with him any more. (At least for a year or so, he was assured quietly, until the dust had settled.)

That Friday had proved one of the more unusual days of his life for, early in the hours of Saturday morning, as he found himself standing before the desk sergeant being released on bail, his wife, Beverley, to his utter astonishment, was brought up from the cells too, having been charged with the murder of a tortoise. (A later autopsy on the animal would prove that its death had been induced by digestive failures, its stomach gluey with After Eights, and subsequent charges against her were also dropped.) That alone would have been a coincidence worthy of a good dinner-party story, but it was improved considerably by the fact that, one after another, each of his three children also appeared in the same position, Nelson charged with impersonating a police officer, Elizabeth with suspected terrorist activities, and Achilles with blackmail and extortion. All in all, not a great day for the Cleverley brand, and only when the ghost showed up to drive them all home did the terror building in their souls start to diminish a little.

'What is wrong with you all?' asked the ghost when she pulled up outside their house, turning from one to the other with an expression on her face that suggested she felt nothing but contempt for them. 'How on earth have you allowed yourselves to turn into these types of people?'

At which point, each of their phones started beeping with notifications of how their adventures were becoming the talk of social media and the pile-on began.

The newspapers, of course, had a field day with it and the stories ran for weeks, the Cleverleys becoming the butt of jokes on all the television and radio panel shows, and while the CPS had ultimately decided not to pursue a prosecution on four of them – Achilles, the only true criminal mastermind among them, was to undertake two hundred hours of community service – their names were mud and they had, as a family, in Elizabeth's words, been cancelled.

'Possibly the most cancelled family in the history of the world,' she'd added, feeling a certain pleasure that they had at least trended on every social media platform during their public disgrace. 'Worse than the Borgias. Worse than the Trumps, for pity's sake.'

In the end, it had been George's idea to come to this most remote region of the United Kingdom, one of the only places left in the country that did not have access to Wi-Fi, and spend some time recuperating from their traumatic experiences. To have no phone or laptop was providing a digital detox that was proving a heavenly experience. Indeed, there was a part of him that was beginning to wonder whether he could move here for ever, grow a long beard and learn Gaelic to converse with the half-dozen or so wildlings that he occasionally encountered on his walks. He'd spent his entire life climbing the greasy pole of the television industry but realized now that he didn't care if he ever saw Portland Place again. Here was bliss.

'How's the book coming along?' asks Beverley, stepping outside to join him and handing him a gin and tonic as she sits down, sipping on her own. She leans across and they kiss briefly. To their mutual surprise, romance has been revived between them in this most desolate of places and they've come to realize that they might not have much in the world any more, but they still have each other. And ten million quid in the bank, of course.

'It's very interesting,' he says. 'Although, obviously, I'm reading it for ironic reasons.'

She smiles, glancing at the front cover. There was a time in her life when her husband had been able to amuse her like this regularly and it seems that that time has returned. Sitting together like this, outside in the fresh air, looking across the sea, they find themselves chatting as amiably as they did when they were a young couple, but it's a relief to be simply living in the present. They can sit here for hours, exchanging small snippets of conversation or just saying nothing at all, and she feels closer to him than she has in years. It's come as something of a delight to both of them to realize that they still love each other.

Some days, Beverley accompanies George on his walks to the village and back, and they stop for lunch and a drink in the one pub that stands down there, sitting by the fireplace enjoying a hearty stew and talking about life, love, politics, history, culture and art until the sun goes down, at which point they head back to the cottage hand in hand. Two days earlier, on their walk home, they even stopped in the woods, throwing themselves upon each other to make love with a vigour they have not displayed in many years.

She hasn't yet told her husband, but Beverley has decided that, upon her next trip to the village, she will go in search of paper and pens, for she has an idea for a semi-autobiographical novel that she's interested in pursuing. She hasn't written one herself since her very earliest efforts, but she feels a strong desire to pursue this book alone. They have no plans to leave Scoraig anytime soon and she quite likes the idea of sitting quietly every morning for a couple of hours and allowing the story to build before her, the characters to take shape, the world she might imagine out of nothingness. She will write about a family, she has decided, not a young woman in search of love from a wealthy, damaged man. A family with faults and flaws, who have gone wrong somewhere but are trying, are desperately trying, to connect with each other again. Their downfall, she knows, will be choosing publicity over privacy, followers over friends. She'll take the events of her own family's lives over many months and encapsulate them into five days. She might even soften them a little by including scenes that took place when the children were younger and she and George were more loving towards each other. She has a title for it already: *The Echo Chamber*. She doesn't know whether

her family will like being featured at the centre of the story or not, particularly as she has decided to portray them with all their eccentricities intact, but she can't think about that for now. As her late colleague Kingsley Amis once said, if you can't annoy somebody, there is little point in writing.

'Look,' she says, nudging her husband as she catches sight of their elder son, Nelson, making his way along the beach towards them, carrying something in his hands. 'What's he got there?'

'I can't tell,' says George, following the direction of her eyes. They watch silently as he climbs the steps towards the cottage.

'Oh Lord,' says Beverley. 'That's not what I think it is, is it?'

'I think it might be.'

'Look what I found,' says Nelson, smiling broadly. 'It was all alone and seemed completely lost. How on earth would a tortoise find its way to the Scoraig peninsula?'

'It's probably been walking for decades,' says George, taking a sip from his drink. 'In search of other tortoises.'

'I doubt it will find any, but who knows?'

'Why did you bring it up here?' asks Beverley. 'Speaking as a mother, shouldn't you have just let it be?'

Nelson shrugs. He'd been strolling along the beach, which he does every day, wearing what he liked to think of as his *Baywatch* uniform, although he'd never confess that to anyone, when he saw the poor unfortunate creature standing on its own and felt a sudden urge to befriend it.

'You should put it back,' says Beverley. 'Let it go where it wants.'

'I thought I might keep it. I could name him Yaroslav the Wise, after the great eleventh-century Ukrainian prince.'

'Yes, we all know who Yaroslav the Wise was,' says George. 'We're not complete ignoramuses.'

'No, it's a bad idea,' says Beverley. 'They're not meant to be kept as pets anyway. And we don't have anything to feed it.'

'The village shop doesn't even sell After Eights,' adds George. 'You're lucky to get a Mars bar most days.'

'I suppose,' says Nelson, placing the creature on the ground, where it turns slowly with a disgruntled sound and begins the process of returning whence it has come, a walk that will inevitably take many months, if not years. He watches it as it moves away and envies it a little. A life of solitude does not seem like such a bad thing, and he's enjoying living in this part of Scotland, with no particular plans to return to the real world. Shane broke up with him when he realized that almost everything Nelson had said to him during their brief romance had been a lie, and he'd been forced to end his relationship with his therapist, Dr Gosebourne, when he learned that she'd been conducting an affair with his father, which had almost resulted in another sibling. In his sorrow, he had retreated into the arms of his parents, who, most unexpectedly, had embraced him and were now doing all they could to make him whole again. He'd never really thought about them in these terms before but, since their arrival in Scoraig, he's grown to realize how deeply he loves them. Sitting down on one of the veranda's steps now, George reaches out a hand and lets it rest on his son's shoulder for a few moments, and he remembers what it was like to be a child, when there were just the three of them. They had been very happy days, and somehow, unexpectedly, they seem to be returning.

'If I had a phone,' says Elizabeth, stepping out of the cottage door and stretching her body out in a great yawn, 'I would take a picture of the three of you looking out to sea and post it to Instagram. It would be an amazing shot.'

'If you had a phone,' says Nelson. 'But you don't.'

'No,' she says. 'Nor do I miss it.'

'Liar.'

'Well, I miss it a bit. But not as much as I thought I would.'

It had taken six weeks for Elizabeth to convince the authorities that she was neither a terrorist nor did she have any plans to take a machete to the Prime Minister's head. While she received a caution for her behaviour, it was nothing compared to the ignominy that fell on her when it was revealed that @ElizCleverley✅ and @TruthIsASword were, in fact, the same person, a revelation that led to a long and distressing conversation between George and his daughter. Once again, the newspapers revelled in a week's worth of revelations, going back through her tweets, likes and replies before contacting every famous person she had ever messaged for their response to her unkindness. Most had been disparaging, of course, saying that she must have some form of mental illness, or perhaps been bullied in school as a child, since she had now turned into such a bully herself, and the more she was reacquainted with the messages she'd sent, the more ashamed she felt of her behaviour.

What was wrong with me? she asked herself as she scanned the hundreds of abusive tweets that had sprung forth from her mind. *Why was I like that?*

Which is one of the reasons that she had agreed to accompany her parents to this part of the world, a place she would never have even considered visiting in the past and where there is absolutely no possibility of returning to the digital grid. Although she can't anyway, having been banned for life by all the social media platforms and finding herself under a court order not to set up any fake accounts. But, like George, she finds that she doesn't really miss any of it. Sitting down next to Nelson on the steps and looking out to sea, she realizes that there's something wonderful about simply enjoying this view, in the company of her family, without having to document it for the world to see. The only likes that matter now are her own.

'What's going on?' asks Achilles, emerging from the beach in microscopic Speedos and ascending the steps towards them, having just come from his morning swim. The sea water still clings to his body, but he's deliberately waited until this moment to shake his head like a dog so all the drops fly out of his hair and drench his assembled family.

'Idiot,' says Elizabeth, wiping her face with her T-shirt.

'Only kidding,' says Achilles, sitting down next to her and, quite to her astonishment, laying his head on her shoulder. She puts an arm around him, as she used to do when they were children, and only when he makes a joke about her try-ing to feel him up does she push him away.

'So what's the plan for today?' he asks, looking around at them all. 'Anyone got anything special in the diary?'

'I intend to continue reading my book,' says George. 'And then to take a walk.'

'Through the woods?' asks Beverley.

'Yes, I thought so.'

'Hm,' she says, reaching out and taking his hand. 'Perhaps I'll join you.'

'Very good,' he replies, smiling.

'And I'm going into the village and taking a bus to Inver-ness,' says Nelson. 'I think I might look for a job.'

'A job?' they all say in unison.

'Has it come to this?' asks Elizabeth in horror.

'Yes, I think I might go back to teaching. I have the qualifica-tions, after all. And it seems a pity to let them go to waste. I might visit the council and see what's on offer.'

'They won't have any London jobs listed,' says Achilles.

'No, but I might stay up here,' he says. 'A new environment. A fresh start. It might not work out but—'

'I think that's a very fine idea,' says Beverley. 'Good for you.'

'And what about you?' asks Achilles, turning to his sister. 'What are you doing?'

'I haven't decided yet,' she says, lying back and closing her eyes, allowing the sun to pour over her. 'Probably nothing at all.'

'A solid plan.'

'I think so.'

'I might join you,' he says. 'Although I'll get a few more swims in too. It's really helping my abs. Have you seen them?'

'Zero interest,' says Elizabeth.

'Well, it is. You should swim with me, Nelson,' he adds. 'Lose some of that blubber.'

'I don't have any blubber,' protests his brother. 'I'm big-boned, that's all.'

'Children, behave,' says George quietly and they all fall silent.

'It's so peaceful up here, isn't it?' remarks Beverley later that night when it's just her and George seated together on the veranda. 'Away from everyone and everything. Just us. Together. And happy again.'

'It is,' replies George, nodding his head.

'If you ask me,' she adds, pointing towards the book in her husband's lap, the stern visage of its subject, Alexander Graham Bell, staring back at her, 'that fucker has a lot to answer for.'

Acknowledgements

I am, as ever, indebted to Bill Scott-Kerr, Patsy Irwin, Larry Finlay, Eloisa Clegg, Aimée Johnston, Simon Trewin, Eric Simonoff, and to all my international publishers for their ongoing support.

Thank you, too, to all my readers.

Ironically, you can still find me on Twitter @john_boyne

This House is Haunted
John Boyne

1867. On a dark and chilling night Eliza Caine arrives in Norfolk to take up her position as governess at Gaudlin Hall. As she makes her way across the station platform, a pair of invisible hands push her from behind into the path of an approaching train. She is only saved by the vigilance of a passing doctor.

It is the start of a journey into a world of abandoned children, unexplained occurrences and terrifying experiences which Eliza will have to overcome if she is to survive the secrets that lie within Gaudlin's walls . . .

A History of Loneliness
John Boyne

Clonliffe Seminary, 1972. Odran Yates arrives after his mother informs him that he has a vocation to the priesthood. He is full of ambition and hope, dedicated to his studies and keen to make friends.

Forty years later, Odran's devotion has been challenged by the revelations that have shattered the Irish people's faith in the Church. He has seen friends stand trial, colleagues jailed, and the lives of young parishioners destroyed.

But when a family tragedy opens wounds from his past, he is forced to confront the demons that have raged within a once-respected institution, and recognize his own complicity in their propagation.

Courageous and intensely personal, *A History of Loneliness* confirms Boyne as one of the most talented chroniclers of his generation.

The Heart's Invisible Furies
John Boyne

Cast out from her West Cork village, sixteen years old and pregnant, Catherine Goggin makes her way to Dublin to start afresh. She has no choice but to believe that the nun to whom she entrusts her child will find him a better life.

The baby is named Cyril by his adoptive parents, Charles and Maude Avery, a well-to-do but deeply eccentric couple who treat him more like a curiosity than a son. You're not a proper Avery, they tell him. And perhaps he isn't. But through them he meets Julian Woodbead who, even from childhood, seems destined for an infinitely more glamorous and dangerous life.

And so begins one man's funny and moving search to find his place in a world that seems to delight in gently tormenting him at every turn. Buffeted by circumstance and, at times, the consequences of his own questionable judgement, Cyril must navigate his emotions and desires in a search for that most elemental human need . . . happiness.

'A substantial achievement'
GUARDIAN

'A bold, funny epic'
OBSERVER

'Written with verve, humour and heart . . . at its core,
The Heart's Invisible Furies aspires to be not just the tale
of Cyril Avery, a man buffeted by coincidence and circumstance,
but the story of Ireland itself'
IRISH TIMES

A Ladder to the Sky
John Boyne

You've heard the old proverb about ambition, that it's like setting a ladder to the sky. It can lead to a long and painful fall.

If you look hard enough, you will find stories pretty much anywhere. They don't even have to be your own. Or so would-be-novelist Maurice Swift decides very early on in his career.

A chance encounter in a Berlin hotel with celebrated author Erich Ackerman gives Maurice an opportunity. For Erich is lonely, and he has a story to tell; whether or not he should is another matter.

Once Maurice has made his name, he finds himself in need of a fresh idea. He doesn't care where he finds it, as long as it helps him rise to the top. Stories will make him famous, but they will also make him beg, borrow and steal. They may even make him do worse.

'A deliciously dark tale of ambition, seduction and literary theft . . . compelling and terrifying, powerful and intensely unsettling. In Maurice Swift, Boyne has given us an unforgettable protagonist, dangerous and irresistible in equal measure. The result is an ingeniously conceived novel that confirms Boyne as one of the most assured writers of his generation'
OBSERVER

'Maurice Swift, the novelist protagonist of John Boyne's A Ladder to the Sky, *is a bookish version of Patricia Highsmith's psychopathic antihero Tom Ripley'*
THE TIMES

The sequel to
The Boy in the Striped Pyjamas

'One of the most assured writers of his generation' *The Observer*

All The Broken Places

JOHN BOYNE

Coming 15 September 2022